To

Dkypy really!

## THE REUNION

Maina Martindale

XOXOXOX!

# THE REUNION

Marina Martindale

Good Oak
Press, LLC

Good Oak Press, LLC
P.O. Box 12195
Tucson, Arizona 85732
info@goodoakpress.com

Editor: Cynthia Roedig
Proofreader: Dolores Sierra
Cover Illustration: Wes Lowe
Cover Design: Good Oak Press, LLC
Typesetting: Good Oak Press, LLC

ISBN: 978-0-983938408

*To Geneva*

# ৯৹ONE৶৹

ROSEMARY MCGEE HAD the next traffic light perfectly
timed until a car from the other lane suddenly cut in front of
her minivan. She slammed on the brakes, narrowly avoiding a collision
as the light turned yellow. Rosemary kept her foot on the brake pedal,
coming to a stop as the signal turned red. Her knees were shaking a little
as she looked at the woman sitting in the passenger seat.

"Are you okay?"

"I'm fine," she replied.

"You're sure?"

"Yes, I'm sure."

"I sure hope that wasn't a bad sign. It's your opening night and I
want everything to be perfect for you."

"It's not a bad sign, Rosemary," she said, trying to reassure her.
"These things happen, especially in rush-hour traffic. Don't worry. We're
okay. We'll get there in plenty of time, so try to relax. You've been on edge
ever since we left the hotel. You're about to give yourself an ulcer, and me
a screaming headache to go along with it."

"Sorry, Gillian. It's not like I know my way around Denver, and
these idiots on the road certainly don't help."

"That's why we have a GPS device. Like I just said, everything is fine."

They waited for the light to change. Once it turned green, the
minivan lurched forward.

1

"You know," said Gillian, "just before that happened, I was thinking about my father, and how convinced he was that I'd have no future whatsoever if I became an artist."

"And when I first met you, I knew you were much too talented to be wasting your time laying out ads for weekly supermarket specials. You've come a long way, Gillian. I'm sure your father would have been proud of you."

"I hope so."

Gillian Matthews was becoming famous in the art world, and now she had a new gallery to add to her collection. All the risks she'd taken to get herself where she wanted to be were finally paying off.

"Right turn ahead," chimed the electronic voice.

"Thank you, Bill," replied both women in unison. Bill was the name they'd given the GPS device.

"It's too bad you never got to meet my father, Rosemary. I'm sure you and he would have found one another—interesting."

"I met your mother."

"Only once or twice, and that was after she had gotten so sick that she really wasn't herself anymore. Trust me, there was no way my parents were ever going to allow any daughter of theirs to become an artist. That was way too beneath them. I'll always remember when Cynthia first went off to college. She was studying to be an elementary school teacher. As far as they were concerned, that was an appropriate career, and I was to follow in her footsteps."

Rosemary let out a sigh as she turned the minivan to the right at the next stoplight.

"I don't know why, Gillian, but for some strange reason I've had a bad feeling about tonight's show. It started about the time we drove over Raton Pass and crossed the Colorado border."

"I don't know why you'd feel that way. It's not like this is my first time having an opening. You brought all our paperwork, didn't you?"

"It's in my briefcase."

"And we already know my paintings arrived safely. When did you last speak to the people at the gallery?"

"About an hour ago," replied Rosemary. "They said everything was just about ready to go."

"Have you spoken to your family today?"

"Lou called this morning. He and the kids are managing just fine."

"Then I'd say we have all our bases covered. You've probably just have a case of opening-night jitters, that's all."

"I hope you're right, Gillian, but for some reason I just can't shake this feeling."

A few seconds later, Bill announced that they had reached their destination. The minivan turned into the gallery parking lot. Anthony Sorenson Fine Art resided in a large, single-story office building that had been converted into an art gallery. They noticed a catering truck parked nearby with its crew busily unloading boxes and taking them into the rear entrance.

"See, Oh Worried One, we have arrived. In one piece, and in plenty of time," chided Gillian.

Rosemary put the minivan into park, shut down the engine, and the two women emerged. They stopped for a moment to smooth the wrinkles from their dresses before Rosemary reached for her briefcase and pressed the remote to lock the doors. As they walked toward the front door a passing car honked at them.

"You've still got it, girlfriend," teased Rosemary as she opened the door for Gillian. "I told you that yellow outfit would make you look hot."

Entering the art gallery, they came upon a reception area in the foyer. Beyond it, the building was divided into two sections. The main gallery was on the right, with the smaller changing exhibit gallery on the left, where final preparations were being made for Gillian's opening. At the back was a hallway leading to the administrative offices.

Rosemary stepped up to the receptionist's desk and introduced herself. A minute later Tony Sorenson, the gallery's owner, entered from the hallway and greeted them. For a moment, he appeared to be a bit out of character. He looked uncomfortable in the stiff, three-piece suit he was wearing, and his thinning, curly gray hair appeared as though it had been very hastily pulled back into a ponytail. Gillian guessed his typical work attire was probably a well-worn pair of blue jeans with a tie-dyed shirt. As they made their introductions, a harried-looking young man, whom Tony introduced as Paul, his assistant, quickly joined them.

"What we need to do now," said Tony, "is take a little tour and make sure everything is absolutely correct."

"Of course," replied Gillian. "Rosemary, do you have copies of our inventory sheets?"

She retrieved them from her briefcase. "Right here."

They stepped into the gallery and proceeded to go over every detail, inch by inch. Gillian's favorite subject matter was architectural and outdoor scenes as well as the occasional still life. She worked mostly in acrylic and watercolor, and she was known for using big, bold, brightly colored shapes. Mounted next to each painting was a small descriptive paper plaque, but they discovered one plaque with a minor error. Paul ran back to his office, quickly printed out a corrected copy, and remounted it next to the painting. Once everything passed inspection, they went to Tony's office to go over the last-minute details.

"Okay." He seated himself behind his desk. "We sent out the media releases two weeks ago. There was a mention of you, Gillian, along with a photo, in last Sunday's paper. And, as I already told Rosemary over the phone, a reporter and photographer from *The Denver Centennial*, one of our weekly papers, will be coming here tonight. They'll want to interview you and take a few photos. They said they'd be here sometime between seven and seven-fifteen. Our friend, Paul, will position himself near the front door so he can watch for them, and he'll let you and Rosemary know the minute they arrive. We don't want to keep them waiting."

"Understood," said Rosemary. "I'll keep an eye on the clock myself so I'll know when to watch for Paul."

"Good," said Tony, "then it sounds like we've covered our bases on that one. We've sent announcements to all of our regulars and we've had a good response. We've also updated our website and Facebook page, so between that, and last Sunday's paper, we hope to have good turn out from the general public as well. I have a feeling this is going to be a very good evening for all of us."

Tony and Rosemary went over the rest of the last-minute details before the meeting broke up. As they stepped back into the gallery, they passed the caterers, who were almost finished setting up.

"See Rosemary, everything is fine. I expect tonight will go flawlessly," assured Gillian. "Tony and his staff are pros. You have nothing to worry about."

"I know, Gillian, but I still have a feeling that something's about to go terribly wrong."

"Well, I can't imagine what it would be." Gillian glanced at her watch. "The show starts in ten minutes. I'm going to go freshen up. I'll be back in a sec."

By the time she returned, people were beginning to arrive. One or two, here and there, trickled in at first. Then more began showing up. Before long the room was crowded. Gillian had her work cut out for her. She had to introduce herself to as many of the guests as she could and talk to them about her art. Unlike some artists, Gillian wasn't shy. She genuinely enjoyed meeting new people and answering their questions. Once again, her knack for charming people paid off. Within forty-five minutes, several patrons had followed Tony down the hallway to open their checkbooks.

"How are we doing?" Gillian whispered to Rosemary as she took a short break at the bar to get a glass of water.

"Not bad, not bad at all. So far you've sold three acrylics and one watercolor. And the night is still young. We have another hour or so to go."

Rosemary pointed out one of the paintings hanging near the back corner. It featured an abandoned tractor parked in front of a rustic old barn.

"There was a man standing there admiring that one for the longest time. Did you by chance go over and speak with him?"

"Not yet," replied Gillian. "I've been so busy that I haven't been able to work my way to that part of the room."

Rosemary looked down the hallway toward Sorenson's office.

"Well, I guess it didn't matter. I see him coming back with Tony. Looks like you may have just sold painting number five. You're doing well, Gillian. Keep it up."

"See Rosemary, your worries were all for naught."

As Gillian sipped her water she watched the two men coming back up the hallway. There was something familiar about the man who'd just purchased her painting. As he stepped back into the room she saw him more clearly. Her heart skipped a beat and she suddenly felt her entire body going limp. She was experiencing one of those freaky moments in time that sometimes happens to people just before they have a terrible accident. Everything around her seemed to be running in slow motion. She felt the water glass slipping from her hand. She somehow managed to snap out of it just in time to regain her grip, but as she did, the glass slammed down hard on the bar. She quickly turned her face away, hoping the man hadn't seen her.

"Are you all right, ma'am?" asked the bartender.

"Yes. Yes, I'm fine."

"What's wrong?" asked Rosemary.

"Nothing, nothing at all. I just lost my grip for a moment." She tried to regain her composure. "You know, I haven't eaten very much today. I guess I must have gone too long without food. I'll be glad when we're finally done here and we can go grab a bite. Meantime, I think those reporters are coming soon, so I'm going to fix my makeup. Would you mind bringing me my purse, Rosemary? I don't remember where we put it."

Rosemary reluctantly did as she was asked. Gillian grabbed her purse and quickly headed down the hallway. As she rushed into the ladies' room, she was relieved to find no one else there. Her entire body was shaking. She placed both hands on the vanity, bent her head down, and took several deep breaths. Many times over the years she'd wondered if he was still in Denver. Now she finally had her answer. But why did he have to come tonight? Her show would be on display for several weeks. He could have just as easily stopped by another night.

She remained at the vanity and kept breathing slowly and deeply. After a few minutes she felt her body start to relax. She thought about it again and realized it was perfectly innocent. She had a different last name now, and he couldn't have known that. This would make his being here purely coincidental. He always had an appreciation for art. For all she knew, he was one of Tony's regulars. Her hands were still a little shaky as she took one last deep breath, reached for a tissue, and gently patted the little beads of sweat that had popped up on her forehead. As she patted, she looked more closely a face in the mirror.

Gillian looked a good ten years younger than her actual age. Despite all the time that had passed, she still looked much the same. About the only noticeable difference between then and now was that her long blonde hair was now a shoulder-length pageboy. She started to reminisce about the past and her mind suddenly filled with a whirlwind of images of all they had shared, the good times as well as the bad. It was like watching a movie, but the scenes were spliced together out of sequence.

"Calm down, Gillian," she told her reflection. "You've got to pull yourself together."

She took a few more deep breaths, and as she did, the events of one particular day began playing back in her mind with crystal clarity. It was the day she first laid eyes on Ian Palmer.

# ❧Two❧

GILLIAN JAMMED HER paintbrush into her palette and glanced at the wall clock. It was almost four twenty-five. Class would be over at four-thirty.

"Damn it," she muttered to herself as she tried to work more white paint into the canvas.

This particular painting was one of those projects that simply wasn't coming together, and the more she worked with it the worse it got. It happened to every artist from time to time, but it was never good when it happened in a university art class the day before the project was due, and the painting in question would count toward the final grade.

"So what's up, Miss Hanson?"

The voice behind her was that of her professor, Dr. Kinney. Kinney was a good instructor, but he could be hardnosed when he wanted to be.

"I just can't seem to get the lighting right on this one, Dr. Kinney."

"Obviously. So now you've overworked it to the point that it's turned into mud. A half hour ago this painting wasn't that bad. You should have quit while you were ahead."

"Should I come back later tonight and try to fix it?"

The university kept the art studio doors unlocked until ten o'clock every night so students could come back and put in extra time, if it was needed.

"At this point, Miss Hanson, it would be a complete waste of time. As it stands right now, you have a few aspects that are still working. As I just said, if I were in your shoes, I'd quit while I was ahead, especially if I had any aspirations of passing this class. You'll get your new assignment next week. Perhaps you'll have better luck then."

As her professor turned away to announce that class was dismissed, Gillian let out a frustrated sigh. She hated it when a painting didn't come out the way she wanted. She took it off the easel and placed it in one of the racks. She looked forward to covering the canvas with a fresh coat of gesso, once Dr. Kinney finished ripping it to shreds during his next critique session. She gathered up her brushes and waited in line at the sink.

"Hey, it happens to all of us sometime, Gillian," said one of her classmates. "You're so much better than the rest of us. You'll still ace this class."

"Thanks, Melinda. I appreciate it."

She cleaned up her brushes, loaded up her toolbox and backpack, and headed for her locker. After depositing her toolbox, she ran down the stairs, out of the art building, and onto the plaza. It was a beautiful March day. She paused for a moment to take in the balmy, late afternoon air. Springtime in Arizona was much too short. It wouldn't be long before the blistering heat of summer set in. She walked across the plaza toward the architecture building. Ryan would be getting out of class soon and maybe they could grab dinner somewhere. A cheerful greeting rang out as she entered the building.

"Hey, Gillian. How's it going?"

A frequent visitor to the architecture college, Gillian was well liked by Ryan's classmates.

"Good Rob. How 'bout you?"

"Not bad, considering we're all stuck on the gallows around here. If you're looking for Ryan, he's not upstairs in the studio. He's down here, in the library."

"Thanks, Rob."

"You're welcome. Good seeing you." He hastily made his exit.

The architecture library was on her immediate left. She stepped in and looked for Ryan. She quickly spotted him at one of the tables, going through a reference book.

Gillian had been seeing Ryan Knight for the past year and a half. It was her first serious relationship and Ryan was the first man she'd ever made love to. The first year they were together everything seemed perfect. They were deeply in love and their romance sizzled. All their friends thought they made a great couple. A few had even dubbed them Blond and Blondie, as they both had blond hair. Everyone, including Gillian, believed that once Ryan graduated they'd start making wedding plans. But ever since Ryan returned from Christmas break he seemed different. He was moody and distant. Gillian kept asking him what was wrong and he kept insisting he was just nervous about graduating that spring. As she approached Ryan, she took a deep breath and prayed he'd be in a good mood.

"Hey there, handsome. You new around here?"

"Not now, Gillian," he growled back.

"Now what's the matter?"

"Nothing's wrong, I'm just busy. There are a lot of things I have to do. So what did you need?"

"Oh, nothing. I just thought that as I'm your girlfriend, you might want to go out and have a burger with me. You have to eat sometime, you know."

Ryan thought it over for a minute." Okay, but I have to come right back after we're done. I'm working late again tonight."

Just like the art building, the university kept the architecture building open until ten o'clock at night so that students could work on their projects.

"That's fine," replied Gillian. "I have to study tonight myself, but I still have to eat, and I'd like to spend a little time with you, if that's okay."

Ryan pushed the book aside, stood from the table and walked away while Gillian, rushing to catch up with him, had to pick up her pace. Just as Ryan neared the door, it opened and another student entered. He motioned Ryan over and they talked. Gillian stopped abruptly. She had never laid eyes on this man before in her life, yet for some strange reason she felt as though she recognized him. At the same time, she felt another strange sensation. It was almost as if a pulse of electricity had just shot through her body.

He was roughly the same height as Ryan, with a slightly more muscular build, deep set brown eyes, and wavy dark-brown hair that just touched the top of his shoulders. And while Ryan was certainly handsome, this other man was, in Gillian's eyes, far better looking. As he continued his conversation with Ryan, he turned, just for an instant, glancing in her direction and inadvertently making eye contact with her in the process. In that split-second moment, she thought she noticed a glimmer, as if she'd somehow caught his eye as well. He quickly shifted his focus back to Ryan.

"Wait a minute," Gillian muttered to herself. "What am I doing?"

The two men wrapped up their conversation and the other one left. Ryan turned and motioned to Gillian to come with him. They exited the building and headed toward the hamburger stand across the street.

"Who was that?"

"His name is Ian Palmer."

"Oh. So who is he? I've never seen him around here before."

"That's because he's a year behind me, but we have a couple of elective classes together. He came in to ask me something about an assignment. He's a nice guy. Sometimes he comes along on Wednesday nights and joins us for a beer after class."

They crossed the street and entered the burger joint. It was a popular place that was typically crowded, and this night was certainly no exception. They ordered their food and found an empty table near one of the windows, but Ryan apparently didn't feel like talking. He seemed content to eat his burger in silence.

"So, what are our plans for the weekend?" Gillian finally asked. "I'd really like to go see a movie. We haven't gone out or done anything fun in weeks. Not since my birthday, and that was what, about a month ago?"

"Sorry, I can't. Gotta work on a project all weekend."

"Again?" There was a definite whine in her voice. "Can't I at least come over to your place when you're done? Maybe I can fix dinner or something."

"No, not this time. Why don't you ask Sam if she has any plans this weekend? Maybe she'd like to go to see a movie."

Samantha Walsh lived in the apartment two doors down from Gillian, and even though they came from completely different backgrounds, they'd become fast friends.

"Well, I suppose I could ask her." Gillian was obviously disappointed. "You know, lately all my friends have been asking me, 'Where's Ryan?' 'How come you two aren't going out that much anymore?' You were always busy before, yet somehow you always managed to find the time for us to get together. What's going on, Ryan? Are you getting bored with me or something?"

Ryan threw his burger down on his plate. "Nothing! I keep telling you that. Why can't you get it?" He glared at Gillian. His blue eyes looked like cold, hard steel. "I don't give a rat's ass about what any of your friends think. Maybe they should try minding their own damn business. Better yet, maybe they should try taking some real courses sometime, instead of some easy credit lecture class where all they have to do is show up, take notes while the professor talks, and then regurgitate it back on a test."

Gillian stood up and put on her backpack.

"Where are you going?"

"Home. I've heard enough, thank you."

Ryan's face softened. He stood up, wrapped his arm around her waist and pulled her in close.

"Hey, I'm sorry. I know I've been acting like a real jerk lately. I'm just stressed out about graduating, that's all. I'm worried about how long it's going to take to find a job and how I'm ever going to pay back all those student loans. Tell you what. We'll get together on Sunday. All day. I promise."

Sunday came and as promised, Ryan stopped by Gillian's apartment that afternoon. They watched a little TV and she whipped up a spaghetti dinner. Gillian was an amazing cook and at least Ryan still appreciated her meals. Afterwards they made love, but she noticed their lovemaking also lacked the passion it once had. She stayed in bed with her head propped on her elbow while she watched him dress. He had great muscle tone and his proportions were perfect. She thought Ryan would make the perfect model for her life-drawing class. But then again, if he actually were to model for her class, she would be jealous. She didn't want any other woman looking at Ryan's naked body, even if it was only for a classroom assignment. He was all hers and she intended to keep it that way.

## ❧THREE❧

GILLIAN WAS TRYING to wake up, but she was in such a deep, heavy sleep that she couldn't break free. Once she finally was able to open her eyes, she noticed the sun shining brightly. It took a moment or two for her to get her bearings and realize it was Saturday. She rolled over and looked at the clock on the nightstand. It was a few minutes past ten. She'd slept for nearly ten hours. She knew she was tired when she went to bed, but she hadn't realized just how exhausted she was.

It had been a hectic week of final exams, followed by Ryan's commencement ceremony on Thursday night. Ryan's mother had come from Indiana, and it seemed like all she talked about was how proud Ryan's father would have been. Ryan had been a young boy when his father was killed in a car crash, and the tragedy still haunted him. It also appeared to Gillian that his mother used the event as a means to manipulate her son. The sudden ring of the telephone interrupted her thoughts. She jumped out of bed and grabbed it.

"Hello."

"Hey, Babe, it's me. Are you up yet?"

"Yeah, just barely. I really slept in this morning. How 'bout you?"

"I've been up since the crack of dawn," replied Ryan. "I had to take my mother to the airport."

Gillian's heart leapt for joy at the news.

"I need you come over as soon as you can. I've got something very important that I need to discuss with you."

Intrigued, Gillian ended the call and started getting ready. As she drove to Ryan's apartment, she thought about everything that had happened over the past few months. There had been good times, like when she tagged along with Ryan and his classmates on their weekly Wednesday night, after-class, beer-and-burger run. Ian Palmer usually joined them as well and it seemed like he was the only one who really took the time to talk to her. She and Ian had become good friends. The weekends, however, had been a strain. Ryan was always busy in the architecture studio and their usual Saturday night dates became a rarity. Gillian hated spending most of her weekends alone in her apartment. There were, however, a few occasions when she and Ian went out for dinner or a movie. Just as friends, of course, and always with Ryan's blessing. Now that the semester was over, and Ryan had finally graduated, she hoped things would soon return to a sense of normalcy. She arrived at Ryan's apartment and knocked on the door. He opened it and greeted her with a kiss, but once she stepped inside, she saw something was amiss.

"What's all this? Ryan, what's going on?"

Cardboard boxes were scattered everywhere. Ryan had been busy packing up his belongings. He quickly cleared off the boxes that were sitting on the sofa bed, which was still pulled out, and sat down. He motioned for Gillian to come and sit next to him.

"Gillian, I have good news. I found a job. I start a week from Monday."

"You did? Ryan, that's fantastic." She gave him a hug. "I knew one of my dad's contacts would come through for you. I just knew it."

Gillian's father was a real estate developer and well-respected businessman in the community. He knew plenty of architects, and Gillian had asked him to put the word out about Ryan.

"No, I'm afraid it wasn't anyone associated with your father. There've been a number of recruiters from architectural firms visiting the college, and I interviewed with several of them. The offer I've accepted came from one in Santa Barbara."

Gillian felt her heart sink. That meant Ryan would be leaving for good.

"Now, here's what I propose, and please, hear me out on this."

Gillian's spirits rose. Had Ryan just said the word propose to her? Before she could react, his lips were covering hers. He was kissing her passionately, just like he did in the old days. Her heart skipped a beat. The moment she'd been waiting for had finally arrived. Ryan was about to ask her to marry him. She returned his kiss just as passionately. She felt his tongue probing her mouth and his hands unbuttoning her blouse. They made love on the sofa bed, and it was better than it had been in a very long time. When it was finally over, Ryan pulled her in close and began stroking her hair.

"Now, Baby, I want you to listen very carefully to what I'm about to say to you. Some of this may seem a little strange at first, but I've got it all worked out. If you'll trust me, and I mean really trust me, and if you'll be patient with me, then Gillian, I'm guaranteeing, right here, right now, that you and I will have a terrific life together."

"Of course I trust you, Ryan. Why wouldn't I?"

Ryan let out a deep, prolonged sigh. "Gillian, over the past few months, I haven't exactly been honest with you. I'm really, truly sorry for it, but it couldn't be helped. Please understand that none of this was my idea. My mother put me up to it." He paused and took another deep breath. "Gillian, ever since the first of the year, I've been seeing Lisa Dawson."

Gillian's heart sank like a ball of lead into her stomach. For months she'd instinctively known that something was terribly wrong. Deep in her heart she feared Ryan was being unfaithful to her, but she would never force herself to believe it. Now her worst fears were about to be realized.

"What are you saying to me, Ryan? Do you mean to tell me you've been cheating on me, behind my back? How could you?"

"Gillian, you have to understand. Ever since high school, my mother's been on my case about Lisa and me getting married someday. It got even worse once she found out Lisa was coming out here for college too. I had to keep reminding her that Lisa only came because Kevin got that football scholarship. Then, when I went home for Christmas, I discovered that my mother had somehow found out about Lisa and Kevin breaking up. So all I heard from her, morning, noon and night, was that the time was right and she wanted me to start dating Lisa. She also kept bringing up Lisa's inheritance. She simply wouldn't stop hammering me about it."

"And you couldn't tell your mother no?"

Gillian was getting angry, and the more Ryan talked, the angrier she felt. At least this explained why Lisa had been constantly underfoot during his mother's visit, and why Lisa had been the one invited to sit with his mother during his graduation ceremony instead of her.

"Okay, okay. I get the point, Ryan. You decided to go along with your mother's scheme, so you took Lisa out, behind my back, I might add. That must be why you kept telling me, over and over again, that you were busy burning the midnight oil every weekend at the architecture building. You were really out with Lisa, weren't you?"

Ryan didn't respond.

"Okay Ryan, I'll take your silence as a yes. So you did your bit.

Hopefully, it's been enough to finally get your mother off your back. So what's next? Where do we go from here? Were you planning on asking me to come to Santa Barbara with you?"

"Not exactly."

"And what is that supposed to mean?"

There was another long pause.

"It means yes, Gillian, I want you to come visit me, as often as you possibly can. One, maybe two, weekends a month. As long as it won't interfere with your studies. And don't worry about the cost. I'll help pay your airfare."

Gillian dared to brave the question. "And what about Lisa?"

"Lisa is coming to Santa Barbara with me. We're engaged, Gillian. I have to marry her."

"What! Don't tell that me you've been sleeping with her too. Did you knock her up?" Gillian was trying to free herself, but Ryan held her down.

"No. She's not pregnant, and I haven't exactly been sleeping with her."

"Oh, so you only went to second base with her!"

"Gillian, please, calm down. Just hear me out. I don't love Lisa. I never have. I love you. You know that. All I've ever felt for Lisa was friendship. But you have to understand my situation. My mother has had it pretty rough ever since my father died. My student loans didn't cover everything, and she's had to wipe out her life savings in order for me to go to college. I have to make it up to her, Gillian, but I'm in such deep debt that it will take me years to get anywhere."

Gillian remained silent as Ryan made his final pitch.

"Don't you get it, Gillian? Lisa is my ticket—our ticket, to the good life. Her dad's getting up in years. She'll be getting a pretty good chunk of change in about another five, ten years at the most. Once she does, I'll make sure we co-mingle it. Then, after another year, maybe two, I'll divorce her. After that you and I can finally get married and I can buy you a nice house, or a new car, or diamond jewelry, or whatever your heart desires. In the meantime, don't worry. What matters is that you and I will keep seeing one another. Then, once you graduate, I'll move you to Santa Barbara. I'll tell Lisa that I found you a job lead, or something to that effect. If I can, I'll even help you buy a condo."

Gillian was at a loss for words. Ryan was still stroking her hair and the side of her face, only now his touch made her skin crawl. He kissed her on the cheek. She felt repulsed.

"See, Baby, it's all going work out. Now you just wait here. I'm going to take a shower and then I have to rent a utility trailer. A couple of the guys are coming over this afternoon to help me load it, and I'm pulling out first thing in the morning. I have to find an apartment in Santa

Barbara as quickly as I can. But tonight, I'm taking you out for prime rib and then we're going back to your place. We're going to celebrate, and I mean celebrate. I'm going to have you screaming and moaning for most of the night."

"What about your fiancé, Ryan?"

"I took her to the airport this morning, along with my mother," he casually replied. "She's back in Indiana making wedding plans. She'll be joining me in Santa Barbara in a few weeks."

Ryan kissed her and stroked her face one last time before he finally got up and went into the bathroom. As soon as Gillian heard the water running she leaped from the sofa bed. She was in such a hurry to get out of his apartment that she stuffed her bra and panties into her purse and quickly put on her shorts and blouse. It took her less than a minute to dress, grab her purse and sandals, and run out the door. She stopped in the courtyard, just long enough to slip on her sandals, and then she ran across to the parking lot as fast as her legs would carry her. She unlocked her car and cranked the engine, but she wasn't going to allow herself the luxury of crying until she got home.

She wasn't aware of the drive back to her apartment. Everything was too surreal. She was living a nightmare she couldn't wake up from. For two years she dreamed of becoming Ryan's wife, not his mistress. In all that time she thought he was the man whom she was destined to spend the rest of her life. Now she realized she'd never known him at all.

As she entered her apartment and closed the door behind her, the choking sob that had been stuck in the back of her throat finally came up. She flung herself down on the sofa and wept uncontrollably. She heard the phone ringing but she didn't bother answering it. When she finally had no more tears left to cry she went into the kitchen and got a glass of water. Suddenly, she felt dirty.

She went into the bathroom, filled the tub with water, and took a long, hot, soaking bath. She wanted to wash every trace of Ryan off her body. After spending a good half hour in the tub she drained it and took a shower so she could wash out the feeling of Ryan's fingers stroking her hair. When she finished, she drew herself another bath, but during her second soaking she realized it would be a very long time before she would feel clean again. She finally got out of the bathtub, combed out her hair, and put on some fresh clothes. Once she was dressed she took the panties and bra out of her purse and dropped them in a trash bag, along with the pair of shorts and blouse that she'd worn to Ryan's apartment. She tied the bag closed and took it out to the dumpster. By the time she returned to her apartment she was starting to feel a little better, and she noticed the blinking light on her answering machine. She rewound it to play back the messages.

"Hey Gillian, Ian here. It's Saturday morning, about eleven o'clock. Hey, I just wanted to say goodbye and to let you know how much I've enjoyed hanging out with you. This afternoon I'm heading home to Colorado, but I'll be back in August. Ryan says you'll be moving to Santa Barbara, but not until you graduate, so maybe I'll run into you sometime. Ryan is one lucky guy. What more can I say, other than have a good summer. Bye."

She rewound the tape again, and as she listened to his message the second time she recalled the old saying that when one door closes another one opens. Maybe it was time for her to stop denying her attraction to Ian. Her mood was quickly shattered by the next message. The call must have come while she was at the dumpster.

"Gillian, it's Ryan. Where are you, and why aren't you answering your phone? It's two o'clock and the guys are on their way to help me load the trailer. It should only take us a couple of hours at the most, and if you're not back by the time we're done I'm coming over to your apartment. So get your butt over here. Now."

Gillian looked at the clock. It was about five minutes after two. She picked up the receiver and quickly punched in a number.

"Hi, Cyn. It's me."

"Hey, Gillian, what's up? How was Ryan's graduation? Sorry I wasn't able to make it."

"It was great, and don't worry about it. Hey listen, I've decided to take a little road trip."

"I see. Are you guys going up to Flagstaff to see Mom and Dad?"

Like many Phoenicians, their parents had a summer home in the mountains.

"No, not this time," replied Gillian. "I have something else in mind."

"Okay then. Where and for how long?"

Typical Cynthia. Always being the overly protective big sister.

"I've decided to do some projects for myself before the summer session starts, so I thought I'd drive up to Sedona or Jerome to shoot some photos and do some sketching. Tell Mom and Dad I'll be gone for a few days and that I'll call them as soon as I get back."

"Will do. You two are certainly due for a break. Tell Ryan I said hi."

"I will. Thanks, Cyn. Bye."

Cynthia assumed that Ryan would be traveling with her, but Gillian didn't want to tell her sister, or anyone else for that matter, that she and Ryan were done. She wasn't ready to be quizzed about it.

The clock ticked on. She quickly packed what she needed, but before she could leave she had one last phone call to make. She took a deep breath, picked up the receiver, and dialed Ryan's number. The phone rang. Once. Twice. Three times. It seemed like an eternity. Finally, someone answered.

"Hi, this is Ryan. Sorry I missed your call, but you know the drill. Leave your name and number after the beep and I'll call you back as soon as I can."

Obviously, he hadn't packed his answering machine yet. She waited patiently for the beep.

"Hi Ryan. This is Gillian. Got your message. You can go to hell!"

She slammed the phone down, grabbed her bags, stepped outside and locked her door. She was about to walk to Samantha's apartment when, by coincidence, Samantha stepped outside. Her long, dark hair shimmered in the sunlight.

"Hey, Sam."

"Hey Gillian, what's up? Going someplace?"

"As a matter of fact, I am. Are you going to be around here for awhile?"

"I think so," she replied. "I'm just on my way to check my mail, but I don't have to leave for work until five. I really don't have anyplace to go between now and then. Why?"

"I've decided I need a vacation, from Ryan. I'll explain later, but for now, could you do me a big favor?"

"Sure. What is it?"

"If Ryan should by chance come over later on today, and if you should happen to see him, would you let him know that I had to go up to Flagstaff to see my folks? Tell him I was called away on a family emergency, and that I'll talk to him later."

Samantha chuckled. She never liked Ryan. "Sure Gillian, I'd be more than happy to. Have fun and I'll see you when you get back."

# ∾Four∾

IT WOULD BE A LONG, difficult summer for Gillian. By the time she returned from her road trip, Ryan had departed for Santa Barbara. She found the note he'd slipped under the door, chastising her for what he called her immature behavior.

She spent the next few weeks telling Ryan over the phone, and by letter, that it was over. Ryan, however, refused to get the message. Somehow he'd convinced himself that she was merely going through a phase and Gillian soon became weary of his harassment. She returned his letters, unopened, and she used her answering machine to screen her incoming calls. Samantha begged her to get a new phone number but she refused. She didn't want to chance Ian calling and hearing that her number had been disconnected. He might draw the wrong conclusion and think she'd gone to Santa Barbara. Samantha also suggested she take out a restraining order against Ryan, but Gillian was hesitant about taking such a drastic step. She honestly believed that if she ignored Ryan long enough he would eventually get the message and go away on his own.

By the time summer turned into fall, Gillian had moved on with her life. She was starting her junior year of college. She was making new friends and even went on a few dates, although nothing more serious than an occasional dinner, movie, or a round of miniature golf. One

Saturday afternoon, while she was busy working on a class project, the phone rang. Ryan's hounding made her jump at the sound. She waited for the beep.

"Hi, Gillian, Ian Palmer. How have you been? Hey, I was just—"

She leaped up and grabbed the receiver. It was the first time she'd heard from Ian since he left the message on her answering machine months before.

"Ian? Ian Palmer? Is that really you? Sorry I couldn't get to the phone in time."

"Yes, it's really me," he replied, "and it's good to hear your voice. How are you, Gillian?"

"I'm doing well; thanks, Ian. It's good to hear your voice, too. How have you been?"

"I've been good, Gillian, and life is treating me good. It's even better now that I'm talking to you. I was calling to let you know I've got two tickets for the football game tonight. Would you like to go?"

"Of course I would, you silly goose."

"All right. Why don't I pick you up around five o'clock? We can grab a burger before the game and catch up on everything."

"Sounds like a plan. I'll see you at five. Do you remember how to get to my apartment?"

"Sure do. See you soon."

"Yes!" exclaimed Gillian as she hung up the phone.

She suddenly felt like a schoolgirl who'd just been asked to her first dance. She dashed to her closet to decide what to wear. She wanted to look her best for Ian, and when he arrived at her door she couldn't believe her eyes. She was overjoyed to finally see him again. His face was beaming as well. He handed her a bright red carnation and gave her a big bear hug. Over dinner she brought him up to date on everything that had happened with Ryan. He was stunned.

"Gillian, I can't believe I'm hearing this. I had a feeling that Ryan was up to something, but I honestly had no idea what it was. None of us knew anything about Lisa. He must have kept her under lock and key. For what it's worth, I never thought he treated you right, but back then I really didn't think it was my place to say anything."

"I know, Ian, and I appreciate it. I just wish he'd get the message and leave me alone."

He steered the conversation to a happier topic. "You know, I thought about you while I was home over the summer."

"Really?"

"Yep. I wondered how you were doing, and how your summer classes were going, but I just wasn't sure if it would be a good idea for me to call you when I got back, so I kept putting it off. I just assumed you were still with Ryan. But then the other day I thought to myself, 'C'mon, Ian, she's a good friend, and what's wrong with two good friends hanging out together?' So I decided to try my luck. I got a couple of tickets to the game, and the rest, as they say, is history."

"Well I'm glad you did."

"Me too."

After the game they stopped at one of the popular student watering holes. A band was playing so they stayed and danced until nearly midnight. Ian was a good dancer and it felt good to have his arms around her whenever they danced a slow dance. When he took her back to her apartment he gave her a little goodnight kiss at the door. Gillian had trouble falling asleep that night. She couldn't get Ian off her mind. A couple of weeks later he called back and invited her to another football game. The second date was as pleasant as the first, although Gillian just wasn't sure if she was ready for another serious involvement.

The night he took her to the third game would be different. An unusual weather pattern had developed and the forecast called for late-season thunderstorms. The weather held out for the game, but afterwards, while on the way to their post-game hangout, the skies opened up and both were drenched. They laughed and danced in the rain like a couple of children.

"Gillian, follow me. Let's go back to my car."

Ian's car was parked a few blocks away. They got inside and as he fired up the engine they looked at each another. Neither one could stop laughing. They both looked like a couple of wet, shaggy dogs. The post game traffic was barely moving and the unseasonable rain made it worse.

"Let's head over to my place to dry off," suggested Ian. "It's fairly close. We can listen to some music and have a drink or two while we wait for the rain to stop and the traffic to clear. Then I can take you home."

"Sounds like a plan to me."

Ian lived in a small apartment building about a mile away from the campus. The building was clearly in need of a fresh coat of paint and for someone to clear all the weeds away.

"It may not look like much on the outside," he said as he unlocked the door, "but I think you'll like it on the inside."

As she stepped through the door, Ian turned the lights on. Gillian was impressed. The apartment itself may have been old and run down, but he had done an outstanding job furnishing the living room. It looked like something from a magazine photo.

"Wow," she said. "Mahogany tables. And a leather sofa and chairs. This stuff must have cost you a fortune, Ian."

"Not really. Some law firm in Denver went bankrupt so I went to their auction. This lot came from their waiting room. I picked it up for a song."

"Well, you certainly have a good eye for design, and I like the way you've done the lighting. Nice and soft. Very cozy and relaxing."

"Thanks. You know, so few people seem to appreciate that. Now, let's get you out of these clothes."

"What?"

"I'm sorry. I guess that came out wrong, didn't it?" Ian's face turned red. "What I meant to say is that you can borrow my bathrobe, if you'd like, and get out of those wet clothes before you catch a cold. It's hanging on a hook inside the bathroom door, and you can hang your things on the towel rack to dry. I'll turn on the stereo and we can listen some music. What kind of music do you like?"

"Just about any kind, except opera."

"Me too. I like to be able to understand the words."

Gillian soon emerged from the bathroom, wearing Ian's yellow terry-cloth robe, and noticed he'd changed into his sweats.

"Would you like a glass of wine?"

"Please."

She took the wine and made herself comfortable on the plush leather sofa as Ian took a seat in one of the leather chairs. They sipped their wine and had a long talk. They discovered they had much in common and both wanted the same things in life. They discussed their childhoods, their families, and how neither had chosen the career paths their parents had wanted them to take. Happily, Ryan's name never came up in the conversation. As the evening progressed, both felt more comfortable in the other's company. Finally, Ian stood up.

"Would you like another glass of wine?"

"Just one more, thank you. Then I guess we should think about you taking me home. What time is it, anyway?"

Ian looked at his watch. "It's about ten minutes to one."

"You're kidding," she replied. "I had no idea it was so late. So one more it is, and then we'll call it a night."

Ian picked up her glass and refilled it, but somehow things got awkward when he handed it back to her and he ended up spilling half of it down her front. Gillian laughed. He got a rag from the kitchen and started dabbing the spilt wine off her chest. Gillian breathed in the sweet scent of his cologne. They gazed into each other's eyes. He followed his instincts and kissed her. It was a long, sweet, soft, gentle kiss.

"I'm sorry," he said. "I shouldn't have been so forward."

"Shut up."

Gillian returned his kiss. After she was done, she leaned back against the sofa, and as she did, the robe came slightly undone, exposing a little bit of her left nipple.

"Gillian, are you sure you want me to be doing this?"

"Yes, Ian. I'm very sure."

Ian sat on the sofa next to her. He kissed her once again, his tongue gently feeling its way into her mouth as he began stroking her shoulders and chest. He slowly worked his hand down to her breast, unsure how she'd react. As he gently caressed it, he heard her softly moan as he felt her nipple turn hard. He pulled off his t-shirt and tossed it aside. He gently placed his hands on her shoulders, slowly laying her down before reaching down and untying the bathrobe. As he pulled it open her body was fully revealed to him. He had never seen anything so perfect, or so beautiful, in his entire life. Gillian looked like a delicate porcelain doll.

He removed the rest of his clothes and lay down on the sofa next to her. He kissed her again as he gently stroked her stomach and her breasts. Gillian dug her fingers into his back. Her touch made his muscles go tense. He began kissing her breasts while he ran his fingers across her hips and down her thighs. As he began exploring inside her, she arched her back and moaned with pleasure before opening her legs to invite him in. He couldn't wait any longer. He mounted her, and as he entered her, his mouth covered hers. They kissed a long, hard, passionate kiss while they moaned in pleasure and thrust their bodies up and down in perfect harmony with one another until they both experienced pure, unbridled ecstasy. For a brief, magical moment in time, their very souls touched and were united as one. When their dance was finally over, they slowly eased themselves down into a calm, gentle silence as they lay wrapped in each other's arms. They may have started the evening as friends, but they would end it as lovers. There was nothing more for either one of them to say.

# ❧Five❧

ROSEMARY BURST INTO the ladies' room. "What are you doing, Gillian? There are people out there waiting to meet you, and—oh my God, you're as white as a sheet. You look like you've just seen a ghost."

"As a matter of fact, I have." Gillian's voice had a strange tone. "You were right, Rosemary, when you said you had a bad feeling about tonight. I should have listened to you."

"What on earth are you talking about?"

"Do you recall my ever telling you about a man named Ian Palmer?"

"Ian Palmer?" Rosemary searched her memory. "Ian Palmer? Ian Palmer? You know, that name sort of sounds familiar, now that I think about it."

Gillian decided to clue her in. "Ian Palmer was someone I knew many years ago. I first met him back when I was in college. That was long before Jason Matthews."

"Oh yeah, now I think I remember, but I'm afraid I really don't know very much about him. In all the years I've known you, you've probably only mentioned him to me once or twice. At least, that's about all I can recall."

Gillian let out a sigh. "I know I've rarely spoken of him over the years, but he's never been very far from my mind. Ian Palmer was the one man, Rosemary, the one man who I never got over. As the years passed, I came to realize that I would be in love with Ian Palmer for the rest of my life, even if I never saw him again. I guess it doesn't matter how many other relationships I've had, or even how many marriages I've had. None of them was Ian. I suppose that's why, in the end, none of them worked out for me."

Gillian reached into her purse, pulled out her compact and started dabbing fresh make-up on her face.

"You know, over the past the twenty-five years, there probably hasn't been a day that's gone by that I haven't thought of Ian. I don't mean for it to sound like I'm obsessing over him. Most of the time they were just memories, or brief, passing thoughts. Then, when Jason arrived on the scene, I thought that maybe the reason why it didn't work out with Ian all those years ago was because I was really meant to be with Jason. Guess I was wrong on that one too, wasn't I?"

"So why on earth are you bringing up this man now? This is your opening night in Denver, Gillian. It's a very big night for you, and you're doing very well. I came in to tell you that someone else just went into Tony's office to buy two of your watercolors. They told me they really love your work and they may come back to buy more."

Rosemary stopped for a minute. "Wait a second, wait a second, that mystery-man. The one wearing the tan suit who just bought the painting hanging in the corner, of the barn and tractor. I haven't had a chance to go over to introduce myself to him either. Now I remember. Didn't you once tell me that Ian moved to Denver? Are you saying...?"

"Rosemary McGee, meet Ian Palmer."

"Oh, my God. Gillian, I don't know what to say. No wonder you look so pale."

Gillian didn't respond. She continued to touch up her make-up as she fought back the tears.

"You know, Gillian, under the circumstances, I think we can break protocol. I'll tell Tony that you've taken ill and I'll take you back to the hotel. We'll order you a stiff drink. A manhattan. We'll make it a double. And you can have yourself a good cry."

Gillian shook her head. She grabbed a fresh tissue and dabbed away the tear rolling down her cheek.

"No, Rosemary, that won't be necessary. Really. I'm not going to let Ian win. Not this time. Just give me a few minutes to pull myself together. I'll be fine."

"You're sure about that?"

Gillian nodded her head before wiping away another tear as Rosemary changed the subject.

"You know, I can't help but wonder what it is about that particular painting that he finds so fascinating."

"Oh, I think I can explain that." Gillian resumed fixing her make-up. "Ian grew up on a farm, somewhere in eastern Colorado. I think it may have been near the Kansas border, but I'm not certain. Anyway, he always said he felt guilty about leaving the family farm to become an architect, and who knows whatever became of the place. That painting must remind him of his childhood. That's probably why he's so drawn to it."

Rosemary glanced at her watch. "Well, I'm proud of you for deciding to stay. I know you've been startled, but I also know you, Gillian. You're a pro. You're not going to let this little unexpected bump in the road ruin a really good opening for you, which reminds me—I came in to let you know that the reporter and photographer from that newspaper just showed up."

Gillian nodded as Rosemary continued.

"It looks like the color's come back into your face, but you'll need to put on some fresh lipstick and straighten your hair a little. I'll go out to tell them you came in to freshen up so you'll look good for the photographer and that you'll be ready in a couple minutes."

"Thanks, Rosemary. I don't know what I'd do without you."

"Anytime. That's what I'm here for. As for Ian Palmer, all I can say is he's apparently been here for some time and he hasn't bothered you. And since he's just purchased one of your paintings, I think we can safely rule out his coming here to cause trouble for you. I'll go out and give him our customary 'thank you' for buying your art. I'll also try to keep him occupied for as long as I can so he won't have an opportunity to disturb you while you're talking to the reporters. You still need to personally thank him, the same way you'd thank anyone who purchases one of your paintings, but you don't need to get involved in a long conversation with him. Just say thank you, nice seeing you again, and politely excuse yourself. I know you can do it, Gillian. Meantime, I need you to hurry up and get ready. There are people, some very important people, out there waiting for you."

"Thanks, Rosemary. I'll be ready in a couple of minutes."

Gillian took a deep breath as Rosemary departed. With her on the job, Ian Palmer wouldn't be a problem at all. She reached into her purse for her lipstick. As she applied it, she noticed the tiny scar over her upper right lip. It was a thin, white line, probably no more than an eighth of an inch long. It was so faint that even she hardly noticed it anymore. The memory of that day, however, would stay with her forever.

# ๛Six๛

A S GILLIAN YAWNED and stretched she felt Ian's arms wrap around her while he murmured softly in his sleep. She lay still for a moment, savoring his sweet embrace. It was the weekend before Thanksgiving and she looked forward to bringing him home to her family holiday dinner. She sincerely hoped that Ian and her father would hit it off. Maybe by the time his graduation rolled around her father could give him a job referral, just as he'd tried to do the year before with Ryan.

Ryan. Just the thought of his name was enough to bring her down. The past few weeks had been golden. Ryan had finally stopped calling her. At long last, he was out of her life. That gave her an extra reason to be thankful.

The sun was up and her stomach was growling. It was time to go to the kitchen to make a pot of coffee. She carefully inched her way out of bed, being careful not to disturb Ian. She picked her nightgown off the floor and slipped it back on, wondering why she even bothered with such formalities when he was there. She tiptoed into the kitchen and had just finished pouring the water into the coffee maker when she heard a loud banging on the door.

"Gillian! I know you're in there. Answer the damn door!"

Her blood turned to ice. It was Ryan. She ran to the door and cracked it open.

"What are you doing here?" she hissed. "I told you six months ago it

27

was over between you and me, so go back to Santa Barbara. Lisa's waiting there for you."

She tried to close the door but Ryan pushed it open, forcing his way into her apartment. He stopped and carefully closed the door behind him. He was about to turn the lock when the phone rang. She turned to answer it but Ryan grabbed her by the arm and stopped her.

"Lisa's gone, thanks to you. She found one of the letters you returned, and after she read it she gave me back my ring and hightailed it back to Indiana. Guess that's good news for you, huh? Pack your bags. As soon as I'm finished with you, you're coming to Santa Barbara with me."

Gillian looked into Ryan's eyes. What she saw chilled her to the bone. Ryan was about to rape her. She tried to break free of his grip, but the more she struggled, the tighter it became.

"Are you out of your mind? I'm not going anywhere with you. Now you either go, right now, or I'm calling the cops."

Ryan was undeterred. "Didn't you hear a word I just said to you? Lisa's gone. You got what you wanted. You can finally drop this charade about our breaking up."

"Let go of me, Ryan. You're hurting me."

"The lady just told you to leave, Ryan. I suggest you let go of her and get going."

Ryan turned away from Gillian. For the first time he noticed Ian, standing a few feet away. He looked back at Gillian, still in her nightgown, then back at his friend, who was wearing nothing but a pair of sweat pants. He shifted his gaze back and forth a few more times. It took a moment for it to all sink in.

"Well Ian, what have we here? I see you've been keeping her warm for me, but I honestly don't know if I should thank you or not." He turned back to Gillian. His grip on her arm grew tighter. Gillian cried out in pain. "And as for you, Little Miss High and Mighty, how dare you criticize me for two-timing you with Lisa. How long have you been doing Ian on the side? Tell me!"

"Don't say a word to him, Gillian. It's none of his damn business. You either let go of her Ryan, right now, or I'll make you let go of her. "

"Sure Ian, no problem. Here's your whore."

Ryan slammed Gillian against the wall and followed up with a punch across her face. At the same instant the door burst open. It was Samantha Walsh.

"Gillian!"

As Samantha stepped into the apartment Ryan turned a somersault in the air. He landed flat on his back with a hard thud at her feet.

"Holy Mother of God!"

Gillian ran into the kitchen. Samantha stepped across Ryan and raced into the kitchen behind her. She grabbed ahold of Gillian, who was badly shaken.

"Are you all right?"

Gillian made soft, whimpering noises as she stared down at the floor. Samantha followed her gaze. A couple drops of fresh blood lay at their feet. She reached under Gillian's chin to lift up her face so she could take a closer look.

"Oh my God!"

"What's wrong?" shouted Ian.

"He cut her face when he punched her."

"Son of a bitch!"

Samantha grabbed a paper towel and started dabbing the blood away from Gillian's face. Even though she tried to be as gentle as she could, Gillian flinched with pain. Ian looked down at Ryan, still lying on the floor. A blinding rage burned in his eyes.

"I ought to put you out of your misery, right here and now."

"Don't bother, Ian," said Samantha as she tended to Gillian. "I think he got the message when you flipped him in the air. He's not worth going to jail. Besides, I don't think we have enough money to post your bail."

Gillian took the paper towel from Samantha. She held her bleeding face with one hand and reached for the phone with the other. Both Samantha and Ian noticed the red marks on her arm and the blood drops on the front of her nightgown.

"I'm calling the cops. If anyone's going to jail right now, it's Ryan." Gillian's speech sounded slurred. Her lip was starting to swell.

"Don't bother, I'm leaving." Ryan slowly sat up and looked at Ian. They all heard the acidic tone in his voice. "And don't worry, I won't be coming back. Now that I've found out you've been doing her, I don't want her anymore. As far as I'm concerned, she's damaged goods. Hell, you can do a threesome with Samantha, for all I care. With her looks, I'm sure she turns more than just tables."

"I'm taking out a restraining order against you, Ryan—today." Gillian set the receiver back in its cradle. "I have two witnesses, and I have a busted lip to prove what just happened here. But now that I think about it, I'm not going to press charges. Not because I'm showing you any mercy, but because you're so repulsive to me that the very thought of ever having to see your face again, even in a courtroom, turns my stomach. But if you ever call me again, if you ever show up at my door again, or if you so much as write me a note, I'll have your sorry butt tossed in jail so fast it'll make your head spin."

Ryan slowly rose to his feet. He, too, appeared shaken. Before exiting, he stopped in the doorway, turning back to Gillian for one final parting shot.

"So long, slut!"

"And on that happy note," quipped Samantha, "I'm going to walk you to your car." She looked back at Ian as she followed Ryan out the door. "Take care of her. I'll be back in a little bit."

Samantha returned to find Gillian resting on the sofa. Ian had helped her change out of her bloodied nightgown and was tending to her injured face.

"Have a look," he said to Samantha. "She's got a little tiny cut, right above her lip. I flushed it out with peroxide and I've got the bleeding stopped. I don't think she'll need stitches. I've put some ice on it, and the swelling's gone down. What do you think?"

Gillian pulled her makeshift ice pack away and pointed to a tiny red area just above her right lip.

"Oh yeah. The swelling's gone down considerably. Thank goodness it's only a tiny cut. Can't be more than an eighth of an inch, if that much. We'll put a butterfly bandage on it for a couple days. By the time it's fully healed, it shouldn't be that noticeable."

Samantha had been a nursing student until she ran out of money. Now she was waiting tables at a truck-stop diner until she saved up enough to go back and complete her degree.

"So, where's Ryan?" asked Gillian.

Samantha had a gleam in her eye. "Well, when he left here he wasn't moving very fast, so I ran and grabbed my purse. Then I walked him to his car, just like I said I would. Once we got there it took him a couple of minutes to regain his composure, so I stood by, very patiently. As soon as he got in, I got in my car. I followed him out of the parking lot, down the street and onto the freeway. And then I followed him down the freeway for several miles."

"That was smart thinking on your part," said Ian. Gillian nodded her head in agreement.

"Thanks. I noticed his car this morning, while I was taking out my trash. I started getting a really bad feeling, so I got a pen and paper and took down his license plate number. Then I rushed back to my apartment so I could call and warn you. Next thing I know, I'm hearing him banging on your door, and when you didn't answer your phone, I came running over. I could hear all the shouting going on inside. I knew it was bad, and I figured you wouldn't mind if I came in without knocking."

Gillian stood up from the sofa and hugged her friend. "Thanks, Sam. You truly are a good friend. I owe you one."

"Thanks, Sam," echoed Ian. "You were good back-up. I appreciate it."

"Oh, I'd say that by the time I got here you pretty much had it under control, Ian. You really kicked his butt. But you gotta hear the rest of the story. This is where it gets really good."

Samantha took a seat on the sofa next to Gillian. "I decided to stop by the diner on the way back. As usual, a few of my trucker buddies were there, so I told 'em all what happened. I gave them the make, model and license plate number of Ryan's car, and asked if they'd mind relaying the information on their CB radios. I'd say by now every truck driver from El Paso to Sacramento is on the lookout for Ryan."

All three burst out laughing. Ian raised his arm and gave Samantha a high five.

"So I take it our friend will be escorted home."

"You got it, Ian," replied Samantha. "I wanted to make sure we're covered, just in case he changes his mind and decides to come back."

"What's going on? What are you guys talking about?"

"It's called boxing, Gillian," explained Ian. "It means one big rig will get in front of him, another behind him, and the third and fourth will pull up in the lanes beside him. He's going to find himself surrounded by truckers for most of the drive back to Santa Barbara."

For the first time that morning, Gillian smiled. "Well then, I can't think of anyone more deserving. Like I just said, you truly are a good friend, Sam."

"I'll get her bandaged while you get dressed, Ian. We need to take a trip to the cop shop so she can take out that emergency restraining order. I'll drive."

31

## ❧SEVEN❧

GILLIAN TOOK A FINAL look in the mirror. Everything was tucked neatly back into place. She dropped the lipstick back into her purse and gave herself a little pep talk.

"Well kiddo, I guess it's now or never."

As she headed back toward the gallery she found Paul waiting in the hallway.

"Are you all right, Gillian? Rosemary said you weren't feeling well. Can I get you anything? Perhaps a glass of orange juice?"

"No, Paul. I'm fine, really."

"Are you sure?"

"Yes, I'm sure. Thanks for the offer."

As she entered the gallery she glanced toward the corner. Sure enough, Rosemary was busy talking to Ian. Judging by their body language, the conversation must have been going well. She turned back to Paul, who pointed out two people in the crowd.

"Now, look right over there. Do you see the lady with the long brown hair and the white sweater, and the African-American man in the blue shirt standing next to her?"

"Yes. It looks like they're both wearing ID badges."

"Very good," replied Paul. "They're the people from the newspaper, and yes, they have their press badges. You need to go over and talk to them. And please, let me know if you need anything."

"Will do. And thank you again, Paul."

Paul waved to the two reporters and pointed to Gillian. As she began walking toward them a rather talkative older woman blocked her path. After spending just enough time with her to be polite, Gillian tried, twice, to end the conversation and step away. Both times, however, the woman followed her and kept talking. This sometimes happened to her at public events. A well-meaning fan would glom onto her and not want to let go. She looked around for Rosemary, but by then she and Ian were no longer in the back corner.

"I'm sorry to interrupt," said a voice from behind her. Once again, it was Rosemary to her rescue. "If you'll excuse us, Ms. Matthews has to meet with a reporter for an interview."

"Thanks," said Gillian as Rosemary whisked her away. "I'm sure she's a sweet little old lady, but this just isn't the time or place. I couldn't get away from her."

"That's what I'm here for," replied Rosemary, smugly. "I'll bring you up to date on Mr. Palmer once you're done. Nice guy, by the way. He's not harboring any kind of a grudge and he says he still thinks of you."

Before Gillian could ask any questions, Rosemary introduced her to the reporters. "Gillian, this is Emma Sanchez. She's a reporter for *The Denver Centennial*. And this is Ron Lewis. He's a photographer, also with the *Centennial*. They would like to speak to you for a few minutes."

Emma led Gillian to one of the settees scattered about the gallery and both women sat down.

"First of all," said Gillian, "let me apologize for keeping the two of you waiting."

"Please, don't worry about it. It's not a problem at all. Ron and I both saw what was going on. We've seen it happen many times before." Her photographer nodded his head in agreement. "Now, let's get started. First of all, can I call you, Gillian?"

"Please do."

"All right, Gillian. As I'm sure you've been told, *The Denver Centennial* is a weekly arts and entertainment paper, and we'd like to do a feature story about you in our fine arts section. Would you mind answering a few questions? Then, when we're done, Ron would like to take a few photos."

"Of course. Fire away."

Emma retrieved her digital tape recorder from her purse, along with a pen and a small notebook. She asked the typical questions the media people always asked. How long had she been painting? Did she have any formal training? What was her inspiration? What were her future plans as an artist? As Gillian talked with the reporter she noticed a familiar scent. It was the cologne Ian always wore. She tried to glance nonchalantly around the gallery but she couldn't see him anywhere. She had a strong feeling, however, that he was standing somewhere close behind her. It was becoming difficult for her to focus on the interview. Fortunately, it was winding down.

"One final question, if you don't mind, Gillian. Is there a Mr. Matthews? And if so, what does he think of your work?"

Gillian felt Ian's presence nearby. She was certain his ears perked up. She chose her words carefully. "Well, yes, there was a Mr. Matthews. At one time he was probably my biggest fan. However, he and I are no longer together."

"Thank you, Gillian." Emma extended her hand. "I think Ron's ready to take a few photos. Barring any last-minute editorial changes, the story is scheduled to run in two weeks. I'll send Rosemary an email and let you know for sure. We'll also be sure to send you a hardcopy, and it will be on our website as well."

The scent of Ian's cologne faded away. She followed the photographer to one of her paintings so he could take a few shots of her standing next to it. Ironically, it was the one of the abandoned tractor in front of the barn. As soon as Ron finished, she thanked him and looked around the gallery. The crowd was thinning. She spotted Ian standing at the bar. As she summoned up the courage to approach him, another woman came up to him and started talking. Gillian's heart sank. She realized she'd been wrong in assuming he'd come alone. After twenty-five years, he certainly would have been married by now. Perhaps it was just as well. At least it looked like he had a beautiful wife.

Gillian returned to doing what she came to do—to meet people and to talk about her art. She kept working the crowd until she noticed almost everyone had gone. She looked at her watch. It was nearly eight o'clock, the scheduled ending time. At eight-fifteen she and Rosemary had an impromptu meeting near the bar with Tony. By then only a handful of patrons remained in the gallery and the caterers were beginning their break down.

"Gillian, Rosemary, thank you both so much," said Tony. "I understand you weren't feeling well this evening Gillian, but obviously, you're a trooper. You still managed to make tonight a smashing success, and you've sold quite a number of paintings. I'm already looking forward to your next show. I'll call Rosemary next week to see if we can possibly arrange something for you later on in the year. In the meantime, ladies, I thank you once again."

They shook hands and Tony left to finish up the paperwork in his office.

"Well, I don't know about you," said Gillian, "but I'm famished. Let's go find someplace to eat."

"Good idea. I'll go get our bags. In the meantime, there's still a certain gentleman here who you need to go over and thank."

Gillian looked in the corner. Ian was still in the gallery, and he was once again immersed in the painting. She looked back at Rosemary.

"Look," Rosemary whispered, somewhat emphatically, "he just wrote out a check tonight for five thousand dollars. You need to tell him 'thank you.' Trust me, he's not going to bite you. I'll be back in a minute and then we can leave. Okay?"

Rosemary exited down the hallway. Gillian took a deep breath. As usual, Rosemary was right. Under the circumstances it would have been bad form, not to mention highly unprofessional, for her not to personally acknowledge him. She cautiously approached him. His back was still turned. It was now or never. She took another deep breath and said a quick little prayer.

"Pardon me, sir. I'm so sorry I didn't get the chance to come over earlier to tell you 'thank you.'"

His shoulders squared at the sound of her voice. "Yes, I know...and I'm so sorry to have startled you, Gillian." He slowly turned to face her. "But I have to admit, watching you trying to keep from dropping that glass was one of the funniest things I think I've seen in a long, long time."

"You knew?"

"Of course, I knew. You never could keep a secret from me, Gillian."

He looked much the same as she remembered. He still had a head of thick, dark brown hair, but it was cut shorter. He now wore glasses, and they somehow made him look smarter and more sophisticated. He was a little thinner and his face had a few lines, giving him a more distinguished look. He wore an expensive looking suit. Ian must have done well for himself. Even back in college, he was driven for success. He reached out and grasped her hand. She looked into his eyes. She could tell he was genuinely happy to see her, but at the same time, underneath it all, was a look of sadness.

"It's good to see you, Gilly-girl."

Gilly-girl. He even remembered his old nickname for her. No one had ever called her, Gilly-girl, before or since. He bent down and softly kissed her on the cheek.

"It's good to see you too, Ian. It's been a long time. A very long time. More than half a lifetime."

Not wanting to allow herself to become too emotionally wrapped up in their sweet reunion, she decided to lay it on the table.

"I see you brought someone with you. Do you want to introduce me to her?"

"Who?"

"The lady you were talking to earlier. I was coming over to introduce myself, while you were standing at the bar. Then she came over and started talking to you. I assumed she was your wife, or your significant other, so I stepped away."

Ian suddenly remembered. "Oh, right, right. The lady with the short brown hair, wearing the black pants and the patchwork sweater."

"Yes, that was her."

Ian shrugged his shoulders. "I have no idea who she was, Gillian. She was just making small talk with me while she waited for her husband. I came here on my own tonight. I saw your picture in the newspaper the other day, so I thought I'd come and say hello to an old and very dear friend, and, if by chance she was available, ask her if she would like to have dinner and, maybe, catch up on old times."

"Well, I—"

"She'd love to."

Gillian hadn't heard Rosemary coming up behind her. "But I've got some work I need to catch up on—"

"Which you pay me handsomely to take care of for you. Here's your purse. I can find my way back to the hotel. I can order in. We've got the GPS device. Remember?"

"But I—"

Rosemary turned her attention to Ian. "We're staying at the Radisson. It's only a few blocks from here. You know where that is?"

"Of course," he replied.

"If you wouldn't mind dropping her off?"

"It would be my pleasure. Thank you, Rosemary. I enjoyed meeting you. Very much."

Rosemary said her goodbyes and made a hasty exit.

"You know," said Ian, "she reminds me a lot of Samantha Walsh. She even looks a little bit like Sam. Now, let me buy you dinner. She tells me you haven't eaten very much today, and that you still love a good steak."

## ❧EIGHT❧

IAN ESCORTED GILLIAN to a late model silver BMW. He opened the passenger door and waited as she got in. She fastened her seatbelt and took it all in as he slipped into the driver's seat. She couldn't believe she was about to take a drive with Ian Palmer.

"Have you ever been to Denver, Gillian?"

"No." She shook her head. "It's my first time here."

"In that case, I guess I'd better show you 'round."

As they drove, he explained that the part of town they were in had been near the old Stapleton Airport, which had been decommissioned when the new Denver International Airport opened north of the city. Over the years it had been redeveloped into new shopping centers and business districts with Ian's firm involved in the design.

"Are you still with Salisbury and Norton?"

"Yes. I've been with them for over twenty years now. I've worked my way up to project architect, which means I'm probably way too overqualified to ever change jobs."

He pulled into the restaurant parking lot and escorted her inside. The dining room was softly lit and very formal. It was in sharp contrast to the college hangouts they frequented when they were younger. Seated in a quiet corner, Ian ordered a half-liter of wine. Once they were served, he raised his glass.

37

"Here's to old friends and new beginnings."

"Here, here." Gillian raised her glass.

"So, now that you know I've stayed with the same firm I've been with since I graduated, I should probably thank your father. He was the one who referred me to the Salisbury office in Phoenix."

"I think my father would have been very proud of you, Ian. Unfortunately, he passed away a number of years ago."

"I'm sorry to hear that. If I'm not being too bold, may I ask what happened?"

She explained that after her father retired her parents did a lot of traveling. They were vacationing at a golf resort in California when her father collapsed and died of a massive brain aneurism.

"At least there was no prolonged pain and suffering and he died doing something he loved. My mother wasn't so lucky. A few years later she was diagnosed with lung cancer."

Gillian's mother had been a heavy smoker her entire adult life, so what happened to her really wasn't that surprising. Still, it was a slow, agonizing death. She decided to change the subject.

"So what about your family?"

"Sadly, both of my parents are gone now too," he said. "My father was a heavy smoker as well; that whole generation smoked. It was kind of like what happened to your father. One day, while he was out working the fields, he had a heart attack. He'd been gone for several hours by the time anyone found him. My mother later died of pneumonia. At least, that was the official cause of death, but she really died of a broken heart. After she passed my sister, Kat, and I sold the farm. It was sad. It was the end of a family era actually, but times change, and life goes on."

He took another sip of his wine. "You know, Gillian, it's uncanny how our minds sometimes work. I don't recall ever showing you any photos of my family's farm, but the barn in your painting was virtually identical to the one we had, and my father had a similar tractor. I simply had to have it. It was like suddenly rediscovering a long lost part of myself. So how is it you've become such a successful artist?"

She began by telling him that after they broke up she went to graduate school in San Francisco.

"It was an exciting time for me. San Francisco was a fun place to live and I made a lot of new friends, but I knew I wasn't going to spend the rest of my life there. Anyway, about the time I was ready to graduate, a bunch of us went to Lake Tahoe for a ski trip, and while I was there I met a ski instructor by the name of Stuart Callahan. We quickly became friends. While I was there I decided, for a lark, to put in an application at the local newspaper in Tahoe City. They offered me a job in their advertising department, so I accepted it."

Before long she and Stuart Callahan were living together.

"You know, I was never passionately in love with Stu, but for some reason I felt very comfortable with him, like I could be myself, you know."

She and Stu got engaged. They came back to Phoenix and had the big wedding she'd always dreamed of, but the marriage only lasted a short time. Stu turned out to be too undependable, and the bills were never paid on time.

"Did you have any children?"

A look of sadness came across Gillian's face." Almost." She took a sip of her wine before continuing. "About six months after Stu and I were married, I had a miscarriage. I wasn't very far along. I hadn't even had the chance to see a doctor or tell my family that I was pregnant. We were on a back-country hike in a remote part of the Sierras when it happened. I started feeling this incredibly horrible pain, and Stu noticed I was bleeding. It took several hours for us to get to a hospital. I had an ectopic pregnancy, which means the baby was growing in the tube, and my tube had ruptured. I nearly bled to death."

Ian reached across the table and took her hand. "I'm so sorry that happened. Did you ever have another child?"

She shook her head. "No. We weren't ready to be parents yet, and after that I wasn't about to get pregnant again. It wasn't until much later, while I was married to my second husband, that I tried again. By then I was in my thirties and it just didn't happen. Maybe it was just as well. I was totally dedicated to my career. Now I'm getting too old to have a baby."

She decided it was time to change the subject. "So, how about you, Ian?"

The waiter arrived with their main course. After he left, Ian answered her question.

"A few months after you and I parted company for good, Salisbury's receptionist went on maternity leave, so a temporary came in for a few weeks. Her name was Laura Mitchell. She was single, so I asked her out. It was kind of like you and Stu. I wasn't madly in love with her, but I felt comfortable around her. She was also a blonde and she sort of looked like you. I guess that's what attracted me to her. After going out with her for about a year, I figured she'd make a good wife, so I married her. We had two sons together, Jeremy and Larry. We were both devoted parents, but over time we simply drifted apart. She may have looked like you, but she wasn't you, Gillian. Still, we'd had two kids together, so I stayed with her. She was the last woman I ever thought would cheat on me."

"I'm sorry, Ian. You're a good man. You didn't deserve that."

"It was Jeremy's senior year in high school, and I got some

unexpected visitors at the office one day. They were a private investigator and his client, a woman whom I'd never met. Turned out her husband was the man who'd sold us our car six months earlier, and he and Laura were having an affair. I couldn't believe it, even with the proof staring me in the face. When I got home that night, I confronted her. She admitted it, but she didn't seem that remorseful. It ended a short time later, but by then there was nothing left between us. We separated a few weeks after Jeremy graduated and left home. I filed for divorce, and she ended up taking a job at a horse refuge near Steamboat Springs. We both agreed that I would stay in the house with Larry until he finishes high school, which will be a little over a year from now. Then I can sell the place and finally close that chapter of my life. So, what happened after you and Stuart Callahan went your separate ways?"

"I came back to Phoenix and got a job in the art department with an advertising agency. That's where I met Rosemary. She worked in their public relations department. After my parents passed away, Cynthia and I ended up with a pretty hefty inheritance. I always hated being a graphic designer. My heart and soul was in drawing and painting."

"Yes, I remember."

"Over the years I kept doing my art on the side and I was in a number of juried art shows. After Mom died, I heard about an art gallery in Scottsdale being up for sale. I decided to use my inheritance to buy the place, and Cynthia decided to invest in it as well. We became business partners, and we brought Rosemary on board. We call it Hanson Sisters Fine Art. It was the best decision I ever made in my life."

"I never had any doubt that you'd make it someday. So, if you don't mind my asking, how did you end up with the name Matthews?"

Gillian let out a sigh. "About ten years ago I got a private commission for a series of paintings. The client wanted something Old West, with a modern day twist, so I drove down to Tombstone and spent a few days taking photos and doing some sketches. While I was there, I met a man named Jason Matthews. He was a bartender who also performed in gunfight shows. He had that rugged, cowboy look, so I decided to use him as a model in the paintings. He was terribly flattered. I don't know how else to say it, Ian. The man completely swept me off my feet. I thought I'd finally found Mr. Right."

Now it was Ian's turn to see a look of sadness in her eyes. "Hey, you don't have to talk about it, if you don't want to."

"No, it's okay. I've told you this much, so I may as well finish. Jason and I ran off to Las Vegas and got married a few weeks later. Cynthia was furious with me. She knew, right from the start, what kind of a man he really was. He was a con man. He sought out single, unattached middle-aged women, like me, and over time he drained their bank accounts. He knew how to make himself out to be the man of their dreams, but sooner or later the mask would come off and his true colors would come out. The fifth year of our marriage was when he finally realized that he would never, ever, be able to get his hooks into the gallery, or into any of my other assets, so he became abusive. He made Ryan Knight look like a schoolboy in comparison. I filed for divorce, but he made it all as ugly as he possibly could. Thank goodness for Rosemary. She stood up for me, just like Samantha did all those years ago, that awful morning when Ryan showed up at my door and you kicked his sorry butt."

The waiter came and took their plates. Ian noticed they were the last customers in the restaurant, and that the staff was starting to clear off the other tables.

"It's getting late, Gillian. Why don't we call it a night? I've got a seventeen-year-old waiting at home for me, and I need to make sure he's staying out of trouble. We'll catch up some more later. Now that I've found you again, I'd really like for us to stay in touch."

"I'd like that too, Ian."

He took the red carnation from the glass vase sitting on their table and handed it to her.

"Remember how I was always giving you red carnations? Somehow I don't think they'll mind if we take it. They have to put out fresh flowers tomorrow anyway."

He drove to the front of her hotel, opened her car door, and walked her to the entrance. He gave her a kiss on the cheek and waited until she was safely inside before going back to his car and driving away. Gillian took the elevator up to her room. She was unlocking her door when Rosemary, who had the room across from her, heard her in the hallway.

"So how did it go?" she asked.

"Good, Rosemary. It went well."

"May I come in? Maybe we can have a nightcap and sit out on the balcony for awhile."

"Of course. I'd like that."

Gillian set the carnation down on the dresser and took a couple bottles of mineral water out of the mini refrigerator. The two women took a seat on the balcony. They had the perfect view of the Denver nighttime skyline.

"So, don't keep me in suspense any longer," said Rosemary. "How did it go?"

"It went well. It seems we're both single these days, and he'd like for us to stay in touch."

"Yes, he did indicate to me that he was no longer married. But

Gillian, whatever you do, do not get your hopes up. It's been twenty-five years. That's a long time and people do change. He lives here and you live in Phoenix. Enjoy your reunion and be friends, but please, don't expect it to be anything more."

# ❧NINE❦

GILLIAN WOULD HEAR from Ian several times over the next few weeks, but not as frequently as she had hoped. He sent her a few emails and he called her once or twice, but only to chitchat. Rosemary and Cynthia again reminded her not to expect too much. It was what it was and they weren't in college anymore. In her head, she knew they were right, but in her heart, she couldn't help but feel disappointed. In the meantime, her life went on, and she'd just picked up another private commission.

Gillian worked out of her home. She converted her utility room into an art studio and it was the perfect location for her as she often got her best ideas late at night. She shared her home with Duke and Daisy, her two miniature dachshunds, who didn't seem to mind her occasionally crazy work hours. She stepped into her den and took a seat at her computer. She needed to look through her source files for visual references, but first she decided to check her email. No message from Ian for the past three days. She thought of emailing him but thought better of it. The last thing she wanted was for him to think she was feeling anxious. She felt one of the dogs nuzzling her foot.

"Well Daisy, nothing from Ian again today. He must be working hard and keeping busy."

Daisy cocked her head as if she was trying to understand what Gillian saying.

"And speaking of work, I guess I'd better start on it myself, if I want to keep you and your brother fed and with a roof over our heads."

She turned back to the computer and started weeding through her photo files. She didn't know how much time passed before she heard two barking dogs and the sound of the doorbell. She went to the door and looked through the peephole. It was Rosemary. She opened the door and discovered Rosemary had a big bouquet of red carnations in a beautiful red glass vase.

"Well my goodness, Rosemary, you shouldn't have. And it's not even my birthday."

"Very funny, Miss Smarty-Pants. This arrived for you at the gallery about a half an hour ago. Care to guess who really sent them?"

Gillian invited her inside. She eagerly took the flowers to the kitchen and added more water to the vase. Rosemary was right behind her.

"Can I get you anything to drink?"

"Yes, please," replied Rosemary. "I'll take a soda, if you've got one, but first let's take a look at the card."

Gillian placed the flowers on the table in the breakfast nook and took the card from the envelope. Her face lit up as she read it.

"You're right, as usual, my friend. The card says, 'Guess what? You have a big surprise coming. Love, Ian.' Well now, that certainly sounds intriguing. I wonder what it means."

She poured Rosemary a soda, along with one for herself. They took a seat at the table so Gillian could admire the flowers. They gazed out the window at the backyard pool. It was the end of May and summer was on the way. The pool looked inviting.

"Well, Gillian, it's like I keep telling you. Enjoy Ian's friendship, but please don't put too much into it. His surprise could be anything. You know how men are. They don't think like we do. For all we know it could be nothing more than his knowing someone who wants to buy one of your paintings."

Gillian sipped her soda. Once again, Rosemary was right.

"Gillian, I know it's none of my business, and you certainly have the right to tell me to butt out, but I've been wondering something. Why it didn't work out with Ian, all those years ago?"

Gillian let out a sigh. "Ian Palmer and I dated, exclusively, for about two and a half years. It was a very intense relationship. During that time, he graduated from Arizona State University with a degree in architecture. My father heard about an opening at the Salisbury and Norton office in Phoenix. Ian applied for the job and was hired. I still had another year of college to go, and I was hopeful that we'd marry once I graduated. However, my graduation came and went, and Ian seemed content with the status quo. He was ambitious. He was putting in incredibly long hours, while I was struggling trying to find my first job, and yes, that did put a strain on the relationship."

"Actually that makes sense, Gillian. Most young men do want to get established in their careers before they're ready to settle down."

"At the time that was my thought too, but then one day, shortly after the Christmas holidays, Ian called me from work and he sounded strange. He said he needed to talk to me right away, so that evening I met him at his apartment. He told me there'd been an opening at the Salisbury office in Denver, that he'd applied for it, and that they'd offered it to him. He said he wanted to go home to Colorado, and he'd be leaving in thirty days. I told him I understood his wanting to live closer to his parents, but I also asked him about us. He told me he just wasn't ready to make a commitment yet. He said he wanted to establish himself in his career before he settled down, like you just mentioned. I told him that was fine. I had things I wanted to do myself, and I'd be happy to wait for him. And that's when he suddenly made a left turn on me. He said no, he wanted me to find someone else."

"You're kidding," said Rosemary.

"I wish I was. I felt like I'd just been sucker-punched in the face. We stayed in touch for a few months after he left. He even came back once or twice to visit me. I had a very good friend back then by the name of Samantha Walsh. In fact, Rosemary, she was a lot like you."

"Really? And here I thought I was one-of-a-kind."

Gillian gave her friend a smile and continued with her story. "Sam always had a good rapport with Ian, and she was just as stunned by his sudden, erratic behavior as I was. During his last visit to Phoenix, she invited him out for coffee. She wanted to find out what was really going on with him. Later on she told me he had a severe case of cold feet. She said Ian kept reassuring her that I'd done nothing wrong, and she said he even admitted I was the best woman who'd ever come into his life. But he never gave her a reason for why he wanted to end things, so she was just as much in the dark as I was. She wasn't sure if Ian even knew the reason himself."

"Did you ever find out what it was?"

"No, but as the weeks went by, Ian became more and more distant. I kept asking him what was wrong, but whatever it was, he refused to tell me. He just said that while he still loved me, he'd also come to realize that it was time for me to move on and find someone else. It got to the point that one day I finally told him I couldn't take the torture anymore. I'll always remember that final phone call. I told him if that was how he really felt, then I didn't want to see him, or hear from him, again. He got really quiet for a moment. Then he wished me a happy life and said goodbye. After that I never saw or heard from him again, until a few weeks ago, when he showed up at Tony Sorenson's gallery."

## ❧ TEN ❧

THE SILVER BMW with Colorado license plates pulled into the parking lot at Hanson Sisters Fine Art. Ian had forgotten about the intensity of the early June heat in Phoenix. As he stepped out of the car, it nearly took his breath away. When he pulled out of the motel in Gallup, New Mexico, that morning, it had been cool and comfortable. He reached back into the car, retrieved the briefcase from the passenger seat, pressed the remote, and locked the car. The air conditioning felt refreshing as he entered the gallery. It was like a slightly smaller version of Sorenson's gallery. He walked up to the information desk and was greeted by a young woman.

"May I help you?"

"Yes. Is Gillian Matthews in?"

"I'm sorry sir, but Mrs. Matthews only comes here by appointment. If you would like to leave your card with me I could call her for you. Or perhaps someone else can help you."

"I see. Well, I suppose I can speak to her sister."

She picked up the phone and asked him for his name. A minute later he heard a familiar voice coming from the hallway on his left.

"Ian? Ian Palmer? Could that possibly be you?" A woman rushed up to greet him.

"Cynthia! How are you? Let me take a look at you." He stepped back and they looked one another over. Cynthia and Gillian bore a strong family resemblance, however Cynthia's eyes were blue instead of green, and her long, auburn hair was pulled neatly back into a ponytail. Like Gillian, Cynthia looked many years younger than her actual age.

"Would you like to step into my office?"

"Yes. I actually have something that I wanted to discuss with you. Is Rosemary here?"

"She's out running an errand, but I can have her join us as soon as she gets back."

"Thanks. And would you mind calling Gillian? I want her in on this too. But please, don't tell her I'm here. It's all part of a big surprise I've planned for her."

Ian followed Cynthia into her office and took a seat in one of the chairs in front of her desk. While she was on the phone, he noticed the several photos of children hanging on the walls.

"Gillian is on her way," she announced as she hung up the phone.

"Are these your kids?"

"Yes, I have three. Two girls and a boy."

Cynthia identified everyone in the photos. Her younger daughter bore an uncanny resemblance to Gillian. Ian remembered Cynthia had just started dating her husband about the time he went back to Colorado. He was happy it worked out for her and he told her about his two boys, who, it turned out, were similar in age to her two girls. They were soon joined by Rosemary, who was both happy and surprised, to find Ian in Cynthia's office.

"So what brings you to our part of the world, Ian?"

"You'll just have to wait until Gillian gets here to find out. It's a surprise."

Before she could respond a familiar voice was heard from the hallway.

"What surprise? Oh my God! Ian, I thought that was your car in the parking lot. What on earth are you doing here?"

Ian greeted Gillian with a big hug, followed by a kiss on the cheek. He asked for everyone to please take a seat as he retrieved a thick file from his briefcase.

"Ladies, I've kept in contact with Tony Sorenson ever since this past April, when Gillian had her show in Denver. I have some news that may be of interest to you. Tony has decided to retire, and he plans to sell his gallery. I've asked him, as a personal favor, to please allow Gillian an opportunity to look it over, and, perhaps, entertain making him an offer before he lists it with a broker. I've gone over everything in this file at least three times now. It's a very profitable gallery and he's asking a fair price for it. I think you ladies could do well for yourselves if you were to buy it."

For the moment everyone was silent. Then Cynthia asked to see the file. "I'll need some time to review this. Can I hold onto it for a few days?"

"Of course."

"My next question is what would we have to gain by buying this? We're already doing quite nicely with our gallery here, and Gillian also has representation in Santa Fe and San Diego."

"I'm aware of that, Cynthia," replied Ian. "I've done my homework. She's done quite well indeed, but I don't think you're aware of just how huge of a hit she's been in Denver. *The Denver Centennial* just did a follow-up story on her."

Cynthia looked at Rosemary, who nodded her head in agreement.

"And lately, I can't seem to keep up with the demand," added Gillian. "I've got a show coming up in San Diego next month that I have to get ready for. Between that, and the private commission I've just finished up, I'm exhausted. However, everything goes in cycles, and so far I've been lucky. I've managed to maintain a good following, even in a slow economy, but a year from now I might not be so popular. It might not be a bad idea, Cyn, for us to at least think about a second gallery. If the demand for my art were to slow down, we'd still make money selling other people's work."

"All right then," said Cynthia. "My sister and I will have to have a longer discussion about this, on our own."

"I understand."

Cynthia began thumbing through the file. "Although judging by the surface, it does appear to have some potential for us. And the building has a multi-year lease, which certainly makes it more attractive. However, it's all going to depend upon how much he's willing to negotiate. How long will he wait for us to let him know if we have an interest?"

"End of business day on Friday. He'd really like to be able to close on something fairly soon."

"Then I'll start reviewing his file this afternoon, and afterwards Gillian and I can discuss it in detail. We'll let Mr. Sorenson know if we have an interest or not."

Ian watched Gillian while her sister was talking. The low-cut, tight-fitting top she was wearing was beginning to distract him. The meeting soon broke up and Gillian walked Ian into the employee break room.

"Well, Ian. When you say you have a big surprise for me, you really do have a big surprise, but what's really going on here?"

"What do you mean?"

"I can't say that I'm not happy to see you, and I can't say I'm not excited about the prospect of buying another gallery, but I'm not sure why you went to all this trouble. I mean really, coming here all the way from Denver, just so you could make a pitch to Cynthia? You could have done that over the phone and overnighted the packet to us."

"Okay, Gilly-girl, I guess you got me. Let's go have lunch. There's more."

There was a Chinese restaurant a few blocks away that was one of Gillian's favorite haunts. As they waited for their soup, she again asked Ian about the real reason behind his unexpected visit.

"Ever since I saw you last April, Gillian, I can't get you off my mind. I feel like Rip Van Winkle. There's a part of me that's been asleep for over twenty years that's finally woken up again. I want us to be more than just an occasional email or phone call. I want us to be real friends. The kind of friends who spend time with one another. You know, like we did when we were kids."

"And if Cynthia and I were to buy Sorenson's gallery, that would mean I'd have to spend a lot more time in Denver. Ian Palmer, you are devious."

They had a laugh while the waitress brought their soup.

"So do you want to know about the rest of my surprise?" asked Ian.

"Of course I do, silly goose."

Ian began by telling her the slow economy had taken its toll on Salisbury & Norton. They were cutting back, and he'd recently been offered a very generous early retirement package.

"I don't get it," said Gillian. "If you're retiring, then why can't you spend more time down here?"

"It's not that simple. For one thing, I haven't accepted their offer yet. I'm going to delay making any decision for as long as I possibly can. Gillian, I'm not even close to sixty years old. I'm much too young for a rocking chair, and I need some time to figure out what to do next. Do I want to hire myself out as a consultant? Do I want to look into teaching? I also have a son still living at home. He's spending the summer with his mother, but come this fall he'll be back with me, and he has another year of high school to go. Then I have another son who's just informed me that he's decided to become a college drop out. I'm going to have to spend some time working on him until he gets his head back on straight."

He went on to say that he'd recently heard from one of his former classmates who had a firm in Phoenix.

"You remember Robert Davis, don't you?"

"I think so. His name sounds kind of familiar."

"Well, he certainly remembers you. He was a year ahead of me. I got to know him on our Wednesday night beer runs, and we've remained close friends over the years. One of their projects has just taken a nosedive. Everything that could possibly go wrong has gone wrong. The client's threatening to sue, and Rob's about to lose what little hair he has left. He's asked me to come in, as an outside consultant, to try to smooth things over and to help clean up the mess. I figured it'd be the perfect opportunity to take a leave of absence from Salisbury and spend some quality time with a very good friend while I'm at it. I'll be here through the end of July."

Gillian couldn't believe her ears. She wanted more than long-distance friendship with Ian and she would get her wish, at least for the short term.

The next few weeks would be golden. While Cynthia was busy trying to hammer out a deal with Tony Sorenson, Gillian and Ian rediscovered the fun of their college days. They went to dinner, to the movies, and Ian even took her to a few Arizona Diamondbacks baseball games. Then came the Fourth of July.

Gillian decided that rather than fight the crowds at a fireworks show, she would invite Ian to her home for dinner and perhaps a late evening swim. She was still an excellent cook and she prepared a fabulous meal. Once dinner was finished and the dishes were washed, it was time to go out to the pool. The summers in Phoenix were so brutally hot that even at ten o'clock at night it could still be over one hundred degrees outside. She grabbed a couple of beach towels and turned out the lights. Ian followed her out to the backyard.

"This time of year I have a nightly ritual. After ten o'clock I go skinny-dipping. You're certainly free to join me, if you wish."

"Gillian, I'm shocked," teased Ian. "I had no idea you were that kind of girl. What do the neighbors have to say about that?"

"Not much. There's a six-foot-high block wall surrounding my backyard, and it's dark. No one can see a thing. Besides, most of them have gone out of town for the holiday."

Not sure what to do, Ian took a seat in one of the lawn chairs. He took his shoes off and made himself more comfortable. Gillian crossed to the other side of the patio, near the deep end of the pool. Ian watched her silhouette in the darkness as she disrobed. She may not have had quite the figure she had when she was younger, but what he was able to see still looked good. She dove into the pool with a splash, and while she was under the water, he couldn't resist the temptation. He got up and switched on the pool light. Gillian quickly rose to the surface and started treading water.

"Ian! What do you think you're doing? Turn off the damn light!"

"Hmm," he mockingly replied. "So what happens if I don't? Are you going to come out and get me?"

He couldn't help himself. It was fun teasing her. They playfully argued back and forth until he finally relented and turned the light back off. Gillian swam to the edge of the pool.

"Ian? Would you mind taking off your glasses before you come back over here?"

"Why? Does this mean you're getting ready to come out? And you don't want me to see anything? Why all the false modesty, Gilly-girl? Aren't you forgetting that there once was a time when I was intimately acquainted with every square inch of you? I remember all of it, you know. Every last detail. There are some things in life that a guy simply never forgets."

"Would you do it, just as a favor, please?"

"Okay, okay." He took his glasses off, carefully setting them on the patio table.

"And where's your cell phone?"

"I left it in the car. Why all the questions?"

"I just thought that after I got out of the pool we could stay out here and look at the stars for awhile, and I'd hate it if we got interrupted."

"I see," he replied.

"Now, would you mind coming back over here? I need to ask another favor of you."

He returned to the side of the pool. "Sure, Gilly-girl. What is it?"

"This!"

She shot up, grabbed his hand, and yanked it as hard as she could. His body made a big, loud splash as it hit the water. As soon as he came back up to the surface, she began to swim away.

"You're in deep doo-doo now, Hanson!" He shook the water off his face. "I'm gonna get you for that."

"Well, first you have to catch me, and since I'm not wearing anything I don't have any drag in the water."

"Well, I can certainly fix that, right now."

Ian swam to the shallow end. Once he was there he began taking off his clothing and throwing it out of the pool. His shirt and trousers made loud, splattering sounds as they landed on the deck. As soon as he was done, he swam after her. They swam back and forth across the pool several times as she taunted him and tried to get away, but he eventually caught her near the shallow end. She playfully struggled against him. Even in the water, the touch of her skin against his was intoxicating. He held her tightly.

"So Gilly-girl," he whispered, "Now that I've finally caught you, what do you intend to do about it?"

He kissed her before she could respond. It was a deep, passionate kiss; the kind of kiss he gave her years ago. His tongue was in her mouth. He ran his hand across her breasts. They were still firm. After the kiss he looked at her. She didn't say a word. Instead, she led him out of the water, picked up the beach towels and laid them across the lawn. She lay down on top of one and motioned for him to join her.

He lay down next to her and reached over and kissed her, just as passionately as before. He slowly began touching her body, and she reciprocated, touching his. He caressed her breasts, her stomach, her hips and her thighs. The more he touched her, the more she gave in return, and the more intense their kisses became. Now her tongue was going into his mouth. He reached down and starting exploring inside her. She moaned, arching her back and writhing in pleasure.

"Don't stop, Ian. Keep going. Keep going."

He went for another deep, passionate kiss as he rolled his body on top of hers. He slowly entered her body as she begged for more. They moved in unison, once again returning to a place where they had not been together in years, only this time it was more powerful than it had been before. She looked up into the night sky and thought she saw a falling star. She cried out in the height of her ecstasy. His mouth covered hers as he climbed the peak right behind her. They soon fell into a state of total, blissful exhaustion. For the second time in their lives, they had begun an evening as friends and ended it as lovers.

## ᚛ᚑ❦Eleven❦ᚑ᚜

IT WOULD TURN OUT to be one of the best summers Gillian ever had. Ian was back in her life, and for the first time, in a long time, all was right with the world. She dove into her art with a newfound enthusiasm. The day before her San Diego show Ian drove her to California in The Beamer, as he liked to call it. Her show was a smashing success, just as her show in Denver had been. They stayed over a few extra days and took a real vacation. Ian had rarely seen the ocean and he loved spending time on the beach. Their romantic sunset strolls were like a sandy paradise.

Ian completed his consulting job the week after they returned. It had been a challenge, but in the end Rob's client walked away happy. He even received a generous bonus on top of his fee. The time had finally come for him to return to Colorado. Larry would soon be starting back to school. Laura mentioned she had a difficult time with him, which came as no surprise. Larry had been having issues with his mother ever since she moved to Steamboat Springs. The school counselor had once told Ian that Larry perceived his mother as having abandoned him. The night before he left he took Gillian out for one last dinner together. It would be a bittersweet evening. The hostess sat them near a window with a beautiful view of the mountains for which Phoenix was famous.

"You seem awfully quiet tonight, Ian."

He sighed. "Gilly-girl, I'm afraid the time has come for me to say goodbye, but only for awhile."

Although the news was not unexpected, Gillian felt her heart sink nonetheless.

"Today was my last day helping Rob, and it all worked out better than any of us had hoped. I think I could really get used to this consulting thing, but not right now. Salisbury has finally agreed to let me stay on, at least for the next few months. Hopefully, I can hold out until May, when Larry graduates. But barring an uptick in new projects coming our way in the interim, it looks like I'm going to have to accept their early retirement package, probably no later than the first of June."

"What happens after that?"

"I don't know, Gilly-girl. I haven't figured it all out yet. The only thing I know for sure is I want for you to be a part of my life. We'll have to work out the details later. Which reminds me, have you and Cynthia been able to work out something with Tony yet?"

Gillian sighed. Now it was her turn to be the bearer of bad news.

"Well Ian, it wasn't from a lack of trying on our part. The bank approved our loan, but it just wasn't enough. Even at Tony's best price, we still couldn't come up with what we needed to close the sale. We tried everything we could think of, but we just couldn't do it."

"Have you said anything to Tony yet?"

"I think Cynthia is planning on calling him either tomorrow or Friday. We're certain he'll be just as disappointed as we are. For what it's worth, my sister and I are both very grateful that you thought enough of us to bring this proposal to our attention in the first place. We both want to thank you, from the bottom of our hearts. And don't worry. Whoever buys the gallery will have to honor my contract. Tony's promised that will be included in whatever deal he makes. I'll still have representation in Denver."

Both were unusually quiet over dinner. Twice during the meal Ian's phone went off. Rob was calling with last-minute questions and Gillian couldn't help but feel annoyed. It was her last evening with Ian for the foreseeable future and she wanted to squeeze as much time out of it as she could. She wasn't looking forward to a long separation.

They made small talk in Ian's car after they left the restaurant, but once they turned onto her street they came across something unexpected. A large, white sedan was parked in front of her house. Ian pulled in the driveway, and as they got out of his car, a sandy-haired man stepped out of the sedan. He approached Gillian and presented her with a badge.

"Are you Gillian Matthews?"

"Yes. What's this about?"

"My name is Kyle Madden. I'm a homicide detective with the Phoenix Police Department. Ma'am, I need to ask you some questions. Can we go inside and talk for a few minutes?"

"Of course."

Gillian escorted the detective inside. She tried to quiet the dogs down as Ian told him to take a seat in the living room.

"Mrs. Matthews, when was the last time that you had any contact with your former husband, Jason Matthews?"

"It's been at least four or five years by now, maybe longer. Why? What's this all about?"

Madden ignored her question. "Do you know anyone by the name of Deanna Matthews?"

"No sir, I do not. I heard through the grapevine that Jason married another woman a few months after our divorce was final. I think that her name may have been Sandy, but I'm not certain. He apparently left the state sometime after that, but I have no idea where he went. He didn't leave me a forwarding address."

"Ma'am, this afternoon we were contacted by a homicide detective in Birmingham, Alabama, where your former husband had been living for the past seven months with his current wife. However, her name was Deanna, not Sandy, and yes, he did marry her a few months after his divorce from you was final." He paused for a moment. "Ma'am, Deanna Matthews was found dead in her home this morning. She'd been shot through the head at point-blank range."

"Good Lord!" exclaimed Ian. "You honestly don't think Gillian would be involved in something like that, do you?"

"No sir, I don't," replied Madden. "All the evidence points to Jason Matthews as the prime suspect. However, Mrs. Matthews, it appears that your former husband is still very much interested in you."

Gillian sat speechless. Her blood ran cold.

"What do you mean?" Ian finally asked.

"They found a stack of news articles about her among his belongings. They also removed a computer from the home. Her former husband has been Googling her pretty regularly."

Gillian finally got her voice back. "I don't understand. We've been divorced for years and we had no children. What could he possibly want from me?"

"From what the detectives in Birmingham have told me, ma'am, there's sufficient evidence to suggest that your former husband has been involved with illegal gambling, and that he's been borrowing money from some, shall we say, rather unscrupulous sources, to cover his debts. He apparently cleaned out his current wife's bank account, and he took out large cash advances on all of her credit cards. Deanna's brother says she called him last night, told him what happened, and said that she planned to confront Jason as soon as he got home. When she didn't answer her phone this morning, he went to check on her. He's the one who found her. The coroner says she'd been dead for about twelve hours."

"Dear Lord, how awful. That poor woman."

"Based on the evidence found at the scene, the Birmingham police detectives believe that she did indeed confront him, that an argument ensued, and that he shot her during that argument," continued Madden. "We also have reason to believe, based on the evidence I just mentioned, that he may either try to contact you or that he may possibly be headed this way. You're something of a public figure, Mrs. Matthews, and he's desperate."

"Not to mention armed and dangerous," added Ian. "Do you think he may try to kidnap her?"

"That I don't know." He turned to Gillian. "Does he know where you live?"

The color drained from Gillian's face. She felt another cold chill running down her spine as she struggled to maintain her composure.

"I—I'm not sure. I bought this place a few months after the divorce was final. To the best of my knowledge, Jason doesn't have this address, but I can't be absolutely certain. I kept in touch with a few of our mutual friends for about a year or so after we split up. I have no way of knowing if any of them might have told him where I live, or if he's even still in contact with any of them."

"Are you still in contact with any of these people?"

"No sir, I'm not. I wouldn't even know where to begin looking for them. I'd be happy to give you their names and last known addresses, if that would be helpful to you."

Kyle nodded and Gillian went into her office to retrieve her address book. He copied down the information she gave him, and as they were talking, an even more worried look appeared on her face.

"Wait a minute. Jason knows where my art gallery is. He used to work there, back when we were married. Do you think he would try to harm any of my staff?"

"Again, I can't speculate. Is that your place of work as well?"

"No." She shook her head. "I actually work out of my home. About the only time I'm there is when I have an appointment or an occasional staff meeting, and Jason knows that."

"I see. I'd be more concerned about his calling on the phone trying to get personal information about you, such as your home address or perhaps using a different name and trying to set up a meeting with you."

"Well, my staff certainly knows better than to give out my home address, and Rosemary, my personal assistant, carefully screens anyone who wants to set up an appointment with me. They usually have to meet with her first, and she and Jason already know one another."

"Then it sounds like you already have some reasonable precautions in place. Meantime, the authorities in Alabama have put out an APB on Jason Matthews. With any luck he'll be apprehended soon. But until that happens, I'm recommending that you consider changing your normal routine, and that you keep your doors locked and be aware of your surroundings at all times. If you see any suspicious activity in your neighborhood, or if Jason Matthews should attempt to contact you, by phone, text, or email, you need to call nine-one-one immediately."

The detective gave Gillian his card and instructed her to call him if she had any additional questions. Ian then walked him to the door. When he returned, he found Gillian on the phone with her sister. He sat down next to her as they talked. After ending her call, she burst into tears.

"Shh... It's okay, Gilly-girl. I'm right here. No one's going to harm you. I promise."

"It's Ryan Knight all over again, Ian. Only this time he has a gun, and I don't think flipping him though the air is going to be enough. I'm scared, Ian. I'm really, really scared. There's a good chance he knows where I live. You weren't here, Ian. You have no idea just how much Jason made my life a living hell before he finally left. There's a very dark, very cruel side to him."

"Then that settles it. Tomorrow morning you're packing your bags. I'm taking you, and Duke and Daisy, back to Denver with me until this nutcase is caught. You'll be safe there, so try to relax. Even if Jason were to drive all night, I doubt he'd have enough time to get all the way here from Birmingham before tomorrow. So why don't you take a nice hot bubble bath and I'll bring you a glass of warm milk. Then I'll go online to find you a place to stay that allows pets."

By the time Gillian came out of the bathroom she found Ian lying in her bed, watching the ten o'clock news. As she cuddled up next to him, he wrapped his arms around her.

"Well," he said, "at least it's not a story on the local news."

"Give it time. I'd better call Rosemary first thing tomorrow morning and give her a head's up as well."

"Probably another good reason for you to leave town until this all blows over. You don't need the media hounding you."

Ian kept his arms around her until she fell asleep. Then, he reached for the remote and switched off the television set.

# ❧ TWELVE ❧

**A**S GILLIAN WOKE UP it took her a moment to remember where she was. She was in her hotel suite in Denver. She'd woken up in this room every morning for the past two weeks. She felt one of her dogs poke her leg with its nose. She looked down and noticed Duke watching her. His wagging tail, along with the expression on his face, told her it was time to get up.

"Come here, baby boy."

The little dog did as he was told. She held him tight and petted him on the head.

"Maybe we'll be lucky, and today will be the day they'll find Jason. Then we can all go home."

Gillian let out a long sigh. She felt as though she was the one being held in a prison. It was a prison of her own making, her punishment for choosing the wrong husband. She was becoming restless. She'd hardly seen Ian since she arrived. He was busy with Larry, who just started back to school that week. She had a show in Santa Fe coming up in a few weeks, and while she brought along her art supplies, trying to get anything accomplished in a hotel suite was nearly impossible. Most of her time had been spent web-surfing, dog-walking, and waiting for the call from Kyle Madden, or some other police officer, informing her that Jason had finally been captured. Until that happened, Jason once again controlled her life. If there was one thing Gillian knew about her ex-husband, it was that he excelled at staying a step or two ahead. He already had a good twelve-hour head start. In all likelihood he was in another state by the time his wife's body was discovered. She got out of bed and had just switched on the coffee maker when her phone rang. Cynthia was calling.

"Gillian, are you ready for some good news?"

"What's up? Have they caught Jason?"

"No, I'm sorry to say."

Cynthia regretted her choice of words. She was so excited that she momentarily forgot about Jason.

"I'm on my way to the airport," she continued. "I'm scheduled to arrive in Denver at two-thirty this afternoon and I need you to come pick me up. We're meeting Tony Sorenson, at the gallery, at four."

"So we're still on then?"

Tony had called Cynthia the same day Gillian departed for Denver. He decided to accept their offer after all.

"It's a done deal. Tony just called. The final paperwork will be ready later today, as promised."

"I see."

Cynthia heard the hesitation in her sister's voice. "Gillian, what's wrong? Have you changed your mind?"

"What's wrong is I'm stuck in a hotel room hiding out from a psychopath. Sorry Cyn, I just haven't thought that much about anything else."

"I'm sorry. Maybe I should call Tony to let him know that our situation has changed and that we need more time to think it over."

"No Cynthia, don't. Now that I think about it, I really do need something to keep myself occupied. I'm going stir crazy in this hotel room while Jason could hide out for months, even years. I simply can't spend the rest of my life living in fear."

By the time she got on the freeway, Gillian was starting to feel like herself again. She'd missed Cynthia and she looked forward to spending some quality time with her. She cranked up the music and sang along as she drove. It was her first outing in some time and it felt good to be in the real world again. Before long the airport exit came up. It was a long drive down Pena Boulevard to the short-term parking garage and she savored every minute of it. She parked the minivan and entered the airport terminal. Denver International Airport was huge. It would take some time for her to reach their prearranged rendezvous point at the baggage claim. Once she finally got there, she discovered several other flights had arrived at the same time. She wondered how long it would take to find her sister.

"Gillian! Over here!"

She looked through the crowd and finally saw her sister waving at her. She pushed her way through until she could reach her.

"Cyn, it's so good to see you. You don't know how happy I am."

Cynthia stepped back to take a closer look. She was concerned about what she saw.

"Gillian, are you feeling alright? You look like you have circles on top of the circles under your eyes."

"It's been rough. Every little sound I hear, I think it's Jason, and I haven't been sleeping well."

"And where's Ian?"

"Doing the best he can, but I haven't been able to see that much of him. Remember, he's got a teenager at home who's still dealing with the effects of their divorce."

"Teenagers can be difficult, Gillian, even without their parents divorcing. I know what that's like. Give Ian some time. Once Larry finishes high school and goes off to college it'll get much better. Meantime, your big sister is here, and I'll be here through the end of the week, longer if need be. We're going to have to put in some time training the Sorenson staff, but in the evenings, we'll have some quality time, just you and me. You're going to be spending a lot of time here, Gillian. Between our starting up a new gallery and Jason being on the loose, I'm thinking that we should relocate you here in Denver."

Cynthia saw her suitcase coming up the chute. She stepped over to the carousel to grab it.

"Is that all?"

"Yep," replied Cynthia. "Now let's blow this Popsicle stand and go buy ourselves an art gallery. And then we need to find you a house to rent."

Gillian had left Ian a voice-mail message before she headed off to the airport. She wanted to be the first to give him the good news. By the time she and Cynthia arrived at the gallery, a big bouquet of bright red carnations was prominently displayed on the receptionist's desk. Gillian remembered Tammy from her opening, and after she paged Tony, Gillian introduced her to Cynthia.

"These are for you, Ms. Matthews." She motioned to the flowers. "Looks like people are already congratulating you."

Gillian looked at the bouquet and smiled. She knew who sent it. She would read the card later, in private.

"Gillian!" Tony emerged from the hallway.

"I knew it!" exclaimed Gillian. "I had you pegged the night my show opened and you were walking around in that ridiculous three-piece suit. I knew you were the type of guy who wore blue jeans and tie-dyed shirts to work."

"Yes, and now I'm going to have to find a new home for that suit, very soon."

She introduced Tony to her sister, and he took a few minutes to show Cynthia around. Gillian's show had been taken down from the smaller gallery and several of her paintings were proudly displayed in a space in the main room. A short time later Tony escorted both women down the hall to his personal studio, next door to his office. Inside, a table and chairs had been set up, and Paul was waiting there, along with several other people wearing business attire. The time had come to sign the final papers and make everything official.

Because Anthony Sorenson Fine Art was a well-established gallery with a strong following, everyone had agreed they would keep the name, and Tony would have representation for his own work. Cynthia announced that she and Gillian had decided to keep the current staff, although those who wished to leave would be free to do so. Paul was visibly relieved. He'd been with the gallery for nearly ten years and knew its inner workings better than anyone, including Tony himself. Once the last paper was signed, placed in a folder, and packed in a briefcase, everyone shook hands and Paul escorted their guests to the front door. Moments later he returned, with a bottle of champagne and the rest of the staff in tow. Tony popped the cork and poured champagne for everyone.

"Ladies and gentlemen, I'd like to propose a toast to Denver's newest fine art dealers. Ladies, you certainly know how to drive a hard bargain. But I want you all to know that fifteen years ago, when this old hippie first arrived in Denver, I knew I'd finally found the right place to build my dream. I started this gallery from scratch, and along the way I've literally put my own blood, sweat and tears into it. It's going to be very difficult for me to say goodbye, but I honestly can't think of two better people on this planet to take over its care. So here's to you, ladies."

He raised his glass. Everyone took a sip and started congratulating Gillian and Cynthia, but before things got too noisy Tony got everyone's attention one more time.

"I have one more surprise for everyone before I go, although I think most of you already know what it is, since we've been planning this little shindig for what, three, four days now? As we speak, there are caterers setting up tables in the main gallery and a grill in the parking lot. Tonight we're closing our doors early, because I'm hosting a barbeque dinner for all of you, along with your spouses, families, and significant others. It's my way of thanking you for all that you've done for me over the years. It's also a chance for all of you to introduce yourselves, and your families, to these two ladies, as they'll be your new bosses."

Everyone left Tony's studio together and walked back into the main gallery where the caterers were already setting up. While they were waiting, Cynthia and Gillian approached each staff member and introduced themselves. Soon the husbands, wives, and significant others began to arrive. Paul introduced Cynthia and Gillian to his companion, Dwayne Hitchings. Ian arrived a short time later. He greeted Gillian with a hug and a kiss.

"Congratulations, Gillian. I knew this would be a good move for you. I'm so glad you two were able to get it all sorted out." He then introduced her to someone he brought with him. "Gillian, this is Jeremy, my oldest son. Jeremy, this is Gillian Matthews. She's been a very special person to me since before you were born."

"Nice meeting you." He extended his hand.

Gillian was taken aback. Memories of seeing Ian for the first time, in the architecture college library, suddenly flashed through her mind. Jeremy looked much like Ian had that day. He was slightly taller than his father, but he had virtually the same face, the same wavy hair, and the same deep-set eyes. His hair, however, was darker and longer than Ian's had been, and his eyes were hazel instead of brown. Jeremy was polite, but reserved. Gillian sensed right from the start that he intended to keep a close watch on her.

Tony announced that dinner was ready to be served. As the sisters took their seats at the table, Jeremy sat down directly across from Gillian. She wanted to make a good first impression. She looked around for Ian, but he was busy talking with Tony.

"So Jeremy," she said, "your father says you've dropped out of college."

"Yep. It was time to take a break from school. At the moment, I'm working as a bartender at a sports bar. The hours can get crazy, but the pay is pretty decent and I make great tips." He went on to say that he had been majoring in electrical engineering and that he enjoyed tinkering with high-tech gadgets. Gillian could tell that Jeremy was a very bright young man, much like his father.

"So enough about me, Ms. Matthews. I was wondering about your plans for the future."

"You can call me, Gillian, and right now my plans are to keep this gallery just the way it is."

"I see. So, does that mean you're planning on moving to Denver?"

"Yes, at least for the short term. My sister and I are still ironing out the details."

Jeremy wasn't one to mince words. He liked to get straight to the point. "Makes sense." He looked her in the eye. "But what I'm really asking is what are your intentions regarding my father?"

Gillian was taken aback, and for the moment she didn't know if he was friend or foe. She knew she had to be careful with her answer.

"Well, to be honest with you, Jeremy, I'm not completely sure right now. No doubt you've been told by now that your father and I were pretty serious back when we were in college, but that was a long time ago. I never expected to see him again. Right now, I'm just taking it one day at a time, but if anything interesting should happen, you'll be the first to know."

"Pardon me. Is this seat taken?"

Gillian looked up and saw Ian standing behind the empty chair next to Jeremy.

"Ian, please, have a seat."

"I see you two are getting acquainted."

"Yeah, Dad, you could say that."

Jeremy made small talk until he finished his meal. Afterwards he got up and started wandering around the gallery.

"I don't know, Ian. Somehow I don't think I made a very good first impression on him."

"Give him some time, Gillian. He's a good kid. For the most part he's coped well with his mother and I going our separate ways. Laura said it took him awhile to warm up to her new significant other, but that he eventually came around. I think, in his own way, Jeremy is trying to be protective of both his mother and me. He doesn't want to see either one of us getting hurt."

Ian spent the rest of the meal chatting with Gillian and Cynthia, but for the rest of the evening Gillian was fully aware of being under Jeremy's radar, and she didn't like it. Larry may have been the son who had a reputation for being difficult, but she wasn't sure if she liked Jeremy or not. What was certain was that he was going to be a problem for her.

## ✎ THIRTEEN ❧

THE NEXT FEW DAYS were a whirlwind of staff meetings and business affairs. Paul connected Gillian with a real-estate agent who specialized in rental properties. She looked at several houses, but so far hadn't found the right one. She and Cynthia were on their way to look at another house, and as soon as Gillian saw it she realized it had potential. It certainly had good curb appeal. Once they stepped inside she discovered the floor plan was similar to her home in Arizona, but with a basement and a fireplace, like many of the houses in Denver. There was also a heated swimming pool in the backyard. Gillian took her time, carefully looking around and asking questions. Finally, she looked at the agent and smiled.

"Let's go back to your office and do the paperwork. I'm ready to bust out of that hotel room."

A few days later Cynthia was ready to leave, and by then everything had been arranged. Gillian had signed a year's lease on the house, with the option to buy, giving her plenty of time to sell her house in Phoenix. The movers were scheduled to arrive the following week. She stopped to pick up her key on the way to the airport, and as she dropped her sister off at the curb they said a tearful goodbye. Gillian would miss having her close by. While they would talk on the phone nearly every day, it wouldn't be the same as seeing each other in person and occasionally playing hooky from the office to sneak out to a movie or an afternoon at the mall. Gillian fought the tears for a good part of her drive from the airport to the art gallery. She would have to touch up her makeup before she went in. She didn't want her new staff to see that she'd been crying.

"Good morning, Tammy," she said when she finally walked through the door.

"Good morning, Gillian. Did you get your sister off to the airport?"

"Yes, I did. Cynthia said to tell all of you goodbye, at least for now."

"Thanks. You have a visitor waiting for you in your office."

"Who is it?"

"She's a middle-aged blonde, sort of looks like you. I tried sending her to Paul, but she said she wasn't here to buy anything. She said her business with you was personal, but because of your situation with your ex-husband we're all being extra cautious, so Paul asked to see her ID. Her name is Laura Palmer."

Laura Palmer. Ian's ex-wife. What could she possibly want?

"Has she been waiting here long?"

"No. I'd say maybe ten, fifteen minutes or so," said Tammy. "We told her you wouldn't be here until later, and that we would be happy to have you call her, but she refused. She said she had some time before her next appointment and that she preferred to wait so she could speak with you in person."

Gillian rushed back to her office. Tammy was right. The two women did indeed bear a slight resemblance to one another.

"Can I help you, Mrs. Palmer?"

"Yes, you may. And please, call me Laura."

She went on to say that she had driven in from Steamboat Springs that morning, and that she would be having lunch with Ian in about an hour.

"I'd like to buy you a cup of coffee, if I may, so we can have a talk. I see there's a coffeehouse right across the street. Would you mind walking over there with me?"

Against her better judgment, Gillian accepted the offer. She remembered the old saying about keeping one's friends close, but enemies closer. They stepped across the street and ordered their lattes. Laura insisted on paying. They seated themselves at a small table in the corner.

"I'll get straight to the point," said Laura. "I want to lay out the ground rules between us, here and now, so we can avoid any future misunderstandings."

Gillian had to hand it to her. She was direct and to the point. That must have been where Jeremy had gotten it.

"Okay, but I'm not sure I understand exactly what you mean."

"I want to be sure that you and I are on the same page, concerning you, me and Ian. He and I have two children together. There will always be that bond between us. And once our children are grown, there'll be weddings and grandchildren. It's not going to be like it was when the two of you were in college. For better or worse, I'm part of the package."

"I see."

"Please don't get me wrong, Gillian. I don't dislike you, at least, not anymore. And it isn't my intention to come between you and Ian. However, as long as I'm here and we're on the subject, I may as well be very candid with you. There was a time when I really, truly, hated you."

Their lattes were ready. Laura got up and brought them back to the table. Gillian had to fight the urge to bolt out the door.

"I guess I should start at the beginning." Laura set their drinks down and took her seat. "That way they'll be no questions asked later on down the road." She took a swig of her latte and looked Gillian in the eye. "I was young, naïve, and in love with Ian, or so I thought, when we were first married, although it didn't take me long to figure out that he was never in love with me. Sometimes he'd call out your name in his sleep. Other times he called me Gillian, and he wasn't even aware he'd made the slip. By the time I fully realized I'd made a serious mistake marrying the man, I was seven months pregnant with my oldest son. One day I confronted him. He insisted you were in the past, but I knew you weren't. You were a ghost. You were his phantom mistress. You were the person he wanted me to be, instead of who I was."

"I'm sorry that happened, Laura, I truly am, but you must understand that I had no contact whatsoever with Ian during those years. Now, if you would like to get your calendar out to compare the dates, I think you'll discover that I was also married at the time, and I was living in Tahoe City, California."

"I know you weren't literally there, Gillian, but you were certainly there in spirit, and your presence never left us. Let me see if I can explain it another way. It's sort of like Prince Charles, Princess Diana and Camilla Parker-Bowles."

"Come again?"

"Remember how the tabloids made Camilla out to be this vile, evil witch, who was the other woman in Charles' life, and how she was blamed for breaking up Diana's marriage?"

Gillian was starting to resent the implication. "I think I recall hearing something to that effect. Of course, back then I was kind of busy trying to make a name for myself in the art world. I really didn't have time to read the tabloids."

"Well, actually, neither did I," replied Laura, undaunted. "But when you're busy raising two kids, you spend a lot of time in the check-out line at the supermarket, and it's kind of hard to miss all the headlines. Here's the point I'm making. The public perception was wrong. Camilla really wasn't the other woman, Diana was. Charles and Camilla had fallen in love years before Diana came on the scene, but social protocol at the time wouldn't allow them to marry. So when Charles married Diana, he did it for the wrong reasons, and it all came to a bad end, at least for Diana. What I'm getting at, Gillian, is that I'm the Diana to your Camilla. You had a prior claim on Ian. He may have married me, but he never belonged to me. He has been and always will be yours. Unfortunately, it took many years for me to accept it, and when I finally did I decided to get even, so I cheated on him."

"Yes, I know. The car salesman."

"He wasn't the first, Gillian, but he was the only one that Ian ever found out about. It was an ugly chapter of my life that I'm not proud of, and one that I wish I could go back and undo. All I did was create a lot of hurt and pain for my family, and now my sons, especially Larry, are paying for it."

Laura took a few more sips of her latte. Gillian was at a loss for words.

"Look, you and I may never be friends, but I want you to know I'm not a threat, and that I'm not here to cause trouble for you. It's like I just said. Ian is the father of my children. There will be times, like today, when I have to meet with him to discuss matters involving our boys. These are the times when you'll have to graciously step aside and allow us to continue to do our jobs as parents. I just want to be sure that you're very clear that I have no ulterior motive. My sons have already been through enough. They don't need the additional strain of our going to war with one another. Besides, I've found the man of my dreams. His name is Will Mason. We haven't made it official yet, but we plan to get married next spring. So you see, I don't want Ian back. However, we've chosen to remain friends for our children's sakes."

# ❧FOURTEEN❦

PAUL AND DWAYNE carried in the last boxes from the minivan and set them on the living room floor.

"Thanks you guys, and thanks for letting me borrow the air mattress," said Gillian. "You don't know how happy I am to finally be out of that hotel suite. I'll be sure to return the mattress to you as quickly as I can."

"No rush," said Dwayne. "We only use it when we have house guests, which doesn't happen too often. Now, if you'll take me to your bedroom, young lady, I can get it blown up for you."

All three laughed as Gillian escorted Dwayne into the master bedroom and found an outlet for the pump. She was happy with the good rapport she was building with Paul and Dwayne. She found Paul to be an astute businessman who shared the same vision for the future of her gallery. She returned from the bedroom just in time for Paul to excuse himself to retrieve the folding table and chairs from the back of Dwayne's pickup truck. They decided to lend them to her as well, so she would have enough basic furnishings to make the house livable until the movers arrived.

Gillian stepped into the kitchen and started emptying the grocery bags. She'd stopped at the store to pick up a few essentials, including dog

69

food. Duke and Daisy were busy outside exploring their new backyard, but it was well past their usual dinnertime, and she didn't need to add two whiney dogs to the chaos that already surrounded her.

"Surprise, surprise, look who's here." Paul had just returned from Dwayne's truck. Ian was right behind him carrying several shopping bags.

"I come bearing gifts. The two big ones are from Paul and the little one is from me."

Ian set the bags on the counter. Gillian eagerly opened them as Paul set up the card table and chairs. Inside the two large bags were sheets, towels, a blanket and a couple of pillows.

"I couldn't have my boss sleeping on a bare mattress," said Paul. "Happy housewarming!"

"Thanks, Paul. Now I'll be warm and cozy."

"Aha, I see you've finally got them." Dwayne had come back into the room. "Would you like for me to make up the mattress for you?"

"No, that's okay," said Gillian. "You guys have already gone the extra mile for me. I can take care of it later."

She opened the smaller bag, the one from Ian. Inside was a bottle of her favorite wine, a small package of paper cups, and a single red carnation. She quickly filled one of the cups with water to use as a makeshift vase for the carnation, which she then placed on the card table.

"Thank you, love." She gave Ian a quick kiss. "It's the perfect little gift."

"Are any of you hungry?" Ian whipped out his phone. "I thought I'd order some pizza."

"No, that's okay," said Paul, "we need to get going. Tomorrow morning it's back to the old millstone. My boss is such a tyrant, you know."

They all laughed as Gillian walked Paul and Dwayne to the door. She gave each a hug as she said goodbye.

"Thanks, both of you, for everything."

"Our pleasure," replied Paul. "You two lovebirds have some fun. I'll see you in the morning, Boss."

Ian ordered the pizza while Gillian fed the dogs, made up the mattress, and placed the towels in the bathroom.

"Look, Ian," she said as she returned, "they even threw in a couple of beach towels. We can have a swim after dinner."

"Not tonight."

"That's right. I keep forgetting about Larry. Sorry, Ian, I understand. Duty calls."

"That's not it."

She turned and looked at him more closely. He seemed upset about something. "Ian, what's wrong?"

The pizzas arrived before he could answer. They sat down to eat, but he was much quieter than usual. Gillian again asked him what was wrong, but he brushed it off, saying he didn't want to talk about it. She also noticed he didn't seem to have much of an appetite.

"Aren't you hungry?" she finally asked.

"Oh, I'm hungry alright, but not for the food."

He stood up from the table, took Gillian by the hand, and escorted her to the master bedroom. Duke and Daisy tried to follow, but he closed the bedroom door.

"Sorry guys, but right now your mommy and I are busy. You'll have to wait 'til later."

He led Gillian to her temporary bed and began kissing her passionately, but there was almost a sense of desperation she'd never felt from him before. He nearly tore all her clothes off, and he was a little rough in the way he was handling her.

"Ouch! Ian, slow down."

"Sorry. I don't know what got into me."

With that he seemed to calm down, but something was still a little off. When it was over, they laid back and silently stared at the ceiling.

"Gillian, can I ask you something?"

"Of course," she replied.

"Do you think I'm a chump?"

"What?"

"You heard me. Do you think I'm a chump? Do you think I'm some dumb farm boy who just fell off the turnip truck?"

"No! Ian, what's this about? Are you angry with me about something?"

"No, I'm not angry with you, but I understand you had an unexpected visitor at the office today."

"You can say that again, and I hope you don't think I was trying to keep it a secret from you. I was waiting for the right time to tell you, but we got a little involved with something other than a polite conversation before I got the chance."

"I understand," he replied. "That's not the issue. So tell me, what did you think of her?"

"Honestly?"

"I wouldn't have it any other way."

"Well, she does look a little bit like me, but you're right about one thing, Ian. She's not like me. Not like me at all."

"What did she say to you?"

"She told me she wanted to be completely honest and upfront with me, and that it wasn't her intention to cause any trouble between us. But she also wanted me to understand that because of the kids she'd always be, 'in the picture,' as she put it, and that during those times when she had to meet with you to discuss the boys, and these are her words not mine, I am 'to step graciously aside and allow the two of you to do your job as parents.'"

"I see," said Ian. "Well, you can disregard that request. If I decide I want you to be included in any discussion I'm having with her concerning the boys, then I want you to be there, whether she likes it or not. Now, what else did she tell you?"

Gillian hesitated. Ian had a right to know the truth, but she hated having the burden placed on her.

"I don't know how else to say it, Ian, other than to just come out and say it. I know this is going to hurt, but you have the right to know." She paused for a moment as she tried to find the right words. "Ian, she admitted to me that she'd been unfaithful to you for some time. I don't think she meant to tell me; I think it just slipped out, but she admitted the car salesman wasn't her first. I told her that you had the right to know, and that I wasn't going to keep that kind of a secret from you. Surprisingly enough, she agreed with me. She said she wanted to resolve all her unfinished business with you so she could marry Will with a clean slate."

"Did she tell you how many there were, besides the car salesman?"

"No," replied Gillian.

"Two."

"What?"

"Two," repeated Ian, "and then, when you add the car salesman, it comes to a grand total of three."

"You're kidding. Ian, I had no idea."

"Neither did I. And I feel like I've really been played for a fool here. I spent some twenty years of my life busting my fanny for that woman so I could give her as good a life as I could possibly give her. And how did she thank me? By being the town whore. Over the course of our marriage, she had three other guys. Three. And each and every one of them was a married man with a family of his own. And it goes way back, Gillian. The first was when Larry was barely five years old."

"I'm so sorry, Ian. I don't know what else to say."

He turned and wrapped his arms around her, pulling her in close and kissing her on the forehead.

"Don't be sorry, Gillian. None of this is your fault, although I think she tried to pin the blame you. She said the reason she did it was to get even with me for trying to turn her into you."

"That's what she said to me as well. She said I was your phantom mistress."

"Gillian, over the years I've come to realize that I was very wrong in letting you go. Back then I was young and stupid, and I was scared to death to make a commitment. Then later on, because of the kids, I honestly felt that I had an obligation to stay with her. But I also want you to know something. Had I found out about her cheating on me the first time, I would have ended it with her, right then and there. Who knows? Maybe once the dust settled I might have gone looking for you back then, and things might have turned out differently. I would have fought for custody of the boys. You would have finally had the chance to be a mother, and Gillian, I know you would have been a damn good mother to my kids. Maybe we could have had one or two of our own. It might have helped make up for the child you lost."

Ian held her in silence until he finally told her that it was time for him to leave. He had to go home to Larry.

# ❧Fifteen❧

JASON MATTHEWS continued to elude capture and it was taking a toll on Gillian. While she felt safer in Denver, having to live incognito was affecting her professionally. Her show in Santa Fe was rapidly approaching. Unless Jason was captured soon, it could turn into a public relations nightmare. Rosemary knew Jason had been monitoring Gillian's activities on the Internet, and so far she'd managed to keep the news of her move to Denver from the media. However, for Gillian to have a successful show in Santa Fe, Rosemary would have to publicize it, which meant Gillian would have to come out of the shadows.

Gillian remained cautiously optimistic. She set up her studio in the basement of her new home and was busy preparing for the show. The move to Colorado had thrown her a few weeks behind, but as she settled into her new surroundings, she began turning more of the day-to-day responsibilities of running Anthony Sorenson Fine Art over to Paul. She was now only going to the office once or twice a week, freeing up more time to devote to her art. She was putting the final touches on her latest painting when Rosemary called.

"Gillian, we have a problem. Are you sitting down?"

"What's wrong? Is it Jason?"

"Yes and no. I just got off the phone with Greg in Santa Fe. It must have been a slow news day for their paper. They decided to run a story about Jason Matthews, and they put a nice spin on it, as your work is in one of the local art galleries. Greg's not happy about it, so they've canceled your show."

"Canceled as in postponed until a later date?"

"No," replied Rosemary. "Canceled as in they no longer wish to represent you."

"What? They can't do that."

"Unfortunately, they feel that since the word is out about your fugitive ex-husband, people might not want to show up at your opening."

"I understand, and to be honest, I've been concerned about my own safety as well. So why not simply postpone it a few months? Jason can't hide out forever."

"Because they're arrogant jerks," replied Rosemary. "You know they've always been a pain in the fanny to work with. However, word has also leaked out, at least in some circles, about you and Cynthia purchasing Anthony Sorenson Fine Art. Greg mentioned they'd heard about it, and I got the distinct impression they somehow have an issue with it. So, when the story hit the papers about Jason, it gave them all the excuse they needed to cancel your show and let your contract go. Of course, they'll still sell whatever work of yours they have in their inventory until then."

"Well now, that's mighty big of them, isn't it?"

"Look, Gillian, I know you're upset right now, but quite honestly, I'm glad to be rid of them. I never could stand Greg, and, frankly, you deserve much better representation. Greg was such a prima donna at times that I wished I could've slapped him across the face, and they were always slow to pay to boot. Gillian, you've outgrown them, and you've certainly outclassed them. Ian did us a mighty big favor when he suggested we buy Sorenson. You're in a much better place now. And speaking of the man, how is he?"

"Not so good lately. He recently had a meeting with his ex-wife. It was the same day she showed up at Sorenson."

"Yes, I remember."

"She's planning to remarry, so she decided to take care of some unfinished business with Ian." Gillian, didn't want to divulge too many details. "And he's been down in the dumps about it ever since."

"Did her unfinished business have anything to do with the two of you?"

"No, not really. It involved some things that occurred while they were still married, but it's reopened some old wounds for Ian. He knows I'm there if he needs me. Unfortunately, it's just one of those things he's going to have to work through for himself, like I had to do when I found out Jason wasn't the man I thought he was."

"I remember. You take extra special care of him, Gillian. He's a keeper."

They wrapped up their conversation and said their goodbyes. Gillian was about to call Paul to let him know that Santa Fe was history, but before she could place the call, her phone rang again. This time it was Ian.

"Hey, Gilly-girl. Have you got a few minutes? I'd like to talk to you about something."

"Sure, what is it?"

"My sister called me this morning, you know, just to talk."

"Okay."

"Gillian, right now I'm kind of like you were when Cynthia came to visit you. You needed some time with your big sister, and now I need a few days with mine. I'm still trying to deal with Laura's true confessions, and Kat always had a way of helping me find the right answers. She lives in Portland, and I've booked a flight there for tomorrow morning. I'll be staying over the weekend, but I'll be back on Monday."

"What about Larry?"

"He's staying with a friend until I get back," explained Ian. "I know Brian's parents. They're pretty trustworthy. I've also asked Jeremy to keep an eye on you until I get back."

"Really Ian, that's not necessary. I'm a big girl. I don't need a babysitter."

"He's not a babysitter, and until they catch Jason, I'm concerned about you. Jeremy will be off on Sunday. We both agreed it would be a good idea for the two of you to spend some time together and get to know one another better. He's a good kid, and he does like you. He's also aware of your situation with Jason, and he said for you to call him, right away, if you have any trouble. And while we're on the subject, is there any news?"

"Yes and no. Yes, he's still finding ways to make trouble for me, and no, there's no news of the cops finding him."

"What kind of trouble are you talking about?"

Gillian filled Ian in on the Santa Fe newspaper picking up the story on Jason, and how it led to the gallery dropping her as an artist. Like Rosemary, Ian was relieved to hear the Santa Fe show was off.

"I know Rosemary's doing her best to keep a lid on the media," he said, "but I've also had concerns about one of our papers here finding out about your relocating."

"We've covered our tracks as best we can, and whenever anyone asks, I simply say that I'm only here for a few weeks to retrain the staff."

"That's all well and good," he replied, "but I'm still going to worry about you. Gillian, if anything were to happen to you, I don't know what I'd do. I don't think I could handle it."

"I'm fine, Ian, really. Go do what you have to do and give my love to your sister."

* * *

Ian was glad he made the trip. He needed a time out to sort through his feelings about what Laura had done, and he spent hours talking it out with his sister. Kat reminded him that despite what had happened, and regardless of who was to blame, he would have to remain cordial to her for their children's sake. By Sunday night he felt more like his old self again, and he and Katherine were relaxing on the patio next to the fire pit for one last visit.

"You know Ian," she said, "it doesn't seem that long ago that you were graduating from college and starting your career. I kept asking you about your plans for Gillian, and you kept telling me you didn't know. So here we are, once again, and once again I'm asking you, what are your plans for Gillian?"

"And once again, Kat, I'm not sure, I definitely plan on keeping her this time around, but I honestly don't know about our getting married. Neither of us has had a great track record when it comes to marriage. I ended up with a tramp. She ended up with a flake her first time, and a homicidal con artist the second time. I don't think either of us is eager to take the plunge again, at least not anytime soon. Right now I'm focused on getting Larry through high school, and she's focused on her new gallery. I'm also up in the air over this early retirement. We both have a lot of hurdles to work through before we can even think about discussing marriage."

"That's all well and good, Ian, but somehow I think there's more to it. As someone who's known you your entire life, what I've observed is that at the end of the day you get scared, so you cut and run. That's what you did the last time. You always had a way of rationalizing it away, but deep down, Ian, I think you have some deep-seeded fear of abandonment. You latch on to the best excuse you can find so you can leave them before they have a chance to leave you."

Ian didn't respond right away. He stared into the fire, gathering his thoughts. Finally, he spoke up.

"Actually Kat, that's not quite right. I've never told a soul what I'm about to tell you. The day before I married Laura, I tried to contact Gillian. I was going to ask her to take me back."

"Really?"

"Yep. I dialed her old number, but she wasn't there. Whoever answered had never even heard of her. It had been well over a year since I'd last spoken to her, so it would have made sense that she'd moved someplace else by then. I called information. They didn't have a listing for her either, so I got the number for her father's business and I called him. Lucky for me, he was in his office and he took my call."

"So what happened?"

"I identified myself. Once he knew who I was, he was cordial, but very cool. He asked if I was still with Salisbury and Norton. I told him, yes, I was. He said he was pleased it had worked out. Then he asked me if there was anything else I wanted. I told him that I wanted to speak to Gillian, and would he please give me her telephone number. He got really quiet. Then he explained that Gillian had become extremely depressed and despondent after she and I spoke for the last time. He said she'd virtually stopped eating, and that she'd lost so much weight he and his wife were worried she was becoming anorexic, so they decided to move her back home for a time. He said they sent her to a therapist, who diagnosed her with depression. After a few months of therapy, she began feeling better and eventually got back to her normal weight, and then they sent her off to an art college in San Francisco. He told me that she was doing well there, and there was no way he'd ever allow me another opportunity to hurt her."

"So what did you say after that?"

"There wasn't much else I could say," he replied. "I gave him my phone number. I asked him to please send it to her, and to let her decide for herself if she wanted to call me back or not. But I knew, deep down, that he wouldn't do it. So I thanked him once again for the referral to Salisbury, and he told me to have a good life. The next day I married Laura."

"So why didn't you hop on the next flight to San Francisco?"

"I don't know, Kat. Guilt, I suppose. I was shocked to hear that I'd caused her so much pain and suffering, and for a time I thought maybe she really was better off without me. But I did think about it later on. About the time I was ready to make my move, Laura announced that she was pregnant. You know the rest of the story."

"You might want to consider telling Gillian this. I think she'd want to know."

Before Ian could respond, his phone rang. It was Jeremy. Kat decided to turn in. Ian was beaming after he hung up from talking to Jeremy. Things were looking up indeed. He stayed outside on the patio, watching the fire slowly burning itself out, eventually falling asleep in his chair. He woke up in the wee hours of the morning, just long enough to go inside and fall back to sleep on top of his bed.

## ❧Sixteen❧

GILLIAN WAS VACUUMING the living room when she noticed Duke and Daisy starting to bark and to run toward the front door. She switched off the vacuum cleaner, wondering if she had a visitor. With Jason still on the loose, any unexpected visitor made her feel edgy. She looked through the peephole. It was Jeremy Palmer. Ian must have sent him.

"Hello, Jeremy," she said as she opened the door. "Nice seeing you again."

"Likewise."

She invited him to take a seat on the living room sofa while she put the vacuum cleaner away. He took an instant liking to the two dogs.

"We had a dog when I was growing up," he said. "His name was Barney. He was a mutt of some kind. He passed away about the time I moved out and Mom and Dad split up. He was sixteen years old. Died in his sleep."

"I'm sorry to hear that."

"Thanks. Once I finish up my degree and I'm able to buy my own house I'll definitely want to get a puppy. That is, when I'm at the point where I have time for a dog. But that's going to be down the road."

"You're going back to school?"

"Yep." His face was beaming. "Contrary to what my father may have believed, my plan all along was to only take a short break from college. As soon as I heard about his situation with Salisbury, I decided to take some time off to see if I could qualify for a scholarship, which I did. Come January, I'll be returning to the University of Colorado, and my tuition will be fully paid. I only have two semesters left before I complete my degree. In the meantime, I'll keep tending bar so I can save up as much as I can for living expenses."

"Good for you, Jeremy. I'll bet your father is really proud of you."

"He will be, once I tell him. I just found out about the scholarship on Friday, so I thought I'd surprise him. You're not going to spill the beans, are you?"

"No, I won't spoil your surprise. He was concerned, however, when you told him you were dropping out of school. This will really cheer him up."

Their conversation was interrupted by Gillian's cell phone ringing in her office. "And speaking of whom, I wonder if that could be him."

She excused herself and stepped into her office to answer her phone. She returned a minute later, phone in hand, with a puzzled expression on her face.

"This is so weird," she said. "For the past few days I've been getting calls from a strange area code with an unfamiliar number, and when I answer, whoever it is, hangs up. I guess someone has a wrong number and they're calling me by mistake."

"May I take a look? If you don't mind."

Gillian handed her phone to Jeremy. He began scrolling through her list of recent calls.

"Well let's see...you and my father have certainly been using up the minutes, haven't you?" He gave her a smile. "But someone else has been calling you a little too frequently in my estimation for it to be a wrong number, and we need to find out who that someone is. So, let me try something."

Jeremy pulled out his own phone and dialed the number that had just called.

"I'm putting this on speaker. Don't make any noise."

They heard the phone ringing. A man soon answered.

"Hello."

"Hello," replied Jeremy. "Is Judy there?"

"Who?"

"Judy. I need to speak to Judy. Is she there?"

"Sorry buddy. You've got the wrong number."

The call disconnected. Jeremy looked at Gillian, who appeared to be in a state of shock.

"Are you all right?"

It took a moment for her to find her voice. "That man. That's Jason. How did he get my cell phone number? I've only had that number for about a year, and it's never been published."

"You'd be amazed at what kind of information you can get your hands on, especially if you're willing to pay under the table for it. Look, I don't want to scare you, but I think you'd better call that cop in Phoenix and let him know."

"I think you're right."

Gillian stepped back into her office, found Detective Madden's business card and dialed the number. She filled him in on what happened and gave him Jason's phone number. He thanked her for the information and reassured her they were still trying to track Jason down. He again reminded her to remain vigilant until Jason was captured. After she finished her call, she came back into the living room.

"Are you all right?"

She didn't want to alarm him. "Yes. I'm fine."

Jeremy didn't buy it. "Yeah, right. Tell you what. Why don't we get out of here for a few hours? It'll do you some good. Dad says you like to go out and take pictures for your paintings. I know some back roads and hiking trails up in the mountains. It's God's country up there. You'll love it."

Gillian thought it over. The fresh mountain air would help ease her mind. "Good idea, Jeremy. Thanks."

She threw her camera and other essentials in a backpack and grabbed a jacket, but when she stepped out the front door what she found, instead of another car, was a black Harley-Davidson motorcycle with huge, chrome pipes. Jeremy put on a leather jacket and a pair of leather gloves before handing her one of the two helmets he'd brought along.

"You ever ridden on the back of a bike?"

"Yep. Jason had a motorcycle."

"Really. What kind?"

"A Triumph."

"Sweet."

Gillian put the helmet on and got on the back of the bike.

"Now, you can hold on to me. I promise I won't bite you."

Jeremy fired it up and they headed down the road, onto the freeway, and out of the city. Before long he exited onto a smaller highway. After another hour, they'd worked their way well into the mountains. Jeremy veered off the main road and onto a dirt road, taking them deeper into the woods. Gillian couldn't get over the stunning beauty of the Rocky Mountains. She'd lived in the Sierra Nevadas while she was married to Stu, but the Rockies were far more spectacular. Finally, Jeremy pulled off to the side of the road, near a small hiking trail, and shut down his motorcycle.

"Now if you'll follow me," he said, "I'll take you someplace really special."

They got off the bike and she followed him down the hiking trail, for about a quarter of a mile, until they came around a bend. It was one of the most spectacular scenes she'd ever come across in her life. There was a clearing of grass and wildflowers, surrounded by aspen and pine tress. A small creek rushed through the meadow with snowcapped peaks towering up behind. She whipped her camera out of her backpack and starting taking pictures.

"It's incredible. I have to paint this. I might even do a whole series on it. You weren't kidding when you said this was God's country."

"Take your time."

There were a number of large rocks along the side of the creek, and once Gillian finished snapping photos they both sat down to watch the water flow by. The sound of the rushing waters, along with the sound of the breeze blowing through the trees, was very soothing. Gillian felt her muscles starting to relax.

"This is a very special place for me." Jeremy picked up a large stick and dangled it in the water. "I was ten years old the first time I came here. I was on an overnight hiking trip with my Boy Scout troop. Once I got my driver's license I started coming back. And when Mom and Dad were splitting up I came up here as often as I could to clear my head."

"That must have been a difficult time for you, Jeremy."

He sighed. "It was, but not in the way you think. I was sad, but I was also relieved at the same time. My parents were never happy together, at least not at any time that I can recall. When I was a kid, I'd go to visit my friends and I'd notice that their parents, or maybe their mom or dad and a stepparent, always seemed to love one another. Kids can tell these things, you know. But then I started noticing that my mom and dad just weren't that close. They weren't mean or nasty to one another, but where was the love? I couldn't see it in their eyes and I couldn't hear it in the sound of their voices. I could tell, not so much by the things that they did, but by the things they didn't do. They simply weren't in love with one another. They loved my brother and me, but over time I figured out that the only reason they were staying together was because of us, and I hated it. I hated all the tension, and I hated all the pretentiousness. I wish they'd gone their separate ways much sooner. I would have been much better off having them living separate, but happy lives. I know that people sometimes stay together for the sake of their kids, but they're not necessarily doing us any favors. At least, not me."

"I'm sorry, Jeremy. Have you ever talked to your father about this?"

"Some, but not a whole lot. I mean, what's done is done. You can't go back and change the past."

"I suppose you're right."

"You know, I remember this one time when I was a kid. I forget the reason why, but I went into the closet down in the basement, and I came across a box full of Dad's old mementos. In it I found some photo albums that my grandmother must have put together. They had old pictures of him on my grandparent's farm back when he was a kid. And there were his high school yearbooks, and then there was this scrapbook. In it were a whole bunch of photos of you and him, back when you were in college, with notes talking about what the different photos were."

"You're kidding," said Gillian. "I had no idea your dad still had that. I made it for him as part of his graduation present."

"I figured you must have, although I didn't know who you were at the time. But what impressed me was how happy the two of you looked together. My dad was never that happy with my mother, and photos don't lie. He really did love you. I hope you'll have better luck this time around."

"Me too."

"Well, for what it's worth, I've noticed he's become a different person since you came here. He's happy, and I've never seen him like this before. But I don't want him getting hurt either. I guess that's why I was a little too direct with you that night at the gallery. Sorry if I came off a little blunt. Anyway, I talked to him about that later on that night, so I understand if you're not ready to make any kind of a commitment yet."

"Well, Jeremy, I appreciate you being so candid with me. You're a good son, and it pleases me to see that you love your dad like you do. I love him too. I've been in love with your father since I was your age. I wanted us to get married back when we were young, but for whatever reason, he wanted to end things, and that was that. I never understood why. All I know is that I was unhappy for many, many years afterwards."

He noticed a change in her demeanor. "Hey, I didn't mean to open up old wounds. For what it's worth, he wasn't that happy either; but now, it appears to be working out for the best. My father found you again, and my mother found someone she's happy with too. Now, if we could only get Larry to see the light, life would be perfect."

"I hear he's having a hard time adjusting."

"You could say that," replied Jeremy. "Larry and I are complete polar opposites when it comes to our parents. Deep down, he thinks Mom left because he was a bad kid, and he's still holding out hope that she'll eventually come back. Of course, her leaving had nothing to do with him, but he hasn't quite figured it out yet. I think once he finally does he can move on as well."

"And what about you, Jeremy? What about your life?"

"What do you mean?"

"Well, you seem to have it all figured out for the rest of your family, but what about you? You're twenty-one years old. You're at an age and stage in life when you should be looking forward to having a bright future ahead of you. Like I just said, I was about your age when I first met your father. Is there anyone special in your life?"

"Nah." He tossed the stick aside. "Women are different, at least in my generation. There are some decent ones out there, but they seem to be few and far between. It seems like most of the ones my age are skanks. I've had my fair share of, shall we say, friends with benefits, but certainly no one I'd want to be with for the rest of my life. Sometimes I think I was born about twenty years too late."

"Well, hang in there. You're young. You still have plenty of time. Maybe you'll meet someone special when you go back to college."

"Maybe, but I'm sure not going to find much while I'm working as a bartender, other than the occasional one-night stand, and yes," he grinned, "I'm taking all the proper precautions."

They stayed in the meadow and talked longer, but as the afternoon wore on they knew they needed to start heading back. They stopped for dinner at a little honky-tonk bar and cafe in some small town on the way back. There was a country music band playing, so they stayed and danced. Jeremy turned out to be just as good of a dancer as his father had been. It was getting late by the time they got back on the Harley and rode back to Denver.

Once they returned to Gillian's house Jeremy offered to stay overnight on the sofa, just in case she was worried about Jason. She appreciated the thought, but she didn't want to involve him in her problems. Before leaving, he double-checked all the doors and windows, just to make sure she'd feel secure. Then he told her goodnight and got back on the Harley.

"Nice going, Palmer." He sighed as he put the key into the ignition. "You finally come across a good one that you could really fall for, but your father has a prior claim on her."

He shook his head, fired up the motorcycle, and rode off into the night.

# ᎒ᏚᎬᏙᎬNᎢᎬᎬN᎒

GILLIAN EXITED THE freeway at the airport off ramp. Ian was on his way home and she couldn't wait to feel his sweet embrace. She parked the minivan and headed into the crowded terminal. She was nearing the baggage claim when she heard a voice behind her.

"Gillian!"

She scanned through the crowd but couldn't see him. Suddenly, she felt a hand touch her shoulder. She quickly spun around.

"I'm right here," said Ian.

They fell into each other's arms.

"I missed you," said Gillian.

"Not half as much as I missed you. Why don't we continue this at my place? I'm not expected back at the office until after lunch, and I need to drop off my bag and pick up my car."

He got his suitcase and they headed out to the parking garage. "So, how did it go with Jeremy?"

"Much better. He's actually a pretty good kid, once you get to know him."

"See? Now aren't you glad you gave him a second chance? He called me late last night, after he took you home. He told me about getting that scholarship. I'm so proud of that kid I could bust. I don't know, Gilly-girl, I think my oldest is all grown up. How did that happen?"

"It happens, Ian. They have to grow up sometime. Did you know that Jeremy has staked out his own special place, sort of his own personal retreat, up in the mountains?"

"Yes, but I've never been there. I'm not even sure where it is."

"I know. He told me that in all the years he's been going up there, I'm the first person he's ever brought along."

The minivan popped into view and they loaded Ian's suitcase. Gillian handed him the keys and hopped into the passenger seat. Ian climbed in the driver's seat, but before he started up the engine he turned to her. The expression on his face was one she hadn't seen for many years.

"Gillian, I think you and I need to have a little talk. Jeremy also tells me that you've been getting some strange phone calls lately, and that when he checked it out, he discovered they've been coming from Jason."

"I'm afraid so. The first one came the day before you left for Oregon, but I thought it was a wrong number. Jeremy is the one who decided to call the number back. I never imagined it was Jason calling me. I still can't figure out how he got my number."

"They say where there's a will, there's a way. So why didn't you call me?"

"I'm not sure. I'm sorry, Ian. I guess I really don't have a good excuse. I was in such a state of shock after hearing Jason's voice that I went completely numb. Jeremy even had to remind me to call Detective Madden."

"Gillian, I've been deeply concerned about your well-being ever since Madden showed up at your door and told us what Jason had done. Now that Jason has your phone number, I'm even more concerned. It's only a matter of time before he finds out you're in Denver. I want your word that if anything like this happens again, you'll call me right away. I don't care if I'm with a client, in the middle of a staff meeting, or having an audience with the Pope, I want to know the minute something happens. Okay?"

"Okay, Ian. I'm sorry I upset you. I really am."

"It's okay, Gilly-girl. I'm not angry with you," he said, reassuringly. "It's just that I can't stand the thought of anything happening to you. So please, promise me that you won't leave me out of the loop again."

"I won't, Ian. I promise."

He turned the key and started the engine. "Anyway, my visit with my sister was just what I needed, and I spent a lot of time hashing things out with her. I know there's enough blame to go around for everyone, but I'm still not going to let that be an excuse for what Laura did. However, what's done is done, and hopefully, for my sons' sakes, I'll be able to forgive her someday."

"For what it's worth, Ian, she came across to me that day as very remorseful. As I told you before, she said she wished she could go back and undo it. To her credit, she's come a long way. She talked about how she hated me at one time, but that she's put it behind her, at least for the sake of the kids. She may have her faults, Ian, but she's a good mother. You two did a terrific job with Jeremy. He's an amazing young man, and I know he's going to go far in life."

They exited the parking garage and headed back toward the freeway. They drove for about a half an hour, making their way into a well-kept but mature neighborhood. Ian pulled into the driveway in front of a two-story house with sand-colored masonry and a dark brown wood trim.

"Here we are, my humble abode." He shut down the engine. "We bought this place when Jeremy was about six months old, and despite everything, it's going to be hard when the time comes to sell it. I have many fond memories of my boys growing up in this house."

He handed the keys back to her, grabbed his bag, and unlocked the front door. Gillian stepped inside and looked around. The house was neat, but a little odd. The dining room was completely empty, and it appeared that some of the furniture in the family room was missing too. Those must have been the pieces that Laura took with her when they went their separate ways. Looking back into the family room something familiar caught her eye. It was the matching mahogany coffee and end tables that had once been in Ian's college apartment.

"You still have these?" Gillian walked over to take a closer look.

"I certainly do. They're good furniture. And here, let me show you this."

He led her downstairs to the basement. It was set up like a den, with a game table, a TV with a video game console, and the leather sofa with the two matching leather chairs that had also once been in his college apartment.

"Well, this certainly takes me back."

Gillian inspected the sofa, remembering the night she and Ian made love for the very first time. As she looked closer she noticed some of the leather was now cracked and torn. Ian explained that it had actually stood up well under the strain of two growing boys.

"I thought about getting rid of it, but I just couldn't. It holds the same memory for me as well."

Gillian ran her hands back and forth across the leather. "You know, Ian, you can probably have this redone. It's still a good piece of furniture. It would certainly be worth the expense."

"You think so?"

"Yes, I do."

"You know, Gilly-girl, I've still got time before I have to be back at the office. What do you say about taking a little trip down memory lane on this old sofa?"

"Ian Palmer, I swear, you have a one track mind."

"And you love it. Admit it."

An hour later they were in the kitchen, seated at the breakfast bar, enjoying some leftover, homemade lasagna. Gillian was even wearing Ian's bathrobe, just for nostalgia.

"You know, Ian, this kid of yours really is a good cook. I can make a pretty mean lasagna myself, but Larry could certainly give me a run for my money."

"Hopefully I can introduce the two of you soon. The other night we had a long talk about his future. He tells me he wants to go to culinary school. He says he wants to become an executive chef and have his own restaurant someday. He says when that happens he'd like for me to design it for him."

Gillian glanced over at the microwave clock. "Uh-oh!" She hopped off her barstool. "I don't mean to cut you off, but I'm supposed to be in a meeting with Paul in less than fifteen minutes. I hate to eat and run, but duty calls."

She ran into the bathroom and quickly dressed. When she came out, she stopped just long enough to give Ian a quick kiss good-bye before she rushed out the front door.

## ᘒEIGHTEENᘕ

GILLIAN RUSHED INTO Paul's office, just in time for their meeting.

"I take it Ian's back."

"He is." Gillian quickly took her seat.

"I thought so, but Boss, you may want to touch up your lipstick. You're a little smudged."

Gillian blushed as she quickly excused herself to tidy up. Her face was still a little red when she returned.

"It's okay, Boss. I'd be more worried if something wasn't happening between the two of you. And to think, this is all my doing. I'm the one who sent your picture to the newspaper last spring, before you had your show."

"Thanks, but since we're a little too old to have kids, you may have to settle for our naming our next dog after you."

"That works for me, Boss, but for now we'd better get back to business."

Paul had several things to go over with her and they went down the list. He took a deep breath as he approached the last item on the agenda.

"This came in the mail on Thursday. I wanted to discuss it with you before I did anything further." He pulled a letter from a folder on his desk and handed it to her. "And remember, I'm just the messenger. Okay?"

The letterhead indicated that it was from The Saint Eligius Ranch Foundation, Steamboat Springs, Colorado. It was a personalized form letter, explaining the foundation's mission of rescuing abandoned, abused, injured or neglected horses, rehabilitating them, and, whenever possible, putting them up for adoption and placing them with responsible owners. The letter went on to announce the foundation's upcoming annual dinner and auction to be held in Denver the following February, and ended with a request for donations of items for the auction. The letter concluded with the photocopied signature of William T. Mason, D.V.M., President and CEO of The Saint Eligius Ranch Foundation.

"I guess we must have made a positive impression on Laura Palmer when she came to see you," said Paul. "But still, I'm a little taken aback."

"Well, if there's one thing I've learned about Mrs. Palmer, it's that she's direct. I gotta hand it to her. The lady's got spunk."

"So, what do we do? Do you want me to place it in the circular file?"

Gillian looked it over once again. It really was a worthwhile charity. Donating a painting to their auction would be a nice write-off as well as an opportunity for the gallery to earn some publicity.

"No. We don't want to throw the letter away. Honestly Paul, I'm a little torn on this one. On one hand, I'm a horse lover myself. My personal feelings for Laura Palmer aside, these people are doing good work."

"But on the other hand?"

"On the other hand, if it was from anyone other than Laura Palmer." She rolled her eyes as she spoke. "I'll have to decide later if I'm going to respond or not. Anything else on the docket today?"

"Nope. That's it, Boss."

Gillian took the letter to her office and placed a call to Ian.

"Hey, Gilly-girl. What's up? Do you miss me already?"

"You know I do, and you won't believe what was waiting for me when I got to the office. A letter from Saint Eligius Ranch soliciting donations for their annual auction."

"I'm not surprised," said Ian. "Salisbury gets one of those letter every year too. I know in year's past we always sent them a check."

"I'm just blown-away that she would have even sent this to me in the first place."

"Well, don't be. She's just doing her job, and she and Will really do good work. If you want to donate something, that's okay. If not, that's okay too. I don't want you to feel like you're under any obligation, either way, because of me."

"Thanks Ian. Maybe I'll just send them a cash donation as a wedding present."

"Now you're talking."

She was about ready to tell Ian good-bye when she heard her cell phone ringing. She asked him to hold on while she checked the caller ID.

"Ian! It's Jason. I'm putting you on speakerphone. Whatever you do, don't make a sound."

She answered her cell phone. "Gillian Matthews." There was no immediate response. "Hello? Is anyone there?"

"Hello, Gillian."

The sound of Jason's voice made her shudder, but she needed to remain calm. "Jason? Is that you?"

"Yes, Gillian. It's me. How are you?"

"I'm fine, Jason." She fought to keep the tremble in her voice down. "I'm just very surprised to hear from you."

"I'm sure you are."

"I'm working on a painting in my studio. Would you mind if I put you on speaker? Right now I just don't have a free hand to hold onto my phone."

"Of course."

She placed the cell phone on her desk and turned on the speaker. "There, now. I can get back to this painting and talk to you at the same time."

"So, Gillian, have you been keeping yourself busy?"

"Yes. There's always a show I have to get ready for. You know that."

"Like the one in Denver?"

Her blood turned to ice. "Yes, that was a good show. How did you hear about it?"

"I have my ways."

"I see. Well, Denver was a nice town, but that show is over. I'm back home in Phoenix now." She prayed Jason would buy it.

"Good to know," he replied.

"Enough about me. How have you been? Are you still with Sandy?"

"Who?"

"Sandy. I heard through the grapevine that you married someone named Sandy right after we split up."

"Oh, you mean Deanna. No, I'm not with her anymore."

"Really? What happened?"

Jason let out a sigh. "Gillian, she threw me out."

"I see. Sorry to hear it. When did that happen?"

"A few weeks ago. Gillian, I need your help. I've fallen on some hard times. I just need—"

"No way, Jason." Her tone was firm. "Not gonna happen."

"Be careful, Gillian." Ian murmured under his breath. "Whatever you do, don't provoke him."

"Look, Gillian." Jason's tone turned icy."My patience is wearing thin. You either help me or I'll show up on your door and make you help me."

"I moved, Jason. About six months after the divorce."

"I know, and I have your new address, although it appears that you've moved out and it's up for sale. I have my way of finding these things out."

Both Gillian and Ian felt the air escaping from their lungs. Somehow Gillian regained her composure. She knew she had to think fast.

"I'm living with someone now, Jason. It's his house, not mine, and I'm not giving you the address. I guess you need to go home and try to work things out with Deanna, or Sandy, or whatever her name is, because I'm sure as hell not taking you back."

"Look Gillian, I'm on my way to Phoenix and I'm going to find you. I don't care who you're living with. I got your cell phone number, didn't I? I found out where you moved to after our divorce, didn't I? So guess what? I can get your new address too, even if you're shacking up with some new boy toy. You can count on it. I put up with you for five stinking years. You owe me and I'm coming to collect."

"I don't owe you jack, now get the hell out of my life."

She disconnected the cell phone, picked up the receiver on her office phone and turned off the speaker.

"Ian, did you get that?"

"Every word. Gilly-girl, you were magnificent. You got the information we needed. He doesn't know you're in Denver. At least not yet, thank God."

Gillian's hands were trembling so hard she could barely hold on to the phone. "If he's on his way to Phoenix I'll have to call Detective Madden to let him know, but I don't have his number with me. It's at home."

"It's okay," said Ian. "If you can hold on for a minute or two I can pull it up on my computer."

"Thanks, Ian." She stepped out to get a glass of water. By the time she returned to her desk, Ian had the information ready for her.

"I wish I could come over and stay with you tonight, but I can't."

"I'm fine, Ian. I really am. He thinks I'm in Phoenix. That's the best lead we've had in weeks. I know tonight I'll sleep better than I have in a long time."

# ❧NINETEEN❧

GILLIAN PRAYED THE nightmare with Jason would soon end. It had been over a week since his phone call and she hadn't heard from him again. Her spirits, however, had received a much-needed boost in knowing that he thought she was still in Phoenix. She decided the time had come to claim more of her life back and that evening she planned to accompany Ian to an office party. Another of the old-timers at Salisbury & Norton had accepted his early retirement offer, although at age sixty-two, this man was considerably older than Ian.

She gazed at her reflection in the mirror after she dressed. Her hair was starting to grow long again, making her look more like she did back in her college days. She brushed and teased it to make it look fuller. Ian greeted her with a passionate kiss when he arrived. He too noticed the changes in her hairstyle and her demeanor.

"You look incredibly sexy tonight," he said. "Maybe we'll skip the party and have our own little celebration, right here."

"Ian Palmer, you are such a bad, bad boy," she flirtatiously replied. "But if you insist..." She returned his kiss, just as passionately.

"Unfortunately, they're expecting me, but there's no rule that says we have to stay very long. Besides, I feel like I'm going to a funeral. We'll stay just long enough to be polite and then I'll take you to dinner."

Salisbury & Norton Architects, Inc. was located in an eight-story, slightly curved, glass-and-steel building near downtown Denver. Gillian had admired it the times she'd driven by, and she looked forward to finally seeing it on the inside. Ian pulled into the entryway and immediately veered into an underground parking facility, pulling into his reserved parking space.

"I'm impressed," she said.

"Rank has its privileges. It took me a long time to get here. Kind of a bummer that I'm not going to be around to enjoy it for very much longer."

They took the elevator from the garage to the seventh floor. The doors opened into a large, spacious work area, filled with desks and drawing tables. At first glance it appeared to be a busy firm, but upon closer inspection Gillian noticed that a number of the desks appeared to be unoccupied. It was apparent that the firm had been downsizing. Offices with large picture windows lined both sides of the main room, one of which was Ian's. It was a beautifully furnished executive suite with a spectacular view of the Denver skyline. Gillian spotted something familiar hanging on one of the walls. It was her painting of the barn with the tractor.

"I wanted you to see this, at least once," he said. "It's been like my second home for many years. However, they've just informed me that they want me to leave sooner than June. Now I'll be lucky if I can hang on until the end of the year."

"I'm so sorry, Ian."

"Me too. I keep telling myself that I'm better off than the younger guys. Some of them are leaving with only two weeks severance pay, and they get to look forward to long lines at the unemployment office. At least I'll still have a decent income, but not what I was making before."

"I understand."

"Do you? Because being an architect is who I am, Gillian. I can't imagine being anything else. It would be like you suddenly waking up one day and realizing that you were no longer an artist."

"I'm sorry, Ian. I didn't mean to sound like I was being insensitive."

Ian regretted his sudden outburst. "No, I'm sorry. I didn't mean to take out my frustrations on you."

He explained that the party was being held on a different floor. They got back into the elevator and took it down to the mezzanine. When the doors opened, they stepped into another large, open area. This one looked like an art gallery. It was filled with architectural models displayed on pedestals and the walls were covered with large, color photographs of buildings Salisbury & Norton had designed. There was a bar and a table of hors d'oeuvres set up, but unlike the artist openings at Gillian's galleries, the atmosphere was hardly festive. Ian introduced Gillian to the guest of honor, along with several of his other coworkers. Before long, he was involved in their conversations. As Gillian stepped away to get something to drink she heard her phone ringing in her purse. She checked the caller ID. The call had a Phoenix area code.

"Hello."

"Mrs. Matthews, this is Detective Madden. I have some news about your ex-husband. Can we talk?"

"Sure. Would you mind holding on for a minute or two?" She turned to the man standing next to her. "Excuse me, I have an urgent phone call that I have to take. Is there someplace where I can talk in private?"

He directed her back up to the seventh floor, explaining that it would be okay to take the call in Ian's office. She thanked him and took the elevator back up.

"Thanks for holding," she told Madden as she sat down behind Ian's desk.

"Not a problem. Please allow me to bring you up to date on your ex-husband's case. Yesterday afternoon, around four o'clock, a police officer in El Paso, Texas, attempted to make a routine traffic stop on a vehicle running a red light. It was the same make and model as Jason Matthews' car, but it turned out to have stolen New Mexico license plates. The driver took off as the officer approached. They put out an APB, but rather than endanger the public, they decided not to give chase."

"I see. Was it Jason?"

"Yes ma'am, it certainly was, as we would later learn. Then, at about eleven o'clock last night, here in Arizona, the Cochise County sheriff's office got a call about a suspicious vehicle near the town of Benson, which, as you probably know, is east of Tucson. There's an old western movie set out in the desert just outside of town."

"Yes, I know the place. Jason took me there once. He told me he used to work there from time to time as an extra."

"I see," said Madden. "Then you're also probably aware that there's a full-time caretaker living on the premises. He was making his rounds last night when he came across your ex-husband's vehicle. It was unoccupied, but he went ahead and reported it to the authorities anyway. Apparently they don't like trespassers."

"No, they don't."

"By the time the deputies arrived, Jason had returned to his vehicle. They ran the plates and they too discovered that they were stolen New Mexico plates, so one of the deputies approached the car and ordered the driver out. It was at that point that your ex-husband drew his gun and fired a shot at the deputy."

"Oh my God. Was the deputy hurt?"

"Fortunately, no," replied Madden, "but the other deputies

immediately returned fire. I'm sorry, Mrs. Matthews, but your former husband is dead. He died at the scene of multiple gunshot wounds and the coroner has confirmed his identity."

It wasn't the news she expected to hear and it took a moment for it to sink in. Jason was gone. He would never be able to hurt her again. She would no longer have to live in the shadows.

"Mrs. Matthews, we need to notify his next of kin, but so far we've been unable to locate anyone."

"There was no family, at least none that I ever knew of. Jason always maintained that he was an only child and that he had no children himself. He also claimed that both his parents were deceased. If there were any uncles, aunts or cousins, he never mentioned them."

"In that case, and I hate to have to ask you this, but if no relatives can be found, do you want to claim the body?"

Gillian didn't know whether she should laugh or cry. "No, I don't. We've been divorced for a number of years, and since we had no children I don't want the body or any of his personal property."

"I understand." The detective ended the call by stating that the case was now officially closed, but she was welcome to call him back, any time, if she had questions. After the call ended she stayed at Ian's desk and stared out the window watching the sunset. The room was beginning to get dark when someone turned on the lights.

"Gillian? What are you doing?"

It was Ian.

"Sorry." She turned to face him. "I had to step away for an urgent phone call. I didn't think you'd mind. I apologize if I was rude."

"Are you all right? You look upset about something."

"The call was from Detective Madden. Ian, it's all over. Jason's dead."

"What?"

She went on to explain what had happened. "Ever since I got off the phone, I've felt as if a war was raging inside of me. Part of me is incredibly relieved this nightmare is finally over, and that I never, ever have to worry about him hurting me again. But there's another part of me that's sad, and almost feels guilty for feeling so relieved. In spite of everything that happened, I was still married to the man for five years. There was even a time when I thought he was my soul mate."

"Come here, Gilly-girl." He wrapped his arms around her and held her close. "You wouldn't be you if you weren't feeling some compassion. It's unfortunate that Jason couldn't have been brought to justice. I don't think anyone wanted to see it end this way, but he brought it on himself."

"Ian? Why is it that I seem to attract all the crazies? Present

96

company excluded, of course, but where are the Ryan Knights and the Jason Matthews coming from?"

"I don't know, Gilly-girl. I think it's probably because there are a lot of bad guys out there, and you're a loving, giving person who has a good soul. You're everything that they're not, so I guess they feel that they have to try to take it away from you."

"I'm so lucky to have found you, Ian. Not once, but twice. Promise me you'll always be there for me."

"I promise, Gilly-girl."

# ❧Twenty❧

ROSEMARY WAS ESPECIALLY relieved to hear the Jason Matthews nightmare had finally ended. She, too, would no longer have to fear for Gillian's safety, and she would also be free to do her job again. The first item on her list was to start publicizing the fact that Hanson Sisters had recently acquired Anthony Sorenson Fine Art. The Sunday following Jason's death a story appeared in the Denver newspaper about Sorenson's new owners, along with a photo spread of Gillian and her paintings.

Ian read the article before cutting it out and placing it in the folder he kept with the other articles about her. He called her that morning, teasing her about being in love with a celebrity, but when he hung up he realized he was beginning to harbor some serious doubts about the future of their relationship. Gillian was, in some circles, a public figure. Her star was rising, while his was fading. As much as he loved her, and as much as he wanted to spend the rest of his life with her, he also wanted to be a man she could be proud of. He didn't want to be perceived as a former architect, living off her fame and success.

Ian was still unsure of how to fill the void when the time finally came for him to leave Salisbury & Norton. He wasn't worried about his income, but he was worried about how to spend his time. He had options. He could hire himself out as a consultant, but there were already a number of others doing the same thing. He thought about teaching and had even applied for a few teaching positions, but so far he'd come up empty. There were simply too many other people out there, equally qualified, in the same position. He sighed as he placed the folder back on his desk and walked down the hall to Larry's room. He knocked on the door.

"Come in."

Larry turned from his computer and faced his father. Unlike his brother, Larry bore more of a resemblance to his mother with his fair complexion and blond hair, although he had his father's deep-set brown eyes.

"What's up, Dad?"

"You got a few minutes? I want to show you something."

Larry sighed as he followed his father into his study and took a seat. "So what did I do now?"

"Nothing, son." Ian handed him the folder. "I just wanted for us to have a little talk. You know that I've been seeing someone. At first I wasn't sure just how far it would go, but now I think that maybe the time has come for me to introduce the two of you."

"I remember you telling me you ran into an old friend. I take it this is her." Larry glanced at the article and came across her picture. "Wow, Jer was right. She really is cute."

"What was that?"

"Jeremy told me a little bit about her. He said he thought she was pretty cute, but he didn't elaborate."

"I see." Ian felt a slight tinge of jealousy.

"So what's the story on her?"

"I first met her back when I was in college. She was the first woman I ever really fell in love with. Over the years, I've come to realize she's the only woman I'll ever truly be in love with."

Larry winced at his father's words. "So why didn't you marry her?"

"I'm not sure," replied Ian. "I've spent many years asking myself that very question. I was young. I got scared. I had cold feet. Sometimes your old man does dumb things and makes mistakes too."

"So what about Mom?"

"I did love your mother for a time, Larry, in my own way, but it just didn't last. And in case you're wondering, I wasn't seeing Gillian during the time your mother and I were married. We'd broken up before I met your mother, and I honestly didn't think I'd ever see her again, at least, not in this lifetime. Then I ran into her again this past April. We hadn't seen or heard from one another in many years. She's no longer married, and I'm no longer married. However, she and I share a past together, and we plan on sharing a future together."

"I see. So does that mean that you're going to marry her?"

"I hope to, someday, but at the moment neither of us is ready for that kind of commitment. When the time comes, it will be after you're out on your own, so I don't want you worrying about it. I'm not going to leave you."

"Like Mom did."

"Larry, we've been over this how many times now? Your mother and I had a long discussion before she took that job in Steamboat Springs. The reason why she took it was because it was the best paying one she could find, and she wanted to be able to help you and your brother go to college. Yes, we've put money away for your education, but if you're serious about going to one of those culinary schools that you were telling me about then you're going to need some help from your mother to get there. Remember when she came down from Steamboat Springs a few weeks ago and took you to dinner?"

"Yeah."

"Well, she and I met for lunch that day to talk about you and how we both plan to pay for you to go to college. She assured me she's in a good position to help cover the cost of your tuition, even if I were to lose my job, which by the way, will be probably be happening at the end of the year."

Larry was stunned. "Jeez, Dad, I didn't know. What are you going to do after that?"

"I don't know. I'm still trying to figure it out, but I don't want you worrying about it. I'll still have an income and I'll still be able to pay the bills. I just won't be making as much as I'm making now. I also wanted you to know that as soon as the holidays are over I'll be putting the house on the market. That was another thing your mother and I had agreed on. We weren't going to sell this house until you finished high school and moved out. The reason was so you wouldn't be uprooted. But in this market, I'm probably going to have to list it sooner than we'd originally planned, and your mother understands my decision. It could easily take six months to a year to sell, and I don't want to be rattling around a big empty house that long once you've moved out."

"So, between your old girlfriend and selling the house, I take it to mean that you and Mom aren't going to try to work things out."

"That's right, son," replied Ian. "We've also been over this how many times before? It's been over between your mother and me for a long, long time. Even if Will and Gillian weren't in the picture, it would still be over between your mother and me. We don't regret being together long enough to have your brother and you, and we both still love you. However, we've both moved on with our lives, and we both want you to move on with your life too. Your high school graduation isn't that far away, Larry. After that, you'll be starting a whole new chapter of your life. If that means going to culinary school, then your mother and I will support your decision. And we'd both be very proud of you, by the way."

Larry sat in silence before closing the folder and placing it back on his father's desk. He stood up to leave.

"Oh, and one more thing before you go. I got an email from your mother yesterday. She and Will are coming to town on Wednesday and we're to meet them, along with your brother, for dinner. You know they're getting serious. I have a hunch they're going to announce their engagement. If that's the case, then I want you to be prepared. I also want you to be happy for your mother, because I certainly am. She's finally found someone who can make her happy, and that's the one thing, son, that I could never do for her. I'm going have Gillian meet us there. She and your mother have already met. Your mother also likes her, so I think it's as good a time as any for the two of you to meet. She's a good woman, Larry. You just told me your brother likes her, and I think you'll like her too, if you'll just give her a chance."

* * *

Larry didn't like the sound of any of it, but he knew there was nothing he could do about it either. Maybe his father was right. Maybe it was time for him to focus more on his own life. When he returned to his computer, he found an instant message from Brian waiting for him. A group of their friends were going to a beer-keg party out in the woods on Friday night. Larry replied that he wouldn't miss it.

# ❧Twenty-One❧

THE BUTTERFLIES roiled in Gillian's stomach as she drove to the restaurant. Not only was she going to face Laura Palmer again, Larry would be there as well. She prayed that he'd be decent. She had to remind herself that Larry was only seventeen, and that she'd hardly been an angel herself at seventeen. Cynthia also tried to reassure her. She said that even if Larry was difficult, he would, in time, outgrow it.

She pulled into the parking lot and spotted Ian's BMW. She found an empty space, shut down the engine and glanced in the rearview mirror for one last check. If she was going to face the firing squad, she at least wanted to look her best. As she reached for her purse she heard the familiar sound of a Harley-Davidson engine. Jeremy pulled into the empty space beside her. She exited her vehicle and greeted him.

"Well hello there, Miss Gillian." He pulled off his helmet. "It's good seeing you again. Sorry to hear about your ex-husband, but I'm glad you're okay."

"Thanks, Jeremy. I'm just relieved it's over."

"I'll bet. And by the way, nice article in Sunday's paper. Dad called and told me about it, so I read it online. He really sounded impressed."

"Oh, Jeremy, it's really no big deal. It just goes with the territory of being an artist. I'm hardly a rock star." They walked together to the front door. "So now we're on to the next crisis. I get to meet your baby brother. Hope he doesn't have fangs."

"Now, now. He's really not some demon seed, although he can be annoying at times. For what it's worth, he was always more of a thorn in

102

my mother's side than my dad's. Besides, I already had a talk with him. I told him you were cool, so believe it or not, he's actually looking forward to meeting you."

They spotted the rest of their party as soon as they entered the restaurant. Much to Gillian's relief, Larry actually smiled and extended his hand when they were introduced. She took her seat next to Ian and, for the next few minutes, everyone made small talk. Will was certainly not what Gillian expected. She assumed he would be a more mature man. Instead, he appeared to be in his mid-thirties. He certainly looked no older than forty at the most, making him several years younger than Laura. He had a full head of thick, dark-brown hair with a thick, dark-brown mustache. He was warm and friendly, and he told her how pleased he was that she was gracious to Laura the day she showed up unannounced at the art gallery. A waiter soon arrived with a bottle of champagne and five glasses. Once everyone was served, Will proposed a toast.

"Well, I'm sure you're all wondering why we invited you to join us this evening, so I'm not going to keep you in suspense any longer." He looked at Laura as his hand covered hers. It was obvious that he was very much in love with her. "It's no secret that this lady and I have become more than friends and more than best friends. We're soul mates. She's the kind of person who only comes along once in a lifetime, and when something this good comes along you grab a hold of it and you don't let go. So the other day I asked this beautiful lady to marry me, and she said yes."

Laura was beaming as she extended her left hand, proudly showing off her diamond ring. Jeremy immediately gave his mother a hug and shook Will's hand. Ian also congratulated them as he jokingly told Will that he hoped he knew what he was getting himself into. Will laughed and the two men shook hands. Gillian saw that Ian was relieved. It was another milestone along his journey of moving on to a new beginning with her. Only Larry seemed quiet and reserved. He gave his mother a lukewarm congratulation as he shook Will's hand.

* * *

Will and Laura discussed their wedding plans over dinner. Their wedding would be the following March and it would be small. Laura asked Jeremy if he would be willing to escort her up the aisle and give her away. Jeremy replied that he'd be honored. As soon as the meal was over, Larry asked to be excused. When he didn't return right away, Jeremy decided to find out what he was up to. He checked the men's room, but Larry wasn't there. He noticed a side exit near the men's room door, and he soon found Larry behind the building, busy texting on his phone. Larry looked up as his brother approached him.

"So what's up, bro?"

"I was about to ask you the same question," replied Jeremy.

"I just needed a time out, you know. All this wedding stuff was getting on my nerves."

"Well, I, for one, am glad to see Mom happy at last."

"Yeah, that figures."

"C'mon Larry, it's time to cut the bull. Mom has officially moved on from Dad, but she's still our mother, and her marrying Will has nothing to do with the two of us. You can be happy for her or you can be a pain in the butt, it's up to you. Either way, she's not coming back to Dad, so it's time for you to put that to rest once and for all. And in case you haven't noticed, he's got someone else now too."

"Yeah, I noticed and she's not bad looking either. I can see why you like her."

"You're right, I do like her. She's a decent woman and she's someone who I'd like to have as a friend as well. She and Dad share a past together, and most likely, she's going to be our stepmother someday. What that means, Doofus, is that the time has come for you to wake up, smell the coffee, and stop meddling in other people's lives."

"Whatever," replied Larry, "and by the way, Mr. Know-It-All, I actually am moving on with my life. While you've been standing here giving me your lecture, I've been busy making plans for Friday night."

"Good. So get your butt back in there. Now."

The two young men came back to their table.

"Everything all right?" asked Ian.

"We're good, Dad," replied Jeremy.

Before long the party broke up. Will and Laura had a long drive back to Steamboat Springs, and Ian mentioned it was a school night. Everyone said their goodbyes as Ian kissed Gillian goodnight in front of the boys. He figured it was time to be out in the open with them.

"I'll call you tomorrow, Gilly-girl."

He turned to leave, but before she could respond Larry piped in.

"Goodnight, Ms. Matthews. You know, you really are a cute one. I can see why my brother thinks you're hot."

Jeremy looked at his brother with daggers in his eyes before turning to his father.

"She's a good lady, Dad. Maybe we can come back here, really soon, and you two can announce your engagement too."

"All in good time, son," replied Ian. "Ready to go, Larry?"

"Yeah, Dad."

"Goodnight." Ian gave Gillian a quick parting kiss. "Jeremy, would you mind walking her to her car?"

"Sure, Dad."

They stood and watched Ian and Larry walk out the door.

"I am so sorry about that, Miss Gillian. About the time I think I can trust the little twerp, he pulls something like this."

"He's still seventeen. We were all little smart-alecks when we were that age."

"Well, tell you what," said Jeremy. "Let me make it up to you and buy you a drink before we go."

"Sure, why not?"

They went into the bar and took a seat. Jeremy ordered a beer for himself and a glass of white wine for Gillian.

"So, are you the oldest, youngest or middle child?"

"I'm the youngest," replied Gillian, "and I used to do the same thing to my older sister when we were kids. I wanted to hang around with her and her friends, and I'd throw a real fit whenever she told me no. She had a couple of boyfriends back when she was in high school, and I liked to torment them too. Every chance I got."

"You? No way."

"Yes, I did. But I remember another time, I think we were both still in grade school, and some boy was giving her a hard time. I remember coming home one day and finding him hanging out in front of our house. Here I was, this scrawny little nine-year-old kid, and I marched right up to him and told him to leave. I can't remember exactly what he said to me, but whatever it was, it really ticked me off. So I leaned back and punched him, right in the jaw."

"You're kidding."

"No, I'm not," she replied. "He went down, and when he got back up he ran home as fast as he could. I didn't hit him hard enough to hurt him, but he got the point. He never bothered my sister again. I even scared myself when I hit him, but my motive wasn't all that pure. I'd already decided that nobody was gonna hassle my sister except me, and he was stepping on my turf."

"Remind me not to ever get on your bad side."

"Hey, it was an isolated incident. In hindsight, I'm amazed that Cynthia ever put up with me. But by the time I became a teenager, she and I started growing closer, and we've been that way ever since. So just be patient with your little brother. He'll grow up soon enough."

They chatted for a few minutes longer, and when it was time to leave, Jeremy walked her out to her minivan. He told her goodnight and waited for her to pull out of the parking lot. He envied his dad. He hoped his father appreciated what a special woman he had.

## ❧ TWENTY-TWO ❦

FRIDAY NIGHT, while Larry went out with his friends, Ian treated Gillian to a long overdue night on the town. After an evening of dinner and dancing they returned to her house where she drew a bubble bath in her big, garden bathtub. She lit some candles and they had a long, romantic soak, followed by a lovemaking session that was one of the best they'd experienced in some time. It was nearly midnight when Ian reluctantly announced that he had to leave. Larry was due home and he didn't want to be out too late.

It was just after twelve when he pulled into the driveway. He noticed the light by the front door was still on. Larry must have forgotten to turn it off when he got home. He pushed the remote control button, waited for the garage door to open, and parked his car. The house was dark and quiet when he stepped inside. It was too dark and quiet. He quickly turned on some lights.

"Larry!"

No answer.

"Larry! Where are you?"

Again, there was no answer. He went upstairs and knocked on Larry's door. No answer. He opened it and turned on the light. The room was empty and the bed hadn't been slept in. He checked his phone. He had no messages or incoming calls for the past several hours. He went back downstairs. There was no note on the kitchen blackboard. He pulled up Larry's number on his phone, but his call went straight to voice mail. He waited for the beep.

"Larry, it's your dad. It's after midnight, so where are you? Call me as soon as you get this message."

He went into the family room, turned on the television set, and waited for Larry. He flipped through the infomercials while he checked the mantle clock every few minutes and tried to cope with his growing anxiety. His phone finally rang around one-thirty. He checked the caller ID, but he didn't recognize the number. Perhaps Larry was calling from someone else's phone. When he answered, he heard a woman's voice on the other end.

"I'm calling for Ian Palmer."

"This is he."

"Mr. Palmer, my name is Rosa Garcia. I'm an officer with the Golden Police Department. I'm calling from the emergency department at Southern Memorial Hospital. Sir, I'm calling to inform you that there's been an accident, and your son, Larry, has been admitted to the hospital."

It was every parent's worst nightmare.

"What happened?"

"I'm afraid I don't know all the details of his injuries, sir," she replied. "However, he was involved in an auto accident earlier this evening, and he arrived by ambulance about an hour ago. We need you to come to the hospital as soon as you can."

"I'm on my way."

He quickly disconnected and called Jeremy.

"Dad, what's up?"

"Are you off work?"

"Yeah," replied Jeremy. "I'm just walking out the door."

"Meet me at the emergency room at Southern Memorial. Larry's been in a car accident."

"How bad?"

"I don't know. He wasn't here when I got home and the police just called me. I'm leaving right now."

"I'm on my way, Dad."

Ian heard the stress in Jeremy's voice. "Calm down, Jeremy. Take your time. I'll see you when you get there."

Ian raced to the hospital, but he was hardly aware of the drive. He entered the emergency room and walked up to the admissions desk.

"May I help you?"

"Yes. My name is Ian Palmer. My son, Larry, was admitted a little while ago." He waited for her to pull up the information on her computer as Jeremy came up behind him and tapped him on the shoulder.

"Larry Palmer. Yes, he was in an auto accident. They're still treating him. One of the police officers will be out to talk to you shortly. In the meantime, I need you to sign some paperwork."

Ian handed over his insurance card and rapidly signed the paperwork. Once he finished, a female police officer approached him. The three stepped into a corner of the waiting room to talk.

"Sir, I'm Officer Garcia. I spoke to you on the phone earlier. This evening I was called to investigate an alcohol-related traffic accident. A drunk driver ran a red light and collided with a car in which your son, Larry, was a passenger."

"Where's Larry?" asked Ian. "Is he alright?"

"They're still treating him, Mr. Palmer. He was lucky. His injuries are relatively minor. The other two boys who were with him weren't as fortunate. Their injuries are far more serious."

"What happened?" asked Jeremy. "From the top."

"This evening your son, along with his two friends, attended a drinking party out in the woods."

"What!" exclaimed Ian. "He knows better than that."

"For what it's worth, Mr. Palmer, we've already determined that he has no alcohol in his system, so no charges will be filed against him. However, the driver and the other passenger who was with him this evening were drinking. They're both underage, so both of them will be facing charges, and the other driver will also be charged with a DUI Your son, however, will be free to go, once the doctor has released him."

"Good to know," said Jeremy. "So what happened?"

"As I was saying, they were driving through Golden when another drunk driver ran a red light and broadsided the car your son was riding in, slamming it into a utility pole. Larry was very lucky. He was the only one wearing a seat belt. I also wanted you know, Mr. Palmer, that he's a pretty remarkable young man. I spent quite a bit of time with him on the scene. Despite being injured and being trapped in the wreckage for an extended period of time, he remained calm throughout the entire ordeal, and he kept reassuring the other two boys that they'd be all right."

The officer gave Ian her card and instructed him on how to get a copy of the accident report. Once they were finished, he stepped outside to call Laura. When he returned, he found Jeremy talking with the doctor.

"This is Dr. Chin, Dad"

The two shook hands.

"As I was telling your son, Mr. Palmer, the impact of the crash caused the car windows to shatter and Larry was hit by some of the broken glass which caused a few minor cuts. He was also hit by some flying pieces of debris, which caused some lacerations on his scalp, some of which required stitches, and we gave him a tetanus shot. He also suffered multiple contusions on his left side. Fortunately, he has no broken bones nor does he appear to have a concussion, but we'd like to keep him here for observation for a few hours, just to be sure. Other than that, he seems to be okay, and we expect him to make a full recovery. He'll need to rest over the weekend and you may want to keep him home from school on Monday. You'll also need to schedule a follow-up visit with his regular doctor later on next week to have the stitches removed. Otherwise, he's fine."

"Can we see him now?" asked Ian.

"Of course, but first I need to warn you about something. He experienced some significant bleeding from some of his injuries. He doesn't need a transfusion, but we've got him on an IV. However, there's quite a bit of blood on his clothing and it looks a lot worse than it actually is."

The doctor led them to one of the cubicles in the treatment area and pulled back the curtain. The heavy bloodstains on Larry's shirt startled both Ian and Jeremy. The right side of his head was covered in bandages and wrapped with gauze and he was holding an icepack on the injured portion. His eyes were closed. He appeared to be asleep.

"Mr. Palmer," said Dr. Chin, "you have some visitors."

"Thanks." He slowly opened his eyes and blinked a few times. "Dad? Jeremy?"

"We're here son," said Ian.

"So what happened, bro? You okay?"

"Yeah," replied Larry. "But I'm not moving really good right now, and I have a really nasty headache."

"I'm sure you do," said Ian.

"I guess I really messed up this time, huh?"

"I don't know, son." Ian pulled up a chair and sat down next to Larry. "You tell me."

"Okay." Larry let out a sigh. "As long as I'm already busted, I may as well come clean and start at the beginning. I don't know whose idea it was, but word was out all over school about a big beer-keg party out in the woods. Everybody was going to be there. Brian sent me an instant message about it last Sunday and I told him I'd be there too."

"So, you lied to me when you said you guys were going to the movies tonight."

"Yeah, Dad, I guess I did. You got me on that one."

"So then what happened?"

"As soon as we got there I went to find Ashley."

Ian glanced at Jeremy. "That's his girlfriend."

"I know, Dad," replied Jeremy.

"Anyway," continued Larry, "I found her. We grabbed a flashlight and some blankets out of her truck and hiked about a quarter mile or so into the woods, away from the others. We were going to, you know, hang out for awhile."

"Did you use protection?" asked Jeremy.

Larry looked his brother in the eye. "What do you think? You're the one who told me not to trust 'em when they say they're on the pill."

Ian couldn't believe his ears. He shot Jeremy a strong look before turning his attention back to Larry.

"How long has this been going on?"

Larry turned his attention back to his father. "Not that long, Dad. She turned eighteen a few weeks ago so don't worry. I won't be getting thrown in jail."

"She may be eighteen, but you're still seventeen, and now I have to worry about an irate father showing up on my doorstep. You and I are going to have a long, serious talk, son, without your brother."

"It's not Jeremy's fault, Dad. At the time I brought it up, he thought we were speaking hypothetically. I didn't tell him I was already doing it with her. And by the way, Ashley has no idea where her dad is and her mother doesn't care if we're sleeping together or not."

"Well, I do."

"Anyway," said Larry, "by the time we finally made our way back to the party things were winding down. The beer keg was already empty, but someone brought some sodas, so we drank a few sodas and hung out for a little while. Then Ashley and her friends left, and Trevor decided that maybe we should leave too. I wanted to make sure I got home before midnight."

"Did you ask Trevor if he'd been drinking?"

"No, but he seemed okay to me, so we got into his car. I don't know why, but for some strange reason I had a feeling that I should ride in the backseat, so I got in behind Trevor. We made our way back into town. Everything was fine. We were all laughing and joking. Trevor and Brian were giving me a hard time about Ashley, but you know, they were just messing with me. Then, all of a sudden, the inside of the car lit up. I looked to my right, and all I could see were these huge headlights coming straight at me."

Larry's eyes grew misty. A tear rolled out the corner of one of them. "You know, Dad, it's true what they say. Your life really does flash before your eyes. I saw you, and Mom, and Jeremy, and I thought to myself, 'so this is what it feels like to die.' And you know what, Dad? I really wasn't scared. I made my peace with God, and I hoped I'd be able to cross over to the other side quickly and without too much pain. My only regret was that I wasn't going to be able to tell any of you goodbye. I was worried about what would happen to the rest of you once I was gone. I wanted all of you to go on with your lives and be happy without me."

Jeremy reached over and squeezed his brother's shoulder as he grabbed a tissue to wipe off the tears that were running down his own face. Larry continued with his story.

"Then I heard this loud crash. The sound of it seemed to go on forever. For a minute the world went dark and I felt myself slamming into something really hard. For a few seconds after that I couldn't breathe. Then I realized it was all over. I looked around. All I could see around me was twisted metal. I wasn't sure, in that moment, if I was dead or alive. I could hear Brian screaming and people running up to the car. Then I started feeling the blood running down the side of my face. That's when I knew I'd somehow survived, and that I had to focus on keeping Brian calm while we waited for someone to get us out. First, they had to cut the top of the car off and then they had to use the Jaws of Life, so all that took awhile. They got Trevor and Brian out first, but that was okay. They were in a lot worse shape than I was. By the time they got to me, the worst was over."

The nurse came in to check on Larry. He asked about his friends. He was told that Brian was still in surgery with a fractured pelvis and femur and that Trevor also had several broken bones and would remain in the hospital for several days. When the nurse left, Larry closed his eyes and said he was tired. Ian and Jeremy stepped out into the waiting room to get some coffee from the vending machine.

"So Jeremy, am I a complete and total washout as a father?"

"No, Dad, not at all. You're just upset. It's been a rough night."

"He's sneaking out and going to drinking parties. And he's sleeping with his girlfriend."

"Dad, I know this will come as a shock to you, but I pulled the same stuff when I was his age. Back then you and Mom were still together, so don't go guilt-tripping over being a single parent. The only difference between him and me is that I didn't get caught, and I still turned out okay. Larry wasn't drinking and the girl is eighteen. He knows the difference between right and wrong. He's just testing the waters, like we all did when we were that age."

"But he's only seventeen, Jeremy. He's still in high school. I didn't have my first—um, encounter, until I was eighteen and out of high school."

"Farmer's daughter?"

"No, farmer's wife." Ian didn't realize until after the fact what he had just allowed to slip out. "And please don't go repeating that. It's not something that I'm very proud of, and I paid a high price for that little sin over the course of many years."

They went back to sit with Larry. He'd fallen into a fitful sleep. Ian suggested that Jeremy go home, but he refused. As the hours passed, the nurse returned a few more times to check on Larry. Laura arrived in the wee hours of the morning. Larry was still asleep. She almost fainted at the sight of his bloodied shirt.

"Oh my God."

"It's okay, Laura," whispered Ian. "It's not as bad as it looks. Try to keep your voice down. He needs to get some rest."

She pulled up another chair and took a seat. "So what the hell happened?"

"He told me he was going to the movies tonight with his friends, but they all went out partying in the woods instead."

"Was he drinking?"

"No, but his friends were."

The nurse came back in as he filled her in on the details.

"Dad, why don't we go out and take a walk?" suggested Jeremy. "We'll give Mom a chance to have some time alone with Larry."

"Good idea. We'll be back in a little bit."

* * *

As soon as Ian and Jeremy left Larry began stirring and slowly opened his eyes. It took him a moment to focus.

"Mom? Is that you?"

"Yes Larry, it's me."

He was overjoyed to see her. "You came? All the way from Steamboat Springs?"

"Yes, I did."

"What time is it?"

She glanced at her watch. "It's almost four-thirty."

"You mean, you drove all night to get here?"

"Yes, Larry, I did."

"How come?"

She took his hand and squeezed it. "Because I'm your mother, Larry. Just because I live in Steamboat Springs doesn't mean I'm not going to be here for you when you really need me."

"But what about Will?"

"He's fine. He couldn't make it, but he wanted you to know that he'll call you later to see how you're doing. He knows he can't replace your father, but he'd really like to be your stepfather, if you'd be willing to give him a chance."

The tears began running down his cheeks. "Even after I was so nasty to the two of you all last summer, you still came all this way, in the middle of the night, just for me?"

"Yes, Larry. That's what mothers do."

"I love you, Mom," was all he said.

\* \* \*

Larry was released shortly after sunup. Jeremy headed home while Laura followed Larry and Ian back to their house. After she and Ian got Larry settled in his room, she went into Jeremy's room to rest. Ian collapsed on his bed and cried himself to sleep. It was past noon by the time he woke up again. He went to check on Larry, who finally appeared to be resting comfortably. He then headed downstairs to the kitchen to make a pot of coffee. He filled his cup, went into the family room, and sat down to think. He made a difficult, life-changing decision. He went back upstairs, showered and shaved, but before he left, he checked on Larry once more. He was still fast asleep. Ian tiptoed down the stairs, got into his car, and headed to Gillian's house. Along the way he prayed she would someday forgive him for what he was about to do.

# ⫷ TWENTY-THREE ⫸

**I**AN STOPPED AT THE impound yard. He had to see Trevor's car for himself, but the sight of it took his breath away. It was hardly recognizable as a car, especially with the top portion, which had been cut away, laying in the dirt beside it. The right half of the backseat had completely disintegrated. It had taken the brunt of the impact. He inspected the area where Larry had been sitting and realized an angel had been looking out for his son. The deep indent from the utility pole was at the driver's seat, leaving the left side of the rear passenger area like a cocoon that had somehow, miraculously, shielded Larry from certain death. He snapped a few photos with his phone. It was an image that was forever burned into his memory.

He returned to his car and drove to Gillian's house. He hated facing her with what he was about to tell her. He dreaded approaching her front door. Her face was beaming when she opened it.

"Ian. What a pleasant surprise. Come on in. Can I get you something to drink?"

"No, I won't be staying that long. Gillian, I have to talk to you about something."

"Ian, you look so serious. Is something wrong?"

"Yes. I'm afraid there is. I think you'd better sit down." His heart sank deep into the pit of his stomach as he followed her into the living room and took a seat.

"What's wrong, Ian?"

"I almost lost my son last night."

114

"Oh my God. Which one? Jeremy?"

"No, Jeremy's fine. It was Larry. He and his friends didn't go to the movies last night like he said. They went to a party out in the woods instead. They were on their way back when they were hit by a drunk driver running a red light."

Gillian looked shocked. "Dear Lord, is he all right?"

"He got hurt, but not that seriously," explained Ian. "Jeremy and I were up all night with him at the hospital. They released him early this morning. He's home resting. Laura is with him. She's going to be staying with him for a few days."

"It's good that you called her, Ian. She's his mother. She should be there. I don't have a problem with that."

Ian let out a deep sigh. What he had to say next was going to be one of the most difficult things he'd had to tell her in many years.

"Gillian, do you remember Laura telling you that there would be times when you would, as she put it, 'have to step aside and allow us to do our jobs as parents?'"

"Yes, I do. And as I just told you, I don't have a problem with her being here. I'd be more concerned if she wasn't."

"That's not it. " He paused, grasping for the right words. "Gillian, I feel like I'm walking a tightrope. I love you. I love you more than I've loved any woman, before or since, and I really hoped I'd be able to have a future with you. But I'm also a parent. I brought Larry into the world. I was there when he came out of the womb, and I was the one who held him while he took his first breaths. And even though Laura and I have agreed to joint custody on paper, I'm still the primary parent, which means I'm the one who's ultimately responsible if something goes wrong. And last night something went terribly wrong."

"Ian, this isn't your fault."

"Yes, it is my fault. Somehow I've failed miserably at my job, and it nearly cost Larry his life. I've just come back from the impound yard. There's not much left of the car my son was riding in last night. He missed being killed by mere inches. I'm his father, Gillian, and right now I have to make a difficult choice. I now have to choose between the woman I love, and my son. It's not fair, but it is what it is."

"Calm down, Ian." There was a sense of desperation in her voice. "You've been through a shock. Let's sit down and discuss this rationally."

"There's nothing to discuss," he argued back. "You're an adult, Gillian. You've managed to accomplish some great things in your life without my being around, and I know you'll continue being successful without me. Larry, on the other hand, is still a child, and he still needs me to be his father."

Her voice wavered. "I understand that, Ian, and you are a good father, but don't you think—"

"This is goodbye, Gillian." His voice was firm. "Please understand that I'll always love you. And who knows. Maybe someday, if we're lucky, we'll get to have another chance, but I don't want you holding out for that. If some other guy comes along and wants to take you out, then I want you to go out with him."

Gillian looked at Ian with a sense of total disbelief. She stood up, but before she could react he turned away and headed out the front door.

* * *

As Ian left Gillian slowly sank back into her chair. The memory of their conversation, years before, when he told her he was going back to Denver, played back in her mind as she went completely numb. She didn't know how long she remained in her chair, although she was vaguely aware of the sun going down. Once the room went completely dark she got up, turned on the lights, fed the dogs, and poured herself a manhattan. She took her drink to the sofa and remained there.

* * *

Ian drove aimlessly through the streets of Denver. He was already having second thoughts. He wrestled with the idea of going back and telling her changed his mind, but thought better of it. Finally, he headed home. When he arrived, he found Larry and Laura waiting for him in the family room. Laura had her overnight bag with her.

"My son is sending me home, Ian."

"We had a long talk while you were out, Dad," said Larry. "And we've come to a new understanding. Mom belongs in Steamboat Springs. That's where she's happy. I shouldn't have tried to interfere in her life, but that's in the past. What matters now is where we go from here." He slowly reached down and picked up his mother's bag. "I'll walk you to your car."

Laura stopped to give Ian a hug. "This will have to be addressed, and I'll back whatever decision you make regarding what to do with Larry. I'll call you as soon as I get home to let you know I've arrived okay, and we'll discuss it then."

She looked at Ian more closely. "Is there something else wrong?"

He shrugged it off. "No. I'm fine. I'm just tired, that's all. It's been one hell of a night."

They said their goodbyes and Larry escorted his mother to her car. When he returned, his father gave him a strong look.

"Well, son, I'm glad you've worked things out with your mother. However, you and I are going to sit down and we're going to have a long, serious discussion."

# ❧TWENTY-FOUR❧

JEREMY AWOKE TO HIS beeping phone. He rolled over and grabbed it off the nightstand. He'd just received a text message from Larry.

"I'm on double secret probation. Dad just dumped Gillian."

He couldn't believe what he was reading. There had to be a mistake. He pulled up his father's number and hit the call button.

"Dad?"

"Hey, Jeremy, what's up?"

"Not much. Just called to see what's going on. How's Larry."

"He's doing much better. And would you believe your brother sent your mother home yesterday? They've had a real breakthrough. He's finally figured out that she never abandoned him, and he's going to let her live her life in peace."

Jeremy was genuinely happy to hear it. "That's really good news, Dad. I guess nearly getting wiped out was a real wake up call. It's like you always taught us--things always work out for the best in the end. So, now that the little twit's finally smelled the coffee, how 'bout you and Gillian? Isn't it time you took it to the next level? Maybe this will be the year that Larry and I get a new stepmother, along with a new stepdad."

There was a long pause. "Dad? Are you still there?"

His father's voice sounded strange. "I'm not seeing her anymore, Jeremy."

"What?"

"I can't do it all, son. I can't be the man she expects me to be, and be a full time parent to your brother."

"Dad, with all due respect, have you lost your mind?"

"Look Jeremy, I'm not going to sit here and justify my reasoning with you. It's my life, thank you, and I'll live it as I see fit. I know that you were fond of her, but it just wasn't meant to be."

Jeremy was flooded with a mix of emotions. Part of him was disappointed his father had ended things with Gillian, but then again, another part of him wasn't. That part suddenly realized he'd just been presented with a golden opportunity to go after her for himself. It would take some time, of course. She wouldn't get over his father that easily, but he was willing to bide his time. Then there was the difference in their ages, but the world was changing. It was becoming more socially acceptable for younger men to become involved with older women. After all, his own mother was about to marry a man several years her junior.

"Jeremy? Are you still there?"

"Yeah, Dad. I'm here. Sorry, I just woke up a few minutes ago. Guess I'm still getting over doing an all-nighter at the hospital. Anyway, I'm sorry to hear about you and Gillian. Any chance of you getting back together with her?"

"Not right now. I told her if someone else asks her out, then she should go with him. I don't want her pinning all her hopes on me. I can't guarantee I'll ever go back to her."

Perfect. Not only did this mean he was free to pursue her, his father had just granted his permission. If all went according to plan, he would really have to thank his father someday.

"Well Dad, I'm sorry to hear that. She's a good lady. You once told me yourself she's the kind who only comes along once in a lifetime. I hope, for your sake, that you get her back, and soon. Otherwise, you're right. Someone else just might come along and claim her. If that should happen, and I really think there's a good chance that it will, then I sincerely hope that you'll be able to handle it."

Ian didn't respond right away. After a long pause he ended the call, saying he had to check on Larry. After they disconnected, Jeremy grinned and looked at his phone.

"Well, old man, your loss is about to become my gain."

He glanced at the clock. It was a few minutes past eleven, and it was Sunday. No doubt Gillian would be home and in need of comforting. When he was ready to go, he decided to leave the Harley at home. After what had just happened to his brother, he'd lost his appetite for riding motorcycles. He picked up the keys to his Jeep and headed over to Gillian's house.

# ❧ TWENTY-FIVE ❧

GILLIAN WOKE UP on the sofa with a splitting headache. Her first thought was that it had all been a bad dream. She looked down and noticed that minus her shoes, she was wearing the same clothes she had on the day before. She dragged herself into the bathroom. Gazing at the bloodshot eyes looking back at her in the mirror, it slowly dawned on her. It wasn't a bad dream. For the second time, Ian Palmer had abruptly walked out of her life.

She went to the kitchen to feed the dogs. She decided for breakfast she'd have the same thing she had for dinner the night before--a manhattan. She pulled the bottles of bourbon and sweet vermouth out of the cupboard and checked their contents. She hoped she had enough bourbon to last the rest of day, but she knew at some point she'd have to pull herself together long enough to make a run to the liquor store.

"Jeez," she muttered, "now I'm even starting to think like a lush."

She poured herself a drink, took a swallow, and parked back on the sofa. At least the bourbon was clearing up her headache. She raised her glass and toasted herself.

"Well, Gilly-girl, here's to the hair of the dog."

She sipped her drink slowly. She wanted her supply of whiskey to last. Finishing the first drink, she poured herself another, and upon emptying her glass a second time, leaned back on the sofa. She groaned as she felt the room spinning around her. Visions of Ian danced through her head. She didn't know if she should pour herself a third drink, or perhaps try to take a nap. Struggling to decide, she heard the doorbell and barking dogs.

"I'm ignoring you," she shouted. "Whoever you are, just go away."

The doorbell rang again. This time she heard a familiar voice.

"Gillian! It's me, Jeremy. Open up! I know you're in there."

"All right, all right."

She got up and ambled to the front door, running her fingers through her hair and trying to smooth the wrinkles out of her clothes. She opened it slowly.

"Well hello, Jeremy." She smiled and tried to sound as normal as possible. "What a nice surprise. Would you like to come in?"

"Thank you."

She tried to walk carefully as she led him inside. "Can I fix you anything to drink?"

"No, I'm good. And by the way, Missy, you can't fool a bartender."

"I'm sorry, I don't know what you mean."

"Bull. You're eyes are bloodshot, your speech is slurred, and you couldn't walk in a straight line right now if your life depended on it. So how many have you had?"

"Let's see. Two, I think. No, three. No wait... You know, I really think it was two. Sorry. Did you mean, like today? Because today it would have been two, I think. But don't ask me about last night. I couldn't tell you how many I had last night. I kinda lost count after awhile."

"This isn't like you, Gillian."

"You're absolutely right. It's not me at all. So terribly sorry about that. You know, Jeremy, you really caught me at a bad time. Maybe we should talk later."

"And what have you been drinking?"

She grinned. "Manhattans. And I made 'em doubles, too."

"No wonder you're higher than a kite. What time did my father leave here yesterday, Gillian?"

"I...donno. I'm pretty sure it was sometime during the afternoon. At least I think it was. He said he couldn't see me anymore, bye-bye baby, Que Sera Sera, and all that other—well, you know. And by the way, I'm not blaming any of this on your brother, just so you know. But you know what, Jer? Talking about your dear old daddy is really, seriously, and unequivocally depressing the hell out of me. So if you don't mind..."

She stumbled into the kitchen, took a glass out of the cupboard, and filled it with ice. She pulled the liquor out of the cabinet and mixed herself another manhattan. As she went to pick it up when a hand suddenly reached over and snatched it away. Jeremy dumped it down the sink. Gillian was astonished.

"Wh—What the hell? Now why would you want to go and do something like that for? Jeez Louise! You know what, Jer? You're just not any damn fun at all. You really, seriously, need to lighten up."

He put his arm around her waist and gently guided her to a chair at the kitchen table. "I'm cutting you off, my dear. So sit down, and I will fix you something else to drink."

"Okay. Whatever you say, Captain."

Gillian began singing to herself as he filled the teakettle with water and placed it on the stove to heat. He started searching the cupboards.

"Have you got any herbal tea?"

"Cupboard over the stove. On the right. Did you want a cup of tea, Jeremy? I could have fixed it for you."

He opened the cupboard and found a box of herbal tea. "I'm fine, thank you. I'm going to make a nice cup of herbal tea for you."

"Well now, that's mighty kind of you. Can you put a shot of bourbon in it?"

"No."

"Why not?"

"Because you've already had enough bourbon for today."

"Party pooper."

Gillian resumed singing to herself and soon the teakettle whistled. He dumped a teabag into a mug and poured some hot water over it. He let it brew for a minute, removed the teabag and handed the mug to her.

"Here you go. Now drink this."

She took a sip. "So, Jeremy, why are you here?"

"Because you need a friend. Here, let's take this outside. It's a beautiful day out there, and the fresh air will do you some good."

He picked up her tea with one hand while he guided her through the living room and onto the patio with the other. He led her to the patio table and sat her in one of the chairs.

"See, now isn't this better? It's really nice out here today. You know, fall officially started about a week ago. I love the fall. It's my favorite time of the year. Now, you be a good girl and drink your tea."

Gillian drank her tea in silence.

"So, are you feeling any better now?"

"No."

Gillian slowly drank the rest of her tea while Jeremy watched her closely. He had never seen her in this condition before and he was genuinely concerned. At least she was being cooperative. Once he got her sober, he would have to get her to eat something and to try to get her to talk it out.

"Looks like you finished your tea," he said. "I'll go make you another cup. You stay right there, and don't move."

"Whatever. Take your time. And I'd like it a whole lot better if you'd put some damn bourbon in it."

He went back into the house. Gillian put her elbows on the table buried her face in her hands. The bright sunlight was irritating her. Something brushed against her ankle. She looked down. Duke was looking up at her and wagging his tail, wanting her to throw his ball. She knew better than to try to bend down to pick it up, so she gently kicked it across the yard. He brought it back. She kicked it a second time, and he brought it back. Duke brought the ball back a third time, and Gillian kicked it again. This time, however, she kicked it a little too far. It rolled into the pool and floated on top of the water.

"Sorry about that, Duke. Here, let Mommy get it for you."

\* \* \*

Jeremy watched her from the kitchen window while the water heated, but when the teakettle whistled he briefly turned away to get another teabag. At that same moment Gillian rose from her chair and staggered to the edge of the pool.

By the time Jeremy looked out the window again, she was no longer sitting at the table. He glanced around the yard. To his horror, he saw her standing at the edge of the pool. She reached down for the ball, lost her balance, and plunged into the water.

\* \* \*

Gillian was normally a good swimmer, but all the alcohol in her system was having an effect, and the shock of suddenly finding herself completely submerged overwhelmed her. Unable to react, she had no choice but to let go and surrender to it. A life without Ian wasn't worth living anyway. She knew it would be over quickly. As she lost consciousness, her final thought was a prayer that somehow, on the other side, she and Ian would be together forever.

\* \* \*

Jeremy dropped the mug and it shattered on the floor. He raced through the kitchen and living room, out the side door, and across the backyard. He momentarily stopped at the edge of the pool and scanned the water. Gillian was lying motionless at the bottom of the deep end.

He dove in, swam down to her and brought her back up to the surface. As soon as he raised her head out of the water he saw that her face was ashen, her lips were turning blue and water was bubbling out of her nose and mouth. He swam her toward the shallow end of the pool as fast as he could. As soon as he found his footing, he felt along her neck for a pulse. He found one, but it was very weak. He started giving her mouth-to-mouth. No response. He tried a second time, no response. He checked her pulse a second time. He felt two more faint beats, then it stopped. Gillian was gone.

"No! Damn it, Gillian! Don't leave me!"

He carried her to the edge of the pool and laid her on the deck. She didn't look real. She looked like a chalky, wax mannequin. He knew he had to act fast. If she didn't respond this time he'd have to begin CPR.

"Come on Gillian! Stay with me!"

He took one final deep breath and blew it into her lungs. Suddenly, her body jerked. He turned her over, face down, and turned her head sideways. Water started spewing out of her mouth as she struggled. He held her down.

"Stop fighting me, Gillian. I'm trying to save you."

She started coughing and vomiting. He held her down until there was nothing left to come back up. By then the color was returning to her face. He climbed out of the pool, scooped her up and carried her back into the house. He set her down on the sofa, ran into her bedroom and pulled the blanket off the bed. He wrapped her in it and carried her out to his Jeep. After strapping her into the passenger seat, he started it up and backed out of the driveway.

"Where are we going?" Her voice was a hoarse whisper.

"To the hospital, Gillian. You nearly drowned."

She remained silent for the rest of the trip.

They pulled into the emergency room parking lot. Jeremy picked her up, carried her inside and ran up to the admissions desk.

"I have a near-drowning!"

The clerk picked up the phone and called in a code. Within seconds a nurse came running.

"Follow me," she said.

Jeremy was on the nurse's heels as he carried her into the treatment area and placed her on the bed in one of the patient cubicles. Dr. Chin immediately rushed in and recognized Jeremy.

"Mr. Palmer. Back so soon?"

"I'm afraid so."

"What happened?"

"Her name is Gillian Matthews. She's a close friend of the family. I was visiting her this morning. She was trying to retrieve a dog toy out of the swimming pool and she accidentally fell in. I dove in and pulled her out."

Dr. Chin briefly glanced at Jeremy and noticed his hair and clothing were still soaking wet. He turned his attention back to Gillian. Jeremy stepped aside while they hooked her up to some oxygen and began treating her. Dr. Chin questioned him while he examined her.

"How long was she under the water?"

"A minute, maybe. No more than two at the very most. I was in the kitchen and saw her fall in the pool. I got to her as fast as I could."

"Has your friend been drinking?"

"Yes. She told me she'd had two double manhattans. She'd had them before I arrived."

"Did you try to resuscitate her?"

"Yes. The first two times she didn't respond, but the third time was a charm. I didn't have to do CPR."

Dr. Chin and his team spent the next few minutes working on her before they wheeled her out of the cubicle. The doctor turned back to Jeremy as he removed his stethoscope from his ears.

"Well, Mr. Palmer, you did good and you got to her in time. We're taking her to X-ray, but so far she seems to be okay. Her lungs sound good and there's no sign of any brain damage. She'll be back in a few minutes, and then we're going keep her here under observation for a little while. Barring any unexpected complications you'll be free to take her home. By the way, how's your brother doing?"

"Much better. In fact, he's even beginning to annoy me."

"Good to hear."

They shook hands and Dr. Chin left to take care of his next patient. A minute later a nurse appeared with a blanket for Jeremy.

"Doctor doesn't want you catching cold, sir."

"Thanks."

He wrapped himself up in the blanket, took a chair, and covered his face with his hands. He decided to call his dad while he waited, but when he picked up his phone he realized it had gone into the water with him. He would have to repair it later. Before long they brought Gillian back in. She reached out for him as they wheeled her by. He gave her hand a quick squeeze and stood by while the nurses finished up. Once they left, he returned to her bedside. She was awake, but she looked very frightened.

"Are you okay?"

She shook her head and began sobbing. Jeremy took her in his arms.

"It's okay, it's okay. I'm here."

Jeremy, you're shivering." She looked him up and down. "Good heavens, you're all wet. You must be freezing. Come up here with me. We can huddle up together and keep each other warm."

Jeremy pulled the curtain closed and laid down next to her on the bed. Before long she was dozing in his arms. He held her close and began stroking her hair.

"Thanks, Ian," she murmured.

Undaunted, Jeremy kissed the top of her head and kept stroking her hair. "Don't worry, baby girl," he whispered. "We'll get you over him. Eventually."

He held her and kept stroking her hair until he began dozing off as well.

***

"Well, well, what have we here?"

The sound of the nurse's voice woke Jeremy. He glanced at Gillian. "She's asleep."

"Well kids, it's time to break it up. She's just been released. You'll have to wake her."

"Gillian?" He sat up and stroked her face. "Wake up, Gillian. It's time for us to go home."

She moaned and began stirring. She slowly opened her eyes, sat up, and looked around. She seemed surprised to see him.

"Jeremy? What are you doing here? What happened?" She looked scared and confused.

"Don't you remember?"

"No." She looked into his eyes.

"What do you remember?"

"Let me think. " She paused for a moment. "I was in the backyard. You were with me, but you had to go get something, and then Duke wanted me to get his ball. It was floating in the pool. After that I was aware that I was going somewhere, but it was very strange. I heard you calling me, but it sounded like you were someplace far away, and it sounded like you were in distress. The next thing I remember is being in a car and you were telling me you were taking me to the hospital. Then I remember the doctor and the nurses, but it's all kind of a blur. And then you woke me up, just now. That's all I know."

"Gillian, you had too much to drink this morning. Then you fell into the pool, and I had to jump in to rescue you. You nearly drowned, and you scared the living hell out of me as well. You're still at the hospital, but you're going to be all right. They're getting ready to send you home."

She fell into his arms. Beneath all her fame and success was a part of her that was very vulnerable, which he found quite endearing.

"Jeremy, was I dead?"

"For a brief time, yes, you were."

Gillian was silent for a moment as she took it all in. "Then I guess I owe you one. Big time."

"Don't worry about it. Let's just get you home."

The nurse unhooked the oxygen and went over her discharge instructions. Gillian would need to be supervised overnight. After signing the paperwork, they left the hospital and headed to Jeremy's place so he could change clothes and pack a bag.

"Look Jeremy, I really appreciate everything you did for me, but you don't have to do this. Your father and I are no longer together. You're not under any obligation to me."

"Miss Gillian, can I say something? With all due respect?"

"Certainly."

"Lady, I just saved your life today." His voice was stern. "I hear in some cultures that once you save a life you're forever responsible for it. Maybe I'm here because I want to be your friend, and because my father has turned into a total moron."

Gillian started to laugh.

"See, I knew if I worked at it long enough I'd get a smile out of you. Now I need to warn you this place is a real man cave that I'm sharing with two other guys, but don't worry. We'll only be a few minutes, and then we'll head back to your place. Okay?"

"Okay."

The house Jeremy was renting indeed resembled a dungeon, but, as he explained, it was cheap. Gillian took a shower one she returned home while Jeremy fed the dogs and swept up the broken coffee mug. By the time she came out she looked like her old self. She even styled her hair and put some makeup on. In his eyes, she looked sexy, but he also noticed that she seemed unusually subdued. She went into the kitchen and made two cups of tea, which she brought into the living room and placed on the coffee table. Jeremy took a seat on the sofa next to her.

"Gillian, would you like for me to call my father and let him know what happened?"

She shook her head. "Thanks, but no. I don't want him knowing about this. He's got his hands full right now with your brother, and I don't want his pity."

"It's not pity, Gillian. The man still loves you and he'd want to know. I think he's just overreacting about my brother."

"Then let's not burden him with my problems, okay? He's done with me, Jeremy. He made it crystal clear. From this day forward, whatever goes on between you and me, stays between you and me. Okay?"

Jeremy liked the sound of it, but now was not the time to start pursuing her. "All right, but what about your sister? Do you want me to call her?"

Gillian stopped for a minute. Cynthia would have to know, but it wasn't a call she looked forward to making.

"No. I prefer to call her myself, if you don't mind."

"When?"

"I don't know, Jer."

"How about now?"

She hesitated.

"Sorry Gillian, but she's your immediate family, and she has a right to know about what just happened here. If you don't call her, I will."

Gillian reluctantly retrieved her phone and punched up Cynthia's number. The phone rang.

"Hello."

"Cynthia, hi. It's Gillian. We need to talk."

"You don't sound well, Gillian. What's wrong?"

"Everything." Gillian's voice broke. She handed the phone off to Jeremy and stepped out of the room.

"Hi, Cynthia, this is Jeremy Palmer. I'm Ian's oldest son. Remember, we met that night at your gallery?"

"I remember you, Jeremy. So what's going on?"

"It's been a bad weekend for all of us."

"What happened?"

He started by telling her about his brother's accident.

"I'm so sorry. Is he okay?"

"Just some cuts and bruises. Other than that, he's fine, but it gave the rest of us a bad scare. Especially my dad. He's decided to end things with Gillian, and she's not taking it very well."

"Damn. I was afraid something like this might happen. No wonder she's beside herself. So if you don't mind my asking, Jeremy, what are you doing there?"

"I talked to my dad this morning. He told me what he'd done. I consider her a friend as well, so I came over to check on her."

He went on to tell her everything that happened after he arrived.

"We just got back from the hospital about an hour ago. She's fine, at least physically, but she's pretty shook up. The doctor says she has to be supervised, so I'm staying in the guest room tonight."

"My God, Jeremy. I don't know how to thank you. You just saved my sister's life. I think I'd better get up to Denver for a few days."

"I think you should as well. How soon do you think you can get here?"

"I have a conference with my son's teacher tomorrow evening. I'll leave as soon as I can after that. I'm at my computer right now. It looks like the earliest available flight will arrive in Denver around two o'clock Tuesday afternoon. I'm booking it as we speak."

"That's fine. I'm off tonight and tomorrow, so I can stay with her until then, and I don't have to be at work until five o'clock on Tuesday. If you'll give me your flight number, I can pick you up at the airport."

He went into Gillian's office for a pen and paper and jotted down the information. "I'll see you on Tuesday. Here, I'll put Gillian back on."

He found Gillian back in the living room and handed her the phone.

"I'm so sorry, Cynthia. I guess I've really let you down."

"Are you kidding? You're my baby sister and I almost lost you. I love you, and I'm going to be there for you. I'll be there on Tuesday. If you need anything between now and then, call me. Get some rest and I'll call you in the morning, okay."

"Okay." She ended the call.

"See, now that wasn't so bad, was it?" said Jeremy. "There are people who care deeply about you and love you, Gillian, and I'm one of them. We're going to get you through this. Now, can you remember the last time you had anything to eat?"

"I'm not sure, Jer. It's probably been a good twenty-four hours. Maybe longer."

"Well then, we'll have to take care of that, right now. My treat."

He ordered some Chinese food and had it delivered. During the meal she even smiled a few times, but the sadness in her eyes remained. It was still early in the evening when she announced she was tired and ready to go to bed.

"Before I leave, Jeremy, I want you to understand something. I admit I'm devastated over your father, but I'm not suicidal. I don't even remember going in the pool, and I'm truly sorry for giving you such a bad scare. I guess you were here today because God apparently isn't finished with me just yet, and I'm eternally grateful to you for saving me. You're my guardian angel, Jer. And because what you did for me today, there will always be a special bond between us."

She leaned over and kissed him on the cheek.

"Well shucks, ma'am." There was a smile in his voice. "I'm just doing my job around here."

She took her leave and closed her bedroom door. Jeremy tidied up the kitchen, and afterwards he tried watching a little TV, but he felt restless. It had been a difficult weekend for him as well, and he really needed to talk it over with someone. Despite what Gillian had said, and despite the growing sense of rivalry he was feeling toward his father over her, he nonetheless thought his father should know what had happened to her. He also needed his father's reassurance. He finally turned on his laptop and logged into his email account. He may have agreed not to say anything to his father, but he hadn't agreed on not mentioning anything about it to Larry. He and his brother sometimes confided in each other, and while Larry could be annoying at times, he wasn't one to betray something told to him in confidence. He composed an email to his brother, describing in great detail everything that had happened that day.

"You know, bro," he wrote, "every time I close my eyes I still see the image of her when I laid her out on the deck. She was gone. She looked just like our grandmother did the day we saw her in her coffin. And all I could think was that I had let her die. Thank God she finally responded after my third attempt. I know I'm the one at fault for leaving her alone out there in the first place and I'll go to my grave blaming myself for what happened to her. I thank God again that she's okay now and that she doesn't have any brain damage. Anyway, I'll be staying with her until her sister arrives on Tuesday. She's pretty shook up, as am I, and I don't think she should be left alone until then. Sorry to dump this all on you, little brother. You just went through your own ordeal, but please, Larry, you have to keep this to yourself. She doesn't want Dad knowing about it and I guess she has her reasons. Thanks for letting me vent. I had to talk to someone."

He signed off, hit the send button and shut down the computer. A short time later he went to bed in the guest room, hoping to get a halfway decent night's sleep.

* * *

Jeremy had no way of knowing that his father was now intercepting Larry's email. Ian read the letter over several times in stunned disbelief. He was horrified to learn that his actions had nearly cost the life of the only woman he ever truly loved. What hurt even more was the fact that she didn't want him to know about it. He should have been the one looking after her, not Jeremy. He desperately wanted to go to her to beg for her forgiveness. At the same time, he felt an incredible sense of gratitude toward his oldest son. He owed Jeremy a debt he could never repay. He wanted, more than anything, to thank Jeremy in person and to reassure him he'd done nothing wrong and everything right. Unfortunately, for the time being, he couldn't do that either. All he could do was to try to comfort Jeremy by proxy. He hit the reply button and began typing his response.

"Jer, you're a hero. You just saved her life. What do you think would have happened if she fell in the pool and you hadn't been there?

130

If anyone's to blame, it's Dad, not you. But I also think if Dad knew what you did for her, he would be so incredibly proud of you. Hopefully, she'll forgive him someday, and then you can tell him about it yourself. Meantime bro, I'm proud of you."

He gritted his teeth as he signed off using Larry's name. As he hit the send button he prayed that Jeremy would forgive him for the deception. He deleted his reply message from Larry's account and marked Jeremy's email as unread. For the second time in the past three days, he cried himself to sleep.

# ❧Twenty-Six❧

JEREMY WOKE FROM a bad dream. While not the most pleasant way to begin the day, he didn't find it unexpected. Despite his having adverted a tragedy, Gillian's nearly drowning had been a traumatic experience for him as well.

He rolled over and closed his eyes, hoping to take a short snooze, when he thought he heard the distant sound of water splashing. His eyes shot wide open. As he listened closely, he heard the sound again, and he realized it was coming from the swimming pool. His heart skipped a beat. He leaped out of bed, once again racing outside. Gillian was swimming laps across the pool. He marched up to the edge.

"What the hell are you doing?"

She swam to the shallow end. "I'm doing what I have to do. Would you mind handing me my towel? It's on the table."

Jeremy fetched the towel as she climbed out.

"It's like the old cowboys used to say." She took the towel and began drying off her face. "If you fall off your horse, you have to get back on as quickly as you can; otherwise, you'll be afraid of horses forever. And if I didn't go back in to swim a few laps this morning, I would have been afraid of the water for the rest of my life."

"You couldn't wait for me to get up?"

"I wanted to get it over with as quickly as I could, and now that it's

132

done I hope I can move on. The landlord is sending the pool guy over this week to drain and cover it for the winter. After this morning, I won't be using it again until next summer. No more late night skinny dips for me."

"Say what?"

"We all have our guilty pleasures." She had a hint of a smile. "One of mine is going skinny dipping; late at night, of course, and only during the summer. I only wear my swimsuit when I have guests."

"Really? I would have never guessed that about you." An interesting visual popped into his head, but before allowing his mind to wander too far, he decided to switch to a safer topic.

"Speaking of horses, did you by chance get a letter in the mail from my mother about donating something to the St. Eligius auction?"

"I did, but I haven't responded to it yet."

"Well, I hope you'll at least consider it. They do good things, and my mother tells me she was very impressed with your art gallery. I know she'd be grateful if you were to donate one of your paintings and she'd give you all kinds of publicity in return."

"I'll have to think about it."

"As long as you're thinking about it, why don't I take you out there?"

"When?"

"How 'bout today?" he replied. "I'm off on Mondays, and I think a nice day trip would do you some good. I know it would me. Over the past three days I almost lost my brother and one of my favorite people in the world. I need a timeout myself."

"Well, we certainly need to take care of you too, Jer."

"Then why don't you go do whatever it is you have to do, and we'll head out as soon as you're ready. And make sure you wear something appropriate for horseback riding."

"Don't you want some breakfast?"

"We'll pick up something along the way."

"Okay, but my treat, since you picked up the tab for dinner last night."

* * *

They entered the gate at St. Eligius Ranch around noon and headed up the narrow roadway. It was about another quarter mile before they reached the main part of the ranch.

"Well, this is it." Jeremy parked the Jeep next to a two-story house. "It's sort of a home-away-from home for me. I keep a pair of cowboy boots stashed in the back for whenever I'm out here. If you'll give me a minute to change, I'll show you around."

"Take your time."

Jeremy got out and popped the cargo door open while Gillian studied her surroundings. A white barn stood across from the house, with several horse corrals next to it. On the other side of the barn was a small building with signage indicating it was the administrative office. Some twenty yards beyond the office was a fifth-wheel trailer that appeared to be permanently hooked up. He opened the passenger door of the Jeep.

"Ready?"

Gillian nodded and stepped out. As they walked toward the front of the house a man stepped out of the barn and greeted them.

"Good morning, Jeremy. Nice to see you."

"Good morning, Ramon. Is my mother around?"

"She's in the tack room taking an inventory."

Jeremy introduced him to Gillian, explaining that Ramon was the main caretaker for the horses. They entered the barn and the tack room was on their immediate left. Laura was inside, busily taking notes on a clipboard.

"Hey, Mom."

She turned and her face lit up. She walked up to Jeremy and gave him a big hug. "Jeremy, what a surprise. What on earth are you doing here?"

"I just thought I'd come to say hello to my mother, and I brought a friend with me."

"Gillian, nice to see you too. Where's Ian?"

"He's not here, Mom."

"We broke up," added Gillian. "Saturday afternoon he showed up at my door. He told me about Larry, and I'm so relieved that he wasn't seriously injured. But then he told me that he couldn't be a full-time parent and be with me. He it said it was over, and that was that." She let out a sigh as the tears welled up in her eyes. She reached into her purse for a tissue.

"So, that explains it," said Laura. "That's why he was acting so strange when he got home. I asked him what was wrong and he wouldn't tell me. I left right after that."

Will came into the tack room and gave Jeremy a smile. "Well, look who's here. Good to see you, son." He turned to Gillian. "Nice to see you too." He looked at her more closely. "Are you all right?"

"I've been better."

"Ian decided to end things with her, at least for the time being," said Laura.

"I'm afraid there's more to the story," added Gillian. "And since I can only recall bits and pieces of it, you'll have to tell them, Jeremy. Word's going to get out sooner or later, and they might as well hear it from us."

"Are you sure?"

She nodded. He filled them in on what had happened the day before, starting with Larry's text message, and ending with his rushing her to the hospital.

"Good Lord," said Laura. Both she and Will gave her a hug.

"The doctor wants her to be supervised," added Jeremy, "so I'm staying in her guest room until her sister arrives tomorrow. Meantime, I thought she could use a change of scenery. I also thought that if you played your cards right, you just might be able to talk this very talented lady into donating a painting to your auction."

"Will, why don't you take her out and show her around?" said Laura. "I'll come join you in a minute."

Will offered his arm to Gillian. "Come with me."

After they left Laura turned to Jeremy. "Are you all right?"

"I don't know, Mom. It scared the living hell out of me. I can't help but wonder if I'm to blame. I shouldn't have left her alone out there in that condition. I was only going to be gone for a minute or two. I didn't even think about the damn pool."

Jeremy's voice broke. Laura wrapped her arms around him.

"Don't even go there, Jer. You don't have a magic crystal ball. What happened happened, and it's really no one's fault. What matters is you were there and you got to her in time. You didn't panic and you knew exactly what to do. Because of you, she's still with us, and you've made me incredibly proud of you as a mother."

"I know, but she doesn't want me telling Dad about it, and I hate keeping something like this from him."

"Jer, this may sound strange, but I think she's right. This probably isn't the best time to tell your father. He's been through a lot with your brother. He needs some time to deal with that, and if he knew about this, it might just push him over the edge. Don't worry. Something like this won't stay a secret forever. He'll find out, when the time is right. And when he does, he'll be just as proud of you as I am."

"Thanks, Mom."

She held him a little longer. "You okay now, Jer?"

"Yeah, I think so."

"Why don't you stay here for a little while and pull yourself back together. I'll go out and check on Will. Then, when you're ready, I'll ask Ramon to saddle up some horses. I think a good ride will help ease your mind."

She stepped outside to look for Will and Gillian. She found them at the other end of the barn. Will was showing her some of the rescued horses.

"Is he okay?" asked Gillian.

"He's fine," replied Laura. "I think it's time for a ride. Have you ever been on a horse, Gillian?"

"My first husband used to teach horseback riding up at Lake Tahoe, and he taught me how to ride as well."

"Good to know. We have about a half dozen horses that we've kept for our personal use. They're mustangs we adopted from the government. They're well trained, but they're spirited. Come with me. I think I have one that might be a good match for you."

She led her to one of the small corrals outside the barn and pointed out a black mare with a white blaze down her face and three white socks.

"We call her Miss Mollie," said Laura. "She's got a lot of stamina, but she'll respect her rider, as long as you know what you're doing, and it sounds like you do."

Jeremy came up behind them. "Miss Mollie? Good choice."

Laura pointed to a large bay gelding in the next corral. "We call him Pretty Boy. He's Jeremy's favorite."

Before long the horses were saddled and they mounted up. Will stayed behind, explaining he had work to do. Laura rode a young buckskin gelding she called Fred.

"He's Miss Mollie's son," she explained. "He was a young foal at her side when we adopted them two years ago. I think he'll turn out to be a fine horse, but he still has some rough edges to work out."

Laura led them away from the barn and onto a narrow trail leading through a lush meadow. Gillian couldn't get over the sheer beauty of it. The aspen trees were turning gold.

"When I first came here, I was an ex-housewife who didn't know one end of a horse from the other," explained Laura. "I was originally hired as a bookkeeper for Will's veterinary practice. The next thing I knew I was writing grants, planning fund-raisers, and doing everything else I could think of to keep money flowing in the door for the foundation to help care for these animals. Back then I was living in the cottage, that's what we call the fifth-wheel trailer, and I soon became friends with Will. He taught me, and both of my boys, how to ride. He also taught me how to help take care of the horses. Along the way I've been kicked, bitten, and occasionally stepped on, but I've learned to cope with it. Horses are easy. Two sons aren't."

"Thanks, Mom," said Jeremy.

"Anytime," she replied. "Some of the ones we get are simply neglected or have owners who, for whatever reason, are no longer able to care for them. Those are the easy cases, and we can usually get them to new owners right away. Others arrive abandoned, injured or starving. They need some TLC, and we're often pretty successful with them as well. But we also get the occasional hard-luck cases. Those are the ones that have suffered some serious abuse, and it never ceases to amaze me just how cruel some human beings can be. They usually need complete rehabilitation, but we're not always successful. There've also been a few that we've had to put down as soon as they arrived. Those are the ones that really break your heart."

They continued across the meadow and began working their way toward the ridge. Laura went on with her story.

"This ranch used to be called The Flying M, and it's been in Will's family for over a century. When Will's father inherited it from his great-uncle, it was still a working cattle ranch. Will's dad was also a veterinarian. He started up the veterinary clinic, and he started taking in injured and abandoned horses. By the time Will finished veterinary school, they decided to stop raising cattle and add a horse sanctuary to the clinic. They sold about half the acreage, and the name, to that big dude ranch resort next door. Will renamed the place St. Eligius, since he's the patron saint of horses and those who work with them. That pretty much sums it up. The foundation survives mostly on grant money and donor support. We also do a number of fundraisers throughout the year. One is coming up soon, and that's the haunted hayride that we do every year with the Flying M. It's the last Saturday in October and we always have a lot of fun while we're at it. We have volunteers of all ages who come and participate, and the boys always come to help out as well."

"Isn't it snowing up here by then?" asked Gillian.

"A little bit, sometimes, but the snow doesn't really start accumulating until around Thanksgiving. Our big event, however, is our gala and auction in Denver, in February."

Fred started acting up. Miss Mollie got agitated as well, but Gillian pulled the rein tight and got her under control.

"You okay, Mom?"

"Yeah. He's just being the equine adolescent that he is. I'm going to run him back in to let him get it out of his system. I've got some work to do as well. You two take your time."

Laura turned Fred around and he took off in a dead gallop. Gillian and Jeremy watched as she raced across the meadow.

"You know, she's really not so bad," said Gillian

"Well, I would certainly hope not."

"Our first meeting didn't go so well." Gillian turned Miss Mollie toward the ridge. "She meant well, but she showed up, unexpectedly, at the gallery one day and really threw me for a loop. Maybe having Ian out of the picture makes a difference."

"You and I didn't get off to the best start either, if you recall."

"Yeah, but you were just looking out for your dad. You wanted to make sure I wasn't some manipulating tramp."

They rode for another couple of hours, stopping occasionally for

Gillian to snap a few photos. By the time they were ready to head back, she decided that not only would she be happy to donate a painting, she would create one exclusively for their auction. Jeremy was pleased. He couldn't wait to give his mother, and Will, the news. They rode back down the hillside and into the meadow.

"Sometimes, on the way back in, we like to run the horses through the meadow," explained Jeremy, "but I think maybe we'll skip it this time. I don't know if you're up to it or not."

Gillian turned to face Jeremy. "You're right." She spurred Miss Mollie forward and the mare took off like a rocket. Just like her son, Fred, Miss Mollie was a good runner.

"Well, how 'bout that?" A big smile broke across Jeremy's face. "You're going to need that head start, Missy."

He spurred Pretty Boy forward and raced after her. His mount was a bigger, faster horse, and he soon caught up to her. They were in a virtual tie by the time they reached the barn.

"Okay, Miss Smarty-Pants, I stand corrected," shouted Jeremy as they slowed their mounts down.

They rode back into the barn, dismounted and handed the horses back to Ramon. Will and Laura insisted they stay for dinner. Over the meal Gillian gave them the good news. Both were excited about the project and looked forward to seeing what she would create for them. Jeremy kept his watch on her. Even after racing him through the meadow, she was still subdued and he saw the sadness in her eyes. Once the meal was finished, Gillian excused herself from the table and stepped away.

"She's been through a trauma and it shows," said Will. "Hopefully, she'll recover over time."

"I'm trying to do right by her," said Jeremy. "You know I love my dad, but there are times when I just don't like him, and this is one of them. The real irony is that the first time I met her, I was worried she'd do something to hurt him."

"She's lucky to have you for a friend," added Laura "but don't give up on your father just yet. They have a long history together, and trust me when I tell you that he's never, ever gotten over her. Once he's over the shock of Larry's accident he'll reclaim her. You wait and see."

It was all Jeremy could do to keep from blurting out that it wasn't going to happen, but it wasn't the time. He wanted his mother to get used to the idea of him and Gillian being friends before they became lovers. Gillian soon returned and offered to help clean up. Afterwards Will and Laura walked them back to the Jeep.

"Thanks so much for your help, Gillian. Call us if you need anything, okay?" said Laura.

"I will. And thanks, Laura."

Laura crossed to the other side of the Jeep to give her son a big hug. "I'm proud of you, Jeremy. I really am."

"Thanks, Mom, for saying that, and thanks for listening."

"I'm your mother, Jeremy. I'm here if you need me."

Gillian slept for most of the trip home. Jeremy noticed that she seemed to tire easily since the incident in the pool. Once they arrived back at her place he fed the dogs while Gillian went straight to bed. He sat up and watched television. It was around midnight when he finally checked his email. He had a response from Larry. Much to his surprise, Larry had known just what to say.

## ❧ TWENTY-SEVEN ❧

THE NEXT MORNING Gillian left Jeremy a note to let him know she'd be at the gallery, but would return in time to accompany him to the airport. She felt sad as she wrote it. She'd genuinely enjoyed his company and would miss him. She left the note on the kitchen counter, picked up her briefcase and stepped away quietly, so as not to disturb his sleep. When she arrived at the gallery she gave the receptionist her usual greeting.

"Morning, Tammy."

"Good morning, Gillian."

"Is Paul in his office?"

"Yes, he is."

She stuck her head in Paul's door. As soon as he saw her he got up from behind his desk and hugged her.

"Cynthia called yesterday and told us what happened. You don't know how relieved we are to see you, girlfriend. You gave us all a big scare."

"It's been rough, Paul."

"But somehow, Gillian, I don't think that you and Ian are through. That man loves you. I think he just needs some space. Give him some time, he'll be back."

"I don't think so, Paul. I'm not so sure I want him back."

"You don't mean that, Boss."

"Yes, I do." Her voice was firm. "I've decided to move on, and I came in this morning to let you know about a new project we're going to be involved with. Jeremy drove me to St. Eligius Ranch yesterday. It's quite a place, Paul. They're doing marvelous things for injured and abandoned horses, so I told them I'd create a painting exclusively for their auction. You and Rosemary will need to coordinate with Mrs. Palmer. I want us to get as much publicity out of this as we possibly can."

"I'm on it, Boss."

Gillian went into her office to catch up on paperwork. She left around lunchtime. When she arrived home, she found Jeremy waiting for her.

"I washed the sheets and made the guest room bed," he said.

"Thanks, Jer. You know, I really am going to miss you. You're a good roommate."

"That's what the two guys I'm renting with keep telling me as well. Are you ready to go?"

"Let's do it."

They walked out to the driveway.

"By the way, Miss Gillian, I'm a young, single guy, so I don't do minivans. We'll take the Jeep, if you don't mind."

She gave him a smile. "Well, at least it's not the Harley."

"Which reminds me, I need to get it on craigslist."

"You're selling it?"

"Yep. The other night Dad emailed me a picture of what was left of the car Larry was riding in. It was worse than I could have ever imagined and it gave me pause for thought. Besides, I could use the money for school."

Jeremy opened the passenger door and waited for her to get in. Once again, she was unusually quiet. Entering the airport terminal, Gillian suddenly felt as if the walls were closing in on her.

"Are you alright?"

"I don't know, Jer. For some strange reason this place is making me feel claustrophobic."

"It's probably some after-effect of what happened to you. Just hold on to me. You'll be fine."

Gillian took his arm and he guided her through the crowds. They soon found Cynthia waiting for them in the baggage claim. Gillian grabbed her sister and held her tight. The tears were streaming down her cheeks.

"It's okay, it's okay." Cynthia tried to reassure her.

"I don't know what's the matter with me today." Gillian reached into her purse for tissue.

"Gillian, it's okay," said Cynthia. "You've been through a lot. I've got my bags and we'll head back to your place. You need to take it easy for awhile." She picked up her overnight bag and turned her attention to Jeremy as he grabbed her suitcase.

"I don't know how to thank you."

"I was just doing what had to be done." He started leading them back to the parking garage. "Anyway, I'm glad you're here. Right now she needs you more than she needs me, and I need to spend some time with my brother."

"I understand. There are certain things that come with the territory of being the older sibling. You always feel protective of them. That never changes."

* * *

Cynthia rode in the backseat of the Jeep as Jeremy filled her in about the project Gillian planned for St. Eligius. She could tell he was excited about it. Once they arrived at Gillian's house, he helped her out of the backseat and pulled her aside while her sister went inside.

"Cynthia, I need to talk to you about something."

"What is it?"

Jeremy retrieved her bags from the back of the Jeep. "Gillian is having nightmares. Both nights I was here she woke me up. I wasn't able to go in her bedroom, because I didn't want to take the chance of her waking up and jumping to the wrong conclusion. I just wanted you to be aware of it."

"Thanks for letting me know, and I'd love to take you out for dinner while I'm here."

"Thanks for the offer, but I'll have to take a rain check. I work from five in the afternoon until one in the morning. That's a little late for a dinner date. Maybe some other time."

He picked up her bags and walked with her to the front door.

"Will do," said Cynthia. "And thank you again, Jeremy. Hopefully I'll get to see you again before I leave."

Jeremy took Cynthia's luggage into the guest room. He came out a minute later and picked up his duffle bag.

"I'll be staying at my dad's for a few days," he said to Gillian. "I need to spend some time with Larry. Do you want me to give you a call tomorrow and see how you're doing?"

"I'd like that. I'll walk you out to your Jeep. I'll be right back, Cyn."

"Take your time."

* * *

Gillian walked Jeremy to the Jeep and gave him a long, lingering hug before he climbed in.

"I'm going to miss you, Jer."

"Me too, but I'll be back."

"I'm looking forward to it."

She kissed him on the cheek. He got behind the wheel, started up the engine, and she waved goodbye as he backed out of the driveway.

"Yeah, I'll be back, baby girl." He watched her in the rearview mirror as he drove away. "You can count on that."

\* \* \*

Cynthia was in the kitchen, rummaging through the cupboards, when Gillian came back in.

"If you're looking for the liquor, Cyn, forget it. Jeremy beat you to it. He's already poured everything out."

"You know, the more I'm hearing about this kid, the more I like him. Too bad he isn't just a tad older. He'd probably be a better match for you than his father was."

"And what's that supposed to mean?"

"I saw the way he was looking at you. He likes you, Gillian. A lot."

"Well of course he likes me. We're friends. It wasn't that long ago that we both thought he'd be my stepson someday. And now that the man has just saved my life, we share a special bond."

Cynthia tried to shrug it off. "Just saying."

Gillian started heading downstairs. Both dogs were at her heels.

"Where are you going?"

"To do some laundry. Then I've got to get back to work. My studio's downstairs. I'm supposed to be an artist, remember?" Gillian made her exit as her sister shook her head.

"So open mouth, insert foot. Nice going, Cynthia." She went into the guest room to unpack.

# ❧ TWENTY-EIGHT ❧

JEREMY PULLED INTO the parking lot in front of Larry's high school. Class had just let out. He scanned through the crowd and saw his brother.

"Yo! Larry! Over here!"

Larry approached the Jeep. "Hey, Jer. What are you doing here?"

"Got your text about losing your driving privileges, so I thought I'd give you a lift home."

"Thanks." Larry hopped into the passenger seat and took off his baseball cap. "Check this out, bro. They shaved half my head, so I had to get a buzz cut."

"Lovely, and I love all the stitches too. Gives you that Frankenstein look. Too bad it's not closer to Halloween."

"Nice." Larry put the cap back on. "So, what's up?"

Jeremy pulled out of the parking lot. "Same stuff, different day. Just thought I'd hang out with you guys for awhile. Between you and Gillian, and your near scrapes with death, I could really use a break."

"Bummer that Dad dumped her. She seemed like a nice lady, what little I saw of her."

"She's a peach. And thanks for the response to my email. You didn't say anything to Dad about it, did you?"

"Time out, Jer. What email?"

"The one you sent me yesterday."

"I never sent you an email. I haven't checked my email since Saturday. I'm on double-secret probation, dude. I told you that when I texted you Sunday morning. That means Dad's monitoring my email, my cell phone log, and my text messages. I guess I had it coming."

Jeremy's heart sank and he was quiet for most of the drive home. Finally, he spoke up. "Larry, did you know that Gillian Matthews nearly drowned a couple of days ago?"

"What? No way. What the hell happened?"

Jeremy pulled into the driveway and shut down the Jeep. "I guess I'll have to show you."

They went straight upstairs to Larry's room and turned on the computer. Larry logged on into his email account and found Jeremy's message in his inbox. It appeared to be unread. He clicked on the link and began reading it.

"Good God, Jer, I had no idea. But you did good, bro. The lady's lucky to still be walking around, and I think you've just motivated me to sign up for a CPR class as well. So how's she doing now?"

"About as well as can be expected. Her sister just arrived from Phoenix and she's going to be staying with her for a few days. Larry, just for laughs, let's check your sent folder."

Larry opened the folder. The reply wasn't there.

"Okay, so now let's check the trash folder."

Larry clicked on the icon. Sure enough, there was the reply. He clicked on the link and opened it.

"Jeremy I swear, I did not write that. But for what it's worth, if I had responded, that's pretty close to what I would've said."

"Thanks, Larry, good to know. So I guess we can figure out who really wrote it, and it looks like Dad needs to learn how to do a better job in covering his tracks. I gotta get to work. Then I'm coming back and having a serious talk with our father. If we had pulled something like this, he'd have our sorry butts for it and you know it. I think it should go both ways."

\* \* \*

The light outside the front door was burning when Jeremy returned. He let himself in, and upon entering, heard his father's voice calling to him from the family room.

"I'm in here, Jeremy. I understand I'm busted, and that you want to have a little talk."

Ian looked up as Jeremy came into the room. He'd never before seen the look he was seeing in his son's eyes. It was a look of pure, intense anger.

"Let me guess, Dad. You've known about this since the day it happened, haven't you?"

"Look Jer, it wasn't my intention to cause you to break a confidence, but right now, under the circumstances, I'm having to monitor your brother's activities until he proves to me that I can trust him again."

"I understand Dad, but what possessed you to send me a reply and make me think that Larry wrote it? Did you really think that I wouldn't find out? If it had been in reverse, and I'd done this to you, you would've handed me my butt on a platter, and we both know it."

"You're right, Jer. I messed up. I admit it. I'm guilty as charged. In hindsight, yes, I should have contacted you directly, but I wasn't thinking clearly. I'd just gone through hell knowing that I literally came within inches of losing your brother, and then I find out I nearly lost her for good as well. On top of that, I'm trying to figure out a way to reach out to you, because you're blaming yourself for something that isn't your fault, but I'm trying to do it in such a way that you won't think you've betrayed her confidence."

"But it was my fault, Dad," argued Jeremy. "I'm the one who took her out to the patio. I'm the one who left her alone out there in that condition, not thinking about the damn pool. She'd been knocking down manhattans. Apparently she started shortly after you left. By the time I got to her, she was three sheets to the wind."

"It's not your fault, Jeremy."

"So what are you saying, Dad? Are you trying to blame her?"

"No, I'm not."

"Well that's good, because trust me, she didn't go into the water on purpose. The woman nearly died, Dad. I got to her as fast as I could, but it almost wasn't fast enough. By the time I pulled her up to the surface she barely had a pulse, and when I tried to revive her she didn't respond right away. Then I felt her pulse as it stopped beating. Do you have any idea what that felt like? She was gone, Dad." Jeremy started chocking on his words, but he kept going. "But I wasn't ready to give up on her, you know. So I started yelling at her and I begged her not to leave me. And then I tried one more time. That's when she finally responded."

Ian embraced his son and held him tight. "I'm proud of you, Jeremy. You did nothing wrong and everything right. I'm the one to blame. I had a knee-jerk reaction after what happened to Larry, and I vented out my frustrations on her. I shouldn't have done that, and somehow, I'm going to have to find a way to make it up to her."

Jeremy's body stiffened and he took a few steps backward. "What? Are you kidding me? Sorry, Dad, but you're not going anywhere near her. She doesn't want to see you, and I'm not going to allow it."

"Jeremy, listen to me—"

"No, Dad, you listen to me." Jeremy's voice was stern. "She's not the way she was before. She's in a very fragile state right now and I'm not going to let you upset her. I'm staying here tonight, maybe tomorrow, because I want to spend some time with Larry. But at the moment, you're not exactly on my list of favorite people, and let's just leave it at that before one of us says something we'll both regret later. Cynthia is staying with her for a few days. Once she leaves I plan on spending a lot more time with her. She needs a friend and I'm going to be there for her, and I'm not going to let you mess with her again."

Jeremy turned and headed up the stairs.

"Jeremy—"

"End of discussion, Dad. I'm going to bed."

## ❧Twenty-Nine↩

THE FOLLOWING MORNING Cynthia went through the house to gather up Ian's belongings and drop them in a shopping bag. She grabbed the keys to the minivan and programmed the address for Salisbury & Norton into the GPS device. She planned on having a serious talk with Ian Palmer. She entered the Salisbury building with a determined look in her eye as she approached the front receptionist.

"May I help you?"

"Yes. My name is Cynthia Lindsey. I'm here to see Ian Palmer."

"Do you have an appointment?"

"No."

"I'm sorry, ma'am, but—"

"Look," replied Cynthia, "I won't take more than five minutes of his time. Trust me, he'll want to see me."

The receptionist reluctantly rang Ian's office. "Sir, there's a Cynthia Lindsey here to see you."

"Send her up. Thanks."

She handed Cynthia a visitor's pass and directed her to the elevator. Cynthia got off on the seventh floor, where someone pointed her to Ian's office. She was shocked when she saw his face. Ian looked like he hadn't slept in days.

"Have a seat, Cynthia. And would you mind closing the door behind you?"

"Certainly." She set the bag on a table. "I just came by to drop off a few things you had at Gillian's."

"Thanks." Ian's voice sounded tired. "How is she?"

"About as well as can be expected. How 'bout you?"

"The same."

"Yeah, I can see that. So, how's your son?"

"All right. He's back in school. Seems to be no worse for the wear. He also seems to have a whole new attitude about life as well. He's learned a hard lesson, but he'll be a much better man for it."

"I'm glad to hear it."

There was an awkward moment of silence before they both started to say something at the same time.

"You first," he said.

"No, you go first."

"Okay, I will. Cynthia, would you believe me if I told you I had a temporary lapse in sanity? I wasn't thinking right when I told Gillian it was over, and now I've backed myself into a corner. I blew it, big time, and I haven't a clue as to how to fix it."

"You're certainly right about that, Ian. You blew it."

"And just so you know, I've been monitoring Larry's email."

"Okay, I'd be doing the same thing if I caught one of my underage kids sneaking out to a drinking party. But what does that have to do with anything?"

"Sunday night, well actually, early Monday morning, I couldn't sleep, so I decided to check up on Larry's email. What do I find, but a message from Jeremy? So, I opened it. I know all about what happened to Gillian. Jeremy's descriptions were quite graphic. And please, by all means, feel free to call me a shameless bastard if you wish. There's nothing you could call me that would be half as bad as anything I've already called myself."

"I know she didn't want you to find out about it," replied Cynthia, "but now that you have, perhaps you should talk to her."

"How? When I tried sending her an email, it bounced. She won't take my calls or return my messages. Somehow, I get the distinct feeling that she doesn't want to talk to me."

"Give her some time, Ian. She's just experienced a major trauma and she's not herself right now. Meantime, for what it's worth, I wanted to let you know that you've got yourself one hell of a good kid in Jeremy. If not for him, I'd be having my sister's funeral today. I'll be forever grateful to him for saving her life."

"Thanks. I'm grateful to him too, but I'm also worried about him. It really shook him to the core and he thinks he's responsible for what happened to her. Now, he's barely talking to me, because I intercepted the email, so he thinks he's betrayed her confidence. He's also made it quite clear that he doesn't want me going anywhere near her. Seems he's made himself her self-appointed guardian. If I didn't know better I'd think...no, let's not go there."

Cynthia considered telling him that his hunches were correct, but then she thought better of it. Gillian was already in a fragile emotional state. She didn't need the added stress of two men fighting over her.

"Well, Ian, I don't know what else to say, other that it looks like we've both managed to weave ourselves into a very tangled web. Since I don't think Gillian is ready to hear that you found out about what happened to her, I'm going to have to keep this little secret of yours as well. Look, why don't you just focus on Larry right now? Give her, and yourself, a time out and chance to heal. I can't guarantee that you'll ever win her back again, but if you should somehow manage to pull it off, there'd better be a ring and a date to go with it. Otherwise, I'm going to wring your bloody neck."

"Understood." He walked her to the elevator.

"Thanks, Cyn. I'm glad you're staying with her. She needs you. Hopefully, the next time we meet, it will be under better circumstances."

The elevator doors opened and she stepped in. The last thing Ian saw before the doors closed was the look of pain and anger in her eyes.

## ❧Thirty❧

CYNTHIA STAYED THROUGH the weekend, but by Monday morning she had to return home to her family. Gillian's spirits were slowly improving, although she was hardly the happy, vibrant woman she'd once been. A new exhibit was scheduled to open at the gallery on Thursday night, and both sisters agreed that work would be good therapy. Late Thursday afternoon Gillian was in her office, finishing up some last-minute details before changing into a cocktail dress. She was about to close her office door when her phone rang.

"Yes, Tammy."

"You have a visitor, Mrs. Matthews."

"Who is it?"

"His name is Larry Palmer."

Larry Palmer. What could he possibly want? She looked at the clock. She had just enough time to squeeze in a quick visit.

"Send him in."

A minute later Larry was at her door. Gillian noticed the shirt and apron he was wearing bore the catering company logo.

"Please, take a seat." She motioned to one of the chairs across from her desk. "So, Mr. Palmer, to what do I owe the pleasure?"

"I just wanted to come and offer you my apology, Ms. Matthews."

"For what? And it's Gillian, by the way."

"Okay, Gillian. I just wanted to apologize for what happened between you and my dad. I feel like it's my fault."

"You have nothing to apologize for, Larry. You were in a serious accident, and you're in no way responsible for what happened between your father and me. I'm just glad you came out of it okay."

"Yeah, but the only reason it happened was because I was out somewhere that I shouldn't have been."

Gillian tried to reassure him. "We all make mistakes, Larry. Apparently there was a lesson that you needed to learn."

"I know. Anyway, after my dad got home from your place, and after my mom left, he told me he'd ended things with you. I told him not to do something like that on my account. I'm trying really hard to make things right with my mother over being so difficult with her about Will, so the last thing I need right now is to get between you and my dad."

"I appreciate that, Larry. Unfortunately, what's done is done. Your father and I simply weren't meant to be, but I don't want you to blame yourself, okay. This isn't your fault."

"Thanks," he said. "Also, Jeremy told me about what happened with your falling in the pool. I'm glad you're okay too. I guess we now have something in common. Just before the car crash, I really thought I was about to die as well. That's kind of a life-changing experience, you know."

Before she could respond, Paul stepped in. "Your boss is looking for you, and I have some business that I need to go over with Gillian, so if you don't mind?"

Larry made his exit as Gillian thanked him and turned her attention to Paul. After they finished their conversation, she changed her clothes, stepped into the gallery, and greeted the artist.

"I thought you said you were going to find a new home for that suit."

"Well hello, Gillian." Tony smiled and shook her hand, "I see the place is thriving. I knew I left it in good hands."

As Gillian chatted with Tony, patrons began to arrive and they both started working the crowd. Several times throughout the evening Gillian and Paul escorted buyers into her office. She had just stepped back into the gallery when she spotted a familiar face.

"Jeremy, what a pleasant surprise. I thought you'd be working tonight."

"They've changed my schedule this week. I'm working the lunch shift, and when my brother told me he'd be working here tonight I decided to stop by to keep him on his toes."

"Sorry to interrupt." Paul motioned to the woman standing next to him. "This lady would like to make a purchase."

"Nice seeing you, Jeremy." She gave him a parting smile as she stepped away. "Enjoy the show."

By eight o'clock most of the crowd had left. The caterers were breaking down and Gillian had some business to go over with Tony. Once they finished she headed back down the hallway to her office and noticed the rear door was still propped open. She knew the catering truck had just left, so she went to investigate. The Palmer brothers were in the parking lot, standing just a few feet away.

"Don't let me interrupt," she said. "I was just checking the door."

"You're not interrupting a thing, Miss Gillian. I was just saying goodnight to my brother."

"And by the way, Larry," she said, "thank you for taking the time to come and talk to me."

"You're welcome."

"Also Larry, I want you to know that just because your father and I have ended things, I'm not harboring any kind of grudge against you, or your brother, so you're both welcome here, anytime."

"Well I would certainly hope so, my dear." There was a flirtatious sound in Jeremy's voice. "After all, I did rescue you from the pool, so that makes me your knight-in-shining armor."

"Ah, jeez." Larry rolled his eyes.

"But the lady, she loves it, don't you, my darling?" Jeremy spoke in his best fake French accent as he put his arm around Gillian.

"You're so full of it, Jer," said his brother.

"Now, now, my oh-so-cynical sibling." Jeremy was still using the funny accent, "You do not need to one-up me."

Gillian laughed as Larry started making gestures of sticking his finger down his throat.

"Oh gag me. Please, someone do something, I can't take it anymore."

Jeremy wrapped his arms around her waist. "Let's just ignore him. Dance with me, my darling. Just the sight of you and I can hear the violins playing." Jeremy began twirling her around the parking lot. The sound of her laughter was music to his ears.

"Shameless flirt," Larry called out. "Quit hitting on her. Look out for him, Gillian. He's a real scoundrel."

A voice came out of the darkness. "Larry! Time to go."

The sound of his voice changed Gillian's demeanor in an instant. She broke away from Jeremy and rushed to the door. "Goodnight, you guys."

"Goodnight, Gillian," replied Larry. "I'm coming, Dad. Night, Jer."

"Night, Larry."

\* \* \*

As Larry got in his father's car Ian approached Jeremy. "So, that was quite a little show you put on."

"How long have you been standing there?"

"Long enough."

"Look, Dad, I'm just trying to cheer her up. She's been through a lot."

Ian wasn't buying it, but it wasn't the time or the place for another confrontation.

"See to it she gets home okay."

"Will do."

* * *

Ian headed back to his car while Jeremy went back inside and headed straight to Gillian's office. He found her at her computer.

"I closed the back door for you," he said.

"Thanks. I've just ordered some pizza. It should be here soon. You're welcome to stay and join us."

"Thanks." He paused for a moment. "Gillian, are you all right?"

"Just hunky dory, although I suppose I should start getting used to running into your father from time to time."

Jeremy hated what he was about to say, but it needed to be out in open. "Gillian, I blew it. Big time."

"What do you mean?"

He tried to explain. "The night of your--accident, after you went to bed, I was feeling pretty stressed, so I sent Larry an email to let him know what happened. I just needed to talk to someone, you know."

"I understand."

He wondered if she'd be as understanding after what he had to say next.

"Gillian, we have a problem. My dad's been monitoring Larry's emails. I had no idea he was doing that, but now the proverbial cat is out of the bag. He knows what happened to you, and he's known about it from the start. I'm sorry. I messed up."

She sat silent for a moment. "Is he aware that I didn't want him to know?"

"Yes, he is," replied Jeremy, "and he's not taking it very well."

Gillian let out a sigh. "Well, I suppose he was bound to find out sooner or later. Anyway Jer, it's not your fault, so I'm not angry with you, okay."

"Thanks, good to know. So, why don't you call him and at least hear him out?"

"I wish I could, but right now I simply can't deal with him."

It was just what he wanted to hear. "I understand, and I won't force you into doing something you don't feel comfortable doing."

"Thanks, Jer, I appreciate it. If you wouldn't mind letting him know that I'm not blaming it on him, we'll let it go at that."

"Will do."

She went back to her computer.

"So, moving on," said Jeremy, "I just sold the Harley."

"Well, that certainly didn't take very long."

"Yeah, I guess I got lucky. Anyway, that gives me a little windfall. I'm also getting a paid vacation from work. Starting Monday, they're shutting the place down for two weeks for remodeling. I don't know about you, but I could certainly use a break. What do you say about getting away from it all? Right now, I think a change of scenery would do us both a world of good."

"I don't know, Jer. Not that it doesn't sound tempting, but I have a lot of responsibilities here."

The pizzas soon arrived and Gillian insisted on paying. Paul came in to take a few slices back to his office.

"You know, Gillian," said Jeremy. "I'm not talking about some cross-country excursion, but Colorado is a beautiful state, especially this time of the year. Maybe we could take a short ride down to Telluride or Durango."

"I don't know. Let me think about it, okay?"

A few minutes later Paul burst back into the room, clearly upset about something. "Boss, we have a crisis, and I mean a crisis."

"What wrong, Paul?" asked Gillian.

"Susanna Richardson."

"Oh that's not funny, Paul," said Jeremy.

"Who says I'm joking, kid?"

"Okay," said Gillian. "So who is this Susanna Richardson, and how is she a problem?"

"Susanna Richardson is a so-called investigative reporter on one of the local TV stations," explained Paul. "She really does hatchet jobs on people, and the more dirt she digs up, the higher the ratings. Her specialty is ruining people's lives, but don't confuse her with the facts. She's all about sensationalism. There's a special place in Hell waiting for that woman someday."

"Lovely." Gillian sipped her soda. "So what does this have to do with us?"

"I just got through listening to a voice-mail message she left for me earlier this afternoon. She wanted to know if there was any truth to the rumor that Gillian Matthews got drunk the other day and almost drowned in her swimming pool."

Gillian nearly chocked on her soda.

"Good Lord," said Jeremy. "How could she have possibly known about that?"

"Rumor has it that Susanna bribes hospital workers," said Paul. "Never mind ethics or patient-privacy laws, she supposedly pays cash for tips, and the law allows her to protect her sources. I'd say it's pretty obvious that someone at that hospital, who had access to patient records, has tipped her off. Now there's blood in the water and that shark is circling you, Boss."

"I wouldn't underestimate her, Gillian," added Jeremy. "She's poison. She could ruin you, and this gallery."

"I understand completely," said Gillian. "It wasn't that long ago that a gallery in Santa Fe dropped me because a local paper there did a story on Jason. So, what do we do now?"

"We get you out of town, Gillian," replied Paul, "as in tonight, or first thing tomorrow morning. Dwayne and I can take care of your dogs, but let's get you out of Colorado for at least a week. Make it two. If she's unable to find you, the story will become old news, and she'll move on to another victim."

"I can go with her, Paul," volunteered Jeremy. "I was just telling her that I have two weeks paid vacation coming up, starting Sunday."

"That's too long of a wait, kid. By then Ms. Richardson and her minions will have staked out Gillian's house, and they'll ambush her. Call your boss tonight. Tell him it's a family emergency. Your dog is sick, your grandmother died, whatever, but you whisk her out of town, right now." Paul turned back to Gillian. "We have the funds for the gallery to pay your travel expenses, and as long as you're gathering source material for your paintings, we can probably write it off."

"Okay Paul," she said. "So where do you suggest we go?"

"Anywhere outside the state of Colorado." Paul looked back at Jeremy. "How old are you, kid?"

"Twenty-one."

"Perfect. Take her to Las Vegas."

"But two weeks in Vegas, Paul?" said Gillian. "That's a bit much."

"Then go someplace else after that, but I want you gone for a good two weeks, Boss. And here's anther thought. Would you two mind traveling as honeymooners? Don't worry, Jeremy, you don't have to actually marry her. But once that barracuda finds out Gillian is out of town, and trust me, she will figure that out, she'll use her sources to try to track her down, but no one will know who a Mrs. Jeremy Palmer really is. Go ahead and book a suite, Boss, if you can find one for a reasonable price. That way you two can share a room and still have separate sleeping areas. And let me know when you're ready to leave. I'll follow you home to pick up Duke and Daisy."

Paul rushed back to his office.

"Well, sweetheart," said Jeremy, "it looks like we're going be having ourselves a shotgun wedding."

"Jeremy, you don't have to do this, you know."

"Hey, for better or worse, I saved your life. Besides, I've never been to Las Vegas. My only stipulation is that I insist on sharing some of the expenses."

"I have a fear of flying, Jeremy, so we'll have to travel by car."

"Only if we take the Jeep. I get to pay for the gas and we can take turns paying for the meals. Deal?"

"Fair enough, oh husband of mine," said Gillian with a smile. "I'm putting together an itinerary now. Pack your swimsuit. We're going on to San Diego after Las Vegas."

Gillian worked on her computer while Jeremy called his boss.

"We're good," he said after he ended the call. "I told him I had a family emergency, and as soon as he heard the name, Susanna Richardson, he told me to take all the time I need."

Paul came back in. "Are we ready to go?"

"I think so." Gillian took a few sheets of paper from the printer and dropped them in her briefcase. "Just need to toss the pizza boxes."

"Good," Paul replied, "and one more thing. This is, for lack of a better description, a disinformation campaign. You guys might want to pick up some costume jewelry. You know, something that looks like wedding rings. That way the hotel staff will think that you're a real married couple, just in case anyone starts snooping around."

"Actually," said Gillian, "I still have my old wedding set from my marriage to Jason. Come to think of it, I still have Jason's ring too. Meant to sell it, but I forgot about it."

"Then use it. You can sell it all, once we've successfully thrown the wolf off the scent."

Jeremy turned to Gillian. "I'll go home and pack. I'll meet you at your place in a couple of hours. We'll hit the road first thing in the morning."

# ∂⊶THIRTY-ONE⊷∂

GILLIAN SQUEEZED THE last suitcase into the back of Jeremy's Jeep.

"I think that's everything, except for this." She pulled a small bundle, wrapped in tissue paper, from her jeans pocket. "Here, catch."

She tossed something to Jeremy. Not being used to early mornings, he was caught off-guard and missed it. It was a gold wedding band. He snapped it up before it rolled into the flowerbed.

"Whoops," she laughed. "I never said I had a great throwing arm. Sorry about that."

"It's okay," mumbled Jeremy.

"Yuck." She unwrapped the woman's wedding set and placed it on her left hand. "There are no happy memories for me when I look at this. Oh well, I've promised myself this will be the very last time I'll ever wear it, or any other wedding band for that matter. I'm done."

"Never say never," said Jeremy, half-heartedly.

She looked at him closely and noticed that he was only half awake. "Why don't I drive the first leg? And you take a nap."

"Thanks." He yawned and handed her the keys.

She went back into the house for a final inspection, making sure nothing was left on and that the premises were secure. She left a message on Cynthia's voice mail to let her know she was leaving and would be in touch with her later. Satisfied, she locked the front door, hopped into the

Jeep, and started it up. Jeremy was already asleep in the passenger seat. He looked so sweet. Just like a younger version of Ian, minus all of Ian's hang-ups.

"Don't even go there," she muttered to herself.

She put the Jeep in reverse, backed out of the driveway, and headed toward the freeway with its Friday-morning rush-hour traffic. They were nearing the town of Idaho Springs when Jeremy began stirring and opened his eyes.

"Morning, sleepy head." She gave him a smile. "Feeling better?"

"Much," he replied as he stretched. "How long was I out?"

"A while, but not too long. We're almost down to a quarter tank of gas. I see a truck stop ahead. Let's fill up and get some breakfast."

"Sounds like a plan. I could really use some coffee."

They pulled up to one of the gas pumps. Jeremy filled the Jeep while Gillian stepped into the diner to get a table. She walked up to the hostess stand and was soon met by a very pretty middle-aged woman. No doubt all the truck drivers hit on her. She reached for the menus.

"How many?"

"Two. I have someone joining me."

As the woman picked up the menus she stopped to look at Gillian again. Her face lit up.

"Gillian!"

Gillian looked back at her, and a look of recognition slowly registered across her face as well. "Samantha? Samantha Walsh?"

"Oh my God!" exclaimed both women as they gave each other a hug.

"I've read about you in the papers," said Samantha, "and I even called your art gallery one day, but they said you weren't in. I meant to call back later, but sometimes I get so danged busy around here. You don't know how happy I am to see you."

"Me too, Sam. I've always regretted losing touch with you. I've wondered a lot about you over the years."

Jeremy came in to join her.

"Jeremy," said Gillian, "I want you to meet a very dear friend of mine."

"My gosh," said Samantha, "he looks just like his father. Gillian, I'm so happy it worked out with Ian after all."

"He's not my son, Samantha. Ian is his father, but I'm not his mother."

"I'm her husband," said Jeremy.

Samantha looked astonished, but before she could ask any questions one of the servers came up to ask her something.

"Don't blow your cover," whispered Jeremy, "you don't know who could be listening."

Samantha turned back around.

159

"It's true." Gillian had a nervous smile. "Samantha Walsh, this is my husband, Jeremy Palmer. Jeremy, this is Samantha Walsh. She was my best friend when I was in college, but we haven't seen each other in years."

The two shook hands and Samantha noticed Jeremy was wearing a wedding band. She glanced at Gillian's left hand and saw that she was wearing a wedding set as well. Gillian saw by the look on her face that Sam was dying to know what was going on.

"It's a long, complicated story, Sam, and one that I'm simply going to have to save for another time. We're on our honeymoon."

"I see. Congratulations. Here, let me show you to your table."

She led them to a table, but returned a short time later with a younger woman in tow. She too was stunningly beautiful, with her long auburn hair, green eyes, and rather voluptuous figure.

"Gillian, this is someone I would like for you to meet," said Samantha. "This is my daughter, Cassie. Cassie, this is my friend, Gillian Palmer, and her husband, Jeremy."

"Nice meeting you." Cassie extended her hand to both of them.

"Would you mind if we join you for a few minutes?" asked Samantha.

"Of course not. Sam, I didn't know you got married."

"I didn't." She and Cassie took their seats. "Cassie's father was a truck driver. We were engaged, but he was killed in an accident before our wedding. It happened up near Flagstaff. It was raining and the road was slick. Someone cut in front of him, he slammed on the brakes and his rig jackknifed. He lost control, went off the road and rolled down the mountainside. I was four months pregnant at the time, and I'm forever grateful that I didn't miscarry and lose her as well. Brendan had taken out a pretty generous life-insurance policy, and later on I used it to buy this place. I wanted to make a fresh start, and I thought this would probably be a good place to raise a child. I'm so happy that she happened to be here today. She's attending the University of Colorado in Colorado Springs, but she has a boyfriend who's been giving her a lot of grief lately, so she's home with me for the weekend."

"They don't need to hear about my problems, Mom."

"He assumes that because of her looks that she's easy and she sees other guys behind his back. But in reality, she's pretty shy, and she's always been a one-man kind of woman."

"Mom." Cassie rolled her eyes. "That's enough. Really."

"And speaking of bad boyfriends," said Samantha, "I wonder whatever became of Ryan Knight."

"Don't know, and don't care," said Gillian.

"Oh no," groaned Cassie. "Please Mom, not the Ryan Knight story again. No offense, but I've been hearing that story my entire life."

"I'd like to hear it," said Jeremy.

"Well then, you all can go ahead." Cassie stood from the table. "I've got a term paper that I really should be working on. I'll be in your office, Mom. It was nice meeting you."

Cassie made her exit. Jeremy watched her as she walked away.

"She's absolutely beautiful, Sam, just like you," said Gillian. "I'd say you did a good job with her."

"I tried, but it wasn't always easy, especially around all these truck drivers. But they all know me, and they know I would hunt them down and kill them if they ever messed with her, so they treat her with respect. There're also a few of them who consider themselves her surrogate uncles. Pity the poor guy who's foolish enough to do her wrong. They'd get to him before I could."

"So, what's the Ryan Knight story?" asked Jeremy. "I certainly didn't grow up hearing it."

"Ryan Knight was a creep that Gillian was involved with at the time she first met your father. After she dumped him, he tried stalking her, until the morning your father kicked his sorry butt."

Samantha was all too happy to tell him the entire story. Even after all the years, she still vividly recalled every detail, and Jeremy eagerly took in every word. He cringed when he heard that Gillian had gotten hurt, but all in all, he was fascinated to learn about this interesting chapter from his father's past.

"You know, Sam," said Gillian, "if I didn't know better, I'd swear you had a secret crush on Ian."

"I've always loved Ian," replied Samantha, "but not the way you think. I loved him dearly as a friend. He was like the brother I never had. So whatever became of him?"

"He's an architect," explained Jeremy. "He lives in Denver, and he's worked for the same firm for as long as I can remember."

"Salisbury and Norton?"

"Yes," replied Jeremy, "although they're pressuring him to take early retirement. My parents split up right after I finished high school and left home. Dad bumped into Gillian at her gallery opening here in Denver last April. They were seeing each other for awhile, but it didn't work out." He reached over and squeezed Gillian's hand. "Dad's loss is my gain."

"And what about you, Jeremy?"

"Right now I'm a bartender, but I'm finishing up my degree in electrical engineering."

"Then it sounds to me like you're going to have a good future ahead of you. You treat her right, you hear."

Samantha excused herself, explaining that she had work she needed to catch up on, but before she left she and Gillian exchanged business cards and promised to keep in touch. When the time came to leave, Gillian discovered that Samantha had picked up their tab.

"I'll have to make this up to her, once we get back." They walked back to the Jeep. "But for now, dear hubby, we need to hit the road."

"Honey, I need my keys," he joked. "And hand them to me nicely this time. Your aim leaves a little something to be desired."

"Thanks, Jer. And I love you too, sweetheart."

Jeremy was pleased to see her laughing and smiling again. They hopped back into the Jeep and continued on their journey. They soon entered the Eisenhower Tunnel, crossed the continental divide, and drove through the mountains and canyons of western Colorado. Jeremy popped in some CDs. He loved eighties rock and roll, as did Gillian. The hours passed and they crossed into the rocky Utah deserts, where they would stop for the night.

"Well Jer, your virtue is safe with me," said Gillian. They entered the motel room and found two queen-size beds. She tossed her bag on top of one, retrieved her phone and placed a call to Paul.

"We got you out of town just in time, Boss," said Paul. "The dragon lady herself called again today, demanding to speak to you."

"And what did you tell her?"

"Tammy told her you were unavailable, took her name and number and ended the call. Of course, she'll be calling back, and we're just going to keep telling her you're unavailable. I also noticed a news van staked out across the street when I went out to lunch. Give her another day or two and she'll start beating the bushes looking for you."

After she finished the call she relayed the information to Jeremy.

"Jeremy, if you want to call your dad and let him know we've stopped for the night, it's okay. I'm not going to get upset."

"That's okay, Miss Gillian. At the moment I'm really not speaking to my father."

"What? Jeremy, I don't want to be the cause of any trouble between the two of you."

"It's not your fault, Gillian. This has to do with his intercepting the email I sent to Larry. Hopefully, we'll work it out, but right now I can't deal with him either."

Gillian didn't like the sound of it, but there was nothing she could do. It was between the two of them.

"So I take it he doesn't know that you and I are taking this trip together?"

"Nope. My mother does, but she doesn't know all the details. At my age, she's not going to call Dad to discuss it with him."

"Well, I'm sorry to hear you two are having troubles. I hope you can resolve it."

"Me too. Thanks, Miss Gillian."

That night Jeremy was once again awoken by sound of Gillian having another nightmare. She was moaning and gasping for air. Suddenly, she woke up and sat up in the bed.

"You're okay?" He sat down next to her and put his arm around her. "You're just having a bad dream."

"I know. I've been having them ever since I fell into the pool. Sorry I woke you. I just wish they'd stop."

"They probably will, in time, but you have to remember, you've had a pretty traumatic experience. You need to give yourself a chance to recover. Why don't you lie back down and try to get some sleep? We've got a big day ahead of us tomorrow."

She lay back down.

"Would you stay with me, just for a little while? I promise, I won't do anything that's inappropriate."

"Sure."

He lay down next to her and put his arm around her. She soon fell back to sleep.

"Soon, baby girl, but not just yet," he whispered under his breath as he too drifted off.

# ❧Thirty-Two❧

T HEY ARRIVED LATE Saturday afternoon. As they drove down Las Vegas Boulevard, Jeremy's eyes swept the street from side to side. He was completely mesmerized by the lights, the buildings, and the crowds.

"I've seen pictures and movies of it," he said, "but it's not the same as actually being here. This place is amazing. It's like one big, giant playground."

"That pretty much sums it up. We're staying at Harrah's. It's across from the Mirage, and right next to The Venetian."

He worked his way up to Harrah's and pulled into the entrance. A bellhop rushed up, unloaded the baggage, and handed Jeremy a claim slip. They entered the lobby, checked in, and took the elevator to their suite. Jeremy opened the door and eagerly stepped inside.

"Well hot diggity dog."

There was a separate living room with a wet bar, and inside the bedroom was a king-size bed with a huge, flat-screen television mounted on the wall. They soon heard a knock at the door.

"That's probably our luggage," said Gillian.

She grabbed her purse, but by the time she turned around, Jeremy had already answered and was tipping the bellhop. Gillian gathered her suitcases and hanging bag.

"Thanks, Jer, and if you'll excuse me for a few minutes, I'll freshen up. Then we'll go check out the strip."

She closed the bedroom door. While he waited, Jeremy changed clothes, brushed his hair and pulled it back into a ponytail. He took a look out the window. They had a great view of the strip. He could even see the volcano in front of the Mirage. Gillian soon emerged from the bedroom.

"After you, my dear," said Jeremy.

They exited Harrah's and stepped onto the strip. Jeremy had Gillian take his arm so the crowds wouldn't separate them. They had their choice of restaurants. All were busy and they'd have a long wait, but they were in no hurry. After dinner they went into the gaming area at another hotel, where Gillian found a blackjack table with a couple of open seats. She pulled some money out of her purse and bought some chips. Jeremy followed suit.

"The object here is to see which player can draw enough cards to come the closet to twenty-one, without going over."

"I'm familiar with it," replied Jeremy.

"Okay, then. Go for it."

After playing a few rounds, Gillian lost twenty dollars while Jeremy broke even. They left the table and wandered back onto the strip. The bright lights twinkled against the nighttime sky, creating a carnival-like atmosphere. They wandered in and out of several other hotels until eventually finding their way into a crowded nightclub. Lights flashed and the music was loud. They worked their way to the bar. Jeremy had to shout above the noise.

"I'll buy you anything but a manhattan."

"I'm off those for good. Just get me a glass of white wine."

He returned with a beer and a glass of wine. Jeremy led her onto the dance floor once they finished their drinks. The music was blaring. The drumbeat had an almost primal sound and the lights flashed on the dance floor in sync to the pulsing sound of the beat. The hypnotic rhythm stirred something deep inside of Gillian. She watched Jeremy. His body, strong and masculine, seemed to writhe with the pulsing sound and flashing lights. She wanted him. She didn't care if he was Ian's son or about any future repercussions. She wanted him, and she intended to have him that night. They danced a few more times and she suggested they have a second round of drinks, but after the second glass of wine, she began feeling a little lightheaded.

"You okay?"

"I think so," she replied.

"Let's get you outside into some fresh air."

He whisked her back outside. "I think I should flag down a taxi and take you back to the room."

"No, Jeremy, I'm fine."

"You sure?"

"Yeah. Tonight is the first time I've had a drink since, you know. I think I've shocked my system a little bit. Let's walk around a while longer. I'll be fine."

They stopped to watch the fountains in front of the Bellagio. The fresh air was starting to clear her head. Gillian pulled her camera from her purse and a passerby offered to take a photo of the two of them in front of the fountains. After posing for some pictures, Jeremy decided to take her back to their room.

"Come on, Jer, I'm fine."

"Gillian, it's nearly midnight, and tomorrow will be two weeks since I pulled you out of the pool. You're still recovering. Let's not overdo it, okay?"

She grudgingly agreed. He walked her back to their suite and waited for her to get settled for the night.

"I'm going back downstairs for a little while," he said. "You get some rest. I'll crash on the sofa tonight."

"That won't be very comfortable."

"It's okay."

"No, it's not. I had them bring up some extra pillows." She pulled the bedcover back. They were lined up in a row, down the center of the bed. "This bed is big enough for both of us. I promise I'll stay on my side. You'll be perfectly safe."

"Miss Gillian, sometimes you make me laugh. You really do." He bent down and kissed her on the cheek. "Get some rest. I'll be back later."

He exited the room and headed to the elevator. Arriving on the first floor, he went into the casino, took a seat at one of the blackjack tables, bought some chips, and ordered a beer from a passing waitress. It was just after three in the morning when he returned to the suite. He changed into his sweats and carefully placed the cashier's check, the result of his winnings, into his luggage. He was about to compose an email to Larry when he heard Gillian having another nightmare. He rushed into the bedroom.

"Jeremy?"

He knelt in front of the bed and began stroking her arm. "I'm here. You just had another bad dream."

"I know..."

"You're okay." He wanted to reassure her. "Go back to sleep. I'll come in and join you in a little bit. I'm getting ready to send an email to Larry. I just won five-hundred dollars playing blackjack."

"What?" She sat up and turned on the light. "You're kidding."

"No, I'm not. Here, let me show you."

He went back into the living room, returning a minute later and presenting her with a cashier's check for five hundred dollars. His face was beaming.

"Jeremy, I'm impressed, but let's be careful, okay? You need to hold on to your money for school."

"I'm fine, Miss Gillian. That check will stay safely in my bag, and it'll go to the bank as soon as we get home. I promise."

As he turned to go back into the living room, he spotted her purse on the dresser.

"Would you mind if I borrowed your camera for a minute? I'd like to email that photo of us to Larry."

"Certainly."

He handed the purse to her. She gave him the camera and turned out the light.

"I'll be back in a few minutes."

He took the camera into the living room and downloaded the photos of the two of them in front of the fountains into his laptop. The email he wrote to his brother was short and sweet.

"I'm in Vegas, bro. Just won $500 at the blackjack table, but I brought the real prize with me."

He embedded one of the photos and hit the send button. Gillian was sound asleep when he crashed on the other side of the big, king-size bed.

It was nearly eleven o'clock when he awoke the next morning. He looked around, but Gillian wasn't there. He soon found the note she had left for him in the living room, explaining that she'd reserved a cabana by the pool and that she'd be at the spa for a good part of the day. Showered and shaved, he went downstairs for breakfast, came back and changed his clothes. He'd been relaxing by the pool for some time when his phone rang. His father was calling.

"Hey, Dad. What's up?"

"What the hell do you think you're doing?"

"Well hello to you, too."

"Cut the bull, Jeremy. I know you're in Las Vegas."

"Really? So, did Larry tell you that, or are you still intercepting the emails between him and me? Thought you would've learned your lesson the last time."

Ian ignored the comment. "Look, Jeremy, I'm not in the mood to argue with you, so I'm going to ask you one more time. What the hell do you think you're doing?"

"Well, Dad, right at the moment I'm down at the pool drinking a beer and getting a little sunshine."

"Where is she?"

"Off to the spa, doing whatever it is that women like to do."

"Five-hundred dollars?"

"Yeah, Dad. I took fifty bucks to the blackjack table and it magically turned into five hundred, and—oh—my—God. What did you go and do to yourself?"

"Do you like it?"

"Yeah," replied Jeremy. "I like it. It's a shock, but in a good way."

Gillian had dyed her hair red. It looked bright and vibrant in the early afternoon sun.

Jeremy stood up. "Do you mind?"

"Not at all."

He picked up a lock of her hair to inspect it more closely. "It's going to take me awhile to get used to it, but I love it."

"Well Jer, it was two weeks ago today that I was reborn, thanks to you. I decided it was time to make some changes."

"Obviously."

She noticed his phone lying on the lounge chair. "Sorry Jer, were you on the phone with someone?"

"Oops. Yes. I was. Woman, you are driving me to distraction."

Gillian laughed. "Go ahead and finish your call," she said. "I'll meet you upstairs."

She stepped away and Jeremy picked up his phone.

"Sorry 'bout the interruption, Dad."

"What the hell is going on?" The anger resonated in Ian's voice.

"Nothing, Dad. We're good. Talk to you later."

Jeremy disconnected the phone and headed back to their room.

\* \* \*

Ian could hear the conversation between his son and Gillian. He had no idea what was happening, and it was driving him mad. He was seated in front of the computer in his den. The photo of Gillian and Jeremy, standing arm-in-arm in front of the Bellagio fountains, was on the screen. As soon as he realized he'd been disconnected, he slammed the phone down on his desk and glared back at their images.

"If you two think you're getting away with this, you have another thought coming."

Larry ran to the den, tapped on the door and stuck his head inside. "I just heard you shouting. Are you all right, Dad?"

"No, Larry, I'm not. Do you know anything about what's going on between your brother and Gillian Matthews?"

Larry let out a long sigh. "I guess it's a good thing that you're already sitting down." He paused for a moment. "Jeremy has had a thing for her ever since you took that trip to Oregon to visit Aunt Kat and he took her out for a ride on his motorcycle. At first he wasn't going to do anything about it, you know, out of respect for you. Then you dumped her, so he decided to go over to console her. That was the day she ended up in the pool. Now he's really stuck on her and apparently she's bonded with him as well."

Ian recalled his telephone conversation with Jeremy the morning he told him he'd ended things with Gillian. He remembered Jeremy's warning that if he wasn't careful, someone else would come along and claim her. Now, he realized, Jeremy had been talking about himself.

"How could I have been so stupid?"

"What's that?"

"Nothing," Ian quickly replied. "Did you see the email Jeremy sent you last night?"

"Yeah. Pretty cool, huh?" Larry saw the image on his father's computer and his mood suddenly turned serious. "Dad, I think you should come into my room. My monitor is larger than yours. I need to show you something."

Ian followed Larry into his room. Larry clicked on the email and blew up the photo as large as possible.

"I noticed something a little odd in the photo, so I decided to take a closer look. See that?" He moved the cursor around, pointing out a wedding set on Gillian's left hand. "And look here." He moved the cursor again, pointing to the gold band on Jeremy's left hand.

"Dad, I hate to be the one who has to tell you this, and I'm just as shocked as you are, but Gillian Matthews is now your daughter-in-law. She and Jeremy must have gone off to Las Vegas to get married."

"What? No way! That's simply not possible."

Ian stormed out of the room. Larry hurried after him.

"Dad!"

"Don't bother me right now, Larry," Ian stepped back into the den, slamming the door behind him. He heard Larry's voice in the hallway.

"Damn it. Thanks a lot, Jer. You didn't even have the decency to tell me about it? What the hell have you done?"

Ian spent the next hour calling every hotel on the Las Vegas strip. So far none had a guest named Gillian Matthews or Jeremy Palmer. The next one on his list was Harrah's.

"Yes, I need Gillian Matthews' room please."

He waited for the pause.

"I'm sorry, sir. We have no guest by that name."

"Sorry. Can we try Jeremy Palmer, please?"

There was another pause.

"Yes, sir. Would you like me to connect you to the Palmer's suite?"

"Come again?"

"Mr. and Mrs. Jeremy Palmer. Would you like for me to connect you to their suite?"

Ian felt as if someone had plunged a knife into his heart. "No, that's all right. I'll call back later. Thank you."

Ian let out a prolonged sigh as he closed his eyes and leaned back in his chair. He had no one but himself to blame. It took a few minutes for him to pull himself together before he went back to Larry's room.

"You were right, Larry. I just got off the phone with Harrah's. Mr. and Mrs. Jeremy Palmer are registered there. They must be on their honeymoon. I'm going to take a walk to try to sort through this. I'll be out for awhile. I don't know when I'll be back."

"Wait, Dad. I'll go with you."

"No."

"Dad, don't you go freaking out on me. Why don't you go downstairs? I'll fix you something to eat. Whatever you want."

"No, Larry, but thank you anyway. I'll be back later. Finish your homework."

Ian spent the next few hours walking. He was in such a state of shock that he was completely unaware of his surroundings. By sundown, he was sitting on a bench at a playground in a small park. No one else was around. Gazing at the empty playground equipment in the twilight, he saw and heard the ghostly images of Jeremy as a small child, laughing and playing. How could that innocent little boy have grown into the man who betrayed him? Darkness was soon upon him, but he had no desire to leave. His mind was filled with images of Gillian and Jeremy, laughing and smiling, while they enjoyed the sights and sounds of the Las Vegas strip. Then he saw the two of them, naked together in their bed. Jeremy was making love to her. Would she respond to Jeremy's touch the way she'd responded to his?

"Oh stop torturing yourself, Ian," he said aloud. "It's over and done with and you allowed it to happen. Now you can't undo it."

He couldn't bring himself to leave. His mind was filled with the memory of that long-ago night in his college apartment. Gillian was on the leather sofa, wearing his old yellow bathrobe, and he was making love to her for the very first time. That was the moment he knew he'd found his one true love, and twice he'd foolishly pushed her away. Tonight she was faraway, laying in her marriage bed, with Jeremy for her bridegroom. She had entered a place from where he could never get her back.

The breeze stirred and he heard the leaves rustling on the ground. The cool October night air seeped through his jacket. He knew it was time to return home, to his own empty bed. He finally stood and walked back to the street. He looked around, but nothing seemed familiar. He walked to the nearest corner. He didn't recognize the names of either street. He looked at his watch. It was after ten o'clock. No doubt Larry would be frantic. He reached for his phone and called home. Larry quickly answered.

"Dad, where the hell are you? I've been worried sick. I've been trying to call you for hours, but all I got was your voice mail."

"I know, Larry, and I'm sorry. I needed some time alone, so I powered down my phone. I lost track of the time, and now I'm not even sure where I am."

He read off the names of the two streets making up the corner where he stood. Larry looked it up on Google.

"Good grief, Dad. That's well over five miles from here."

"Can you come pick me up?"

"Does this mean I get my driving privileges back?"

"Well, son, I guess it does. Problem is, your truck keys are locked in my desk, and I have that key with me. You'll have to come in The Beamer. The extra key is in the top drawer of the nightstand next to my bed."

"I'll find it, and I'll be on my way. I should be there in about fifteen, twenty minutes or so. Don't go wandering off. Okay?"

"I won't."

Twenty minutes later the BMW arrived and pulled up to the curb. Larry started to get out.

"Stay there, son. I don't feel like driving." Ian got in the passenger side and Larry headed home.

"Are you all right, Dad?"

"No, Larry, I'm not."

"I'm gonna kill Jeremy when he gets back."

"No, you're not." There was a despondent tone in Ian's voice. "I'm the one who pushed her away. She's been through an ordeal, just like you have, and she's not thinking clearly. Hopefully I can forgive her, someday, but I'm not so sure about your brother. I should have listened to you two weeks ago, Larry. If I had, none of this would have ever happened."

Arriving home, Larry tried to talk his father into eating something, but Ian refused. As soon as Larry went upstairs, he grabbed his phone and sent a rather terse text message to his brother. A few minutes later he received a reply.

"Calm down, bro. Things are not as they appear. You have to trust me. Will explain when I return."

# ❧THIRTY-THREE❧

IAN TOSSED AND TURNED for most of the night. He couldn't get the images of Jeremy and Gillian making love out of his mind. At dawn, he finally dragged himself out of bed, showered, shaved and headed downstairs. Breakfast was waiting, but Larry looked as though he had a rough night as well.

"I sent a text message to Jeremy last night," said Larry.

"Really? Did he respond?"

"Yep. He says things aren't as they appear, and that he'll explain when he gets back."

"He certainly has some explaining to do all right." Ian placed Larry's truck keys on the kitchen counter. "I think you've earned these back, but if you mess up—"

"It won't happen again, Dad. There's nothing quite like thinking that you're about to die to give you a whole new perspective on life."

Ian didn't respond, other than to tell Larry to have a good day and he'd see him that evening. As soon as he arrived at his office, he poured himself a much-needed cup of coffee. He'd just turned on his computer when the phone rang. He heard a woman's voice.

"Good morning, Mr. Palmer. This is Susanna Richardson, Channel—"

"I know who you are, Ms. Richardson."

"Good. So you want to cut to the chase. I like that. I'm working on a story about an associate of yours. Her name is Gillian Matthews."

Ian's guard immediately went up.

"Apparently Ms. Matthews had a recent mishap. Something about getting drunk and falling into a swimming pool—"

"I have no comment."

"Oh come now, Mr. Palmer. Surely you're concerned about water safety and warning the public about the dangers of getting into the water after consuming too much alcohol. If someone as successful and well-respected in the community as Ms. Matthews can have such a—"

"I said I have no comment. Goodbye, Ms. Richardson."

Ian slammed down the phone. He wondered how someone like Susanna Richardson could have heard about Gillian's near-drowning. Perhaps, for Gillian's sake, it was good that she had left town. Too bad it was because she ran off to Las Vegas to elope with Jeremy. He tried to get started on his work, but he was unable to concentrate. As he debated taking the rest of the day off, his phone rang again. This time it was the front receptionist.

"You have a visitor, sir. Her name is Samantha Walsh."

Ian thought he was hearing things. "What was the name again?"

"Samantha Walsh."

"Send her up."

Samantha Walsh. Where on earth had she come from? He'd thought about her over the years. Like his sister, Kat, Samantha was someone whom he could confide in. Her sudden appearance during what had to be the darkest time of his life truly was a blessing. Perhaps he had a guardian angel after all. He soon heard a soft tapping at the door.

"Ian?"

She was standing in the doorway. He stood up and they looked each other over. She was much the same as he'd remembered.

"Samantha? It really is you. Please, come in. You don't know how incredibly happy I am to see you."

They greeted each other with a long embrace before he offered her a chair.

"Ian, all this time I had no idea you were so close by. If only I'd known. I've been living in Colorado for the past eighteen years. By the time I got here, I assumed you'd moved on from Salisbury and Norton. I was so wrapped in my own life that I never tried looking you up. Now I regret it. I know that's not much of an excuse, but at least I'm here now. You really look like you could use a friend."

"I could indeed, Sam."

"Ian, I own a truck-stop diner. It's on the Interstate, just outside Idaho Springs. And you won't believe who came in my door last Friday morning."

"Let me guess. Gillian and my oldest son, Jeremy."

"At first I thought he was her son too, but he wasn't. Imagine my surprise when she told me they were on their honeymoon."

"You mean they were already married?"

"Yes," replied Samantha. "They were both wearing wedding rings. She also had a halfway decent diamond engagement ring."

"Interesting. I just assumed they got married when they got to Las Vegas, but obviously they must have gone to a justice of the peace here. What else did she tell you?"

"Not much, only that she would explain it all later. Ian, what the hell happened?"

"It's a long story Sam, but for now I'll try to keep it short. I got married about a year and a half after you and I last spoke. That's how I got the two boys, but it didn't work out. She just wasn't Gillian, and I managed to make her life miserable because of it. No one could ever take Gillian's place."

"I know. I never did understand why you let her get away all those years ago."

"Suffice to say I was young and stupid," admitted Ian. "Over the years I didn't think I'd ever see her again, but six months ago she had an opening at an art gallery here in town. I saw her picture in the paper and I simply had to see her. I've been divorced for a number of years, as was she, so we reconnected. Everything was wonderful, Sam. We had a second chance and I was going to do it right this time. She moved up here from Phoenix and I planned on being with her for the rest of my life. Then, about two weeks ago, my whole world suddenly turned upside down."

He filled her in on Larry's car accident, his rash decision to break up with Gillian, her near drowning the following day, and Jeremy's heroic rescue.

"My God. You've been through a lot, Ian, and so has she. And I can see why she would have bonded with Jeremy, but marrying him? So soon after you'd ended things with her? That just doesn't make any sense. Gillian can be impulsive at times and she certainly has a bit of a wild side to her, but she's never thrown caution to the wind like this. That woman loves you. I saw it in her eyes the other morning whenever your name came up. Something doesn't smell right. There's more to this than we know."

"Cynthia spent a few days with her, right after the incident in the pool," said Ian. "While she was here, she came to see me, and she told me Gillian wasn't herself. I'm wondering if she's had some sort of mental breakdown."

"When I saw her she was calm, rational, and definitely not in love with your son. I could see that she's very fond of him, but she's certainly not in love. Unfortunately, Ian, I also saw the look in your son's eyes. He's pretty smitten with her, but I'm not convinced it's true love either. Like I said, there's something else going on here, and I intend to find out what it is."

"I appreciate the thought, Sam, but it's too late. They're married. We can't interfere in their lives now."

"It wouldn't be the first time that someone woke up the next morning and realized they'd made a terrible mistake," said Samantha. "So for now, let's just remain calm, wait for them to get back, and we'll figure out a game plan then. Your son's a nice boy, but she belongs with you, Ian, not him. Somehow we'll have to find a way to make this right."

"Sam, you've always been a good friend, and I'm incredibly happy to have you back in my life, especially now. Can I at least buy you a cup of coffee? We've got some twenty years of catching up to do."

"I'd love to Ian, but I have to get back. Duty calls. But I do want to talk to you again, and soon. Let's try to get together sometime in the next week or two."

"Good idea. I'm already looking forward to it."

"You need a friend, Ian, and I'm on your side. Trust me, this so-called marriage to your son won't last. You're going to get her back, and I can help make sure that happens. However, I need to ask you a question first, and you need to give me an honest answer."

"Okay. What is it?"

She paused for a moment. "Ian, they're married. That means they're sleeping together. Are you able to deal with that?"

Ian let out a sigh as he closed his eyes and leaned back in his chair. He hesitated before responding. "That, Sam, is the very question that kept me up most of the night last night. I've thought long and hard about it, and my answer is yes, I'll take her back. I know it'll complicate things, but it's done and we can't go back to change it. It's something that all of us are simply going to have to learn to live with."

Samantha stood up and walked behind Ian's chair. She put her hands on his shoulders and kissed him on the cheek. "I'll leave my card on your desk. You call me the minute they get back. We'll get together then to come up with a strategy. In the meantime, get some rest, my friend, because you're going to need it. You stay here. I can walk myself back to the elevator."

# ⨳Thirty-Four⨲

"**C**AN I MOVE now, Miss Gillian?"

"No, not yet," she replied. "You're going to have to hold on just a little bit longer."

Her pencil flew across her pad. She was working on a sketch of Jeremy with the beach and the San Diego Bay in the background.

"Now?"

"Not yet. Just give me a few more seconds...there, all done."

Jeremy heaved a big sigh of relief as he relaxed and plopped down in the sand. Gillian laughed.

"You know, it could have been worse, Jer. I could have posed you in the buff."

"Now there's a thought." His face began turning red.

"Anyway, here you go." She signed the sketch, tore the paper from her sketchbook and handed it to him. He marveled at it.

"Can I keep it?"

"Yes, Jeremy. I did it for you."

He leaned over and kissed her on the cheek. "I don't know how to thank you."

"It's just a little something from me to you."

He handed it back, asking her to hold onto it for safekeeping. She tucked her sketchbook and tools in her tote bag, leaned back on her towel, and watched the waves roll onto the shore. They'd been in San Diego for a little over a week. They spent their days enjoying the sun and the surf, even taking in some sailing and jet skiing. For Gillian, however, San Diego was bittersweet. It had only been a few months since she'd been on the same beach with Ian.

"I spoke to Paul again today," she said. "It's been a number of days now since anyone's heard from Susanna Richardson, and no story about me ever ran. We're pretty sure it's safe for me to return, and I have to get back. I've gathered a ton of reference material on this trip. Now I need to go back into the studio to start creating some new pieces."

"I know what you mean. I have to be back to work in three days myself. If we leave first thing in the morning, we should have just enough time, but it's gonna be hard. I could have stayed here forever."

"I understand, but it's time for us to go home. And by the way, just so you know, I've also made a decision. I am going home, as in back to Arizona."

"When?"

"When my lease is up, end of next July."

"You're sure that's what you want?"

"I'm positive, Jer. When I first arrived in Denver, my sister and I both thought it would be a permanent move, but things have changed. Paul's done an excellent job running the gallery while I've been away and he no longer needs my supervision. So, come next summer, I'll be leaving Colorado for good."

Jeremy did a quick calculation in his head. He'd have about nine months, and that would be more than enough time to win her over.

"You know, Miss Gillian, a lot can happen between now and then."

"If you're thinking about your father, Jeremy, it won't be happening. Sometimes all the love in the world just isn't enough."

The smile faded from her face as they watched one last sunset over the ocean.

* * *

Two nights later the Jeep pulled into Gillian's driveway. She went to unlock the front door as Jeremy got her bags.

"I guess we got out of here in the nick time." She pulled Susanna Richardson's tattered business card from the doorframe and handed it to Jeremy before she unlocked her front door. He slipped it in his pocket and carried her suitcases inside. She immediately went into her bedroom, returning a moment later with a small, satin, drawstring bag. She removed the wedding set she was wearing and dropped both rings into it before turning to Jeremy and giving him a smile.

"Well, Mr. Palmer, I'll be taking that ring back now, if you don't mind, and you are now, officially, a single man again. Been nice being married to you."

He removed the ring and dropped it into the bag. "Thanks for the honeymoon."

"Anytime. And I'm going to miss you."

She walked him back to his Jeep and gave him a hug.

"I'm going to miss you too, Miss Gillian. Would it be all right if I called you, from time to time, just to say hi?"

"Of course, silly goose. You saved me. You'll always be a part of my life."

She gave him one last kiss on the cheek before he got back in the Jeep and started it up. She stood by and waved while he backed out. He watched her in the rearview mirror as he drove away.

"No, Miss Gillian, we haven't seen the last of one another. In fact, this is only the beginning. But right now, I need to take care of some unfinished business."

A few minutes later he pulled into his father's driveway. He shut the engine down, reached for his phone and called his brother.

"Hey bro. What's up?" Larry's greeting sounded less than enthusiastic.

"Look out your window."

Jeremy watched as his brother peered out one of the second story windows.

"So, when did you get back in town?"

"About a half an hour ago. Is Dad in?"

"Yep."

"Good. Then why don't you come downstairs and let me in. It's time for a little family meeting."

A minute later Larry opened the front door.

"Where's Dad?"

"In here." Larry led his brother into the family room. "Dad, we have a visitor."

Ian looked up. He didn't look too happy to see Jeremy. "So...you're back. Where is she?"

"She's at home, Dad."

Ian started to say something else, but Jeremy quickly cut him off.

"Look, I'm only going to explain this once, so you might want to take some notes. I don't know what you think you may have seen, or what you think you may know, concerning my relationship with Gillian Matthews, but I'm here to tell you that was all a ruse, and it was done to protect her from Susanna Richardson."

"Really?" said Larry.

"That's right, Larry. That night at her gallery, after Dad took you home, I went back to her office to check on her. She was a little startled after seeing Dad, so I wanted to make sure she was okay. Then Paul came in, all flustered. Apparently, someone at the hospital tipped off Susanna Richardson about Gillian's near drowning, and she was planning on doing one of her famous hatchet jobs on her. Would either of you like to venture a guess as what would have happened to Gillian's career, or to Sorenson's gallery, if that had happened?"

The other two men remained silent until Ian finally spoke up.

"Just so you know, Jeremy, Susanna Richardson called me at the office the following Monday."

"Really? So, what did you tell her?"

"I told her I had no comment."

"Thanks. Good to know. You handled it perfectly."

"You're welcome, Jeremy."

There was a hint of sarcasm in Ian's voice. Jeremy continued with his explanation.

"Once we realized she was after Gillian, Paul decided that we'd better get her out of town, fast, so early the next morning she and I got out of Dodge. We both knew Ms. Richardson would try to hunt her down, so Paul came up with the idea of our traveling as honeymooners. She wouldn't know to look for anyone named Gillian Palmer, would she?"

Jeremy reached in his pocket and handed the business card to his father. "This was waiting on Gillian's front door when we got back. Looks like I got her out of town just in time. And since the story never ran, I'd say I did a damn good job of protecting her. Don't everyone thank me at once."

"But what about the wedding rings?" asked Larry. "I saw them in the photo of the two of you in front of the Bellagio."

"All part of the ruse. That was her wedding set from her marriage to Jason Matthews." He raised his left hand and started wiggling his fingers. "See, all gone. We were never actually married."

Larry seemed to be satisfied with the explanation. "You won five-hundred dollars playing blackjack, bro? That's awesome."

"It's all about playing close attention. I'll show you how to do it sometime."

"You mean, counting cards?"

"I wasn't counting the cards, you little twit."

"What did you do with the money, Jeremy?" asked Ian.

"I got a cashier's check, and tomorrow morning it goes into the bank."

"Okay," replied Ian. "Larry, it's a school night."

Larry groaned in protest but didn't argue about it. "It's good to have you home, Jer."

"Likewise. Talk to you later, bro."

Larry made his exit. A cold silence remained after he left. Finally, Ian spoke up.

"Okay, Jeremy, here's the thing. I could ask you, point blank, if you slept with her, but since I'm not seeing her right now, I guess you could say that technically, it's none of my business."

"You got that right."

"And even if I were to ask, you'd probably deny it, and I'm not so sure that I'd believe you. I know you're attracted to her, so don't bother denying that. She's a very sexy, very beautiful woman, and you and I are alike in a lot of ways. I can understand if you're drawn to her, but she's also a good twenty years too old for you."

"Oh come on, Dad. If our genders were reversed, no one would give it a second thought."

"Whatever, Jeremy, I don't care. The point is, I know your interest in her goes well beyond friendship." Ian's eyes bore into Jeremy's. "Well, son, I hate to break it to you, but I'm claiming her back."

"Wait a—"

"No, you wait a minute," growled Ian. "She and I have a long history together, and it goes back long before you were born, which means I've have the home-court advantage."

"Sorry Dad, but she's done with you. She told me that several times."

"I understand she's angry with me." The confidence resonated in Ian's voice. "And right now, under the circumstances, I know I deserve that anger. But she can't stay angry with me forever. At some point, she'll start getting over it. The minute that happens, I'm making my move on her." Once again, Ian bored his eyes into Jeremy's. "And by the way, just so you know, even if you are sleeping with her, I'm still claiming her back. So, my advice to you is this—once I decide I'm ready to take her, you'd better get the hell out of my way. Because if you don't, I'll turn you into road kill."

"Finished?"

"Not by a long shot."

"In that case," responded Jeremy, "I just happened to have spent the past two weeks traveling in very close quarters with her, but I'm not going to tell you if I slept with her or not. That's for me to know, and for you to wonder about."

Jeremy paused for a moment to give his father the chance to fully comprehend it.

"So, you think you have the home-court advantage with her? Please allow me to refresh your memory on that other history you have with her. You dumped her, twice. You broke her heart, twice. The first time she forgave you. The second time we all nearly lost her for good. She's made it quite clear that she won't be giving you the opportunity to dump her a third time. And since I'm the one who saved her life that day, I have a bond with her that you never will. Still think you can win her back? Good luck on that one, Dad. You'll need it."

Ian let out a sigh as he struggled to remain calm. "Jeremy, you're my son. Despite everything you've done, including sleeping with the woman I love, I still love you, and I don't want to see you get hurt. So I'm warning you one last time. Back off. Otherwise, I won't be held accountable for anything that may happen to you."

"Fair enough. Game on. I plan on seeing my brother from time to time, but I'll make a point of doing it when you're not around. Good night, Dad, and good luck."

* * *

Ian eased back into his chair as Jeremy made his exit. He felt a tremendous weight lifted off his shoulders. He realized he'd somehow failed to connect the dots when Susanna Richardson called his office, and he was elated with the knowledge that Gillian had never actually married Jeremy. He knew, deep down, he would get her back. It was only a matter of when. For the first time, in a long time, he would sleep soundly that night.

# ❧THIRTY-FIVE❧

IAN WAS IN HIS OFFICE, going over a set of blueprints, when the phone rang.

"You have a visitor, Mr. Palmer. Samantha Walsh."

"Send her up."

Samantha arrived a couple of minutes later. Her face was beaming. "Ian, sometimes the news is so good that it just has to be delivered in person. Gillian called me last night. She told me the whole story. They're not married. It was just a cover. She was hiding out from Susanna Richardson."

"I know," he gleefully replied. "Jeremy stopped by my house last night too. He said the same thing. I'm going to get her back, Sam."

"Now you're talking. It's time for us to do a power lunch. We have to plan our strategy."

They left Ian's office and walked to the restaurant across the street. Once they were seated Samantha wasted no time.

"The first thing we need to do, Ian, is to find a good distraction for that kid of yours and I have just the thing." She reached into her wallet, pulled out a photo, and handed it to him.

"Wow. Now she's a real looker, and she kind of looks like you."

"Well, she should. She happens to be my daughter."

"You're kidding."

"No, I'm not. Her name is Cassie. Her daddy died before she was born and I had to raise her all by myself. Somehow I managed to do a good job and she turned out pretty straight and narrow. I introduced her to your boy the morning he and Gillian stopped in. I watched him. He was looking her over, in spite of himself."

"And Jeremy's always complaining about all the women he's met being tramps. He's had a few flings, but certainly not with anyone he'd want to make any kind of long-term commitment to. I think that's one of the reasons why he's attracted to Gillian. She's a class act, and he's not experienced anything like that before. He bonded even more with her after the incident in the pool."

"Understandable, and perfectly normal, but he's confusing that with romantic love. They're two entirely different things."

The waitress came to take their orders. Once she left Samantha turned back to Ian.

"Cassie told me she liked Jeremy, a lot, but she also thought he was married. She's involved with someone else at the moment, but it won't last much longer. I'd give it a few weeks, a month or two at the most. Certainly by the first of the year she'll be available. Too bad she's going to school in Colorado Springs."

"UCCS?"

"Yes."

"Sam, that's perfect. Jeremy goes to the same school. He took a semester off, but he's going back in January."

"That's right," she said. "I remember him saying something about working on his degree in electrical engineering. I didn't realize it was the same college she's going to. Well now, that certainly helps."

"So what do we do now?"

"For starters, I'll let Cassie know he's not married. She'll be very happy to hear it." She paused for a moment. "Wait a minute, I just thought of something. Cassie turns twenty-one next month. Where's this place that your son tends bar? I might suggest she go there to celebrate."

"You gotta pen?"

Samantha grabbed a pen from her purse. Ian drew a map on a napkin.

"It's called O'Malley's Grill. Fun place and it's popular with the younger crowd. She'll love it. He's there Tuesday through Saturday." He handed the map to her and over their meal they discussed their children.

"You know, Ian, the more I'm hearing, the more I'm convinced these two are a perfect match for one another. We just need to be patient and let nature take its course. But you realize, this is only the first step. Gillian is still very angry with you and she's completely shut you out. Once Jeremy is out of the picture, you'll still have your work cut out for you, and you're going to have to work fast. She's moving back to Arizona next summer."

"Really? Well then, maybe it's a good thing I'm being forced into early retirement after all. My younger son turns eighteen in January and finishes high school in May. If I have to, I'll follow her there."

She smiled. "That's the spirit."

The waitress delivered their check and they argued over who would pay. Ian eventually won out.

"I'll walk you to your car," he said.

"Thanks. You know Ian, if someone had told me, all those years ago when Gillian first introduced us, that we'd be in-laws someday, I would've said they were nuts. But it's going to happen. I can feel it in my bones. Give it a year, maybe two at the most."

"I hope you're right Sam, but for now, let's not talk about having any grandkids together, okay?"

"Deal."

# ⁓Thirty-Six⁓

**G**ILLIAN ACCEPTED LAURA'S invitation to help with the St. Eligius haunted hayride. It was an opportunity to get to know her client better and perhaps have some fun at the same time. She'd been lonely since returning to Denver. Jeremy had gone back to work and her occasional visits with Samantha were all-too brief. She was gathering up her costume when Jeremy arrived.

"I'm so glad you were able to get the night off, Jer. It wouldn't have been the same without you.

He gave her a warm smile. "I wouldn't miss it. Are you ready to go?"

"Just about. Come on in my bedroom. I'll show you what I've got."

"Well now, that's certainly sounds intriguing, Miss Gillian."

They both laughed as she pointed out the long black dress laid out across the bed.

"I found this the other day at a thrift store. It sort of looks Victorian. And here..." She pulled a long black velvet cape out of her closet. "I've had this forever, so if it gets dirty I won't worry about it. And look, it even has a hood. What do you think?"

"Looks good, but make sure you put on some long underwear underneath it, and maybe a sweater as well. It'll get pretty cold out there once the sun goes down, and wear a pair of gloves."

She opened a dresser drawer, grabbed her long johns and a pair of black leather gloves, and dropped them in her duffle bag, along with a black wool cardigan sweater.

"And here's the best part, Jer." She reached for the shopping bag resting on top of her dresser. "I'm bringing along a make-up kit. By the time I'm done with all of you, you'll even scare yourselves."

She dropped the makeup and the rest of her outfit into the duffle bag and handed it to Jeremy. She stopped to leave some food for her dogs and they headed out to the Jeep. They pulled into Ian's driveway a few minutes later, and Gillian felt herself tensing up.

"Don't worry, Miss Gillian. Larry says he's out and he'll be gone all day."

He grabbed his phone and called his brother. A minute later Larry came out and hopped into the backseat.

"What's this? Jer, I thought she was a blonde."

"She was, but not anymore. She had that done while we were in Vegas."

"Do you like it?" she asked.

"Yeah," replied Larry, "you look hot."

Gillian laughed as Jeremy backed out of the driveway and headed down the street.

"Thanks. It's all part of my rebirth. New look, new life."

"So, you're going to keep it red?" asked Larry.

"Yep, and I've done something else too, but I'll have to show it to you later."

"What's that?" asked Jeremy.

"I got inked."

"What!" For a moment Jeremy looked as though he was going to wreck the Jeep.

"I got inked. I got a tattoo."

"Where?"

"Just above my right ankle."

"Cool," added Larry. "So what'd you get?"

"Interestingly enough, I got something in honor of your father, although I'm not sure why. It's a little red carnation. That was our flower, back in the day."

Jeremy suddenly became quiet.

"You okay, Jer?" she finally asked.

"I'm not sure. That just really surprises me."

A short time later they pulled into a burger joint. Jeremy turned to Gillian as soon as he parked the Jeep.

"Okay. I can't stand it any longer. I gotta see it."

"Suit yourself."

She unbuckled her seat belt, removed her right boot and sock and rolled up her pants leg. She then placed her right leg in Jeremy's lap and turned her foot sideways. Just above her ankle was a little red carnation. It was about two inches long.

"Let me see." Larry leaned forward from the backseat.

"Take a look," she replied.

"Well, I'll be damned," Jeremy finally said.

"Hey kids," said Larry, "can we save it for another time? I'm starving. Then after lunch I can drive, and you two can sit in the backseat and admire it for the rest of the trip."

"Shut up, you little twit."

"Love you too, bro."

Over lunch Jeremy explained that the hayride would actually be at The Flying M. "They'll hitch up teams of horses to the hay wagons, and Larry here is one of the drivers. You know, they even pay him for this gig."

"I work there every summer, dude," replied Larry. "Which means I'm on the payroll and you're not. Live with it."

"Miss Gillian, did I mention that my little brother is buying our lunch today?"

Gillian laughed as Jeremy went on to explain.

"They'll have a maze set up with skeletons hanging from trees, spooky displays, and, of course, some live actors, and the hay wagons drive through it. I'll be wearing a ghostly cowboy outfit with a fake noose around my neck. I'll be on horseback, occasionally buzzing the wagons, and scaring the you-know-what out of them. You'll be stationed somewhere in the maze and you'll have some other volunteers with you. Basically, you run up to the wagons, scream, and they'll scream back. They'll have some portable gas heaters set up behind the maze so you'll have some light and something to help keep you warm while you're waiting. That's all there is to it."

"Sounds like a good time," she said.

"We enjoy it. We've been doing it every year ever since Mom started working there, but there is one thing. We both know the layout of the maze, so please, Gillian, try not to go wandering off anywhere without one of us, okay?"

"Got it."

Larry followed through and insisted on picking up the tab for lunch as Jeremy admitted that his little brother really was growing up. They arrived at St. Eligius Ranch by mid-afternoon and were greeted by Laura, who was already in her costume.

"What did you do to your hair?" she asked.

"Like it?"

"Yeah. You know, I've been thinking about getting mine highlighted."

She took Gillian to one of the extra bedrooms to change. She emerged a few minutes later in the black dress with green makeup on her face. Jeremy thought she looked like a young, sexy version of a witch. She set up her makeup kit on the dining room table.

"Okay, who's next?"

Jeremy stepped up. He was dressed in the creepy cowboy outfit with a noose sewn onto the shirt collar.

"Lovely. Do you want me to put a rope burn on your neck?"

"Could you? That'd be great."

"You bet."

He took a seat and she applied the makeup. The others came over to watch and they all marveled at her work. As soon as she finished, Laura got a mirror and handed it to Jeremy.

"Whoa." He studied his reflection. Along with the rope burn, she'd painted a detailed skull on his face.

"Who's next?"

"Don't look at me," said Larry. "I'm driving the hay wagon. How 'bout you, Mom?"

Gillian did similar makeup jobs on Laura and Will. After checking herself in the mirror, Laura handed Larry her camera to take a group photo.

"That'll go great on the Christmas card." He laughed as the others took turns looking at the image on the back of the camera. Laura finally checked the time.

"Whoops," she said. "We need to get going."

"Why don't you ride over with me, Miss Gillian?" suggested Jeremy. "I'm going over there on horseback. You don't mind riding behind me, do you?"

"Not at all."

They gathered up the rest of their gear and headed out to the barn where Ramon had Pretty Boy saddled up and ready to go. Jeremy unfolded a piece of paper he pulled from his coat pocket. It was a map of the maze.

"Looks like you'll be working with someone named John in this section here." He pointed it out to her. "I'll take you over there."

He mounted Pretty Boy, extended his hand, and pulled her up behind him. By the time they arrived at her station, the sun was setting low in the sky. The gas heater was already lit, but the other volunteer hadn't yet arrived. Jeremy helped her off the horse.

"Do you want me to wait here with you?" he asked.

"I'm good. Have fun, and I'll see you later."

Jeremy rode away. Gillian was warming herself at the heater when she heard footsteps behind her. Someone in a Grim Reaper costume had just joined her, and whoever it was seemed to be staring at her. Finally, he spoke up. Gillian noticed he had a raspy voice.

"I'm sorry. I was told I'd be working with a blonde lady."

"Well, I was a blonde until a few weeks ago. Now I'm a redhead." She extended her hand. "The name's Gillian, by the way."

"John. Pleased to meet you."

They shook hands. John explained that he was one of the locals, and he seemed to be curious about her. The sound of clopping hooves, nervous laughter and chatter told them the first wagon was approaching. Gillian pulled up her hood. At John's cue she ran up to the wagon, calling for help, while he chased after her. Their brief performance brought startled screams from the passengers. The wagon rolled on and they returned to the heater.

"So why would a blonde lady want to become a redhead?" he asked.

"It's a long story. Let's just say I'm celebrating a new lease on life. The old me was the blonde, the new me is a redhead."

As they talked she caught a whiff of something familiar. It was the cologne that Ian always wore. The scent was a distraction, and she had reminded herself that it was a popular brand and other men used it too. John soon became quiet. A short time later another hay wagon came by and they repeated their scary performance in the dark maze. After the wagon left, Jeremy came by to check on her.

"How are you doing?"

"So far, so good. Wait a minute, Jer. It looks like you've got a little smudge. Let me fix it for you."

He leaned down as she removed one of her gloves and gave him a quick touch up.

"There, that's better."

"Thanks." Jeremy wrapped the reins around the saddle horn and reached down with both hands to pull her hood up. "You need to keep this on so you can stay warm. I don't want you catching cold."

"Got it. Thanks, Jer."

"You're welcome. I'll come back a little later to check on you again."

Jeremy rode away. Gillian turned back and noticed John watching her intently. It was starting to make her feel uncomfortable.

"I take it he's your significant other," he finally said.

"Actually, he's my best friend. Probably the best friend I've ever had."

"How so?"

Despite her growing discomfort with his questions, something deep inside told her John was trustworthy. She decided to follow her instincts.

"It's a long, complicated story. I'll just sum it up by saying I wouldn't be here talking to you right now if it wasn't for him. That man literally saved my life not too long ago. I don't remember it, but I'm told I fell into some water and nearly drowned. He's the one who rescued me."

"I see."

"You know, it's kind of ironic. Here I am talking to you, dressed up as The Grim Reaper, when I've met the real thing."

"Was it scary?"

"To tell you the truth, it really wasn't, and it's the only part of the entire incident that I can remember clearly. I was heading toward a light and I wasn't planning on coming back."

"Why not?"

Gillian sighed. "I'd just lost the love of my life. I had no reason to remain here and I wanted to cross over. Then I thought I heard my friend, Jeremy, calling me. The next thing I knew I was back at my backyard pool, only I wasn't in the water. Somehow, I was suspended over it. Jeremy was in the pool and he was holding a body in his arms, which I knew had to be mine. I saw his face. He had a look of shock, guilt and sorrow. He was shouting at me to stay with him, and I knew, right then and there, that if I didn't come back it would destroy his life, so I had no choice. I had to come back, even though I didn't want to. I watched him lay my body out on the deck, and then I felt something like a tug. The next thing I knew he was rushing me to the hospital. That's why I'm still here."

She started smelling the cologne again and she looked at him more closely. The costume he wore didn't reveal much about him. He was wearing a full mask, with a robe and hood, and he appeared to be bundled up underneath it. A strange thought crossed her mind, but it couldn't be. Larry said his father was spending the day in Fort Collins with friends. John remained silent for several minutes. Finally, he found his voice.

"Well...Gillian, wasn't it?"

"Yes."

"Well, Gillian, your life is a precious gift. It's something that you must never, ever take for granted. You may think you came back for your friend, but that's not the reason why you're still here. You're here because your life is far from over, and you're meant to be here. I'm sure your family and friends, and your true love, are elated that you're still with them. And who knows, maybe your true love will return to you someday."

"Thank you, John. I appreciate your insight, but as far as my true love goes, I'm sorry to say that some things just aren't meant to be. Nice thought, though."

"Never say never."

The hay wagons returned several more times, but for the remainder of the evening, John said very little. Gillian was relieved when she finally heard the sound of Jeremy's approaching horse.

"That was the last one," he said. "Are you ready to go, my dear?"

Jeremy extended his hand and helped Gillian get back up behind him. She wrapped her arms tightly around his waist.

"Good night, John. It was nice meeting you."

John waved goodbye as the horse cantered away.

\* \* \*

John listened closely to the sound of the fading hoof beats. Once they were gone he pulled down his hood and removed his mask. He heard his phone going off in his pocket.

"Is she still there?" asked the woman on the other end of the call.

"Jeremy just picked her up. Thanks, Laura. I owe you one."

He disconnected his phone and looked down the maze. Gillian and Jeremy were probably already halfway back to St. Eligius.

"My God, Gilly-girl, what have I done to you?"

## ❧THIRTY-SEVEN❧

JEREMY WAS WORKING a typical Saturday evening shift when he spotted a familiar face standing across the bar.

"Cassie, right? From Idaho Springs?"

"That's me. And you'd be Jeremy. The married guy who wasn't really married."

"That'd be me, all right." He wiped the water spots off a glass. "So, what can I do for you?"

"Well, today's my twenty-first birthday."

"Happy Birthday."

"Thanks. I thought I'd order myself something to celebrate with, but I don't know what to get."

"First timer, huh?"

"Yeah, and I have some friends here with me, which means I have my designated driver." She pointed out three other girls seated at a nearby table." So bartender, what do you suggest?"

"I have just the thing." He filled the glass with ice. "It's called a fuzzy navel. It's peach schnapps and orange juice and I think you'll like it. And just so you know, I have to see your ID."

He checked her driver's license. It was indeed her twenty-first birthday. He mixed her drink and added the garnish, even throwing in a little paper umbrella.

"Thanks. How much to I owe you?"

"It's on me. Happy birthday."

"Well, thank you again."

Jeremy watched her as she rejoined her friends. He overheard bits of their conversation. They were teasing her about coming on to the bartender. She appeared to be out of place with the rest of them. Her three friends were the type he took home from time to time for a one-night stand, but she was different. She was the kind of girl with whom you took your time. The kind of girl you didn't make a move on until she let you know she was ready. In his reality, girls like her were rare. He started getting a bad feeling, so he decided to keep an eye on her. He noticed that she seemed to be watching him as well, and they smiled back and forth at one another. She and her friends ordered their dinners, and afterwards the waitress brought her a piece of cake with a candle as everyone sang "Happy Birthday" to her. It was just after ten o'clock when a seat opened up at the bar. As soon as it did, she came back to order another drink.

"So how was it, birthday girl?"

"It was good." She took the empty seat. "And I think I'll have another."

"Coming right up."

They made small talk while he mixed her drink. As he counted back her change, he noticed a group of guys walking in and joining her friends. They were a rough-looking bunch. All were covered with tattoos and had body piercing. Their leather jackets identified them as bikers.

"Looks like you have company." He motioned toward her table.

Cassie looked behind her and observed the group who had joined them. She was stunned.

"What on earth? Karen said something about wanting to meet up with some guy in Denver. I guess that must be him and his friends, but I had no idea. What was she thinking?"

"So I take it they're not your type."

"Not by a long shot." She turned back to Jeremy. As she did, he noticed two of the bikers were starting to ogle at her.

"Don't look now, but it appears to me that they're trying to decide which one of them gets to sleep with you tonight."

"You've got to be kidding me."

"I wish I was."

Cassie was starting to look nervous.

"It's okay," assured Jeremy. "You just stay right here with me. If they start making trouble, I'll take care of it."

"Thanks, Jeremy. There's no way in hell that I'm going anywhere near them. I don't care if I have to walk home tonight."

One of the girls came up to the bar and handed Cassie her coat. "Time to go. We're heading over to The Crazy Coyote."

Before Cassie responded, Jeremy spoke up. "Sorry, too late. She's coming home with me tonight."

"Really?" Her friend looked Jeremy up and down, and he gave her a strong look in return. She quickly turned back to Cassie. "Well then, good for you. Do you want us to come get you in the morning?"

"No, that's okay. I'll manage. Thanks."

Her friend stepped away and the group left without incident. Once they were gone, Jeremy spoke up.

"Sorry if I put you on the spot, but The Crazy Coyote is a biker bar. Trust me, you didn't want to go there."

"Thanks, Jeremy. I'm so sorry. This is so embarrassing."

"Well, don't be sorry, and don't be embarrassed. You have nothing to be sorry about. Finish your drink, and we'll see about getting you a cab."

"All the way to Colorado Springs?"

"Colorado Springs? Aren't you kind of far from home?"

"Well, as I mentioned before, Karen said something about wanting to find some guy in Denver, and my mom said something about this place, so that's how we ended up here."

"I see," said Jeremy. "Well, at the risk of butting in, you need to find a better class of friends. If you don't mind waiting another couple hours or so, I can probably get out of here early and run you home."

"Are you sure you don't mind, because I'd really hate to impose."

"It's not a problem. Besides, I know my way around Colorado Springs. I go to UCCS. I'm just taking a semester off."

"You're kidding. I go to UCCS too. What's your major?"

"Electrical engineering."

"Funny, you don't look like a geek to me."

"Thank you, I think."

She gave him a grin. "Hey, I'm just giving you a hard time."

Jeremy liked the fact that she had a good sense of humor. "So how 'bout you?"

"English. I plan to be a writer some day, but I'm also studying business administration so I won't starve to death in the interim."

She sat patiently at the bar and finished her drink. It was nearly midnight when Jeremy's boss told him he could leave, and soon they were on the road to Colorado Springs.

"So, what's your story, Jeremy?" She leaned back into her seat as he merged onto the freeway.

"Well, I was born and raised in Denver. I have a younger brother. I played shortstop on my high school baseball team, and of course, I ski."

"I know my mom and your dad go way back, but what about your mom?"

"She and my father divorced right after I moved out. She's now living on a ranch some twenty miles out of Steamboat Springs and she's about to remarry. So what about you?"

"Oh, I think you got an earful about me from my mother the morning you and Gillian stopped in the diner. I'm the bastard daughter of a truck driver who I never got the chance to meet, and it's something I've had to live with my entire life. I love my mom, and I know she did her best, but I missed out on having a dad. I always wanted to have a real family. You know, with parents who were actually married."

As Jeremy listened to her talk he left pangs of guilt over his own father. "I'm sorry, Cassie. Maybe someday you'll end up with a guy who has a good relationship with his father, and then you can have a father-in-law." He paused for a moment. "So are you seeing anybody?"

"I just got done kicking someone to the curb. He was too jealous. Lucky for me, I found out he was interested in someone else, so he's her problem now and good riddance. Right now I plan on taking a break from the whole dating scene for awhile. And you?"

"There's someone whom I've been interested in for sometime, but so far it's not gone anywhere. She's still getting over someone else."

"Was it someone she was serious about?"

"Very. He says he plans to get her back, but she says she won't go."

"I'd be really careful about that one if I were you," said Cassie. "People on the rebound typically don't stay with the next one who comes along. They'll hang around just long enough to lick their wounds and then they move on. And if the guy she's in love with plans to get her back, you can pretty much bet the farm that she'll go back to him, eventually, even if she says she won't. You strike me as a good guy, Jeremy. I'd hate to see you get caught up in a situation like that, because you'll end up with a world of hurt. You deserve better."

Jeremy steered the conversation to a different topic. They discussed their likes, dislikes, wants and desires. Both were surprised to learn they had so much in common. The drive to Colorado Springs ended too soon. Jeremy pulled up to her apartment building and walked her to her door.

"Hey Cassie, it was really great talking to you. I'll be moving back down here right after the holidays. Maybe I can call you sometime. We could go have dinner or see a movie. Just friends. No pressure."

She took a pen and paper from her purse and jotted down her phone number and email address.

"Anytime." She handed the paper to him. "Thanks for coming to my rescue, and Happy Thanksgiving."

"You too, and happy birthday. Good night."

# ஃ THIRTY-EIGHT ஃ

GILLIAN CLEARED THE last of the snow from the driveway before returning to the kitchen and checking the time. Everything was coming together right on schedule, and Samantha and Cassie were due in another hour. She had plenty of time to make a phone call before she changed her clothes.

"Happy Thanksgiving, Jeremy."

"You too."

"So what are your plans for the day?"

"Not much. I'm watching football, and in a little while, I'll nuke myself a TV dinner."

Gillian was astounded. "What? You're joking. Why aren't you spending the day with any of your family?"

"It's supposed to snow fairly heavily later today in Steamboat Springs, and I don't want to risk getting stranded there. I have to work tomorrow."

"Okay, so then why aren't you with your father and your brother?"

"Because my father and I still aren't speaking."

"Jeremy, it's Thanksgiving and he's your father. Please, whatever it is, let it go and call him. I know he'd want to see you."

"I appreciate the thought, Miss Gillian, but I'm afraid it's just not an easy fix."

It was obvious that Jeremy would be spending the holiday alone, and he was too good of a friend for her to allow that to happen.

"Tell you what. I've got a turkey in the oven and there's plenty of room at my table for one more. Why don't you join us?"

"I can't, but thanks anyway."

"Why not?"

"Because, I'd be imposing."

"No, you wouldn't," she argued back. "Samantha and Cassie are coming, and I'm sure Cassie would love to see you. I heard there was some trouble at the bar the other night and you gave her a lift home."

"I just did what I thought was right. While she was talking to me, a group of bikers came in and joined her friends. They were like a pack of hungry wolves and she's a decent girl. Who knows what might have happened to her."

"Well I'm glad you stepped up to the plate. I'm sure her mother would love to thank you too, so why don't you join us? That is, if you don't mind being with three women."

"Would I mind?" His voice sounded upbeat. "Are you kidding? I'd love it, but only if you let me bring the wine, and I know just the wine to bring."

"Good, then it's settled. Come on over when you're ready."

* * *

Jeremy arrived about an hour later with a bottle of premium wine. As he was putting it in the refrigerator, he glanced over and watched Gillian basting the turkey. He thought she looked incredibly sexy. The doorbell rang as she was working.

"Can you get that for me, Jeremy?"

"Of course."

He opened the door and found himself face-to-face with Cassie and her mother. Cassie seemed happy and surprised to see him.

"Well, if it isn't Jeremy, the bartender who took me home."

"And, if it isn't Cassie, with a double entendre. Be careful. I don't want your mother getting the wrong idea and sending a bunch of angry truck drivers after me."

"Won't happen, Jeremy," said Samantha. "I'm grateful that you were there to give her a lift home, although I'd like to kill those idiot friends of hers."

"You and me both." He invited them in and led them to the kitchen.

"I brought pumpkin pies," announced Samantha. She set her bags on the counter. As she exchanged pleasantries with Gillian, she noticed something.

"What the hell is that?"

Gillian's tattoo boldly stood out between her stilettos and the hem of her skirt. She glanced down and gave her friend a nod.

"That," she replied, "is one of my whims. I got it right after I got back from Las Vegas."

"What were you thinking?"

"I'm really not sure. One day I was out running errands, noticed the tattoo parlor, and thought to myself, 'why not?'"

"That's not like you, Gillian. I know you can be a little impulsive at times, but not like this."

"I'm just different now, Sam. It's not every day that you get to come back from the dead you know."

"And you got a red carnation?"

"I know, I don't know why I picked that one, but I did."

Samantha looked at Jeremy. "Your dad was always giving her red carnations, back when they were your age." She turned back to Gillian. "I know why you did that. You want to wear Ian's mark--permanently."

"I guess. Or maybe I just wanted something to remember him by. I'm only going to be here a few more months, Sam, then I'm going back to Arizona."

Their conversation was making Jeremy uncomfortable, although he was covering his emotions.

"Jeremy," said Cassie, "how 'bout going into the living room with me and lighting a fire in the fireplace?"

"Good idea."

Cassie took off her coat. Underneath she wore a pair of tight-fitting pants with a tight-fitting blue turtleneck sweater, hugging her perfect, hourglass figure. Like Gillian, he found her incredibly sexy. They quickly stepped away.

* * *

"You know, Sam," whispered Gillian, "I'm glad to see him with someone closer to his own age. He's a good friend, but sometimes I worry he's seeing a little too much in me."

Samantha wanted to ask her a question, but decided to wait for a better time. Both women stayed in the kitchen and busied themselves with the final dinner preparations. Gillian had set an elegant table and soon the platters and serving bowls were filled to the brim, just waiting to be passed. Over dinner Jeremy announced that he was ready to give his thirty-day notice to his landlord, and that the following week he'd have to spend a day in Colorado Springs looking for an apartment.

"It's been really interesting living in the dump I've been living in, but I'm looking forward to moving on. With any luck I can find something decent."

"I might know just the place," said Cassie. "My friend Sheila lives there. It's nothing fancy, just a little studio apartment in a small complex near the campus, but it's clean, it's quiet, and best of all, it's cheap. She's moving out the end of December, so I'll call her in the morning. Maybe we can work something out for you."

"That'd be great, thanks."

Samantha smiled to herself. It was looking more and more like Jeremy would become a good friend to Cassie. After dessert, Cassie suggested that he take a walk with her to work off some of their dinner.

"Good idea," he said. "Would you two ladies care to join us?"

"Not me, thanks," said Gillian.

"Me neither," said Samantha. "We don't get to hang out together very often. You kids go, and take your time."

Jeremy and Cassie grabbed their coats. Sam and Gillian overheard their discussing the apartment in Colorado Springs as they went out the door.

"They seem to have taken a liking to one another," said Gillian.

"Yes, they have. Gillian, can I ask you something?"

"Of course."

"Exactly what is the nature of your relationship with him?"

Gillian grabbed the wine bottle and refilled their glasses. "Let's go have a seat in the living room."

They picked up their wine glasses and Samantha followed Gillian to the sofa where they made themselves comfortable.

"Jeremy is a very special friend, Sam," explained Gillian. "We got off to a bit of a rough start, but then it worked out. I truly believed that he'd be my stepson someday, but Ian threw the brakes on that."

"Gillian, if this is none of my business just say so, but is there anything more to it than just a friendship?"

Gillian hesitated for a moment. "You mean, have I ever slept with him?"

"Yes."

"Good heavens no. I'll admit that first night we were together in Las Vegas, I had a moment, and I mean a very brief moment, of temporary insanity while we were out on the dance floor. He's a good dancer, I'd had a glass of wine, and I sure thought about it, but nothing happened between us that night, or any other night for that matter. Later on, when I thought about it again, I realized I'd wanted to turn him into another Ian, and I could never use Jeremy like that. He saved my life, Sam. Whoever he eventually ends up with will have to understand that we will always have a very special relationship. It's not romantic, but we share a very special bond—one that will last for both of us for the rest of our lives. So please, Sam, don't worry about your daughter. I'm not going to be jealous of her. In fact, I think they're a good match."

Samantha felt as if a tremendous weight had just been lifted off her shoulders. She gave her friend a knowing smile. "Gillian, do you have a hundred dollars?"

"Of course. Why?"

"Because a hundred dollars says that by next Thanksgiving he really will be your stepson."

"Oh come on, Sam," laughed Gillian. "I can't take your money like that. I'm not taking Ian back. No way, no how."

"Of course not. You just go out and have yourself tattooed in his honor."

Both women burst out laughing, and then Samantha turned serious. "Quit kidding yourself, Gillian. You're going to take him back, and you know it."

"Am not."

"Fine. Then I'll lose the hundred bucks. It'll be the easiest money you ever made."

Gillian gave her friend a smile. "All right then. One hundred dollars says I won't be married to Ian Palmer a year from now."

"You're on." The two women shook hands on their bet and Samantha grinned once more. "Just be prepared to pay up."

Jeremy and Cassie returned a few minutes later and everyone pitched in to help with the clean up. Samantha and Cassie left once the dishes were done. They had a long drive back to Idaho Springs. It was nearly midnight by the time Samantha finally had a chance to compose her email.

"It's all good news, Ian," she wrote. "You can finally rest easy. Gillian tells me she and Jeremy never slept together, and I know her well enough to know when she's telling the truth. Jeremy told us he's moving to Colorado Springs on New Year's Day, and he and Cassie are growing closer as friends. Give it another month or two after that and he should be completely over his crush on Gillian. We both know he and Cassie are perfect for each other. They just don't know it yet. Meantime, future in-law, Gillian still insists she won't take you back, but Ian, she just had herself tattooed with a red carnation. It's right above her right ankle. If that's not a declaration of her undying love for you, then I don't know what it is."

\* \* \*

Ian read Samantha's email the following morning. He felt overjoyed to finally learn his worst fears about Jeremy and Gillian had never come to pass, although he choked on his coffee when he read the part about the tattoo. Once the initial shock wore off, he was intrigued. Still, it wasn't time to celebrate just yet. Not only would he have to find a way to win her back, he was also going to have to figure out how to build bridges with Jeremy. Neither task would be easy, but now that he finally knew the truth, he had hope.

## ஓ Thirty-Nine ஒ

THE DAY IAN HAD dreaded the most was finally upon him. It was his last day at Salisbury & Norton. The timing was like a double-edged sword as it also happened to be the Friday before Christmas--the same day Salisbury & Norton traditionally held its annual employee holiday party. They offered to combine his retirement party with the holiday party, but he declined. Why add the insult of festive lights, Christmas trees and menorahs to having to wear a false smile and pretending to be happy when he wasn't. Ian had devoted half his life to Salisbury & Norton. His plan had always been to leave on his own terms. Now, he was being prematurely pushed out the door, yet another casualty of downsizing in a weak economy.

He spent his final day packing up personal belongings, closing his company email account, taking phone calls from well wishers, and spending time with co-workers who filed in and out of his office to say goodbye. It was a few minutes past three when he shut down his computer for the last time. He let out a long sigh before loading his car and turning in his badge. He felt as strange sensation as he drove out of the parking garage for the last time. It was as if a giant door had suddenly slammed shut behind him. When he arrived home, Larry greeted him with a puzzled look on his face as he carried in a cardboard box full of odds and ends.

"What's up, Dad?"

"Early retirement, that's what." He headed upstairs. "There's another box in my car. Would you mind getting it for me?"

Larry went into the garage and picked up the box in the passenger seat. He noticed a painting in the backseat. He carried the box upstairs to his father's den.

"What's going on? I thought you'd be staying on until next spring."

"That's what I thought too, but apparently it made their accounting easier to have me out before the end of the calendar year, so I'm done. Finished. Kaput. End of story. Twenty-five years with Salisbury and Norton, and now it's goodbye, Merry Christmas, and kiss my ass."

Larry followed his father back downstairs. Ian made a quick exit into the garage, returning a minute later with the painting. Larry noticed it was of an old tractor in front of a rustic old barn. He followed his father into the family room. Ian took a seat in his easy chair, while Larry inspected the painting as it leaned against the coffee table.

"We'll have to find a place to hang it." He examined it more closely. "Gillian Matthews did this?"

"Yep. I bought it at her show at Sorenson's Gallery last April. I had to have it. I don't know how much you remember about your grandparent's farm, but the barn looked at lot like the one in the painting."

"Yeah, I remember, although I don't recall our going there very often."

"I guess that's my fault, Larry. I was the rebel son, and because of that, I avoided your grandfather for many years."

"What do you mean?"

"That farm had been in our family for generations. It had been passed down, from father to eldest son, since the end of the Civil War. When my parents sent me to college, it was to get a degree in business administration, and they sent me to Arizona State because of the reputation of its business school. However, I had no intention of spending my life being a farmer. I wanted to be an architect. It's what I'd wanted since I was younger than you. Little did my father know that Arizona State also had a pretty good architecture college, and once I arrived, I changed my major to architecture. I didn't tell my father that I'd made the switch until the summer before my senior year. Let's just say it didn't go over well."

"What about Grandma?"

"My mother understood," said Ian. "She said I had to do what I thought was best for me, but my father didn't see it that way. Never mind what I wanted, I was breaking generations of family tradition and that just didn't sit well with him. So I decided that I was going to work my way to the top, no matter what it cost me, just to prove to him that I was right. But you know, in the end, it really didn't matter. My father never forgave me, and, as of today, it's all over. I've been officially put out to pasture. I'm sure the old man, wherever he is, is having a good laugh at my expense."

"Somehow I don't think so, Dad. If Grandpa did harbor any ill feelings toward you, Jeremy and I never knew about it."

"I see. So did he ever talk about me to you?"

"Sometimes. And whenever he did, it was always good. I know for a fact that in his own way, Grandpa was proud of you. I could hear it in the sound of his voice. Jeremy says Grandpa once told him times had changed, and that it had gotten to be too hard to pass family farms down. He said he was relieved you went into another line of work."

"You're joking."

"No, Dad, I'm not. Ask Jeremy."

"Then why the hell didn't he ever tell me that?"

Larry shrugged. "I don't know. Maybe he meant to, but he just didn't get the chance."

Ian let out a long sigh. His eyes grew misty and he had to blink several times.

"My father was always distant, and throughout my entire life, there were four simple words that I longed to hear from him, but never did. Those four words were, 'I love you, son.' I guess it just wasn't his way, you know."

"I'm sorry, Dad."

"Me too, and because I didn't have the best relationship with my father, I really tried to make up for it by being the best dad that I possibly could to you and your brother."

"I know that. I know I haven't exactly been the best son either, but I'm trying to do better, I really am. I just wish you'd work things out with Jeremy."

"Your brother and I have hit a big bump in the road all right. Hopefully, someday, he and I will be able to work through it."

"Anyway, about your retirement, don't worry," said Larry. "I have some good news. You know I only have two more classes to go before I graduate, which means next semester I'll be done with school before noon, so I've found a job with better hours. I'll be working as a line cook at the country club starting in January. If you need help paying the bills, just let me know, okay?"

"I appreciate the offer, Larry, but we're fine. I'll still have an income, and between your mother and me, you're covered for college, or culinary school, or both for that matter. I'll be out looking for other work after the holidays. Just make sure you're working won't interfere with your studies."

"It won't. It's only on Thursday, Friday and Saturday nights, and they stop serving food at nine o'clock. I already told them I have to be home no later than ten o'clock, and they understood."

"Well Larry, you've just made your old man very proud of you. So why don't I take you out and buy you dinner?"

"That works. Thanks, Dad."

"We'll both need to start packing as soon as we get home. Tomorrow morning you'll need to drop me off at the airport before you head off to Steamboat Springs."

\* \* \*

Ever since his divorce, Ian had spent Christmas in Oregon with his sister and her family, while his sons spent the holidays with their mother. This year, however, Jeremy was only able to join the rest of his family on Christmas day. The holiday season was a busy time at O'Malley's Grill. He wanted to put in as many hours as possible before his final shift on New Year's Eve. The family spent the day skiing, and after he and Larry finished their final run, they stopped for a cup of hot chocolate while they waited for their mother and Will.

"So how's Ms. Matthews these days, bro?" Larry took his seat as Jeremy sat down across from him.

"She's good. She's spending the holiday in Idaho Springs with her friend."

"You still chasing after her?"

Jeremy let out a long sigh. "I don't know, Larry. Yeah, I still like her and we'll always be close friends, but lately I'm having second thoughts about it ever being any more than that. I really miss Dad, you know."

"He misses you too."

"That's good to hear. Meantime I've met someone else. She's the daughter of Gillian's friend, the one in Idaho Springs. We're just good friends, but you know, the more I'm around Cassie, the more I like her."

"You're talking about Cassie Walsh, right?"

"Yeah," replied Jeremy. "How did you know?"

"Because Dad took me to the truck stop a couple of weeks ago and I met Cassie and her mother. Damn, Jer. She's good looking and she has a sweet personality to go with it. So there I was, trying to make a really good impression on her, and I struck out. All she did was ask me about you."

"You don't say."

"Yep. For reasons I'll never understand, she seems to like you, bro."

"Well, for what it's worth, I've driven down to Colorado Springs a few times to see her. Like I just said, we're becoming good friends."

"Just friends?"

"Yep. Just friends."

"How long have you known her?"

"I met her a couple months ago," explained Jeremy. "Gillian and I stopped at the diner for breakfast on our way to Las Vegas. She had no idea that her long-lost friend owned the place, and while we were there Samantha introduced us to Cassie."

"Well bro, now you've got me more than a little concerned about you. I know you, and by now you should have carved a notch on your bedpost with Cassie's name on it. And since you haven't, it means you're taking your time, which means you're really falling hard."

"Larry, she's not a tramp, okay. We're just good friends. That's all."

"Whatever, Jer. All I'm saying is she's good looking and she likes you, but if you wait too long someone else will come along and beat you to her. And by the way Jer, just so you know, I overheard you and Dad arguing the night you got back from Las Vegas. You're stepping in Dad's turf and you need to back off. You just told me you're having second thoughts and that you miss Dad. That's your conscience talking to you. It's telling you that it's time for you and Dad to put this behind you and start acting like father and son again."

"Well thank you, Dr. Larry. I'll think about it, okay."

"You do that," replied Larry. "It would be really nice if I could start the New Year with my father and brother speaking to one another again."

"Sorry bro. I know you've been caught in the middle here."

"Don't be sorry. He's our dad. Just do what's right."

## ❧Forty❧

JEREMY CLOCKED OUT of O'Malley's Grill for the last time on New Year's Eve. At high noon the following day, Gillian, Larry and Cassie rendezvoused at his house. They helped him pack and load his belongings before they headed for Colorado Springs. He'd been able to lease the apartment Cassie had told him about and it was a major improvement over his living conditions in Denver. They'd barely finished unloading into the new apartment when two of his buddies showed up with a case of beer. Gillian and Larry said their goodbyes, while Jeremy asked Cassie to stay.

The following day Larry picked his father up at the airport. As soon as Ian arrived home, he changed into his work clothes, borrowed Larry's pickup truck, and drove to the nearest home-improvement store. It was time to put the house on the market and he planned to spend the next few weeks revamping every room.

Gillian had another show at Sorenson in January and once again the newspaper wrote a nice article. Ian wasn't there, but, as always, he clipped the article and placed it in the folder with the others. Now it was time to return to her studio to produce the painting she had promised for the St. Eligius auction. Paul and Rosemary teamed up with Laura to plan the publicity, and the result was a feature article in a local magazine. Gillian looked forward to attending the gala, and Jeremy volunteered to be her escort. It would be her first time seeing him since his move to Colorado Springs. She had just finished dressing when he arrived.

"You sure look handsome in that suit," she said. "And how's Cassie?"

"Thanks, and Cassie's been down with the flu all week."

"Sorry to hear that. Is she feeling any better?"

"I think she will be a few more days. Meantime, as long as I'm in town, I thought I'd stay over the weekend with Larry and see if I can work things out with my father while I'm at it."

"Well it's about time, Jer."

As they were talking, she noticed he looked a little pale.

"Are you feeling okay?"

"I think so, but something I had for lunch today sure seems to be disagreeing with me."

"Seriously Jer, if you're not feeling well I can go on my own."

"Trying to get rid of me, aye?" he said, mockingly. "Gillian, I'm fine. I just have a little upset stomach, that's all. I'll have a soda as soon as we get there and I'll be okay. Besides, I haven't seen you in awhile and I've missed you."

"Me too. I'll get my coat."

Jeremy had a soda once they arrived, but he still looked a little pale. When dinner was served, Gillian noticed he hardly touched his food. Laura saw it too and mentioned that she thought he might be coming down with something. Jeremy, however, insisted it was simply an upset stomach. The auction began shortly after dessert. Gillian's painting of a magnificent black stallion running through a lush meadow garnered one of the highest bids of the evening. After the painting sold, Gillian looked back at Jeremy. His pallor was worse than before. She turned to Laura.

"He's definitely not feeling well," she whispered. "Would we be breaking protocol if we left early?"

"Not at all. I'm stuck here for the moment, but I'll call you as soon as the auction's over. And Gillian, thank you."

"You got it." She turned to Jeremy. "Come on, I'm taking you home."

"Go with her, son," said Laura.

"Thanks Mom. Sorry I'm not able to stay."

"Don't worry, just get better."

Jeremy insisted on driving the Jeep back to Gillian's house, but after a few blocks, he abruptly pulled into a gas station and quickly ran behind the building. He sheepishly returned a few minutes later.

"I'm so sorry, Miss Gillian. I must be sicker than I thought. Would you mind driving the rest of the way?"

Gillian got out and walked to the driver's side of the Jeep. Once Jeremy was settled in the passenger seat she felt his forehead.

"Jeremy, you're burning up. I think you've come down with the flu."

"Damn. This is how it started with Cassie, but I don't want you to get it."

"I'm fine, Jer. I had my flu shot. Was your father expecting you tonight?"

"No, he wasn't, but Larry was. I was going to surprise my dad. Guess I'll have to try again another time. If you don't mind, I'll rest up at your place for a little while, then I'll head home."

"Jeremy, if you're not up to driving a few miles to take me home from the auction, then you're definitely not well enough to drive all the way back to Colorado Springs tonight. Let's just get you back to my place and we'll put you to bed in the guest room."

For once Jeremy didn't argue. He sent a text message to his brother while Gillian drove. When they arrived at her place, she got his bag and laptop, helped him settle in the guest room and gave him a dose of liquid nighttime cold medicine.

"Thanks, Miss Gillian."

"Don't mention it. You took care of me when I needed it, so now it's my turn. That's what friends are for. Do you need anything else?"

"No, I'm good. I think I'll just turn in. Goodnight, Miss Gillian, and thank you."

"Goodnight Jeremy. Let me know if you need anything, okay?"

"Will do."

She closed the guest room door and let the dogs out. After they came back in, she got ready for bed. She had just put on a flannel nightgown when Laura called.

"How's he doing?"

"I'm afraid he's come down with the flu," explained Gillian. "He mentioned one of his friends having it. He's not in any condition to drive back to Colorado Springs tonight, so I've put him up in my guest room."

Gillian was suddenly interrupted by an unexpected knock at the door. She tried to quiet the dogs so they wouldn't disturb Jeremy.

"Laura, I've got someone at my door. Would you mind staying on the line?"

"Certainly."

Gillian turned on the porch light and looked through the peephole. "Damn. It's Ian."

"Would you mind letting me speak to him?"

"Of course." She opened the door and handed the phone to Ian. "It's Laura. She wants to talk to you."

Gillian turned and walked back into the kitchen. Ian followed as he continued the conversation with Laura. He soon ended the call and handed her phone back.

"Well, you've certainly made a friend in her. She really appreciates your stepping up to take care of him, as do I."

"You're welcome." Gillian's voice was cool. "He's in the guest room."

"Thanks. Oh, by the way, love the red hair, not that you didn't turn me on when you were a blonde."

Duke and Daisy followed Ian as he stepped into the guest room to check on Jeremy. Gillian put the teakettle on to heat. A couple minutes later he came back into the kitchen.

"He's out like a light, but I can tell he's got a fever. By the way, both dogs are up on the bed with him."

"That's fine. I gave him a dose of cold medicine a little while ago. With any luck he'll sleep through the night, but I'll go back and check on him before I turn in."

She reached into the cupboard for a couple of mugs. "Ian, I think you and I need to have a little talk. I want to clear the air with you about something."

She made some herbal tea and motioned for him to follow her into the living room. Seated on the sofa, she looked him in the eye. "Okay, Ian, I'm going to venture a guess and say that your falling out with him has something to do with me and that you're probably thinking I've been sleeping with him, haven't you?"

"Gilly-girl, this isn't the time or place."

"Yes, Ian, it is. So allow me to put your mind at ease. We do share a special bond. It has to do with his fishing me out of the pool the day I nearly drowned, but believe me when I tell you that I never, at anytime, did the deed with your son. Satisfied?"

"I appreciate that, Gillian. However, the trouble between us started when I intercepted an email between him and his brother. It was two days after Larry's accident, and it was a time when I had to closely monitor Larry. Imagine my surprise when I found out something that I apparently wasn't supposed to know about, and that something was that you had nearly drowned that day. You never could keep a secret from me, Gillian, and damn it, I had a right to know."

"No Ian, you're wrong. I had no obligation to tell you anything. You'd just ended it with me, remember? From that day forward, whatever may or may not have happened to me, or whatever I did or did not do, was none of your concern."

"Gillian, I overreacted and I made the biggest mistake of my life. For months now I've been trying to figure out a way to reach out to you, but you've completely shut me out. My God, Gillian, you nearly died because of something I did."

"Let's not go there, okay Ian? It happened. It's in the past and now it's time to move on."

"Oh no, you're not walking away that easily. We're going to work through this."

"No, we're not," she replied. "I'm the one who decided to go on a drunken binge, not you."

"The reason you went on that binge was because of me. I completely blindsided you and I take full responsibility for what happened to you as a result. I know the only reason that you decided to come back from the other side was so Jeremy's life wouldn't be destroyed, and I'm--"

"How could you possibly know that? There was only one person who I ever told that to."

The wheels began to turn in Gillian's head. She looked Ian in the eye as the realization slowly dawned on her. "You sneaky, underhanded, son of a—. It was you! You were the one in the Grim Reaper outfit in the hayride maze!"

"Keep your voice down. You'll wake Jeremy. But surely you knew that Ian is the Scottish name for John."

"What the hell were you thinking, Ian?"

"I had to see you Gilly-girl. I had to see for myself that you were all right, and at the time, that was the only way I could do it. Do you have any idea how it felt for me to hear you say that because of me, you thought that you had no reason to go on living? That you wanted to cross over, as you put it, and not come back?"

Ian's voice started to shake. He paused for a moment while he took a deep breath and tried to pull himself back together.

"We're talking about your life, Gillian." He spoke more slowly and with a somewhat calmer voice. "About you're living or dying. That's kind of a big deal to me. I'm trying to reach out to you. I'm trying to tell you that I deeply regret what I did. Gillian, I'd sell my soul if it meant that I could go back in time and undo what I did that day when I came over here and told you it was over. Good Lord, I'd almost lost my son and I wasn't thinking clearly. But I want you to know that I still love you, and that I intend to make it up to you, even if it takes me the rest of my life to do it."

"Ian, I accept your apology, but I can't take you back. Jeremy will be here for the next few days. You are, of course, welcome to see him, but please call me ahead of time so I can step out before you get here." She stood up and began walking away. Ian was on her heels.

"Oh no you don't. You're not shutting me out again."

She spun around and faced him. Her eyes were welling up with tears. "Oh yeah," she hissed. "Just watch me."

She stormed into her bedroom. Ian was right behind her. "Damn it, Gillian." He closed the bedroom door behind him.

She turned around and faced him again. "What the hell do you want, Ian?"

He grabbed her by the wrists and pulled her close. "This."

He kissed her, hard and passionately. Gillian struggled against him, but the more she struggled, the tighter he held her. When he finally came up for air, Gillian was breathing hard. He came back for a second kiss. She still struggled, but her resistance was beginning to wane. He stopped to unbuckle his belt. She watched him, but said nothing. He saw she was still breathing heavily. She knew what was coming. Part of her wanted to push him away, but another part of her wanted him, just as it always had. In that moment, that part of her was in charge. She offered no resistance as he took her in his arms and passionately kissed her a third time before he turned down the bedspread and pulled off her nightgown. He picked her up and laid her across her bed. She watched him undress. He joined her in her bed and kissed her again. He began kissing her breasts. Gillian moaned in pleasure as his hands began exploring her further down. He pulled her legs apart and as he entered her, his mouth covered hers. Before long she climaxed, and he followed right behind her.

"So Gilly-girl," he finally whispered, "Do you still want to shut me out?"

"This doesn't change a thing, Ian," she whispered back. "I just had a moment of weakness, that's all."

"Oh really." He sat up. "If that's what you want to believe, then go ahead. But at some point, Gilly-girl, you're going to have to quit lying to yourself."

"I'm not lying."

"Of course not." He grabbed her right ankle and kissed her tattoo. "But this little red carnation tells me an entirely different story. And I love it, by the way."

Gillian lay quietly in her bed and watched him dress. When he was done, he kissed her once more before opening the bedroom door.

"Good night, Gilly-girl." He stood in the doorframe. "We'll have to continue this conversation later. And don't worry about getting up, I can see myself out."

\* \* \*

Jeremy awoke to the sound of his father's voice. He heard Gillian's bedroom door closing and the sound of his father's footsteps walking toward the guest room. They stopped in front of his door. He closed his eyes while his father stepped in to check on him. After he left, Jeremy heard the front door open and close, and the sound of his father getting into his car and driving away. He let out a sigh.

"Well, I'll be damned. The old man won out after all."

# ❧FORTY-ONE❧

GILLIAN TAPPED ON the guest room door.
"Come in."

She slowly opened the door. Jeremy was lying in bed with the two dachshunds curled up next to him. He face still looked pasty.

"How are you feeling this morning, Jer?"

"Like I just got hit by a freight train."

She reached down and felt his forehead. "You're still running a fever."

"Tell me about it. I've got chills, I have no energy, and my entire body aches."

"Unfortunately Jer, it's going to have to run its course."

Jeremy groaned as she stepped out. She soon returned with a glass of orange juice and a paper cup with a couple of pills.

"This is some over-the-counter stuff that will help your symptoms. Other than that, and bed rest, there's not much we can do. Can I fix you anything to eat this morning?"

Jeremy sat up, took the pills and drank the juice. "Not yet, but thanks. Gillian, can I ask you something?"

"Of course."

"Was I dreaming or was my father here last night?"

Gillian let out a sigh. "He was here. He stopped by to check on you, but he didn't stay for very long."

"Really?"

"Yes. You were asleep."

"Was that all?"

Gillian turned a faint shade of pink. "He and I had a talk, and I'm afraid I may have spoken my mind a little too loudly once or twice. Sorry if it disturbed you."

"It's okay. I just wanted to make sure that you're all right."

"I'm fine, Jeremy. Really."

"You're sure?"

"Positive." She picked up his glass. "I'll bring you more orange juice, and then you need to get some rest. I'll come back to check on you later."

Just as she returned with the orange juice, she heard a car pulling up in the driveway. She set the glass down and looked out the window. It was Ian.

"And speaking of the devil."

"You okay?"

"I'm fine." She sounded nervous. "In fact, his timing is perfect. I need to run to the grocery store. I'll be back soon." She stepped out and closed the door behind her.

"You're fine? Yeah, right," muttered Jeremy.

\* \* \*

Gillian put on her coat, grabbed her purse and opened the front door just as Ian was approaching.

"He's awake. You two need some time alone, Ian, so I'm going out for awhile."

"Wait a minute. Gillian!"

He was too late. By the time he entered the house, she'd already exited toward the garage.

"Damn it woman, you're driving me insane." He shook his head as he knocked on the guest room door.

"Come in, Dad."

Ian slowly opened the door and stood in the doorway. He and Jeremy silently stared at one another before Ian finally spoke up.

"Good morning, Jeremy. How are you feeling?"

"Like road kill."

Ian recognized the inference, and there was another awkward silence between the two men. "Would you mind if I sat down?"

"Help yourself."

Ian took a seat on the edge of the bed. "Jeremy, I owe you an apology."

"For what?"

"For not trusting you when I should have. You saved Gillian's life. You have every right to feel protective of her, especially when I'm the one responsible for her ending up in the damn pool in the first place. You also did the right thing when you whisked her out of town to protect her from Susanna Richardson. And since I'd ended it with her, at least for the time, whatever may or may not have happened between the two of you really wasn't any of my business."

"But I'm just as much to blame as you, Dad." Jeremy sat up. "She's an amazing woman. Yes, there was a time when I wanted her for myself, but that time has passed. Did you know that right after we got back from Las Vegas she got herself tattooed?"

"I seem to recall hearing something about that."

"It's a red carnation. Apparently that has some meaning for the two of you."

"Yes, son, it does. Red carnations were our flower."

"That's what she told me as well. The first time I saw that tattoo I knew she'd always be yours, but it took me awhile to accept it." He paused for a moment and let out a sigh. "And there's another reason why I've decided to stop pursuing her. Losing you was just too high a price to pay. I've really missed you, Dad."

"I've missed you too, Jer." He gave Jeremy a hug. "Welcome home, son." Ian gave him an extra squeeze.

"Dad, I want you to understand something. I never slept with her. Not that I wasn't tempted, but nothing happened, okay. Sorry I led you to believe otherwise."

"It's okay, Jeremy. She told me the same thing last night."

Jeremy was starting to look chalky.

"You okay, son?"

"Not really. I'm feeling kind of light headed."

Ian spotted the glass of orange juice and handed it to Jeremy. Once he drank it, he settled back down in the bed.

"I need you to understand something, Dad. Because I saved her life, there will always be a special bond between us. For as long as we're both alive, I'll always be looking out for her best interests."

"I'm fully aware of that, Jeremy. You didn't just save her life. You brought her back from the dead. Because of that, the two of you share something I won't. I've accepted it."

"I'm glad you did." Jeremy paused for a moment. "Dad, I heard you coming out of her bedroom last night and she's acting a little squirrelly this morning. I'm going to venture a guess and say that you got to see the tattoo, didn't you?"

"Yes, I saw the tattoo. I meant it when I said I was claiming her back."

"And I understand that. Believe it or not, I'm on your side, because I've come to realize that she'll never be truly happy again until the two of you can work things out. But, she's built one hell of a wall around herself. If you want to rebuild her trust, then you're going to have to be patient and let her work through it." Jeremy closed his eyes and sighed. "I love you, Dad, but you need to go home. I have to get some rest, because right now I feel like death warmed over."

Ian leaned down and gave Jeremy a final hug. "I love you too, son, and it's good to have you back. We'll talk more when you're feeling better."

"Thanks, Dad. And would you mind giving Mom a call for me? I know she and Will stayed in town overnight and she probably wants to see me before they head home, but I'm just not up to anymore company today. Tell her I'll call her later, okay."

"Will do."

"Thanks, Dad."

Ian stepped out and called Laura. By the time he returned, Jeremy had gone back to sleep. He left a fresh glass of orange juice on the nightstand and headed home.

# ❧Forty-Two❧

JEREMY SPENT THE NEXT few days recuperating in Gillian's guest room. He went online and tried to keep up with his studies as best he could, but he still tired easily. His spirits lifted the night Cassie called to say she was well enough to return to class. They talked for over an hour. When they finally hung up, Jeremy returned to his laptop, only to find himself unable to concentrate. He was staring out the window, thinking of Cassie and watching the snowfall, when his phone rang again. This time it was Larry.

"Hey bro, what's up?"

"Jeremy, we have a problem and I'm not sure what to do."

"What's wrong?"

"It's Dad. Now he's got the flu and he's really sick. I just went to check on him and he's delirious, so I called the emergency room. Between the flu outbreak and the snowstorm, they told me it could take as long as eight hours before a doctor could see him. So what do I do now?"

"I don't know, Larry. I'd come over, but I'm still down myself, so let me think for a minute...did you try giving him some cold medicine?"

"He's completely out of it, Jeremy."

Jeremy got up to look for Gillian. He found her in the kitchen.

"What are you doing out of bed?"

"Larry says Dad's down with the flu and apparently there's a problem. Larry's beside himself and I'm not in any condition to go over there."

"Is that Larry on the phone?"

Jeremy nodded.

"Let me talk to him."

Jeremy handed the phone to her and headed back to bed. She knocked on his door a few minutes later and handed him his phone.

"I have to go help your brother. I'll be back as soon as I can, but with this snowstorm, it might take me awhile. Can you manage on your own for a few hours?"

"I'll be fine, but take the Jeep." He gave her the keys. "You'll never make it in the minivan."

* * *

It was snowing so heavily that it took her a good half-hour to reach Ian's house. When she finally arrived, Larry immediately rushed her upstairs. Ian was huddled underneath the bedcovers and appeared to be asleep. She gently touched his shoulder.

"Ian?"

"Hey, Gillian." He slowly opened his eyes and smiled at her. "What's up? Why are you here?"

"Larry called me. He said you're really sick."

"Larry? Larry's here? I thought he was at work."

"I'm right here, Dad."

Gillian felt his forehead and looked back at Larry. "He's really burning up. We'll have to do something to bring his fever down."

She stepped into the bathroom, filled the sink with cold water and dropped in a few washcloths. When she came back into the bedroom, she turned the bedcovers down and began removing Ian's pajama top.

"I'm going to apply some cold compresses," she explained. "This may take awhile, but he'll be okay."

"Do you need anything?"

"Later on, I'll need you to bring a pitcher of water and some cold medicine, if you've got it."

"Will do."

Larry stepped out as Gillian went back into the bathroom. She returned a minute later and started applying the compresses.

"There, now, doesn't that feel better?"

"Gilly-girl, what are you doing here?"

"Larry called me. You have the flu, Ian. I have to get your fever down."

"Larry's here?"

"Yes, Ian. He's here."

She found a fever thermometer in the medicine cabinet. His

temperature was indeed very high, and while she didn't want to alarm Larry, she feared she would have to call the paramedics if she was unable to get his fever down. She spent the next hour applying the compresses and rechecking his temperature. Much to her relief, his temperature finally started to drop. He opened his eyes again.

"Gilly-girl, what are you doing here?"

"You have the flu, Ian. You were running a high fever. You were even delirious. Larry got scared and he called me."

"I know I have the flu. I must have caught it from Jeremy. I thought I heard your voice a little while ago, but I thought I was dreaming. I guess I must have been really out of it."

"You were, but only for a little while. You're doing better now. Your fever's going down and you're going to be okay."

He reached over and squeezed her hand. "Thank you, Gilly-girl."

"You're welcome."

"See, we can actually have a civilized conversation with one another."

"Please don't read anymore into this than what it is, Ian. Larry needed help, so I came."

Ian chuckled. "Whatever you say, Gilly-girl." He squeezed her hand again.

A short time later she removed the last compresses, helped him into a fresh pair of pajamas, and parked him in a chair while she changed the bedding. Once he was settled back in bed, Larry knocked on the door.

"How's he doing?"

"Much better," replied Gillian. "Come in and see for yourself."

"Thank goodness. Dad, you really had me scared there."

"I'm okay, Larry, all things considered."

"He needs his rest," said Gillian. "I think we're ready for you to bring something for him to drink, and then I'll sit with him for a little while."

"You got it." Larry stepped away.

"So how's Jeremy doing?" asked Ian.

"Much better, but he's not quite well enough to go home just yet. Probably will be in another day or two."

"I can't thank you enough for taking care of him."

"He's a friend, Ian. Like I said before, Jeremy took care of me after I fell in the pool. It was my turn to take care of him."

Larry soon returned with a pitcher of juice. Gillian stepped into the bathroom and found a bottle of ibuprofen. After Ian took the pills, Larry left again.

"I think you'll be okay now, Ian. You need to get some rest and I have to go check on Jeremy."

"Gillian, before you go, would you mind laying down here with me? I just need to hold you for a little while."

She hesitated for a moment before she climbed on the bed. Ian wrapped his arm around her and pulled her in close. Once he drifted off to sleep, she carefully inched herself away and headed downstairs. Larry was waiting for her.

"He's gone back to sleep," she said, "but you'll need to check on him later on."

"I will. Thanks for helping."

"You're welcome. Hopefully his fever won't spike again, but if it does, call me. Meantime make sure he drinks plenty of fluids and stays on the ibuprofen."

"I will, and thanks. I was about to make some hot cocoa. Would you like a cup before you go?"

"Thanks Larry. I think I will, but I can't say too long. I need to get back to your brother."

She followed him into the kitchen and took a seat at the breakfast bar.

"By the way," he said, "I don't mean to sound ungrateful, but I'm surprised you came."

"You needed help. It's a scary thing when a parent becomes seriously ill. I wasn't about to leave you on your own. I just hope that you don't come down with the flu as well."

"So far so good."

"Seriously, Larry, if you start feeling ill, call me. He's going to be down for at least a week, and if you get sick, he won't be able to take care of you."

He opened the refrigerator door and took out a large plastic container. "I made something for Jeremy. It's our grandmother's famous Italian wedding soup. It's his favorite. I meant to drop it off at your place, but then Dad got sick. Would you mind taking it to him?"

"Thanks, Larry, I'd be happy to. " She smiled. "You know, I remember when your father used to make this, back when we were in college. It was delicious."

He glanced at the microwave clock. "It's getting late, and I think it's finally stopped snowing. Drink your cocoa. I'll go shovel the snow off the driveway."

She checked on Jeremy as soon as she arrived home and found him fast asleep. She went into the kitchen and heated up a bowl of the soup before going to bed and collapsing into an exhausted sleep.

# ᴥFORTY-THREEᴥ

**A** FEW DAYS LATER Jeremy finally felt well enough to return to Colorado Springs. Before stepping out of the guest room for the last time, he sent Cassie a message to let her know he was on his way home and that he hoped to see her soon. Gillian walked him out to the Jeep.

"Here we are, parting again."

He smiled in agreement. "Seems to happen a lot with us. I don't know how to thank you."

"Hey, that's what friends do. We take care of one another. Just take it easy for awhile and don't overdo, okay? I don't want you to have a relapse."

She gave him a hug before he climbed into the Jeep and started it up. As the engine warmed up he turned to her.

"Miss Gillian, would you do me a big favor?"

"Sure. What is it?"

"Will you at least think about giving my dad another chance?"

"I don't know, Jer. You know I'm only going to be here a few more months."

"Hey, a lot can happen in a few months, and I think he's learned his lesson. Will you please just think about it?"

"Okay, I'll think about it, but only because we're such good friends."

They said one last goodbye before he backed out of the driveway and headed down the street. He'd miss Gillian, but he looked forward to returning home. As he merged onto the freeway he suddenly felt a strange sense of anxiety and anticipation that he didn't quite understand. He'd only planned to be away for a weekend, but he ended up being gone for over a week. Of course he'd feel anxious about returning home. As he drove and the miles to Colorado Springs diminished, he kept seeing Cassie's face. Again he rationalized it away. She was, after all, a good friend. He hadn't seen her for some time, so, naturally, he would have missed her. He decided that if he didn't hear back from her in the next day or two he'd have to call her. Maybe they could get together sometime to see a movie.

He felt happy and relieved once he arrived home, but as he unloaded the Jeep, his anxiety returned. He brushed it off as a residual effect from the flu. He unlocked the door and was relieved to find the apartment exactly as he'd left it. Maybe that explained the strange way he was feeling. He cranked up the furnace, unpacked his bag, and had just finished lighting a fire in the fireplace when he realized he was hungry. Warming his hands over the fire, he thought about ordering a pizza, but before he could act, he heard a knock at the door. He opened it and saw Cassie's smiling face.

"Hey, you." His face was beaming as he smiled at her in return. "You must have gotten my message."

"Sure did." She stepped inside and set a couple of grocery bags on the table. "I figured you probably didn't stop at the store on your way back, and that whatever is in your fridge is growing fur by now, so I brought us a chicken dinner and a bottle wine. Nothing fancy, I'm afraid."

"Thanks, Cassie." He inspected the bottle. "Actually, you did well. It's the same brand as the house wine O'Malley's served." He fetched a couple of wine glasses and uncorked the bottle.

"You're a good friend, you know that."

She smiled. "That's what they tell me."

He filled the glasses and handed one to her. Over dinner his strange anxiety came back and it felt stronger than before. Once again, he shrugged it off as an after effect of the flu and being away from home. Dinner finished, he refilled their wine glasses, threw another log on the fire, and spread a blanket on the floor in front of it. They sat down on the blanket and sipped their wine. She looked even more beautiful in the firelight, and several times he had to fight the urge to kiss her.

"Hey Jer, can I ask you a question?"

"Sure."

"You don't have to answer if you don't want to, but lately I've been wondering about something. Whatever became of that lady you told me you were interested in? The one you said was on the rebound from someone else."

"Turns out you were right about her. She's still saying she won't take him back, but she started sleeping with him again. Now I'm glad it never went anywhere with her and me." He decided to take a leap of faith. "So what about you, Cassie? Are you still on your time-out from the dating scene?"

"I suppose, although I've found someone I really like, a lot."

Jeremy's heart sank like a rock. He suddenly realized the anxiety he'd been feeling all evening had been over her. She was more than just a friend to him. She had been for sometime, but he'd allowed his preoccupation with Gillian to get in the way. Larry had warned him about waiting too long and now it was too late. Cassie had moved on and found someone else. He'd have a heavy price to pay for his denial.

"Uh-oh." Cassie was looking at her watch. "It's almost ten o'clock. I've got class tomorrow, and so do you."

"I'll walk you to your car."

She put on her coat and grabbed her purse. They'd just stepped out the door when she slipped on some ice. Jeremy caught her before she fell.

"Whoops! Are you okay?"

"I'm fine, Jer, as long as no one saw me." She let out a little laugh. "I have my pride, you know."

She tried to take another step, but slipped again, and once more Jeremy caught her before she fell. His eyes met hers as he steadied her. This time, he followed his instincts and kissed her. It was a warm, sweet, passionate kiss. He looked into her eyes and realized instantly that he'd jumped to the wrong conclusion. He took her hand, led her back inside, closed the door and kissed her again. This time, she kissed him back.

"Cassie, are you sure about this?"

"I'm sure, Jer. Are you?"

"Darlin', I've never been more sure of anything in my life."

They took off their coats and she kicked off her shoes. He led her back to the fireplace, knelt down and gently guided her down on the blanket. He lay next to her and took her in his arms. Their bodies were warm and glowing in the firelight as they silently held each other in the afterglow. Jeremy nuzzled the top of her head and realized that for the first time in his life, he'd just experienced the pure joy of making love to a woman he truly loved.

# ❧Forty-Four❧

IAN GLANCED AT HIS watch as he finished touching up the paint on the dining room wall. It was going on nine o'clock and Larry was due home soon. He looked around and marveled at his accomplishment. It was the last coat of paint in the last room of the house that needed to be painted. His task was complete. Gathering the brushes to be cleaned, he wondered what he would do next. In the nearly three months since his forced departure from Salisbury & Norton, he had yet to land another job, and it certainly wasn't from a lack of trying on his part. There were simply too many equally qualified people out there competing for fewer and fewer jobs. Once again, he had to remind himself that he was luckier than most. He still had an income, which meant he had other options. He'd thought about doing some traveling, and perhaps starting a travel blog, but the thought of traveling alone just wasn't appealing. He let out a sigh as he dropped the brushes and rollers into the sink and looked at the large piece of canvas drop cloth. Just as he tossed the folded cloth in a corner, Larry walked in.

"So, how was it?"

"Mom is now officially Mrs. William Mason." Larry took off his coat and loosened his tie.

"Well, hallelujah."

"We did have one last-minute change though."

"What was that?"

"Jer and I decided that I should be the one to walk Mom up the aisle to give her away so I did."

"I'm proud of you, Larry. You've come a long way."

"It's like you always said, Dad. Life goes on and things have a way of working out the way they're meant to be. And while we're on the subject, I think we can stick Jeremy with a fork, because he's done. I'm afraid his happy, carefree bachelor days are numbered."

Larry went into the kitchen to get a soda. Ian followed him and joined him at the breakfast bar.

"So, I take it he brought Cassie with him."

"Yep."

"Did your mother like her?"

"She seemed to. She made a point of tossing the bridal bouquet to her."

"How did your brother react to that?"

"I was expecting him to pass out or something, but he didn't. Instead he walked up to her and gave her a big, long kiss right in front of everyone. He's always the showman."

"Well Larry, that's actually a good thing," said Ian. "I don't want your brother making the same mistake I made. Not that I regret having the two of you, but I wasn't much older than he is when I let Gillian go and I've been paying for it ever since."

Ian thought he'd made a real breakthrough with Gillian the night she took care of him when he had the flu. However, he hadn't seen or heard from her since, and she still refused to return his calls or emails. He was at a loss on how to break through the impenetrable wall she had built around herself.

"So, are you all packed, Larry? We're pulling out first thing in the morning."

* * *

It was spring break and Larry had decided to attend a culinary school in the Phoenix area. The plan was to drive to Arizona and spend a few days there. Once they arrived, the balmy springtime weather proved to be bittersweet for Ian. It was a constant reminder of the time when he'd first met Gillian. The first item on their to-do list was to visit the school. It was one of the top culinary schools in the country, and upon completing his studies, Larry would certainly have a bright future ahead of him. He was already talking about moving to Las Vegas once he finished. Ian had to face the fact that his youngest was growing up. Larry had turned eighteen two months before, and his high school graduation was only two months away.

The following morning Ian called his old friend, Rob Davis. Rob said he had some news and wanted to know if they could meet for lunch. Larry had brought along his laptop and seemed content to stay at the hotel, explaining that he had some homework he needed to finish. Rob was already waiting when Ian arrived at the restaurant.

"Ian, good seeing you again."

"You too," he replied as they shook hands. "So how's your client from Hell?"

"It's all good. We got the job done, thanks to you. Sorry to hear about your having to leave Salisbury and Norton sooner than you planned, but I think I may have a solution to your problem, assuming you'd be willing to relocate."

"I've thought about it. My house is on the market and my youngest leaves the nest in May. After that, I'm a free man."

"Good for you, so here's the deal. I'm an active member of our college alumni association, and I've kept tabs on the architecture school ever since I graduated. Ian, as long as you're in town, you need to go and see the place. It's bigger and better than it was when we were there. They've added new buildings and more programs."

"Interesting," said Ian.

"And you'll find this even more interesting. They have an opening for an architecture professor, starting in August, but so far they haven't found the right candidate."

"Really?"

"I kid you not. Didn't you tell me that you got your master's degree after you went back to Denver?"

Ian nodded. "I sure did. Salisbury offered to send me to graduate school, and I jumped on it."

"That's what I thought. So this morning, after I got off the phone with you, I took the liberty of making a few calls. They would like to talk to you." He had the information written down on the back of one of his business cards. "This is who you need to call. I've already spoken to him, and he's expecting to hear from you."

He handed Ian the card.

"I'm afraid I don't recognize the name."

"None of the faculty who were there when we students are around anymore. They've all either retired or have passed away." Rob paused for a moment. "Hey Ian, when you were here last summer, didn't you say something about reconnecting with Gillian Hanson?"

"Yes, I did. She's in Denver right now, but she's planning on coming back this summer."

"I always did like her, not that I don't love the lady I'm married to. But you know, back then, had I found out that Ryan didn't take her to Santa Barbara with him, I would have gone after her myself."

"You know, Rob, I've sometimes wondered whatever became of Ryan."

"I haven't heard from him in years. All I know is he eventually went back to Indiana, so apparently things didn't work out for him in Santa Barbara. I'm just glad Gillian never married him. She was much too good for him."

"She was indeed."

The following morning Ian walked around the Arizona State University campus. Parts of it were virtually unchanged from the time he was a student, while other areas were very different. A strong sense of deja vu swept over him as walked across the plaza from the art building to the old architecture building. It still looked the same, except for the different signage on the front. He entered the building and to his surprise, the library, where he and Gillian had first laid eyes on one another, was no longer there. The room was now being used for other purposes. He walked through the front gallery and out the back door. Even though he'd been told about it, he was, nonetheless, stunned by what he found. The old alleyway behind the building was gone. In its place was a walkway and a big new building, which now housed the architecture department. Rob was right. The place certainly had changed, and it would take some getting used to. After his meeting, he retuned to the hotel feeling optimistic. Perhaps the advice he'd given his sons over the years, about things always working out for the best, really was true.

# ☙FORTY-FIVE❧

"**I** DON'T KNOW WHAT else to tell you, Ian," said Samantha. "I know that up to now you've been patient with her, but I think you're going to have to start taking a firmer stance. You know, be more assertive with her. Does she know you got that teaching gig?"

Ian was having a cup of coffee at the truck stop diner. In the two months since his return from Phoenix, it had become his regular hang out.

"No," he said, "and please, don't say anything about it to her. It's supposed to be a surprise, assuming I ever get anywhere with her."

"Well, I've got good news. You'll have a chance to see her next week. Did you get Jeremy's email?"

"The one about meeting up in Denver, at O'Malley's Grill, for his birthday? Yes, I did."

"Good, so here's what I have in mind." Samantha explained that she would come to Denver early that day to spend the afternoon with Gillian. She would also insist on driving to O'Malley's. Then, after her manager called to update her on the day's activities at the diner, she would announce that she had an emergency and had to leave right away.

"At that point, Ian, I'll ask you to drive her home, so find some excuse for Larry to come in his own vehicle. Whatever happens after that will be up to you."

\* \* \*

Jeremy's birthday arrived, and so far Samantha's plan seemed to be working. She and Gillian arrived at the O'Malley's right on time, and when they reached their table Jeremy stood up and greeted Gillian with a big hug.

"Happy birthday, Jer," she said. "I see you survived final exams."

"Just barely. One more semester and I'm outta there. Meantime, I'm finished tending bar for good. I'll be doing a paid internship this summer with a firm here in Denver."

"I see someone's moving in on your date," teased Larry to Cassie.

"Oh they have this relationship," she teased back. "She'll always be the other woman in Jeremy's life, but since she's also like my aunt, I guess I'll just have to forgive her."

Gillian greeted everyone before sitting down next to Jeremy, on the opposite side of him from Cassie. He joked about being with his two favorite women. Will and Laura arrived a short time later, but by the time Ian showed up the only empty chair was the seat on the other side of Gillian. She gave him a cool but polite greeting and immediately focused her attention back on the others.

Over dinner Larry mentioned his plans to go to culinary school in Arizona. Gillian announced that she too would soon be leaving for Arizona, and before long she and Laura came up with a plan for her and Larry to caravan to Phoenix together. Ian remained silent during their conversation, although Samantha gave him a knowing wink. Before dessert arrived, everyone passed their cards and gifts to Jeremy. A short time later the waitress arrived with a slice of cake and a birthday candle. Everyone sang Happy Birthday to him, but when they finished Jeremy left the candle burning.

"Before I make my wish I have an announcement I'd like to make." He reached for Cassie's hand. "A lot has happened since the night this lady came into this very bar to celebrate her twenty-first birthday. She and I have, for all intents and purposes, been living together for some time now, and we've decided that paying rent on two apartments was a waste of money. So, come the first of June, we'll be renting a place together. But as soon as we signed the lease, I started having second thoughts. I got to thinking about something her mother once said, about sending a bunch of angry truck drivers after any guy who did her wrong, and I sure want to be around long enough to celebrate my twenty-third birthday."

"Now Jeremy," said Samantha, "I don't think that necessarily applies to you, but—" She deliberately left her sentence hanging while the others laughed.

"Thanks, Samantha, that's good to know. I've also been talking to my dad a lot lately, and we've been discussing a serious mistake he made when he was about my age. He let go of the woman he loved. While I'm glad it worked out that my brother and I are both here, I'm also hoping that they'll soon be able to make things right, because they really do belong together."

Gillian smiled politely, for Jeremy's sake.

"So, keeping all of that in mind," said Jeremy, "I'm making a very special birthday wish this year, and I guess I'll find out, really quick, if it's going to come true or not." He pulled a little black velvet box out of his pocket and looked at all the others. "You know, I suppose I should do this the old-fashioned way." He opened the box, stood up from the table, knelt down on one knee, and looked Cassie in the eye. The tears were already rolling down her face.

"Cassandra Walsh, will you do me the honor of being my wife?"

For a brief moment Cassie was speechless as everyone held their breath. To his relief, Cassie nodded her head and whispered, "Yes."

Everyone clapped and cheered as Jeremy slipped the ring on her finger and then stood back up. He pulled out Cassie's chair so she could walk around the table to show off her ring.

"See, Ian, I was right," exclaimed Samantha. "We're going to be in-laws."

She got up from her seat and gave him a hug before congratulating Jeremy and Cassie. Laura also walked up and congratulated Ian.

"That's one down, and one to go," she said. "And you know, despite everything, I still think we managed to do a good job as parents."

Samantha barely heard her phone ringing amidst all the confusion. She stepped away to take the call. By the time she returned, everyone had returned to their seats and a waitress was serving a bottle of champagne.

"Well, duty calls. There's some sort of a problem at the diner. I gotta run."

Groans of disappointment rose up around the table. Gillian reached for her purse.

"No, stay. Enjoy the party." She gave Ian a final wink. "Ian, would you mind running her home for me?"

"No, really, Sam, I can—"

He quickly cut Gillian off. "I'd be happy to, Sam."

Before Gillian could argue, Samantha rushed over to give her daughter, and Jeremy, one last congratulatory hug.

"Good luck," she whispered to Ian as she flew out the door.

* * *

Gillian was silent during the ride home. Ian finally spoke up.

"Gilly-girl, can I ask you something?"

"I suppose."

"Are you jealous?"

"What?"

"Look Gilly-girl, I know that you and Jeremy are close. Are you jealous, now that he's engaged to Cassie?" It felt strange to say the words.

"No, Ian, I'm not jealous. In fact, I'm quite the opposite. For a time I was concerned about how Jeremy would manage once I left, and now I don't have to worry about it anymore."

"That's good, although it's going to take me awhile to get used to the idea of having a daughter-in-law. But at least this one isn't you."

She shot him a look. "And what's that supposed to mean?"

"Last fall, when you were on the run from Susanna Richardson, Jeremy emailed a photo of the two of you in front of the Bellagio fountains to Larry, and Larry pointed out the wedding rings you were both wearing. I thought the worst. I called every hotel on the strip and found out the two of you were registered at Harrah's as Mr. and Mrs. Jeremy Palmer. At the time, I really believed the two of you had eloped, and Gillian, it had to be one of the darkest days of my life. I couldn't get the image of you and him together out of my mind. For awhile there I really thought that you were beyond reach."

Gillian mulled it over for a moment. "Ian, I've already told you that nothing happened between us, but just for the sake of argument, let's say that something did. What would you have done?"

"I would've fought to win you back, even if it meant mowing Jeremy over. However, he stopped by the house the night you two got back to town and he told us it was all a ruse. It was the best news I could have possibly heard."

"I'm sorry that happened, Ian. It was never my intention to hurt you."

"I know that. As I recall, it wasn't your intention for me to even know about it in the first place. But then again, you've never been able to keep a secret from me, Gilly-girl."

Gillian remained quiet for the rest of the drive. When Ian pulled into her driveway, she unbuckled her seatbelt and opened the car door.

"Thanks for the lift, Ian. I can see myself inside."

She stepped out of the car and Ian shut off the engine.

"I'm walking you to your door, whether you like it or not."

"Fine."

She opened the front door and was greeted by two happy dachshunds. After giving each a quick pat on the head, she stepped inside the foyer and turned on the lights.

"See? I'm safely inside. Night, Ian."

"Not so fast. " He stepped across the threshold. "I need to make sure there's no one lurking inside."

"Except for you, of course." Gillian rolled her eyes. "Fine. Suit yourself. Then leave."

Ian walked through the house, checking every room. When he finished, he found her in the kitchen, making a cup of tea.

"I'll have a cup of that too, thanks."

Gillian grudgingly got another mug out of the cupboard. She set it down hard on the countertop, making a loud noise. "Anything else, Lord Palmer?"

"I'll let you know, thanks."

"Don't you have someone waiting for you at home?"

"Larry? He said something about meeting up with friends. He'll be out late."

"Isn't he on double-secret probation, or something to that effect?"

"Not anymore. " He took a more serious tone. "Larry turned eighteen four months ago and his high school graduation was last Friday night. He's now, officially, an adult, which means I can now come and go as I please."

"That's nice." Gillian handed him his cup of tea. "But don't get too comfortable, Ian. As soon as you finish that I want you out of here."

"Trying to get rid of me, are you?"

"Gee, Ian, do ya think?"

Ian smiled inside. He was starting to get under her skin. He took a few sips of his tea before he walked into the living room, took a seat, kicked off his shoes and turned on the television set.

"What the hell do think you're doing?"

"Making myself comfortable while I drink my tea." He flipped through the channels. "Oh look, the Rockies game is still on."

"Damn it, Ian, I want you to finish your tea and then I want you to go."

He heard the frustration in her voice. Samantha's plan was definitely working. "Just go do whatever you want to do. I'm fine here."

"Look, Ian, it's getting late and I want to get ready for bed."

"Not a problem, Gilly-girl. Whatever."

"It is a problem, Ian. We both know what happened the last time you were here and I was wearing a nightgown."

Ian ignored her and watched the ballgame. Gillian stared at him in stunned disbelief.

"That tea is good. I think I'll have another cup." He stood back up. "Don't worry, I can get it myself. If you want to get ready for bed, that's fine. If you want to keep standing there, that's okay too. And just so you know, Gilly-girl, if I really wanted to, I could get you out of that dress just as easily as I got you out of that nightgown."

Gillian's face turned red. Her eyes blazed with anger. "You arrogant, condescending, son of a bitch!"

She picked up a little porcelain figurine and threw it at him. Ian caught it and set it down on the coffee table. She grabbed a vase and threw it at him. He caught that too.

"Gillian, did I ever tell you that I was on my high school baseball team?" He was interrupted by another ceramic knick-knack being tossed at him, which he caught and set down as well. "I played catcher. So if it makes you feel better, go ahead, keep pitching. But try not to throw any knives, okay."

Gillian picked up a brass figurine. "Okay, then. Let's see you try this one out for size."

She hurled it as hard as she could, but it curved to the right. Ian leaned over to catch it, but as he did he lost his balance. He crashed to the floor and rolled over on his back. His eyes were closed and he wasn't moving.

"Ian?"

No response. She ran up and knelt down next to him. "Ian!"

He still wasn't moving. "Oh my God. Ian, are you all right? Please, say something."

She leaned over and touched his face. His eyes popped open as he reached up and grabbed her wrists. He pulled her down close and kissed her. She struggled against him, then she began to relax slowly. Kissing her a second time, he reached up and unzipped her dress.

"See Gilly-girl, I told you I could get you out of that dress," he said with an I-told-you-so smile.

"You sneaky bastard, you were faking it."

She jumped up and stormed off to her bedroom. Ian got up and followed her. By the time he got there, she was halfway out of her dress. She spun back around and faced him.

"You really did scare the you-know-what out of me, Ian, and you shouldn't have done that."

"I'll do whatever it takes to crack that armor of yours." He took her in his arms again, and as he kissed her, her dress fell to the floor. He picked her up and carried her to the bed.

# ❧Forty-Six❧

**I**AN WOKE UP THE following morning alone in Gillian's bed. He quickly dressed and found her in the basement, working on a painting.

"This is getting to be a bad habit, Ian." Once again, there was a chill in her voice. "There's simply no point in our getting involved again. In a few weeks I'll be leaving Colorado, and I won't be coming back."

"What about last night?"

"Last night should have never happened. We'll just say it was my way of telling you goodbye, and we'll leave it at that. Okay?"

"What about your gallery?"

"Cynthia and I have made Paul a partner, and we're now set up so we can run things from Phoenix. My work here is done. It's time for me to go home."

"What about us?"

"Like I just said, there's no point. My life is in Arizona, and your life is here. I've loved you for over twenty-five years, and I'll love you 'til the day I die, the second time, I might add, but we're just not meant to be."

"What do I have to do to get through to you?"

She stopped and looked him in the eye. "You can't. My mind is made up. You've walked out on me twice, and I'm simply not going to allow it to happen a third time. It was fun, but now it's over, and we're done."

234

"What makes you think I'd walk out on you a third time?"

"Old habits die hard, Ian."

Ian felt himself tensing up. He had something else that he wanted to say, but he decided against it. It wasn't the right moment. He'd have to bide his time until they got back to Phoenix. He couldn't wait to see the look on her face when he showed up at her door. In the meantime, his frustrations were getting the best of him.

"You know, Gillian, I liked you a whole lot better back when you were a blonde. You've turned hard and cold since you became a redhead. I'll see myself out."

Larry was in the kitchen getting ready to serve up breakfast when his father walked in, wearing the same clothes he had on the night before.

"I won't ask."

"Good," replied Ian. "Because I wouldn't have told you anyway."

"The agent called about an hour ago." Larry handed his father a plate. "Someone else is coming to see the house this afternoon, and I need to talk to you about something."

"What is it?"

Larry fixed his plate and took a seat at the breakfast bar next to his father. "This is it, Dad. Today is my last day living here. I want to spend some time with Mom before I go, so I got my old summer job back at The Flying M. I'm leaving first thing in the morning. Then, come the end of July, Gillian Matthews and I are moving to Phoenix. She called me a little while ago, and she said it's all arranged. We'll both be staying with her sister until I find my own place. She also said she'd help me look, if I need it."

"What happened to her house in Phoenix?"

"She said she sold it. Apparently she meant to cancel the listing, but before she got around to it she got a full-price offer. Guess we'll both be looking for something. Anyway, I thought that maybe today, if you wouldn't mind, we could hang out together, just the two of us, while I pack and load my truck."

Ian was taken aback. His youngest was leaving the nest. He knew this day was coming, but it was still a bit of a shock to hear the words.

"You bet, Larry, but I'm going to let you in on a little secret. I want your word that this stays between us, at least for now, got it?

"Sure, Dad."

"I'm moving to Arizona too."

"You are!" Larry's face lit up. "Dad, that's awesome. How'd that happen?"

"I've accepted that teaching position at Arizona State."

Larry grinned from ear to ear. "You did? You just made my day. Does Gillian know?"

"Not yet, and that's why it's a secret. Your brother doesn't even know about it yet."

"Somehow, Dad, I think Jeremy has other things on his mind."

* * *

Ian spent the day helping Larry pack and load. That night they went out to dinner and a movie.

The following morning Larry got in his truck, started it up, and waved goodbye as he drove away from the house for the last time. Once the truck was out of sight, Ian went back inside and headed upstairs. As he passed Larry's room he stopped and stood in the doorway. All that remained was a lonely bed and a few boxes containing the items that Larry had either outgrown or no longer needed. A local charity would be by to pick it all up on Monday morning. Ian suddenly felt empty inside. He closed the door and went into his den, where he found himself staring at the walls. As much as he looked forward to returning to Arizona and starting a new career, he knew that when the time came it would be difficult for him to say goodbye to Colorado. It had been his home for most of life, and he knew that once he left, other than the occasional visit, he would never return.

Three weeks later Ian finally had an offer on the house. It wasn't what he, or Laura, had wanted, but after discussing the matter they both decided to accept it. Selling the house was the last piece of business from their divorce, and both were ready to complete that chapter of their lives. Once the house was under contract, Ian sent the leather chairs and sofa off to be redone, while he decided what to keep and what to give to Jeremy. A few weeks later the movers arrived. When they left, Ian took one final walk through every room of the empty house that had been his home for over twenty years. After coming down the stairs for the very last time he locked the doors, dropped his keys on the breakfast bar, and stepped into the garage. The Beamer was loaded with his luggage and Gillian's painting of the old barn and tractor. He backed the car onto the driveway, stepped out, and pressed the button on the remote one last time before sliding it back into the garage. Once the garage door closed it would no longer be his home. He lingered in the driveway for a minute before climbing back in the car and heading to Colorado Springs. He would spend the next few weeks with Jeremy and Cassie, while he worked on lesson plans for the courses he'd be teaching.

# ❧FORTY-SEVEN❧

LAURA HAD EXTENDED an open invitation to Gillian to stay in the cottage, as they called the fifth-wheel trailer, at St. Eligius Ranch. The week before her departure Gillian took Laura up on the offer. She spent the week horseback riding, taking photos, sketching and relaxing. Gillian would miss Colorado. She wanted to take in as much of the mountain scenery as possible before she left. She would, of course, return to Denver from time to time for her own shows at Sorenson, but those visits would be brief. She did, however, promise Jeremy that she would see him whenever she came. She would miss Jeremy. He truly was her best friend. Then there was his father.

Ian Palmer had been and would always be her one true love, and for some reason she'd been thinking of him more than usual lately. She even had her hair bleached back after he told her he preferred her as a blonde. There was a part of her that wanted nothing more than to take him back, but too much had happened between them. The time had come for her to move on for good.

Her last day in Colorado finally arrived. It was a Sunday, and Laura had planned a big family dinner that evening as a send off for her and Larry. It was about nine o'clock in the morning when she came into the barn and found Will.

"Have you seen Ramon?"

"He's out running an errand," replied Will. "Can I help you with something?"

"I just need to have Miss Mollie saddled up."

"I can take care of that for you."

"Thanks." Gillian followed Will to the corral and watched as he saddled the horse.

"How long are you going to be?" He handed her the reins and waited for her to mount.

"I should be back by two. Three o'clock at the very latest. Then Larry and I have to get ready to go. We're pulling out first thing in the morning."

"We're going to miss you."

"And I'm going to miss you too." She settled in the saddle and tied her leather satchel to the horn. "I've really enjoyed my stay and I can't thank you and Laura enough."

"You know you're welcome back anytime."

"I appreciate that, Will. Maybe someday I can come back. Meantime, my phone's right here." She motioned to it in a holster on her belt. "Call me if you need anything."

"Will do. Have a safe ride."

"Thanks." She looked back as Miss Mollie trotted away. "See you this afternoon."

Will waved goodbye and stepped back into the barn to tend to some of the other horses. When he finished, he went back into the house to watch the Rockies game.

\* \* \*

Gillian rode across the meadow toward the eastern ridge. She planned to ride all the way up to the top, where she would have a bird's-eye view of St. Eligius, as well as The Flying M. She had nearly worked her way there when she came to a small clearing and startled a flock of birds that had been resting in the trees. They squawked loudly and flew straight at Miss Mollie, spooking the mare. She reared. Despite being a skilled rider, Gillian was unable to get the horse under control. Miss Mollie spun, stopped abruptly, and reared up again. The quick, jerky motion caused Gillian to lose her balance and she slipped out of the saddle, landing hard on her right leg and falling to the ground. The impact knocked the wind out of her and she lay helplessly, watching the mare run off. It took a minute for her to regain her composure.

"Damn."

She brushed herself off once she was finally able to sit back up. She took a few deep breaths. At least she didn't have any broken ribs, but she felt a sharp pain in her right ankle. She knew she must have twisted it when she fell. She reached for her phone, only to discover it was missing. She crawled around the ground looking for it, but it was gone. She let out a frustrated sigh.

"Well, Gilly-girl, it looks like you've gotten yourself into a real pickle this time. Guess there's not much you can do now but wait for someone to come looking for you."

\* \* \*

It was about half-past ten when Ramon returned. He walked into the barn and discovered Miss Mollie, saddled and unattended. He led the mare outside to one of the hitching posts, and as he began unsaddling her, noticed the satchel. He looked toward the trailer and shook his head.

"City girl," he mumbled to himself.

He untied the satchel and placed it in the tack room. He knew she'd come looking for it sooner or later, and when she did, he'd give her a gentle reminder about not leaving the horses loose. He put Miss Mollie back in the corral and went about his other chores.

\* \* \*

Jeremy and Cassie arrived at the ranch a short time later, and before long he and Larry came into the barn and asked Ramon to saddle up Pretty Boy and another horse. They rode into the meadow and Gillian's spirits lifted when she spotted the two riders leaving St. Eligius.

"They must have found Miss Mollie," she told herself. "Someone's finally looking for me." She waved her arms and shouted. "I'm up here, you guys! Come on, I'm up here!"

\* \* \*

Ian arrived some thirty minutes later. Cassie greeted him from the front porch. She was on the porch swing, curled up with a book.

"Here's your key." He handed it back to her. "And thank you again for your hospitality."

"It was our pleasure, Dad. I'm going to miss having you around."

"Thanks, Cassie. I'm going to miss you too. So, where's Jeremy?"

"He and Larry went out for a ride. He's out there trying to talk his brother into coming back to Denver when he finishes school."

"They always were close. Have you seen Gillian?"

"Not yet. Will said she went out for a ride this morning, and would be back sometime later on this afternoon. When were you planning to tell her about moving to Arizona?"

"I'm not sure. Hopefully, I'll get the chance tonight. If not, I'll just show up here first thing in the morning, and won't she be surprised?"

Ian excused himself and went inside the house.

* * *

Gillian intently watched the two figures on horseback. After a couple hours, she noticed them turning back toward the ranch. Her heart sank.

"Damn." She tried to reassure herself. "It looks like I'm going to have to rely on my own resources."

She glanced at her watch. It was nearly one o'clock. She had many hours of daylight left, but with her injured ankle she knew it would take some time to work her way down the ridge on her own. She somehow managed to get back on her feet, but when she tried putting her weight on her right leg she felt an excruciating pain. Her ankle was either sprained or broken. She looked around and spotted a tree branch lying on the ground some twenty feet away. She hobbled over to it and raised it up. It was a little heavy, but she could still use it as a makeshift cane. Slowly and carefully, she started working her way down the mountain.

* * *

It was going on four o'clock when Will came back out to check on some of the horses. He ran into Ramon in the barn.

"Do you know if Mrs. Matthews is back yet?"

"What do you mean, back yet?"

"I saddled Miss Mollie up for her this morning, while you were in town," explained Will. "And she should have been back at least an hour ago."

"She came back a long time ago."

"What do you mean?"

"I got back here about ten-thirty this morning, Dr. Mason. I found Miss Mollie loose in the barn, so I unsaddled her and put her back in the corral. If you'll wait here, I've got something that belongs to Mrs. Matthews."

Ramon stepped away and Will went out to the corral. Sure enough, Miss Mollie was there. Ramon came out and handed him Gillian's leather satchel. Will took it to the trailer. He knocked on the door. He heard the dogs bark, but there was no answer.

"Gillian! It's Will. Are you in there?"

He knocked a second time, and again there was no response. He tried the door. It was unlocked, so he slowly opened it. It was apparent that the two dogs were unattended.

"Come on you two, follow me."

He walked back to the house, with Duke and Daisy following behind. Ian and Jeremy were in the family room watching a baseball game on TV. When Will came back in, they greeted the two dogs.

"Have you heard from Gillian today, Jeremy?" asked Will.

"No, I haven't."

"Then I need you to call her, right now."

Jeremy reached for his phone and hit the call button.

"Is there a problem, Will?" asked Ian.

"I'm not sure."

Jeremy looked at Will. "She's not answering, so it's going to voicemail." He left a message, asking her to call him back right away.

Ian spotted the satchel. "What have you got, Will?"

"It's Gillian's." He opened it up and checked the contents. "It's got a bottle of water, pencils and a sketchbook."

"You're joking." Ian came over to take a closer look. "She always keeps close tabs on her sketchbooks. Where did you get this?"

Will ignored the question and headed toward the kitchen. Ian and Jeremy followed closely behind. He found Laura in the dining room, setting the table, while Cassie and Larry were busy in the kitchen preparing dinner.

"Have any of you seen or heard from Gillian lately?"

"I haven't seen her since breakfast," said Laura.

"Same here," said Larry.

"Then turn the stove off."

"Will, what's wrong?" asked Laura.

"It looks like she may be missing."

"What?" exclaimed Ian.

"Gillian left here about nine o'clock this morning, and she was riding Miss Mollie," explained Will. "She was due back no later than an hour ago, but she's not here, and apparently no one has seen or heard from her since this morning. Ramon was out when she left, but he says that when he got back he found Miss Mollie wandering loose in the barn, and Gillian's bag was still on the saddle."

"What time was that?" asked Ian.

"About ten thirty this morning."

Ian did a quick calculation in his head. "Do you mean to tell me that she's been missing for nearly seven hours now?"

"I'm afraid it looks that way, Ian."

"Try to stay calm, Dad," said Jeremy.

"Shouldn't we call the authorities?" asked Cassie.

"She hasn't been missing long enough," said Will. "I'm guessing we've got about three to four hours of daylight left. I'm going to have Ramon and the boys saddle up the horses and we're going to go look for her. Laura, are the two-way radios still in the tack room?"

"Yes. There are four of them, and they're all still working."

"Go get them, right now. Leave a radio here with Cassie and Ian, and we'll take the rest with us. You and the boys are coming with me."

"I'm going with you," said Ian.

"But do you know how to ride, Ian?"

"I grew up on a farm. My father taught me how to ride a horse when I was five years old. It's like riding a bicycle."

Ian joined the others in the barn and helped saddle the horses. Cassie stood by with a radio and a pair of binoculars.

"I'll stay out here and keep a close watch," she said. "If she shows up on her own, I'll let you know."

She gave Jeremy a quick goodbye kiss and watched as he and the others quickly rode out to the meadow, split into groups of two, and headed off in different directions. Once they were gone, she grabbed her phone and called her mother.

* * *

It had been long, slow and painful, but Gillian had made considerable progress working her way down the ridge. She found a tree stump and sat down for a brief rest. Her ankle was throbbing, but since she'd been able to put some weight on it she figured it probably wasn't broken. She glanced at her watch. It was going on four o'clock. She was hungry, thirsty, tired, and in considerable pain, but she knew she had to keep going. Her goal was to make it off the ridge and into the meadow by sundown. Surely they realized she was missing by now. Maybe once she was clear of the trees someone would spot her.

After resting for about fifteen minutes, she gritted her teeth and forced herself back on her feet. She took a few cautious steps forward. She was on rough, uneven terrain and she soon made a misstep, causing her to lose her balance and fall. She cried out in pain as she landed, but before she could react she heard one of the last sounds she ever wanted to hear. It was the sound of a rattling hiss. She glanced around and noticed her makeshift cane had rolled several feet downhill.

"No! No! Please don't tell me..."

She could hardly breathe as she watched the rattlesnake slowly emerge from beneath the pine needles. It was a small snake, probably no more than a couple of feet long. Her mind suddenly flashed back to one of the nightmares she had months before. She realized she'd seen this very moment in her dream. In that dream, the snake had bitten her, and she did not survive.

# ❧Forty-Eight❧

C ASSIE LISTENED INTENTLY to every word on the two-way radio. Will and Laura had ridden off in one direction, Larry and Ramon in another, Jeremy and Ian in a third. They had managed to cover a considerable amount of territory, but so far there was no sign of Gillian. It was about five-thirty when she heard Will tell everyone to meet at the rendezvous point.

\* \* \*

"We've been north, south, and west and so far nothing," said Will. "So now we go east."

"Do you think she's up on the ridge?" asked Jeremy.

"Possibly, but it's rugged terrain up there. We can certainly get started on it, but we probably only have a few hours of daylight left."

"Then let's get going," said Ian, "we're wasting time yapping down here."

A serious look came across Will's face. He radioed Cassie one more time to ask if she'd seen anything. Cassie replied that so far there was no sign of her.

"Before we go up there we need to face some cold, hard facts," explained Will. "The woman's been missing for a good eight hours now. She's had plenty of time to call on her cell phone, and even if she went all the way to the top of the ridge, she's had more than enough time to walk back down by now."

"What are you saying, Will?" asked Ian

"I'm saying this isn't looking good, Ian." Will let out a sigh before continuing. "I want all of you, especially you and Jeremy, to be prepared. Wherever she is, it's a safe bet that she's injured, and we don't know how seriously. It'll be getting dark soon, which means the temperature will start to drop. There are also bears, mountain lions and rattlesnakes out there. If we don't find her soon we may be looking at a recovery and not a rescue. Like I just said, we've got about two to three hours of daylight left to find her. After that I'm calling it. That means we head back, call the sheriff, and try again in the morning."

They paired off again and headed toward the ridge.

\* \* \*

Gillian slowly moved to check her watch. She'd been there for well over an hour and the rattlesnake was still by her feet.

"Why do you insist on torturing me so? We both know what you're going to do to me, so why don't you just get it over with?"

She'd spent the time looking back on her life. She'd been blessed with loving parents, a wonderful sister, artistic talent, and a successful career with a little bit of fame to go with it. She thought of Jeremy and how, thanks to him, she'd been given almost another year of life that she otherwise wouldn't have had. Perhaps her time really had come the day she fell into the pool. She knew she had to return for Jeremy, and now his life was on track. Thanks to her, he'd found the love of his life. Her only regret was Ian. She realized she should have forgiven him months ago and now it was too late. She worried about what would become of him once she was gone. She didn't want him to spend the rest of his life with the guilt of their unresolved issues. She desperately wished that somehow, someway, she could see him one last time. Her spirit would rest easy if she could tell him he was forgiven. The tears streamed down her face.

\* \* \*

Ian and Jeremy were searching near the top of the ridge. Suddenly, Ian stopped his horse and his face lit up. Jeremy rode up next to him.

"What is it, Dad?"

"I know where she is, Jer. Don't ask me how, but I know where she is."

Ian moved his horse forward and rode further up the hill. Jeremy stayed close behind. They found a small clearing and Ian slowed down.

As he scanned the area something odd caught his eye. He rode up to it, dismounted, and picked it off the ground. It was Gillian's phone. He also noticed the ground nearby looked disturbed. He pointed it out to Jeremy.

"Look at that. She was here, Jer. She must have fallen off her horse right over there. Finally, we're getting close." He placed the phone in his pocket, mounted his horse, and was about to pick up his radio when he heard Will's voice.

"Okay guys, we're done. I want everyone off the mountain."

"Will, I just found her cell phone," Ian radioed back. "She's somewhere close. You guys can go, but I'm not leaving until I find her."

"Ian, it'll be dark soon."

"I'm fully aware of that. I've got a radio, and if I have to stay out here overnight with her, then I'll stay out here overnight, but I'm not coming down this mountain without her."

"Understood. Keep me posted. Good luck, Ian."

"I'm staying with you, Dad."

"No, you're not. You have someone down there waiting for you, and I don't want you up here, just in case something does go wrong. I'll find her, and when I do I'll let you know, the minute it happens. Okay?"

Jeremy knew it was no use trying to argue. He reluctantly turned his horse around. "Okay, Dad, but call me the minute you find her."

"I will. I promise."

"Bring her home safe, okay?"

"Don't worry, Jeremy. She's going to be all right."

Jeremy headed back down the mountain alone. He prayed that his father was right, but he couldn't shake the horrible feeling that she wasn't going to make it.

\* \* \*

Samantha arrived a couple hours after Cassie called her. She was waiting with her as the others trickled back in. By the looks on everyone's faces, they knew the situation wasn't good. Jeremy was the last to return. Cassie ran up to him as he got off his horse and handed the reins to Ramon. She wrapped her arms around him and began sobbing. She quickly noticed that Jeremy was choking up as well. They walked out behind the barn. Samantha followed the others inside the house.

"I called her sister," she announced. "She's on her way from Phoenix. Her flight should land in Denver in about another hour or so, and then she'll rent a car and head out here."

"Thanks Sam, for letting me know," said Laura. "I was going to try to call her sister myself, but I wasn't sure how to get in touch with her. I have an extra room left for the two of you."

"Thanks, Laura. I'm afraid we're all going to be in for a long night."

Will stepped away to call the sheriff. A deputy arrived a short time later to take the report.

\* \* \*

Ian began working his way down the ridge. If Gillian was injured, she would have taken the easiest route she could find, so he followed what he thought would be her trail. He began calling out for her.

"Gillian!" He paused. "Gillian!"

He thought he heard her voice, but he wasn't sure. He rode a down a little further.

"Gillian!"

"Ian!"

Her voice was faint, but the sound was exhilarating. He followed the direction from which it had come and called out again.

"Gillian!"

"Ian! I'm over here! Hurry!"

This time her voice was louder. He kept riding and soon spotted her. She was alert, but down on the ground. He got off Miss Mollie, tied the reins to the nearest tree, and ran toward her.

"Ian, stop! Don't come any closer."

The sound of the rattling and the hissing abruptly stopped him in his tracks. He scanned the ground and spotted the snake. It crawled past Gillian's feet and up toward her face. It was appeared to be a younger snake. That meant it would be even more poisonous. His blood ran cold.

"Gillian, have you been bitten?"

"Not yet, Ian, but it's going to happen and when it does, I won't make it. You can't get me to a hospital in time."

"Yes, you will make it. Just stay calm and try not to move. I'm going to get you out of this."

He spotted the branch she'd used as a walking stick. He ran over to get it, but by the time he picked it up the snake had stopped near Gillian's neck. To his horror, it was coiling up. He knew that snakes were essentially deaf, but they were very sensitive to vibrations on the ground. He had to be careful.

"Ian, I need you to listen to me. There's a metal file box in my minivan that contains all my important papers, including a copy of my will. The key is in my purse. I've made you executor of my estate, and I'm leaving everything to your two boys."

"That's very thoughtful of you, Gillian, but you won't be checking out just yet."

"I foresaw this in a dream, Ian. I'm not going to make it. It's my time. I was supposed to go last fall when I fell in the pool, but I got a short reprieve when I came back for Jeremy. Now it's up."

"You don't know that, Gillian."

"Yes, Ian, I do. I want you to know that I really do love you, and I'm so sorry for shutting you out. I shouldn't have done that and I can only hope that you'll forgive me someday. I want you to go on with your life, Ian, and I want you to be happy without me. You can do that for me, can't you?"

"Just stay calm, Gillian, and don't move. Someone is definitely about to die here, but it's not going to be you."

"Ian, I don't have much time left. Will you promise me something?"

"What's that?"

"Will you promise to stay here with me until it's over?"

The snake was fully coiled and ready to strike. Ian knew he only had one chance to save her. The snake made its move, and in that same instant, he clubbed it with the branch as hard as he could. Gillian closed her eyes and let out a blood-curdling scream.

For a few seconds neither of them moved. Ian slowly lifted the branch and Gillian opened her eyes. The snake was dead, but it was twitching. Its fangs were within an inch of her face. She let out another scream as Ian reached down and tossed it aside. He pulled her up into a sitting position and searched her for a snakebite.

"Did it get you?"

She shook her head. Her body was trembling hard and tears were flowing down her face. He knelt down and held her tightly. He felt his own tears rolling down his face. He knew he'd come within a split second of losing her. For the next few minutes neither of them spoke as they held each other.

"You have no idea how much I've missed you," he finally said.

"I've missed you too. Promise me you'll never leave me again?"

"It won't happen again. I promise." He suddenly remembered. "Gillian, I have some news for you."

"What?"

"I'm coming with you. To Arizona."

"You're kidding." She used her sleeve to wipe her face.

"No, I'm not. I've accepted a teaching position at Arizona State. I start in a few weeks."

"You did? You mean you're leaving Colorado? For good?"

"That's right. For good."

"How long have you known about this?"

"For awhile now. I meant to tell you about it the night of Jeremy's birthday, but you never gave me a chance. You were too busy hurling things at me."

"I'm so sorry, Ian. I know my behavior's been over the top lately. I just haven't been myself for a long time."

"It's okay." He began stroking the side of her face. "It's all in the past. And by the way, thanks for getting rid of that red hair."

"You were right about that too, Ian. It wasn't me."

"We'll talk more about it later, but right now I need to get you back. We've been searching for you for hours and we'd just about given up hope."

"That's going to be a trick, Ian. I was thrown off my horse and I've sprained my ankle."

"Don't worry, I'll get you back. Uh-oh. I can't believe I forgot about the radio." He got up to retrieve it. "Hey guys, this is Ian."

"I'm here, Dad," replied Jeremy. His voice sounded tired and despondent.

"Here, let me have it," whispered Gillian. Ian handed the radio to her. "Hey you guys, were you all out looking for me?"

"Oh my God!" exclaimed Jeremy. They heard the cheering in the background. "Where the hell have you been, lady? We've been looking everywhere for you. You've had us all worried sick."

She handed the radio back to Ian.

"We'll fill you in as soon as we get back. She's hurt, but not seriously. We're on our way."

He helped Gillian to her feet and handed her the tree branch to lean on. He untied Miss Mollie and helped Gillian get on behind the saddle before he carefully mounted up in front of her.

"I want you to hold on really tight to me, just like you did that night Jeremy picked you up in the haunted maze. I'm going to push this horse as hard as I can push her."

She gave him a squeeze. "You got it."

They rode Miss Mollie down the rest of the ridge and soon reached the meadow, but by then it was nearly dark.

"Ready, Gillian? Because I'm not wasting any more time."

"Let's go."

He slapped the horse with the reins and she lunged into a full gallop. Ian leaned forward and loosened the reins, driving her as hard and fast as she'd go. Jeremy and the others were waiting in front of the house. They heard the sound of approaching hoof beats.

"There they are!" shouted Larry.

The horse raced toward the front of the house, skidding to a stop as Ian reined her back in. As soon as the dust settled, Jeremy reached up and pulled Gillian down. He quickly carried her inside while Ian dismounted and ran in behind him. Jeremy set Gillian down on the couch as Will came up to check her.

"She's got a sprained ankle," said Ian.

"Which one?"

"Right leg," said Gillian.

"Laura, get an icepack," said Will.

"Got it." She dashed toward the kitchen.

"Jeremy, hold her down," said Will. "Gillian, I'm going to have to pull this boot off you, and it's probably going to hurt like hell when I do."

Jeremy held her by the shoulders as Ian took her hand.

"It's okay, Gilly-girl. I'm right here."

"Ready?" asked Will.

Gillian nodded. She cried out as Will pulled her boot off. He gently removed her sock and began checking her. Gillian winced in pain a few times.

"It's pretty swollen. I'd say you probably have a bad sprain, but I can't feel anything that's broken."

Laura returned with an icepack and something for Gillian to drink.

"Thanks, Laura." She elevated her leg. Ian sat down next to her and applied the ice to her ankle.

"Well, I'd say the two of you worked things out," said Jeremy.

"Yeah," replied Ian. "We had a talk. You could say we worked things out."

"So what the hell happened?" asked another female voice.

"Samantha!" Gillian extended her arms as Sam rushed in and gave her a hug. "When did you get here?"

"Not too long ago." She motioned to the others standing by. "So don't keep us all in suspense. Tell us what happened."

"It was a freak accident." Gillian described how the birds spooked her horse and she wound up being thrown and spraining her ankle. "I was going to call for help, but somehow my phone disappeared and I never did find it."

Ian pulled her phone out of his pocket. "You mean this?"

Her face lit up. "Ian, where was it?"

"On the ground, about twenty feet from where you fell. That's how I knew I'd find you."

"Thank you." She gave him a kiss as he handed the phone back to her.

"So then what happened?" asked Samantha.

She described her close encounter with the rattlesnake, and how Ian clubbed it just in the nick of time.

"You were very lucky, young lady," said Will.

"I agree," added the deputy. "At least I'll get to put a happy ending on my report." He stopped to shake Gillian's hand. As soon as he was gone, she spoke up.

"You know, for awhile there I really thought my time had come, and it wasn't like before, when Jeremy was there to rescue me from the pool. All I wanted was to see Ian one last time. Of course, I had no idea that he was even here, so you can imagine how elated I felt when I heard his voice calling me. And when I looked up and saw him, it was like seeing an angel. So I'm giving this man one more shot, and seeing if the third time really is the charm."

# ☙FORTY-NINE☙

**B**EFORE SHE EXCUSED herself from the dinner table, Gillian once again thanked everyone for coming to her rescue. She and Ian said their goodnights and he carried her back to the trailer. Jeremy tagged along with extra icepacks and an elastic bandage for her injured ankle. Once they were inside, Ian gently set her down on the bed and Jeremy came over tell her goodnight.

"Well darling, we'll always have Las Vegas." He gave her a hug.

"Out!" exclaimed Ian, pointing to the door.

"See you in the morning." Jeremy gave her one last hug. "Glad you're back safe and sound. Night, Dad."

Ian shooed him away. Jeremy laughed as he closed the door behind him and walked back to the house.

\* \* \*

Jeremy found Will in the kitchen, making a pitcher of margaritas, while Laura and Samantha were setting up a poker game at the dining room table. Naturally, he wanted to be dealt in. Cynthia arrived a short time later and was greeted by Samantha, who introduced her to the others.

"I got your message, Sam, and thanks for letting me know that she's okay. You don't know how relieved I am."

"You'll have to thank Ian," replied Samantha, "he's the one who finally found her."

"He did? Well, good for him. Where is she? Can I go see her?"

"You might want to wait 'til tomorrow morning," said Jeremy. "She's staying in the trailer out back, and Dad's in there with her."

"Really? Well, it's about bloody time she took him back. So what happened?"

Samantha and Jeremy filled her in. As they were talking Will handed her a margarita and she looked at the poker table. A smile broke out across her face.

"Well, I guess something had to give. Too bad it took a rattlesnake to finally wake her up." She took a sip of her margarita and reached inside her purse. "Deal me in."

* * *

Ian put a fresh ice pack on Gillian's ankle. "So how are you feeling, Gilly-girl? Can I get you anything?"

"I'm fine, Ian. I'll just rest it for a little while." She patted the spot next to her on the bed. "Why don't you come up here and join me?"

"Hold that thought. I'll be right back." He headed toward the door.

"Where are you going?"

"To get my bag. Promise you won't run off while I'm gone."

"I'll try not too."

When he returned, he pulled his boots off, climbed up on the bed and wrapped his arm around her. It felt good to just be able to hold her again.

"You know, Ian, with this injured ankle, I'm probably going to need help with some basics, like taking a shower."

"Really?"

"Afraid so."

"Well, it's a dirty job. I suppose someone will have to do it, and it might as well be me." They both laughed. "You don't know how good it feels to hear you laughing again, Gilly-girl." He ran his fingers through her hair. "So, let's get you out of these clothes."

He helped her into the bathroom and joined her in the shower. They laughed and joked as they washed each other down and shampooed each other's hair. Once they were cleaned up they relaxed in their bathrobes. Ian helped Gillian back on the bed and got a fresh icepack.

"It looks like the swelling's starting to go down." He placed it on her ankle. "You're not in any pain, are you?"

"Not right now, Ian. It seems to be feeling a lot better."

He stroked her little tattoo.

"Ian, if you don't like that I can see about getting it removed."

"Are you kidding? You're wearing my brand, my dear, for the world to see. Did you know that Samantha emailed me Thanksgiving night and told me about it?"

"She did?"

"Yes, she did. I knew, right then and there, that it would only be a matter of time before I'd get you back, but you sure didn't make it easy for me."

"I know, Ian. And I'm sorry."

"It's okay, but please, do me one favor. Don't get any more tattoos, okay?"

She raised her right hand. "I won't."

He stepped away and checked his overnight bag. It was still there, safely tucked away in a corner. He pulled it out and dropped it into the pocket of his robe.

"Gillian, I have something for you."

"What is it?"

"It's a surprise. Can you close you eyes for a minute?"

She looked up, saw the serious look on his face, and realized that whatever he was planning wasn't some kind of practical joke. She leaned back on the pillows and closed her eyes.

"What I have for you, Gillian, is something that I meant to give to you sometime ago. I bought it for you last summer, right after I returned from visiting my sister, and I'd planned on giving it to you last Christmas. Then my youngest had to go sneak out to a drinking party, and we all know what happened after that. But this comes with a promise that I'll never walk out on you again." He reached into his pocket, removed the contents from a box, picked up her left hand and slipped it on her ring finger.

"Okay, Gillian, you can open your eyes."

She looked at her hand and saw the diamond engagement ring. The stone sparkled and glimmered as it reflected the light. It was the most beautiful thing she had ever seen, and she was completely overwhelmed.

"Ian?" Her voiced quivered. "Does this mean what I think it means?"

"Yes, it does. Gillian, I was foolish enough to walk out on you, twice. Then I almost lost you for good. I'll always blame myself for you're nearly drowning—"

"Stop right there, Ian. The time has come for you to stop blaming yourself for what happened to me that day, because I have never, ever blamed it on you. It was an accident. It wasn't anymore your fault than it was my fault or Jeremy's fault. It's just something that happened. What matters is that I'm still here. Do you remember what you said to me that night in the hayride maze? You told me that my life is far from over, and you were absolutely right. I have a lot of living left to do, and yes, Ian, I'll marry you. I want nothing more than to spend the rest of my life with you."

Ian climbed up on the bed next to her and held her closely. Finally, he kissed her. It was a deep, passionate kiss. He reached over and untied her bathrobe, just as he had done many years ago. Gillian was still the most beautiful thing he'd even seen. After he made love to her, they lingered in each other's arms and talked. Each promised to never lament about the past again. The only thing that mattered now was that they would be spending the rest of their lives together, however long that would be. They eventually drifted off to sleep, still in one another's arms. A few hours later Ian was awakened by the sounds of Gillian having a nightmare. She sat up and let out a long sigh as she fought back the tears.

"Are you alright, Gilly-girl?" He sat up and wrapped his arm around her.

"I'm sorry, Ian." She let out another sigh. "I had nightmares nearly every night for weeks after I almost drowned. They finally stopped and I thought it was all over. Now it's happening again. I don't know what's wrong with me."

"I don't think there's anything wrong with you, Gilly-girl. You just had a very close encounter with a rattlesnake and I think you're reacting to it. You're okay. And can I let you in on a little secret?"

"What's that?"

"You weren't the only one who was having nightmares. As soon as I learned about what had happened to you in the pool, I starting having them too, and so did Jeremy."

"You're kidding."

"No, I'm not. Gillian, we're the people who love you the most, and we're all family. We're all connected to one another, so when something happens to one of us, we all feel it. So why don't you lay back down here with me. You'll be fine."

She settled back into Ian's arms and soon dozed off. When she woke up again, it was to the scent of fresh coffee and the sounds of clattering in the kitchen. She opened her eyes and saw the sun was up.

"Good morning, sleepyhead." Ian brought her a cup of coffee. "I'm making you breakfast in bed."

"Well now, that's a pleasant surprise. What are we having?"

"One of my special creations. You had some leftovers in the fridge, so I'm making omelets."

Gillian wasn't sure if that would be a good idea or not, but when breakfast arrived it was surprisingly tasty. Ian rejoined her on the bed.

"You know, Ian, I'd forgotten just how good of a cook you are. This reminds me of when we were in college. You always had a knack for whipping up something wonderful out of virtually nothing."

"Yes indeed. My soon-to-be chef son must have inherited that from me."

They reminisced about their college days over breakfast. Money had been tight back when they were students, but both were good cooks. Many of their date nights had been home-cooked dinners at one another's apartments. Both agreed it had to have been some of the happiest times of their lives. Finally, she set her empty plate aside.

"Well, Ian, as much as I'd love to stay here in bed with you all day, we have to get going. We've got a long drive ahead of us today."

"I wanted to talk to you about that, Gilly-girl. What would you say about staying in Colorado for one more day?"

"What do you have in mind?"

"Parenting 101," he replied.

"What do you mean?"

"What it means is that even though the boys are both adults, I, and now we, are still parents. We have to teach them by example. Even though Cassie and Jeremy are engaged, I've had mixed feelings about their living together without benefit of clergy. And now that we're about to travel across three states with Larry, I want us to set a good example for him."

"You mean, staying in separate rooms?"

"Nope. I have something else entirely in mind. Gilly-girl, did you have your heart set on having a big wedding?"

"No, not really. Been there, done that. To be honest, Ian, I'd much rather take the money we might spend on a big wedding for ourselves and give it to Jeremy and Cassie for their wedding."

"In that case, Gilly-girl, what would you say about our going into town, today, and making it legal? We've waited for this for over twenty-five years, and I don't want for us to wait any longer. Samantha was planning on staying overnight last night. So were Jeremy and Cassie. So, what do you say about gathering up the clan before they start heading home?"

# ❧FIFTY❧

GILLIAN WRAPPED HER ankle after she was dressed, but she was still unable to walk. Ian had to help her back to the main house, and when they arrived they found it strangely quiet. No one was around when they came inside, so Ian sat her down in a chair in the family room. He went to the kitchen and found Laura making a pot of coffee. He noticed she looked a little weary.

"How is she?" Laura asked.

"Much better. We've decided to stay over an extra day, but we'll stay in town tonight. We'll take care of the trailer before we go."

"Thanks, Ian. I appreciate it."

"Actually, Laura, I should be thanking you. You've really reached out to her. Under the circumstances, a lot of women wouldn't have been so gracious."

"She has a good heart. She loves the boys as if they were her own, and she's doing me a huge favor taking Larry back to Arizona with her and looking after him once he gets there. I know he'll be in very capable hands."

They were interrupted by the sound of dogs barking. Laura went to the front door.

"Good morning, Ramon."

"Good morning, Mrs. Mason. I found these in the storeroom." He pointed to the pair of crutches he was holding. "Dr. Mason's father used them back when he had his knee operation, and he left them behind when he moved to Gunnison. Would it be okay if we gave them to Mrs. Matthews?"

"Of course. Come on in."

After a few adjustments, Gillian was able to maneuver around on her crutches.

"Thank you, Ramon. This really helps."

"You're welcome, Mrs. Mathews. You know, I feel really bad about what happened to you yesterday. I kind of feel like it's my fault."

"It's okay, Ramon," she said. "It wasn't your fault and I'm back safe and sound. Thank you for the crutches, and thank you for helping to look for me. I really appreciate it."

They shook hands and Ramon left. A short time later a very disheveled-looking Cassie stumbled into the room. She was still in her robe.

"Good morning, Cassie," said Ian.

"Morning, Dad." She ambled into the kitchen, returning a minute later with her coffee mug in hand.

"Are you okay?" asked Gillian.

She sat down and joined them. "I'm not sure."

"What happened?"

"After the two of you left, Will made margaritas and our mothers set up a poker game. Then your sister showed up."

"Oh no, don't tell me. She asked to be dealt in, didn't she?"

Cassie nodded and Gillian looked at Ian.

"My sister's a real card shark. I swear she cheats, but she'll never admit it." She turned back to Cassie. "So how much did you guys lose?"

"Actually, she met her match in Jeremy, and it ended up being a draw, at least for the two of them. But Will kept pouring the margaritas, and the game didn't break up until three o'clock this morning."

She finished her coffee in silence. When her mug was empty, she stood from her chair.

"And now, I shall attempt to revive Jeremy. Wish me luck, because I'm probably going to need it."

Ian burst out laughing after she stepped away. Over the next hour, the others slowly trickled in and managed to perk up a bit as they drank their coffee, black and strong. As soon as Cynthia arrived, Gillian got on her crutches and greeted her sister with a big hug.

"So, I hear you finally met your match."

"I let the kid win."

"Sure you did."

"Well," said Ian, "now that all of you are back in the land of the living, more or less, Gillian and I have some news that we would like to share."

"What's up, Dad?" asked Jeremy.

"Last night, after we went back to the trailer, I finally, after some twenty-five years, did the right thing. I asked this lady to marry me, and she said yes."

Everyone congratulated them. Gillian's face was beaming as she showed off her ring.

"So have you set a date?" asked Cynthia.

"As a matter of fact, Sis, we have," replied Ian. "Gillian and I are going to town today, and we're making it all legal before I get the chance to mess up and walk out on her again. So, who'd like to come with us?"

Cynthia, Samantha and Cassie quickly surrounded Gillian and began making plans. Laura took Ian aside to congratulate him.

"Will and I will have to pass. You don't need your ex-wife there, even if she is happily remarried, and we have things that need to be done around here. We're expecting a new arrival."

"You're kidding. Laura, I had no idea. When is the baby due?"

"No, I'm not pregnant." She gave him a smile. "Will has a three-year-old daughter named Isabella. She's an adorable little girl, but her birth mother has decided she no longer wants her, so I'm in the process of adopting her. We're meeting with the attorney this afternoon. After that, we have to get her room ready for her. We're hoping to have her here by the weekend."

"You know, Laura, in spite of everything that went wrong between us, you were still a good mother to my kids, and you'll be a good mother to this one too. I know you always wanted a little girl. I'm happy for you."

"And I'm happy for you too, Ian. No hard feelings?"

"No hard feelings." They shook hands. "But Laura, before you go, could you do me one last favor?"

"Sure, what is it?"

"Can I borrow your copy of our divorce papers? Mine are packed away somewhere in a storage locker."

"Of course. I'll go get them. You two go and have a good life."

"You too."

After breakfast Cynthia went out to the minivan and brought a hanging bag back to the trailer. Samantha and Cassie were there with Gillian, and they had to decide which dress she should wear. Gillian already had one in mind.

"This is what I was wearing last year when I had my opening at Sorenson." She took out the yellow dress. "That night was the first time Ian and I had seen each other in over twenty years."

"Yeah, but then he's seen it before," said Samantha, "and that could be bad luck."

"What about this one?" Cynthia pulled out a laced-trimmed, ivory-colored dress. "It even looks a little bit like a wedding gown."

"It's perfect, and I've never worn it, but I don't have any shoes to go with it. Most of my things are in storage right now."

"That's an easy fix," replied Cynthia. "Let's get you packed and clean this place up. Then we'll head into town to find you a pair of shoes, and maybe a hat."

Once Gillian's essentials were loaded into Samantha's car, Cynthia went back into the house. She found Ian and both his sons in Larry's room. They were busy going through Larry's clothes, trying to find something suitable for Jeremy to wear.

"We're heading into town," she announced. "We have some things to take care of before we meet you at the courthouse."

"Sounds like a plan, but before you go, I need to get something for you."

They walked out to Ian's car and he opened the glove box. "I got a room in town for myself last night." He handed one of the keys to her. "In a few minutes, I'll be heading over there to change clothes. After that you may as well use it as a dressing room. Where is she? I'd like to tell her goodbye."

"Oh no you won't. It's bad luck for the groom to see the bride before the wedding. Call me when you're ready."

Cynthia got in the rental car and followed Samantha into town. She would have to drop the car off while she was there. She volunteered to take the minivan back to Arizona, since it would be a few days before Gillian would be able to drive again. The four ladies spent the next few hours shopping. They decided that Cynthia should be the matron of honor, so she would need a dress as well. Afterwards they headed to the motel so the two sisters could get ready. By the time they were done, Gillian was a beautiful bride, despite being on crutches. They were finishing the final touches when Ian called Cynthia.

"Good news," he said. "I found a little chapel that's available this afternoon at four o'clock, and I've got the ring. All we need is the license and we're good to go. Is she ready?"

"She's as ready as she'll ever be."

Cynthia stood by her sister during the ceremony and Jeremy served as best man. Samantha took pictures, Larry tossed a little rice he'd found in Laura's kitchen and they all went to dinner to celebrate. As soon as the champagne was served, Samantha raised her glass to propose a toast.

"Years ago, when Gillian first brought Ian to my door and introduced him to me, I knew she'd found the right guy. Granted, it's been a long and somewhat-interrupted courtship, but it just goes to show that in the end, true love always prevails."

"Here, here," said the others.

"Wait, I'm not done yet," said Samantha.

"Uh-oh," said Gillian.

"What?" Samantha turned her attention to Gillian. "Surely you didn't think I'd forgotten about that, did you?"

"No." Gillian laughed and shook her head in embarrassment.

Samantha turned her attention back to the others. "Last Thanksgiving, while Jeremy and Cassie went out for a walk, Gillian and I had a rather interesting discussion. While trying to explain her reasoning for having herself tattooed in Ian's honor, she also said, most emphatically, that no way, no how, would she ever take him back. So that night I made a bet with her. I bet her one hundred dollars that come next Thanksgiving she and Ian would be married. And like a moth to the flame, Gillian eagerly took me up on it." Samantha turned back to Gillian, who was still laughing as her face turned red. "So my friend, the time has come for you to pay up. And don't worry, since I'm the mother of the next bride, it's all going to a good cause."

Gillian graciously reached into her purse and handed a crisp one hundred dollar bill to Samantha to the sounds of everyone's applause. After dinner they all headed slowly out to the parking lot, not looking forward to words that now had to be said.

"I'm really going to miss you, Sam." Gillian held her friend close. "You were always there for me, all those years ago, and it's been so incredibly good having you back in my life again that I just can't say goodbye. I wish I could talk you into coming back to Arizona with me, but I know you can't. You have a business here, and I know you want to stay close to your daughter."

Everyone knew Jeremy and Cassie would stay in Colorado once he finished college. Jeremy had said many times it was where he intended to raise his own children. He'd also been offered a position with the same firm where he'd had his summer internship. He would be starting in January, as soon as he returned from his honeymoon.

"I'll miss you too, Gillian," said Samantha, "but now that you're finally married to Ian, we'll all be in-laws."

Saying goodbye to Jeremy would be even more difficult for Gillian than saying goodbye to Samantha. They briefly stepped away from the others. After they talked for a few minutes, he kissed her on the cheek, then he came back to say goodbye to his father and his brother. All three were a little misty-eyed by the time Jeremy and Cassie finally got into the Jeep and began their journey back to Colorado Springs. Once they were gone, Ian and Gillian walked Samantha to her car. After one last goodbye from Gillian, Sam got into her car and started it up.

"As soon as I get home, I'll email your wedding pictures. Once you're settled in Arizona you can put an album together." She waved goodbye as she pulled out of the parking lot. Larry then escorted Cynthia to his truck.

"We'll meet you back at St. Eligius first thing in the morning," said Ian. "I want us to be in Albuquerque by tomorrow night."

"You got it, Dad. See you in the morning. Goodnight."

They waited for Larry to pull away before heading back to The Beamer. Ian helped Gillian in, but once he got behind the wheel he hesitated and let out a long sigh. He took his glasses off and began rubbing his eyes.

"Ian, are you all right?"

"Yeah." He let out another sigh. "I'm just having a moment. You know, it's not easy saying goodbye to one of your kids. Nor is it easy for me to leave Colorado. Other than college, and my first year and a half with Salisbury, I've always been here."

"We don't have to leave, Ian. We can still stay here. Cynthia can take Larry to Phoenix."

He reached over and took her hand. "I'm fine, Gilly-girl. Kids grow up. They start their own lives. That's the way it's meant to be. Besides, there's nothing left for me here, but I have a whole new career waiting for me in Arizona that I can't wait to start. And Larry will be close by."

He fired up the engine and they started back to the motel. "So, Mrs. Palmer, I guess it's just you and me."

"I guess so, Mr. Palmer."

"As soon as we get to Phoenix, we'll drop Larry and the dogs off with your sister, and we'll have just enough time for us to squeeze in a short honeymoon before the fall semester starts. Where would you like to go?"

"How 'bout Las Vegas? It's not that long a drive from Phoenix, and they have really nice suites at Harrah's, although it might be a little tricky for me to negotiate the strip on these crutches."

"Vegas it is, and Gilly-girl, don't worry about trying to get around. You really won't be using your crutches that much while we're there, but bring your camera."

"Say what?"

"I'm going to take you out long enough for someone to take a picture of us standing in front of the Bellagio fountains. And then I'm going to email it to a certain kid of mine."

# ❧EPILOGUE❧

I AN UNLOCKED THE front door and turned back to Gillian. "Well, Gilly-girl, it's an old tradition."

He scooped her up and carried her across the threshold, setting her down in the empty living room of the home they'd just purchased. It was a few miles from the ASU campus, and it included the perfect room for Gillian's new art studio, as well as space for their home offices and a guest room. There was also a pool and hot tub in the backyard. Gillian looked forward to resuming her secret penchant for late night skinny dips. It was a habit Ian looked forward to acquiring. As they waited for the movers, they decided what furniture would go where. They'd already spent the past few weeks determining which pieces to keep and which to pass on to Larry. There was no way they were getting rid of the items from Ian's old college apartment. It was still top-of-the-line furniture with too many good memories attached.

"The movers should be here any time." Ian glanced at his watch. "But first, I need to get something."

He stepped out, returning a minute later with the painting of the barn and tractor. He went back out to retrieve his toolbox, and when he returned again Larry was with him.

"Good morning, other Mother," he said. "I thought I'd come over to help you guys unpack."

"Thanks Larry, I appreciate it. And don't worry, we'll help you with the stuff we're sending home with you."

"Thanks. I'm looking forward to finally sleeping in a real bed instead of on the floor." He walked up to the sliding glass door and gazed at the pool outside. It looked cool and inviting.

"Too bad we won't have time for a swim today. I don't know how you all can stand the heat."

"Better get used to it, Larry," said Ian. "It gets just as hot in Las Vegas as it does here."

"I know. That's why I'm going back to Colorado once I finish school. Besides, I don't know anyone in Vegas."

"Does your brother know about this?" asked Gillian.

"I called him two days ago. He was ecstatic. I had to keep reminding him that it'll be a few years before I get back there."

As Gillian began rummaging through the toolbox, they heard someone at the door. "That's either Rosemary or the movers." She pulled out a hammer and a picture hook. "Would one of you guys get that for me?"

She stepped back, found the perfect spot, and hammered the hook into the wall. She was dropping the hammer back in the toolbox when Ian returned.

"Gilly-girl, look who's here." The man standing next to Ian looked familiar, but she couldn't quite place him.

"Happy housewarming." He presented her with a bottle of wine.

"Thank you. I'd offer you some, but I don't have any glasses yet." She handed the bottle to Larry, who stepped away to put it in the kitchen.

"That's quite alright," he replied. "So Ian, I had to see it for myself. After all these years, it's about time you finally married Gillian Hanson."

She looked at the man again and finally recognized him. "Rob! Rob Davis. How are you?" She walked up and gave him a big hug.

"It's good to see you, Gillian."

"You too. Now I remember. That day when I walked into the architecture building, you were the one who told me Ryan was in the library, not the studio. That was the first time I ever saw Ian. He walked into the library about a minute after I did to talk to Ryan about something. Looking back, it really was love-at-first sight. I just didn't know it at the time."

"I remember it well, Gilly-girl," said Ian. "I can still see the look in your eyes."

She stepped away and hung the painting. "Do you like it there, Ian?"

He stepped back and took a look. "It's perfect, Gilly-girl. Just perfect."

## THE END

# ❧Larry Palmer's Italian Wedding Soup❧

### The meatballs

1 pound ground beef, ground chicken or ground turkey
OR ½ pound ground meat with ½ pound ground pork
¼ cup breadcrumbs
1 teaspoon Italian seasoning blend
1 teaspoon salt
½ teaspoon pepper
1 egg

Preheat oven to 350°. Combine all ingredients in a mixing bowl and knead together like a meatloaf. Roll into small meatballs, about ½ to 1 inch in diameter. Place on a baking sheet lined with parchment paper and bake for 25 to 30 minutes, or until brown. Yields approximately 40 to 50 meatballs. Set aside.

### The soup

2 tablespoons olive oil
½ medium sized yellow onion, chopped
1 tablespoon minced garlic
3 carrots, peeled and sliced (optional)
2 stalks celery, sliced (optional)
10 cups, (2 ½ quarts) chicken stock
½ cup dry white wine (such as Chardonnay)
1 egg, well beaten
1 cup small pasta (such as stars or small sea shells)
2 teaspoons salt (if desired)
½ teaspoon pepper
1 tablespoon dill
12 ounces fresh spinach, washed and trimmed
OR 1 can of spinach or 1 package of frozen spinach (defrosted)

While meatballs are baking sauté onion, garlic, carrots and celery, (if desired) in olive oil in a stockpot for approximately 5 to 6 minutes. Add chicken stock and white wine and bring to a boil. Once soup mixture is boiling beat egg in a small mixing bowl with a whisk until slightly frothy. Pour egg slowly and incrementally into soup mixture, whisking the soup mixture continuously until all of the egg has been added. Add pasta, salt, (if desired) and pepper and allow mixture to simmer for about 6 to 8 minutes, or until pasta is soft. Add meatballs and dill. Cover and simmer on low for another 10 minutes. Add spinach and simmer for another 1 to 2 minutes before serving. Once soup is ladled into bowls top with grated Parmesan cheese.

# ABOUT THE AUTHOR

Just like Gillian Matthews, the heroine in her debut romance novel, *The Reunion*, Marina Martindale began her career as a graphic designer and artist, and several of her paintings have been featured in juried art shows. Over time, however, she discovered that writing was her true life's passion.

"I love creating conflicted characters," says Martindale. "I think they're more like the people we meet in real life. I also like the complexity of romance. It's an opportunity to delve deep into the human condition and try to understand what it is that motivates us to make the choices in life that we make."

In *The Reunion*, Martindale draws her inspiration from some of her own real-life experiences. The story itself, however, is fiction.

"Not all of us are lucky enough to get to marry our true love and spend the rest of our lives living happily ever after," adds Martindale. "I think many of us have someone in our past who we think of as, 'the one who got away.' We may stop and think about them from time to time, but have we ever really sat down and wondered what would happen, if, just by chance, we were to run into our long lost love? That's the premise for *The Reunion*. It's a story of love, forgiveness, and second chances."

Marina Martindale resides in Tucson, Arizona. In her spare time she enjoys photography, quilt making, and cooking.

For more information about Marina Martindale, and *The Reunion*, as well her other novels, including *The Journey*, the sequel to *The Reunion*, please visit her official website at www.marinamartindale.com, or her blog at www.marinamartindale.net.

CPSIA information can be obtained
at www.ICGtesting.com
Printed in the USA
FFHW02n0130031018
48659494-52661FF